NO SECOND CHANCES

A Daniel Whelan Mystery

Lyndon Stacey

This first world edition published 2016
in Great Britain and the USA by
SEVERN HOUSE PUBLISHERS LTD of
19 Cedar Road, Sutton, Surrey, England, SM2 5DA.
Trade paperback edition first published
in Great Britain and the USA 2016 by
SEVERN HOUSE PUBLISHERS LTD

British Library Cataloguing in Publication Data
A CIP catalogue record for this title is available from the British Library.

ISBN-13: 978-0-7278-8610-1 (cased)
ISBN-13: 978-1-84751-713-5 (trade paper)
ISBN-13: 978-1-78010-774-5 (e-book)

All Severn House titles are printed on acid-free paper.

Severn House Publishers support the Forest Stewardship Council™ [FSC™],
the leading international forest certification organisation.
All our titles that are printed on FSC certified paper carry the FSC logo.

Typeset by Palimpsest Book Production Ltd.,
Falkirk, Stirlingshire, Scotland.
Printed and bound in Great Britain by
TJ International, Padstow, Cornwall.

In loving memory of my mum, Pat, without whose support I might never have followed this path.
Also in recognition of the many amazing people who work tirelessly to rescue and rehome the discards of the greyhound racing world.

ONE

The sun had dropped behind the hills and the light was fading as Daniel approached Abbots Farm. It had been a long day; one when it felt as though anything that could go wrong had done. At gone six o'clock, this was his last drop of the day and it was with relief that he swung the TFS delivery lorry into the driveway between the granite gateposts.

The gates were open, which was unusual, but it suited Daniel as it saved him getting out to use the intercom or enter the security code. The truck's wheels strummed across the round bars of the cattle grid and onto the quarter-mile gently curving stretch of tarmac that led to the house and stable yard.

'Nearly finished, Taz,' he said over his shoulder. The German shepherd dog had given up on the day over an hour ago, disappearing behind the seats to curl up on his beanbag, with his nose tucked into his bushy tail.

Suddenly, a flash of white caught Daniel's eye and a low-running shape bounded out of the gloom to his left-hand side on a collision course with the front wheels of the lorry.

Swearing, he slammed on the brakes and swerved right. The big tyres squealed in protest as the vehicle shuddered to a halt, half on and half off the drive. The liver-and-white spaniel whose appearance had triggered the evasive action had darted away and now stood looking up at the cab, tongue lolling and eyes shining green in the beam of the headlights. Moments later, it was joined by another dog that paused for a moment then bounded away, head down and tail wagging furiously, no thought in its head besides hunting.

Daniel knew the dogs. They belonged to the owners of the house and he was pretty sure they shouldn't be out on their own at this time of day, especially with the gates standing open. He pulled the handbrake on and climbed down from the cab, picking up Taz's lead and feeling in his pockets for the treat pouch from which he occasionally rewarded him. As he did so, the German shepherd, instantly awake, stepped through from behind the seats and made to follow.

'You stop there, mate,' Daniel told him and reluctantly, the dog did so, eyeing the lead with eagerness. A lead usually meant action for him, and to be told to stay was a disappointment.

Stepping down onto the grass at the side of the lorry, Daniel noticed a chill in the air. It was early October and the Indian summer was finally giving way to autumn. Although the days remained warm, the evening temperatures had begun to drop significantly.

Any worries about the dogs being troublesome to catch were swiftly banished, for as soon as his feet touched the turf, the spaniel that had run out in front of the lorry came fawning around him, muzzle split in a grin and tail a blur of white.

'Hello, Bailey. What are you doing out here by yourself? Does your mum know where you are? I bet she doesn't.' Daniel fed the dog a treat and deftly looped the rope slip-lead over its head. Moments later, seeing its mate eating, the second spaniel loped over with hope in its eyes.

'Hello, Scotch. Have you come to join the party?' Daniel asked. While the second dog crunched on its biscuit, Daniel took hold of its collar and then led them both towards the cab. Hoisting them in, one by one, he spoke a sharp word to Taz, who was inclined to take an indignant view of the invasion, and the bigger dog retreated with bad grace to his position behind the seats, grumbling when one of the spaniels thrust its head through to investigate. Daniel couldn't blame his dog. Spending a large part of every weekday in it, he viewed the lorry as his own territory and the two newcomers were clambering all over the seats in their habitual springer spaniel frenzy.

'Sit down!' he told them firmly but with little optimism as he put the lorry into gear and resumed his journey. To his surprise Scotch and Bailey did as they were told, sitting bolt upright on the seat and panting at what seemed an impossible rate, their breath spreading a fuggy warmth through the cab. Daniel opened the window a little wider.

Abbots Farm was a stone-built manor house nestling in a secluded valley on the edge of Dartmoor and surrounded by around twenty or so acres of its own pasture and woodland.

Business consultant Harvey Myers lived there with his wife, Lorna, although for much of the time, Harvey was away, working.

Since he had been driving for Tavistock Farm Supplies, Daniel had made regular monthly deliveries to the address, and it wasn't long before he and Lorna realized that their paths had crossed several years before, when she had worked as a civilian for the Bristol Metropolitan Police; the same division Daniel had served in.

The drive passed through a second gateway onto a sweep of gravel in front of the building, and normally Daniel would have driven past the house to the stable yard, where he would unload his delivery of horse and dog food and bales of wood shavings into the large stone barn. Today, however, he found his way partially blocked by a black Transit van with darkened windows parked untidily outside the white-painted front door.

Daniel pulled up behind it and, telling Taz to stay put, climbed down from the cab once more, followed in scrambling confusion by the two spaniels. The front door stood open, which explained why the dogs had been running free, and knocking on the paintwork, he called out, 'Lorna?'

He could hear voices from the rear of the building and almost immediately a door opened and a heavily built man appeared in the opening, haloed by the light from the kitchen beyond.

'Mr Myers?' the man enquired, looking at Daniel.

'No, sorry.' Daniel took a couple of steps towards the man and peered round him. In the kitchen he could see another male figure in a heavy leather jacket standing between the door and a slim woman in jeans and a loose cotton shirt.

Daniel's senses came to full alert. Something about their body language didn't look right.

'Lorna? Is everything OK?'

'Daniel?' As she took a step towards him, the man put out a hand to stop her and she flinched. She was wearing her long sandy blonde hair tied back and even in the half-light Daniel could see the stress in her face and hear it in her voice as she said, 'These men are looking for Harvey but I told them he's not here.'

'In that case, I expect they'll be on their way, then,' Daniel observed mildly, wishing he had Taz at his heels rather than a couple of dizzy spaniels.

'We'll leave when we're fucking ready to leave,' the man in the doorway growled, curling his lip at Daniel. He was fortyish with razor-cut dark hair and rather coarse but otherwise unremarkable features.

'Do you want me to call the police?' Daniel asked Lorna, but her reply was sharp with alarm.

'No! Please, Daniel, don't! It's OK.'

'Listen to the little lady,' the closest man advised. 'She knows what's good for her.'

'What do you want with Mr Myers?' Daniel asked.

'I think that's between him and us, don't you?' was the reply. 'Who did you say you were?'

'I didn't.'

'He's a friend,' Lorna said.

'Well, in that case,' the man said, leaning close to Daniel, 'the best thing you can do is make sure the little lady gives our message to her hubby and keeps her pretty little mouth shut or we'll be back to visit her again and next time we mightn't be so polite! My mate, here, has an eye for a pretty lady.'

To accentuate his words, the man in the leather jacket leaned towards Lorna and winked suggestively. He had a face only a mother could love and she shrank back with a look of deep disgust. One of the spaniels, sensing a game, fawned round the man's feet and he aimed a kick at it.

Lorna cried out as the dog yelped and scurried under the table.

'Touch her and I *will* call the police,' Daniel stated calmly, though he knew that, due to the location, the chances of them arriving before the two men made their getaway were close to nil, unless they just happened to be in the area.

Leather Jacket obviously knew this because he sneered, 'Yeah?' and reached out a hand in Lorna's direction.

'Leave her alone!'

'Or what?'

Quick as a flash, Daniel swayed towards the man in the doorway, grasped his arm and twisted it out and up behind his back. Intent on the scene in the kitchen, the man was caught off guard and found himself turned and slammed face first into the wall with his hand somewhere in the vicinity of his shoulder blades. He grunted his discomfort and swore viciously at Daniel.

'Or . . . I break your mate's arm,' Daniel replied, leaning all his weight on the bigger man to hold him still.

Leather Jacket froze, his bovine face registering shock, and Lorna took her opportunity to duck under his outstretched arm and retreat to the far side of the kitchen. She was now near enough to the garden door to open it and get out but she made no move to do so.

Leather Jacket appeared to have lost interest in her now and he began, instead, to advance towards Daniel and his captive.

'I don't fink you will,' he said.

Daniel leaned harder on his man, noticing a small tattoo on the back of his neck as he did so. His victim squealed, 'He bloody will! Stay back!'

Leather Jacket stopped and raised his hands a little.

'All right. So what now? Way I see it, you've got to let 'im go sometime and then you're dead meat, incha?'

Daniel was aware that his position wasn't great but he had an ace up his sleeve that neither of them knew about. Thankful that he had left the cab window open, with a shrill whistle he summoned the cavalry.

Just seconds later there came the clicking of claws on the stone flags and a low rumbling growl sounded.

'Shit!' Leather Jacket exclaimed, backing off. 'The size of the fuckin' thing!'

'And he has teeth to match,' Daniel promised him, confidence surging now his partner had his back. Looking past the two men to where Lorna stood watching, he asked, 'Are you *sure* you don't want the police?'

She shook her head, quickly. He wondered what threats they had used to inspire such a look of desperation but he had to respect her wishes and besides, he had no great desire to bring himself to the notice of the authorities, either.

He returned his gaze to Leather Jacket. 'OK. Now, this is what's going to happen. You are going to very slowly and quietly walk past me and the dog and head for the door. You will get into your van and start the engine. When I hear the engine, I will let your mate here go and he will follow you. You will then both drive away and not come back – now or ever. D'you understand?'

'I'm not going anywhere near that fuckin' dog!' Leather Jacket averred, eyeing Taz nervously.

'He won't hurt you unless I tell him to. Just don't touch me or make any sudden movements.'

Still the man hesitated, licking lips suddenly gone dry, but Daniel's captive was losing patience.

'For fuck's sake hurry up and get out! The bastard's breaking my arm!'

'What he said,' Daniel agreed. 'Only I wouldn't hurry, if I were you.'

His eyes never leaving the dog, Leather Jacket walked in almost comical slow motion towards Daniel and his captive and sidled past, maintaining his crablike progress as he drew level with the German shepherd, who bristled and licked his lips.

'Let him go, lad,' Daniel said to the dog.

Clearly disappointed, Taz did as he was told, turning his head to watch the man pass and, just as the manoeuvre was completed, produced one of his most blood-curdling snarls. Forgetting Daniel's warnings, Leather Jacket turned on his heel and ran for the door. Daniel had to suppress a smile. It had to be said, the dog had excellent dramatic timing.

Moments later Daniel heard the sound of the Transit's engine and leaned forward to speak close to his captive's ear, ignoring the fresh spate of swearing the extra pressure provoked. 'Your turn, now. Do exactly what your charming friend did and make sure you don't do anything my partner there might consider threatening, got it?'

The man nodded and Daniel leaned again. 'Sorry. I didn't hear you . . .'

'Yes. Fuck you!' the man said sullenly.

Daniel released his grip and stepped back, poised for trouble, but the man had evidently had enough. He rubbed his sore arm and edged past the dog with respect but not quite the degree of trepidation his colleague had displayed. At the front door, he paused and looked back to where Lorna watched from the kitchen.

'This doesn't change anything,' he told her. 'When you see your husband, don't forget to tell him the boss wants to see him, like yesterday! If we don't hear from him by the end of the week you'll both be sorry. And you, mate,' he added to Daniel. 'You'd better hope I never see you ever again, cos I never forget a face and I owe you, big time!'

Without waiting for reaction from either Daniel or Lorna, he disappeared into the gloom and seconds later they heard the van accelerating away up the drive towards the road.

Taz padded to the door and looked out, as if to assure himself that the men really had gone, and then returned to Daniel, grinning widely and tail waving.

'Good lad,' Daniel told him, ruffling his fur, but his attention was quickly claimed by Lorna who, now that the crisis was over, buried her face in her hands and began to sob uncontrollably.

TWO

'Hey, it's over now, they've gone,' Daniel said, going to her side and putting an arm round her shoulders. The two spaniels crept out from their hiding places and shimmied towards their mistress, their tails doing overtime.

'But you heard what he said,' Lorna managed, between sobs. 'If Harvey doesn't get in touch, they'll be back.'

'So where *is* Harvey?' Daniel asked. 'Why can't he get in touch?'

'He's abroad, working. Hong Kong. I told them that but they wouldn't believe me. They said I was lying and that he's here – back in England, but he's not. I should know, for God's sake! I'm his bloody wife!'

'Well, he'll have to come back, now, won't he?' Daniel stated. 'Did they say what they wanted with him?'

'No. Oh. God, Daniel! I was so scared! I was terrified that Zoe would walk in while they were here.'

She began to cry harder again and he put his arms round her and drew her close, feeling her body trembling, even between the sobs. Zoe, he knew, was Lorna's fifteen-year-old daughter, who attended day school in nearby Tavistock. She was the product of a previous relationship but had been accepted into the family at age five by Harvey, who had a son and a daughter of his own from his first marriage.

'It's OK. Nobody got hurt. Well, not very much, anyway,' he amended.

'Thank God you came! You were amazing!' Lorna said pulling back and fishing in her pocket for a handkerchief. 'What made you come into the house?'

'Well, the gate was open and I found these guys heading out on a hunting trip,' he added, glancing down at Scotch and Bailey, who grinned back at him with a total lack of shame for their misdemeanours.

'Oh my God! They must have slipped out when the men came in. They're no bloody good at all as guard dogs!'

'How did they get in? Were the gates open?'

'No. I opened them,' Lorna admitted ruefully, dabbing her eyes with the handkerchief and then using it to blow her nose. 'They buzzed and I thought it was you, so I just said, "Hi, Daniel," and one of them said "Hi" back. It never occurred to me that it was anyone else.'

'Well, it wouldn't,' Daniel said. 'Don't beat yourself up about it. From what I saw of them, they would probably have just driven through the gates if you hadn't opened them.'

'I just don't understand why they were here,' she said, her eyes filling with tears again. 'What did they want with Harvey? What has he done?'

'If I was to hazard a guess, I'd say he owes someone money,' Daniel said. 'Those two had hired muscle stamped all over them. Did they say who sent them?'

'No. They said to tell him the governor wants to see him. I asked who the governor was but they just said Harvey would understand. But why would he owe them anything? He has money. He wouldn't need to borrow. Why would he get mixed up with people like that?' she exclaimed, her brow furrowing above large, dark-lashed hazel eyes. A few tendrils of hair had escaped their binding and hung in wisps around her face and even in her agitated state Daniel thought, not for the first time, that she was a very attractive woman.

'I'm sorry. I can't tell you. Hopefully Harvey'll have some explanation when you see him.'

Lorna sniffed disconsolately.

'He's not answering his phone. I've tried to ring him three times today because his accountant is trying to get hold of him, but he's not answering. Oh, Daniel, it's a nightmare! What if I can't reach him before they come back?'

Daniel didn't have an answer and, sensing that she was close to tears again, he gave her a quick hug, saying into her hair, 'I doubt if they'll be in any hurry now they've had a taste of the dog. What do you say I go and shut the front door before the house fills with midges, and you put the kettle on?'

'OK.' She nodded and sniffed again, but before he could release her, a low growl from Taz heralded the appearance of a figure in the kitchen doorway.

'*Mum?* What's going on?' a youthful female voice enquired, sharply.

Instantly, Lorna pulled back from Daniel, wiping her nose again. 'Zoe! Thank God!'

'What do you mean, thank God?' the girl enquired, talking to her mother but looking accusingly at Daniel. 'What's going on? Who's this? What's he doing here?'

Stick-slim, with long thin legs encased in skinny jeans and an oversized jumper with sleeves that left only her fingertips protruding, Zoe Myers had long silky blonde hair, a fine-boned face and wide, heavily made-up eyes. A small stud sparkled on the right side of her nose and she wore a fringed scarf draped loosely about her neck. She was pale and Daniel thought she looked as though she didn't get enough sleep.

'I'm delivering horse feed,' Daniel said. 'Though obviously not right at this moment.'

'Well, I can see that, can't I?' she snapped.

'I found the dogs running loose near the road, so I brought them in,' he explained, unsure how much Lorna would want her daughter to know.

'Daniel's a friend,' Lorna told her daughter. 'I was upset and he gave me a hug, that's all. He just happened to be here.'

'Upset, why?'

Lorna summoned a smile and wiped her eyes. 'Nothing important, sweetheart. Just something someone said. I was just going to make a cuppa, do you want one?'

'You don't cry over "nothing important",' Zoe persisted, still regarding Daniel with deep suspicion.

'Please, darling, leave it. I'm OK, now,' her mother said, picking up the kettle. 'Tea or coffee?'

'Fine, if you don't want to tell me,' she said sulkily. 'Coffee.'

'I'd better get on and unload the lorry.' Daniel headed for the door, feeling that he was surplus to requirements.

'I'll bring you a coffee down in a minute, if you like,' Lorna offered.

'Thanks.' He whistled to Taz and left the room, hearing Zoe exclaim indignantly, 'You wouldn't believe it! Some cretin in a black van nearly crashed into the bus! Just up the road there. He came round the corner in the middle of the road, going about a hundred miles an hour. The bus driver was livid!'

For the next fifteen minutes or so, Daniel was fully occupied in offloading Lorna Myers' order and he was just hoisting the last of the sacks of horse feed onto the pile in the barn when she appeared in the doorway carrying two steaming mugs.

She held one out to him.

'Perfect timing,' he said, attempting to dust himself down with a few sweeps of his hands and taking it from her.

Lorna sat on one of the newly delivered plastic-wrapped bales of wood shavings, and after a moment Daniel followed suit, watching her from under his brows as he sipped. She looked understandably stressed.

'I've just tried to ring Harvey again. It went straight to the answering service,' she said. 'I left a message.'

'That's a pain. You'll just have to keep trying.'

'I'm sorry Zoe was so rude,' Lorna said, after a moment.

'Well, it must have been a bit of a shock, coming in like she did and finding you hugging a stranger.'

'I don't usually fall to pieces like that.'

'Well, I don't suppose you usually have a couple of thugs barging in to your kitchen and throwing their weight about,' Daniel pointed out. 'Most people would be upset. In fact, a lot of women I know would have had a complete meltdown! I think you were pretty amazing but I do think you should reconsider calling the police. Those guys meant business.'

'I know. I was terrified. But I don't want to get Harvey into more trouble. I'm just hoping it's some sort of misunderstanding and he'll be able to call someone and sort it all out when he gets back. And, besides, they said . . .' Her voice shook and petered out.

'What did they say?'

'They said it wouldn't do any good to tell the police and if I did, they'd know, and they mentioned Zoe. That's what really frightened me.'

'OK. Tell me from the start.'

'Well, I was in the kitchen and when the front door opened I still thought it was you, so I called out, "Hi, Daniel. Is there a problem?" but then they just walked right in and one of them said, "Not if you're a good girl and tell us where Harvey Myers is!" Well, I didn't stop to think, I just went for the phone but the one with the leather jacket got there first and pulled the plug out of the wall. So I told them Harvey was abroad, working, but then I didn't want them to think I was all alone so I said that my two grown-up sons would be back from work soon. I thought it might scare them off but they said I was a liar, and that Harvey only had one son and he was working in Cambridge – how did they know that, Daniel?' she asked fearfully.

'There are ways of finding stuff out, especially these days, but I admit, it does make it more worrying. What else?'

'Well, that's when they said not to tell the police. What did they mean about it not doing any good?'

'Probably just to scare you,' he said. 'Unless . . .'

'What?'

'Well, sometimes money has been known to change hands in return for a little selective blindness, shall we say? You used to work at the Met – don't tell me you never heard rumours . . .'

'Yeah, of course, but . . .'

'So when are you expecting Harvey back?' Daniel didn't know exactly what Harvey Myers did for a living, though he was aware it was very high-powered and that it often took him abroad for days or weeks at a time. From his previous conversations with Lorna, he had gained the impression that she was sometimes a little lonely. However, her husband obviously thrived on his jet-setting lifestyle and the pecuniary advantages were plain to see in the size and style of the property and the quality of the horses in the stables.

She shrugged. 'I don't know exactly. He flew out just over two weeks ago and he said he wasn't sure how long he'd be, but it always depends how things go. I imagine if he seals the deal early it could be later this week, if not . . . well, sometimes he's gone for three or four weeks or more. It has been as long as six when there's something big on.'

'But surely he'll come home if you tell him what's happened.'

'I expect so, if he can. But it might be difficult for him. There's a huge amount of money involved in these deals he brokers, from what I understand.'

'Well, excuse me if I'm speaking out of turn, but it's his mess and he needs to come and clear it up!'

'Yeah, I know.' Lorna looked tired and upset. 'If I can't get him on his phone, I'll email him.'

'Is he usually this difficult to get hold of?'

'Depends where he is. He's generally in contact every couple of days. Sometimes a phone call, often just a text or email. I know it sounds a bit casual but to be honest it's not usually a problem. His work's very demanding; I think they work hard and play hard. I don't like to keep bothering him.'

'So when did you last hear from him?'

Lorna looked uncomfortable.

'I've just looked at my phone. It was actually over a week ago. He sent a text.'

She took her mobile from her pocket.

'He says, "*All going well. Very busy weekend coming up so may not be in touch for a day or two. Hope all well. Love you.*" ' She looked at Daniel. 'That's why I haven't worried. It's typical Harvey.'

'He works through the weekend?'

'Yes. I suppose so. That's what he says . . .' She pushed a wisp of hair behind her ear. 'To be honest, I have no idea. Is that crazy? I've never asked.'

'No, not crazy, exactly. Sometimes we just accept stuff without thinking. It's easier. But surely you can get in touch through his work?'

'Well, I *can*, but he doesn't like me doing that, I don't know why. Last time I did it, we had this huge row, so I really try not to.'

Daniel kept his opinion of Harvey's inconsiderate behaviour to himself, saying instead, 'Well, presumably the people he works for will be able to get hold of him, if all else fails, whether he likes it or not. For now, is there anyone who can come and be with you?'

'Not really. Zo will be here, though.'

'I really meant someone older. A friend, perhaps. Or didn't you once say Harvey's daughter stays occasionally?'

'She does, but usually only when Harvey's here. We don't really get on. She's never forgiven me for marrying her father.' She glanced at him in alarm. 'You don't think they'll come back tonight?'

'No. I very much doubt it. I think you'll be OK for a day or two. They'll give you time to contact Harvey and him time to stew in it a bit.'

'Oh, God!' she said, staring into her coffee mug. 'I can't believe this is happening. It's like something on TV.'

'I suppose there's nowhere else you can go for a few days.'

'I can't leave the horses.'

'No. I guess not. Unless you could get someone else to look after them. I'd offer but I'm not sure Fred can spare me at the moment.'

'Of course you can't – why should you? But if I did know someone, wouldn't *they* be in danger, then?'

Daniel nodded. 'I suppose that's a possibility.'

They sat in silence for a few moments, the light in the barn illuminating the swirling dust motes disturbed by Daniel's activities. In the stables across the yard, one of the horses snorted and another scraped the floor, restlessly.

'Did you manage to make your peace with Zoe?' Daniel asked, then.

'She's not happy. She thinks I'm keeping secrets.'

'Which you are.'

'I know, but I don't want to worry her. Do you think I *should* tell her?'

'Maybe not until you've had a chance to talk to Harvey. As I said, I think you'll be safe enough for a day or two, but if they don't get what they want, then yes, I think you'll have to. She should be warned not to go anywhere alone – stick with the crowds, just in case.'

'You think she'll be in danger?' Lorna looked horrified.

'I think it's wise to take precautions, is what I'm saying. They've already told you they know about her. But hopefully it won't come to that. Get hold of Harvey and get him to sort it all out.'

'I will.' She rubbed her face and sighed deeply. 'Oh God! Why is this happening? I want my old life back.'

Daniel drained his mug and stood up.

'I'm sorry, Lorna, but I'd better be going. Fred'll think I've crashed the lorry or something.' He took his wallet out and found one of Fred Bowden's business cards. 'I'll write my home and mobile numbers on here. If you're at all worried, call me, any time, day or night. And if you can't get me, call Fred. He's a good bloke. He's ex-army and his son's CID.'

'Yes, I know Fred. Thank you, Daniel. Thanks for everything.'

'And let me know how you get on with Harvey, OK?'

'Yeah, I will.'

Daniel gave a low whistle to Taz, who was busy ratting among the forage bins, collecting a quantity of dust and cobwebs on his ears and whiskers in the process, and went out to the lorry.

Daniel thought of Lorna Myers several times over the next twenty-four hours and after work the next day mentioned the confrontation at Abbots Farm to his boss, who, it turned out, had known Lorna for many years. They were having a coffee in Fred's office at the yard, as they often did prior to going their separate ways, and Taz was lying next to Daniel's chair. Mindful of Lorna's wish to avoid police involvement, he played down the drama of the situation, merely saying that she had been understandably upset at having the two men arrive unannounced demanding to see Harvey.

'Oh, dear, poor Lorna! I wonder what Harvey's been up to . . .'

'I don't know. I got a partial on the Transit's plates and ran it past Tom but he's pretty sure they were fake or stolen.' Tom was Fred's son and worked in the regional CID. 'So whoever these bastards were, they didn't want to be traced. No surprises there, then. So what's Harvey like? I've only ever seen him once and that was just a hi and goodbye.'

'Harvey Myers? Oh, he's OK. Don't really know him that well, myself. I went to the wedding but I've probably only met him half a dozen times since. He seems to be away more than he's at home. A bit of a workaholic, I gather. I don't think Lorna minds too much. They're fond enough of each other, I think but I don't think the Grande Passion was ever very grand, if you know what I mean. She'd been through a bit of a rough time and wanted security for herself and her daughter, and he didn't like coming home to an empty house when he'd been working away. When he's not there, Lorna keeps busy with the horses. It's worked very well, as far as one can tell.'

'I knew her when I was at the Bristol Met,' Daniel told him. 'She worked on the switchboard for a while, it must have been just before she met Harvey. A lot of the guys had a bit of a crush on her, I remember.'

'You included?' Fred asked with a sideways look.

Daniel shook his head. 'Me? No, I was a newly married man. I had eyes for no one but Amanda; thought the sun shone out of her every orifice! Just goes to show how ridiculously immature I was. As I remember it, Lorna would come for a drink with the lads after our shift sometimes, but I don't think she ever went out with any of them. It wasn't that she wasn't asked, though, that's for sure.'

'It doesn't surprise me. Zoe's father was a police officer. Tom knew him, which is how I knew Lorna. Anyway, once he found out that Zoe was on the way, you couldn't see him for dust! I imagine Lorna didn't want to risk getting stung like that again, and who could blame her? Mind you, he probably did her a favour, there – he was a total waste of space as far as I could see.'

'I thought it was something like that. The trouble is, the more she played hard to get, the more the lads wanted her. No wonder Harvey seemed like a good bet.'

'In more ways than one,' Fred said, nodding. 'I'm pretty sure she was in financial difficulties. Her brother got himself into debt on the horses and went to her for money – which she didn't have a lot of, being a single mum. He promised to turn his life around but then proceeded to lose that money at the bookmakers' as well. Ended up killing himself with booze and pills. Not sure she's ever really got over it. Well, you don't, do you?'

'Oh, God! Poor girl! I didn't know that. It's no surprise that she settled for security.'

'I don't have to tell you not to repeat any of this, of course.'

Daniel favoured him with a pained expression.

'And there was me, thinking of taking it straight to the papers.'

'Yeah, sorry, mate.'

'Well, I'd better let you get home before Meg starts to think we're having an affair,' Daniel joked, putting his empty mug down and getting to his feet. Beside him, Taz stood up, stretched and yawned.

'Yeah, bugger off!' Fred said disgustedly. 'Always hanging around here, drinking my coffee. Can't get rid of you.'

Daniel laughed. In his pocket, his phone began to trill and he took it out. It wasn't a number he recognized and he wondered if it could be Lorna's.

'Hello?'

'Is that Daniel Whelan?' The voice was female but not Lorna.

'It is.'

'Oh. Hi. It's um . . . Zoe Myers. We met yesterday.'

'Oh, hello, Zoe.' Daniel raised his eyebrows at Fred, who looked back intently. 'What's happened? Is your mum OK?'

'Yes, fine – I mean, as far as I know. I've been at school all day but it wasn't about Mum, anyway.'

'Oh.' Daniel was a little taken aback. 'How can I help you, then?'

'Um . . . Mum says you used to be a policeman . . .'

'I was,' he confirmed, wondering a little uneasily where the conversation was leading.

'Um . . . could I talk to you? In confidence, I mean. You wouldn't tell Mum?'

'That depends . . .'

'No! You mustn't tell her. *Please*. She's got enough to worry about, with not being able to get hold of Dad and everything.'

Daniel couldn't argue with that, but he was wary of making promises he might later regret.

'She told you about that, did she?'

'Not exactly,' Zoe admitted. 'I overheard her leaving a message on his answerphone and she sounded upset. What's going on?'

'You should ask your mum about that, not me. I thought you said it wasn't about your mum . . .'

'It's not. So, please can I talk to you? *Please?* I need help and I don't know who else I can ask, but Mum can't know, it's important.'

Considering that she had met him for the first and only time just the day before and had then shown every sign of disliking him intensely, Daniel thought she must indeed be desperate.

'OK. I won't promise but if I can help you without telling her, I will. That's the best I can say – take it or leave it.'

There came a low groan from the other end of the phone. 'Oh, God! I don't know . . .'

'Well, take some time to think about it, if you like, and get back to me,' Daniel said helpfully.

'No!' Her sharp reply surprised him. 'I haven't got time. I need to talk to you, now.'

'OK. Well, the choice is yours.'

'I haven't *got* any choice,' Zoe said with a touch of bitterness. 'When can you come? Now?'

'Come where? Are you at home?'

'No. I've just finished school. I'm in Tavistock. Can you meet me in the town centre? There's a coffee shop near the abbey that stays open late, do you know it?'

'I expect I can find it,' Daniel said. 'Won't your mum wonder where you are?'

'She thinks I'm at an after-school club,' Zoe said, with a lack of shame that suggested to Daniel that it might be an alibi she often used.

He arranged to meet her in twenty minutes and disconnected, looking thoughtful.

Fred Bowden raised his eyebrows. 'Trouble?'

'I don't know. Very possibly,' Daniel said, stowing the phone in his pocket once more. 'No, scratch that. Almost certainly.'

He outlined the conversation and Fred shook his head.

'Rather you than me, mate,' he said with feeling.

'I know but she sounded pretty desperate. I couldn't just turn my back, could I?'

Fred, who knew a little of Daniel's history, shook his head. 'Knowing you, I suppose not. But you need to stop beating yourself up about that girl, my friend. It was a long time ago and it wasn't your fault, whatever you choose to think.'

'Yeah well, maybe I'll stop when the nightmares do,' Daniel said bleakly. The incident, involving a drug addict and his teenage hostage, had effectively ended his career in the police force, and had haunted his nights ever since.

Fred shook his head again and walked towards the door, putting a hand briefly on Daniel's shoulder in passing.

Daniel found the coffee shop with no trouble and once inside, quickly located Lorna's daughter sitting at a table against the side wall. The premises were small, with perhaps a dozen tables, about three-quarters of which were occupied. It didn't seem a natural choice for a youngster, but perhaps that was the reason for its choosing, Daniel thought. Maybe she didn't want to run the risk of being seen or heard by her school friends.

Zoe waved a hand when she saw him and he weaved his way between the close-packed tables to sit opposite her.

'Hi,' she said, a little shyly. 'Thank you for coming.'

Once again, she was wearing a sloppy jumper, which today exposed one shoulder and the strap of a red vest top beneath. Her hair hung in a long silvery-gold plait over the other shoulder and her hands were partly hidden by lacy black fingerless gloves. Her collarbone stood out in a sharply defined ridge and Daniel wondered if she was anorexic.

A waitress materialized beside them and he ordered coffee and a slice of chocolate cake. Zoe's coffee cup was empty and she accepted the offer of a refill with a slightly abstracted air. Daniel added a second slice of cake to the order and sat back to wait for the youngster to unburden herself.

This, after the apparent urgency of the phone call, she seemed reluctant to do, and Daniel wondered if she'd had second thoughts.

'Have you changed your mind?' he asked, after a couple of minutes during which she seemed absorbed in fiddling with the lace of her mitts. Her hands were small and the nails a shiny black. He half-hoped she had changed her mind, but for Lorna's sake, it would not have felt right to just walk away, at this stage.

'No!' she looked up. 'It's just . . . It's difficult.'

'I gathered that much.'

'I'm seeing this guy . . .'

'And your mum doesn't approve?' Daniel hazarded a guess. His first thought was that she had got herself pregnant, but he swiftly discounted that. Eminently possible, it was nevertheless something a fifteen-year-old girl might disclose to a member of her peer group but emphatically not to a male stranger twice her age – besides which, her interest in him had been as an ex-policeman.

'Mum's never even met him!' Zoe exclaimed. 'So what gives her the right to judge him? It's totally unfair!'

Daniel didn't think it would help to point out that as Zoe was underage, her mother had every right to be concerned about her relationships.

'Is he older than you?' he asked, backing a hunch.

'A little,' she conceded.

He raised an eyebrow.

'He's not *old* old. He's only nineteen! It's not like he's thirty or something,' she protested.

Ouch, Daniel thought ruefully. Still, four years could make all the difference when they bridged the age of consent.

'So why don't you invite her to meet him?' he suggested, smiling a brief thank you to the waitress, who had arrived with their order.

Zoe waited until they were alone once more, then said, 'I have. She refuses. But that's not the problem, anyway.'

'OK. So why don't you tell me what is – or do I have to keep guessing?' He pushed the second slice of cake in her direction and was pleased to see that after a quick glance of enquiry she had no hesitation in taking a mouthful.

'I know what you're thinking but it's not just a teenage crush,' she said then, around a mouthful of chocolate sponge. 'It really isn't. This is the real thing. We want to be together – to get married and do the whole settling-down thing.'

'You can't get married, you're only fifteen,' Daniel pointed out, beginning to sympathize with Lorna's objections but no nearer to discovering where he came into the equation.

'Sixteen in January,' Zoe stated, brushing that technicality aside as of little importance. 'The trouble is that we'll need somewhere to live and Shane can't afford a van, so he needed some money to buy his horse back and enter this race – but it was only going to be for a week or two . . .'

'Whoa! Wait a minute!' Daniel said, sifting the sudden rush of information. 'You're planning on living in a caravan?'

'They're not, like, any old caravan, they're beautiful,' she said defensively. 'Shane showed me his sister's van one time and it was lovely – nicer than my room at home.'

Daniel was conscious of a sinking feeling of inevitability.

'Shane . . .?'

'Brennan.'

'He wouldn't by any chance be a Traveller, would he?'

'So what if he is?' she demanded, her voice rising. 'He's all right. He's really nice. The discrimination against them is totally unfair! Anyway, he's an Irish Traveller, not a New Age or a Gypsy!'

Oh well, that's all right then, Daniel thought, but he kept his tongue between his teeth. He sensed Zoe was within an inch of walking out on him and in spite of his misgivings, from what he'd heard so far he didn't want to risk that.

'OK, calm down,' he said. 'People are looking.'

Zoe glanced round briefly, then returned her accusatory gaze to Daniel, who attempted to sort out the facts from the hysteria.

'You mentioned him wanting money to buy a horse for a race. He wants to buy a *racehorse*?'

'Not a thoroughbred racehorse!' Zoe exclaimed impatiently. 'Trotting – you know, in harness. Anyway, there's this trotting race – a really big one they have every year – and the prize is this really amazing caravan. So Shane has been helping train this horse that was really, really fast but then the man who owned her put her up for sale, so Shane thought if he could buy her, he could enter the race and win the caravan, but the trouble is, he hasn't got enough money.'

'What about his dad? Wouldn't he lend him the money?'

'But if he did, Shane wouldn't win the van, would he? It would be his dad's.'

'As a plan it has one glaring weakness,' he pointed out. 'Has it ever occurred to either of you that this horse might just not win the race?'

'Well, of course, it's not a hundred per cent certain but Shane says she's the best he's ever seen.'

Daniel suspected there might be more to the story than Shane was letting on even to Zoe, but he let it go. 'OK. So where do you come in?'

Zoe's gaze dropped and she began to push bits of cake round her plate with her fork.

'Well, obviously, I haven't got much money, myself, and I couldn't ask Mum without telling her what it was for . . .'

'And your father? Harvey, I mean.'

Zoe looked guarded. 'I did kind of ask him, but he said he hadn't got that kind of money in cash.'

'Didn't he want to know what it was for?' Daniel was surprised if Harvey had even considered it, unless he was trying to win brownie points with his stepdaughter. He wasn't sure what kind of a relationship they had.

'Well, yeah, kind of . . .'

'And he was OK with it? Has he actually met your boyfriend?'

'Once. By accident, really. I was out with Shane and we bumped into him.'

Daniel was finding it difficult to imagine a social situation where a Traveller lad and a high-flying businessman might have 'bumped into' one another. 'And he approved?' he asked sceptically.

Zoe gave a sulky shrug. 'He seemed cool with it. Anyway, he couldn't say a lot.'

'Why do you say that?'

'Oh, nothing. Forget it.'

'Was he with someone?'

'Someone . . .?'

'A woman?'

'Oh, no, nothing like that.'

Daniel took a long sip of his coffee and regarded Zoe over the rim of the cup. She looked uncomfortable.

'Just out of interest,' he said, putting the cup down. 'What sort of money are we talking about?'

After a moment's hesitation, Zoe mentioned a sum in the mid four-figures, and seeing Daniel's eyes open wide, hurried to justify it.

'It's not a lot, really – compared with what some people spend. Some of my mum's horses cost three times that much.'

Daniel didn't feel that the comparison was a fair one. He knew that two at least of Lorna's stable had the potential to be Grand Prix dressage horses.

'It may be a silly question, but wouldn't it be better just to spend the money on a caravan in the first place?' he asked. 'Not that I think it's a good idea at your age, but you're clearly very determined and it would cut out the chance element.'

'I think the really nice vans cost a lot more than that, besides, Shane wouldn't let me pay. Traveller men are very proud, you know. Personally, *I* wouldn't mind *what* the van was like but Shane says he wants the best for me and he wants to pay for it. He calls me his princess.'

'But he's happy for you to buy this horse he wants?'

'But that's just *borrowing*,' she explained as to one who was being slow on the uptake. 'Until he wins the race, and then the horse will be worth loads more and he can sell it again.'

'All right. I'm assuming you're not about to ask me to lend you the money, because even if I wanted to, I haven't got that kind of money lying around. So why *did* you want to talk to me? I hope you're not expecting me to plead with your mum for you. Even if I knew her well enough to interfere – and I don't – I wouldn't do it.'

'No, I know that. Anyway, I've got the money, now – at least, I did have . . .' She toyed with the last bits of her cake, her long dark lashes hiding her eyes.

'So where *did* you get it, in the end?'

'It was left to me by my gran.'

Daniel looked at her through narrowed eyes.

'Is that the truth?'

Zoe took refuge in her coffee cup, but under Daniel's continuing scrutiny she all but squirmed.

'Yes, it's the truth! Well, in a manner of speaking. My granny left me her jewellery.'

'Jewellery isn't cash,' Daniel pointed out. 'Please tell me you haven't sold it.'

'No! I wouldn't do that. I pawned it. It's still mine. I mean, it's just like borrowing. I can get it back any time.'

Daniel gave her a hard look.

'You didn't pawn it with any reputable broker. You're too young.'

'Shane did it for me.'

Daniel suppressed a groan, but she saw the look on his face and hurried to her boyfriend's defence.

'I trust him. The Travellers are very honourable people.'

Among their own kind, maybe, Daniel thought, but said, instead, 'OK. So if everything's good, what's the problem?'

'He's gone missing,' Zoe admitted in a small voice. 'Shane has. I don't know where he is.'

THREE

'It's not what you think!' was Zoe's predictable response to Daniel's silently raised eyebrow. 'Something must have happened to him. He would never just go off without telling me.'

'So if you're so sure he'll be back, why are you enlisting my help to find him?' Daniel asked. 'That *was* what you were going to do, wasn't it?'

Zoe nodded miserably.

'It's the pawnbroker. We only borrowed the money for a month because it was cheaper, and if we're late, he'll sell the rings.'

'How long have you got left?'

'Two weeks. Well – ten days,' Zoe amended. 'Please, can you help me? If Mum finds out she'll go absolutely crazy! Especially now, on top of this stuff with Dad.'

Daniel favoured her with a long look, under which she coloured a little and took a sip of her cappuccino.

'When did you last see Shane?'

'Last week. He has Monday off work, so we spent the day together.'

'When you should have been at school.'

'It's just one day,' Zoe protested. 'Didn't you ever bunk off school as a kid? You won't tell Mum, will you?'

'I ought to,' Daniel said, dodging the question. 'So you haven't heard from him since then?'

'He messaged me on Tuesday but that was the last time.'

'So, it's not been that long.'

'For us it is,' she said. 'Normally we're in touch all the time, messaging and that. Now he won't even answer his phone and his sister hasn't been at school, either.'

'You think she's gone too? You don't think it's possible the family have just moved on somewhere for a bit?'

Zoe shook her head.

'No! Well, I don't know, do I? They're Travellers . . . Leila's often off school for no reason. But Shane wouldn't go without telling me, especially not with my money; he knows how important it is for me to get the rings back.'

Daniel regarded her for a long moment, trying to decide how much of what he was hearing was the truth.

'Give me one good reason why I should help,' he said at length. 'You're the daughter of someone I deliver animal feed to. I only met you yesterday. You could be lying through your teeth.'

'I thought . . . I mean, you were hugging my mum, so I thought you were friends,' Zoe said helplessly.

'She was upset,' Daniel said. 'What was I supposed to do? Drive off? And come to that, how do *you* know you can trust *me*? You know nothing about me.'

'Mum obviously trusts you,' Zoe said. 'And you were in the police.'

Daniel uttered a short, humourless laugh. 'Some of the biggest villains uncaught are in the police force, I can tell you that for nothing,' he said. 'OK. Say I did agree to help you – just what exactly do you expect me to do?'

'Well, help me find out what's happened to Shane,' she said as if she was asking him to get something from the shops for her. 'I'd do it myself but I can't because I haven't any transport and, well, I don't much like going into the Traveller village on my own.'

'Well, thank God you've got that much sense, at least,' Daniel commented with feeling. 'So Shane lives in a settlement, does he? That's one thing to be grateful for. I don't fancy chasing a bunch of caravans all over England!'

Zoe, who'd flushed darkly at Daniel's first words, now looked up at him with guarded hope in her eyes.

'So you'll do it? You'll help me?'

'Against my better judgement; I'll see what I can do but I'm making no promises. I still think you'd be better making a clean breast of it to your mum but I agree the timing could be better. I take it she hasn't been in touch with Harvey yet.'

Zoe shook her head, frowning. 'No. What's going on there? I mean Mum's trying to pretend there's nothing the matter but I can see she's seriously stressed.'

'I'm sorry, but you'll have to ask her. It's not for me to say.'

'I *have* asked, but she won't tell me. She just says she needs to speak to Harvey about something. I mean, I don't get why it's so urgent.'

'Yeah, well look, I have a dog in the car who's gagging for a walk, so I'd better go.' He finished his coffee and pushed his chair back.

Zoe opened her eyes wide.

'You said you'd help me!'

'I will, but not right now.'

'Why not?'

'Because I need time to think,' Daniel told her. 'Now, I need to know where Shane lives and anything else you can tell me about him. Come on, I'll give you a lift home and you can fill me in on the way.'

'I don't want Mum to know I've been talking to you.'

'Then I'll drop you at the top of your drive or you can tell her you missed the bus and I saw you walking. Come on, shake a leg . . .'

The next evening found Daniel once again in the company of Zoe Myers. In the intervening time he had slept, done a day's driving and found out as much as he could about the local Traveller settlement, which was on a site known as Hawkers Yard near the rural hamlet of Ottersmoor. There was plenty of news coverage about it in the archives of the regional papers but it was mainly in the shape of letters of complaint from other local residents and articles from a couple of years previously, when the idea of making an illegal site permanent had first reared its unpopular head.

A call to Fred Bowden's son, Tom, produced information relating to a number of minor offences both proven and suspected, but nothing of great note. The surname Driscoll cropped up more than most and Daniel gathered that the Driscolls were one of the leading Traveller families in the area. On Shane Brennan himself, there was nothing beyond a caution for causing an obstruction on the public highway, the result, apparently, of an impromptu trotting race.

'What are you mixed up in now?' Tom asked. 'Because whatever it is, if it involves the Driscoll family, I'd strongly advise you to leave well alone.'

'Daughter of a friend; boyfriend trouble. As far as I know, it's got nothing to do with the Driscolls, but I'll bear it in mind.'

'In my experience they're pretty much all related,' Tom grunted. 'But keep me in the loop, OK?'

When he'd spoken to Lorna earlier in the day, there had been no word from Harvey and she was clearly very stressed. 'If I don't hear from him tonight, I'm going to ring his work,' she told Daniel. 'He won't like it, but that's tough!'

Daniel refrained from saying that Harvey's feelings should be the least of her worries, merely repeating his instructions that she was to contact him if she needed anything.

'You've obviously been there before, so how do you normally get to Ottersmoor?' he asked now, as Zoe settled into the passenger seat of his ageing Mercedes. On this occasion, her oversized jumper partnered a long ethnic-inspired skirt. The lacy mitts were again in evidence and big hooped earrings swung under the curtain of silky hair.

'There's a school bus,' she replied. 'Some of the kids from the site get it, but mostly Shane would pick me up on his bike.'

'Motorbike?' Daniel asked, feeling ever more in sympathy with Lorna's views on the suitability of her daughter's boyfriend.

Zoe nodded.

'If he's got a motorbike, couldn't he have sold that to fund this horse he wants?'

'No, cos he needs it to get to work,' she said. 'And anyway, it's seriously old. Shane says it's not worth more than a couple of hundred quid.'

'Where does he work?'

'For his uncle, at the greyhound kennels in Barnsworthy.'

'Billy Driscoll?' The name had come up several times in the course of Daniel's Googling and he remembered a connection with greyhounds.

'Yes!' Zoe was clearly surprised. 'Do you know him?'

'Of him. I've been doing my homework. The Driscolls are pretty well known in the area, it seems.'

'Well, Johnny Driscoll is, like, the head of the family – of the whole site, really, if that makes sense?'

'Yeah, I know roughly how it is with these Travelling communities,' Daniel said. 'So Billy is what – his brother? His son?'

'Brother,' Zoe confirmed. 'Johnny owns the kennels, Billy runs it for him. And there's another brother called Davy who's a few sandwiches short of a picnic. I've only met him once but he's a bit creepy.'

'That's right. Wasn't there something about him finding a Saxon ring on the property?' Daniel recalled an archived newspaper article with a picture of Billy Driscoll proudly showing it off.

'I don't know. Shane's never said anything about that. He doesn't like it there very much,' she confided. 'It's not the job; he likes the dogs, he just doesn't get on with Billy. He says he's a bully and doesn't care about the dogs. Shane rescued one a few months ago. It was his favourite but Billy was going to get rid of it. It was only three.'

'So if he's so unhappy, why doesn't he leave?'

'He would but it's, like, impossible to get a job round here once people find out you're a Traveller. It's seriously unfair!'

'And you want to marry into that world?' Daniel quizzed mildly.

'It's not Shane's fault. He's not like that!' she retorted hotly. 'And anyway it's racist to discriminate against them.'

'So it may be, but it happens and that's a fact. You'd better get used to it.'

'Well, I won't let it stop me being with the man I love,' Zoe declared, and Daniel decided to let it go for the present. He had a feeling that the idea of being a star-crossed lover might very well be part of the allure for Lorna's daughter and any perceived opposition would merely harden her resolve.

'Good for you,' he murmured, and was rewarded by a sidelong glance bristling with suspicion.

Slowing down as they reached Ottersmoor, Daniel saw the long stretch of white-painted stone wall that enclosed the Travellers' settlement. He glanced at Zoe and caught her looking a little apprehensive, now that the moment had arrived. He could understand that. In spite of her avowed confidence that Shane wouldn't have played her false, she must have considered the possibility, if only in secret, and now she might be on the verge of discovering the truth.

Daniel swung the car between the concrete gateposts and into the central avenue from which side roads branched off in pairs on a grid pattern. He slowed down.

'Where now?'

'It's the last road on the left,' Zoe replied. 'And then the third van on the right.'

In the early hours of the evening, darkness still half an hour away and the children home from school, Hawkers Yard was a hive of activity, much of which stopped abruptly as Daniel drove in. Perhaps two dozen pairs of intensely interested eyes followed the progress of the old Mercedes estate as Daniel drove down the central avenue, and doubtless many others observed them from behind net curtains.

The children, many of whom fell in behind the car as it passed, had a certain look about them, compounded of arrogance, bull-ishness and a measure of wariness, that Daniel felt he would have recognized anywhere. There were a number of girls among them, dressed to impress in miniskirts and strappy or strapless tops despite their tender years and the coolness of the evening.

The caravan Zoe directed him to was, like those around it, large, fairly new and immaculate, its immediate environs cheered by AstroTurf and numerous pots of late-flowering annuals. A flight of steps flanked by more flowers led to an open doorway screened by a curtain of iridescent glass beads.

As Daniel parked the car on the roadway in front of the van, the curtain twitched aside and a statuesque woman stepped out onto the top step. She had tightly curling black hair drawn into a ponytail and coal-dark eyes. Gold hoop earrings and bangles gleamed against her deeply tanned skin. She held a baby straddled on one hip and a toddler peered curiously round her legs, one pudgy hand entwined in her long skirts, the thumb of the other plugging its mouth. The woman's gaze narrowed as Daniel stepped out of the car but when Zoe appeared on the other side, she relaxed a little.

''E's not 'ere, love,' she stated, before either of them had time to speak. ''E's gone with the old man.' Her voice held the Irish burr characteristic of her people.

'Where have they gone?' Zoe asked.

'I dunno, love.' She spoke to Zoe but her gaze kept flickering between the girl and Daniel. 'Men's business. I don't get told an' I don't ask.'

'But . . .' Zoe's voice reflected her disappointment. 'I don't understand. He didn't say anything about going away. Why did he go without telling me?'

She shrugged. 'Like I said – men's business.'

'But when's he coming back?'

The woman shifted the baby to a more comfortable position and looked beyond her visitors towards the small crowd that had gathered.

'Siobhan O'Malley, your mother's looking for you! Where've you been?'

'I bin along of our Jimmy,' came the jaunty response. 'Our ma knows where I am.'

'That's not what she told me. Cut along home now, before your father comes looking.'

Daniel looked over his shoulder and, seeing him, the young girl in question tossed her head then turned and headed away from the group with the hip-swinging gait of a catwalk model, casting a backward glance to make sure she had been noticed. She couldn't have been more than ten or twelve years old.

Apparently satisfied, the woman on the steps returned her attention to her visitors.

'Dunno, love,' she said in answer to Zoe's question. 'Could be this week or could be next. Mightn't be till Christmas, for all I know.'

'But it can't be that long, surely?' Zoe protested. 'Did he . . .? I mean, was anything left for me? He had something of mine.'

'Didn't say nothing to me about leaving anything,' she said, uninterestedly. 'But 'e ain't no thief. If it's yours you'll get it back eventually. Who's yer friend?'

Zoe ignored the question, saying instead, in a voice that was on the verge of cracking, 'But I must have it now; Shane knows that. Why isn't he answering his phone?'

'Because 'e left it behind. S'on my kitchen table,' the woman stated, her eyes still on Daniel.

'Hi. I'm Daniel Whelan,' he supplied. 'A friend of Zoe's.'

'That's a name from the homeland.'

'I'm Irish on my father's side but from way back. And you are?'

'Maire Brennan. Shane's my boy. Look, Zoe, you're a nice girl but you don't belong here with our kind. Go and find yourself a nice country boy to settle down with.'

'But you don't understand!' she persisted. 'I have to speak to Shane, it's important!'

'It really is,' Daniel put in. 'We're not going to make any trouble for him, we just need to speak to him.'

'Well, I don't say as I'd tell you iffen I *did* know but God's honest truth is that I don't,' the woman said with an air of finality, taking a step backwards and pulling the curtain aside with her free hand.

'But that's crazy! You *must* know where your own bloody son is!' Zoe blurted out.

Maire's eyes flashed angrily, and from the doorway of a neighbouring van, a male voice was heard, enquiring if she wanted any help. Moments later a man appeared on the step wiping tattooed arms on a towel. He was built like a power-lifter and wore black jeans and a red vest, which revealed bronzed skin covered in tattoos.

She waved her hand. 'No, I'm OK,' she replied, then to Zoe, 'You keep a civil tongue in your head, miss, or there's nobody who'll be telling you anything!'

'Nobody is, anyway,' Zoe retorted.

The man in the red vest descended the steps and took a pace or two towards Daniel and the girl before standing with his feet slightly apart. He flicked the towel up onto his shoulder and bunching one fist he rubbed it in the palm of the other. Daniel noted that his knuckles were already raw and bruised. The man didn't say anything but then he didn't really have to.

Daniel caught at Zoe's arm.

'Come on, Zoe. It's time we went. Get in the car.'

She rounded on him furiously.

'You're supposed to be helping me!'

'Neither of us can force the lady to tell us what she doesn't know.'

'You believe her?'

'As a matter of fact, I do. But even if I didn't, there's nothing we can do about it. She has every right to keep it to herself if she wants to. It's her family, after all. Come on, let's go.'

Zoe glared at him, then shook her arm free with a petulant gesture and headed for the car.

Daniel waved a hand at the Irish woman, who had been regarding the exchange from the other side of the bead curtain.

'Sorry to bother you.' A nod in the direction of the silent man went unacknowledged.

'You need to keep a tight rein on the lass,' Maire Brennan advised. 'She's a quick temper on her and it'll get her into trouble if she's not careful.'

'I'll try. But it really is important, so if you hear from Shane . . .'

'I'll tell him you were here,' she said with a nod. 'Can't promise more than that.'

'Thank you.'

As Daniel slipped back into the driver's seat of the Merc, Zoe favoured him with a sulky look.

'Dunno why you're thanking her. She was lying through her teeth.'

'You don't have a very high opinion of your future mother-in-law,' Daniel observed with a touch of amusement.

Zoe flushed.

'She won't be my mother-in-law, anyway, at this rate,' she countered. 'What am I supposed to do now?'

'I don't know,' Daniel admitted, turning the car around. 'But swearing at people isn't the answer, it just puts their backs up. We'll find somewhere for a coffee and come up with Plan B. In the meantime, snap out of that mood before I regret agreeing to help you.' If the truth were told, he'd begun to regret his decision almost as soon as it had been made but his reasons for doing so remained and it wasn't in his nature to go back on his word.

Zoe subsided into silence, but the atmosphere didn't noticeably lighten. Daniel pulled out of Hawkers Yard onto the road, trying to think where he would be likely to find a café open at this time of the evening. Remembering passing a garage with a Costa sign a few miles back, he turned that way, but before he had driven more than fifty yards, a girl stepped out of the trees to his left and waved a hand.

Zoe grabbed Daniel's arm with both her hands, causing him to swerve momentarily.

'For God's sake!' he exclaimed, shaking her off.

'No, you have to stop! That's Leila – Shane's sister. Perhaps she knows something.'

Obediently, Daniel pulled in next to the girl: a well-endowed teenager with bleached blonde hair, dressed in a skin-tight pink miniskirt and leather jacket. Her vest top was cut low and Daniel wondered, not for the first time, at the paradoxical values of the Travelling folk. Living in old-fashioned chastity until they married, the girls were often allowed to dress from an early age in a way that could at best be described as beyond their years, and at the worst, tarty.

Leila leaned towards the opened window, displaying an expanse of deeply tanned cleavage for Daniel's delectation.

She was a little out of breath, which fact was explained by her first words.

'I heard yer talking to Ma, so I came out here so's to catch yer after. I knew she wouldn't tell yer anything,' she added in her husky Irish tones.

Zoe flashed a triumphant look at Daniel before turning back to the girl.

'So she does know where your brother is!'

'Not exactly,' Leila said, straightening up and looking back down the road. 'Look, can we go somewhere else. Ma'll catch me a clip round the ear if she thinks I've gone behind 'er back.'

'You can come with us,' Zoe said promptly. 'We're getting a coffee. We'll drop you back after.'

Resigned to having no say in the matter, Daniel nodded.

'You'd better get in.'

'You haven't been at school,' Zoe said as Leila opened the door and slid in. 'And why haven't you been answering your phone?'

'Battery's flat, isn't it? And I can't find the charger; think our Tommy's nicked it.'

'Well, I can't get hold of Shane and I couldn't get you either,' Zoe complained. 'Couldn't you have borrowed one?'

'Well, I didn't know you were trying to get me, did I?' the Traveller girl pointed out reasonably. 'Ma kept me back from school to help with the little ones.'

Luckily, due to Daniel having needed the back seat free for transporting something, Taz was for the time being confined to the area at the extreme rear of the estate car. He whined and shifted to and fro behind the mesh guard upon finding Leila just inches from his nose and she cast a wary look over her shoulder at him.

'Cor, he's a big one!' she breathed. 'Glad he's shut away.'

'He's a softie,' Daniel assured her. 'Most of the time . . .'

He drove on, a waft of musky scent assailing his senses, and Zoe instantly started to question her friend but Leila seemed unwilling to unburden herself straightaway, and he wondered with amusement if she suspected that she'd miss out on the coffee if she dispensed her news too speedily.

Fortunately for the girls' continuing friendship, they soon came upon the garage with the coffee bar and within a very short time were seated on perch stools at a high round table with an assortment of beverages and cakes in front of them.

Leila beamed at Daniel.

'Didn't expect this!' she told him, but Zoe interrupted impatiently.

'Never mind that! Where's Shane?'

Leila didn't seem to resent the other girl's rudeness.

'I don't actually know *where* he is,' she said, provoking a groan of deep frustration from Zoe. 'But,' she went on, 'I know why he went, cos I overheard them arguing.'

'Who?' Zoe demanded.

'Shane and me da, and Billy Driscoll. Well, it was difficult not to hear, really. A right slanging match there was. Should think the 'ole neighbourhood heard till me ma told 'em to keep their voices down.'

'What were they arguing about?'

'Don't know 'xactly. Your name came up quite a lot but that can't have been all of it cos everyone always knew Shane was walking out with a country girl, but that night Billy was mad, I mean *really* mad, so it musta bin something seriously bad!' she recounted with relish. 'Uncle Billy was yellin' and threatening our Shane, and our da was trying to quieten him down but he wasn't having any of it. In the end, Johnny comes along and wants to know what's going on. Then he tells our da it'd be best if he got Shane out of the way for a bit. Shane wasn't happy but Billy says if he ever catches him around here again, he'll make him sorry he was ever born! So then Ma says . . .'

'What? He's not coming back?' Zoe cut in sharply.

'I don't know. I'm just telling you what Billy said,' Leila said, taking refuge in her chocolate muffin.

'But you don't understand! I have to see him!'

'Well, it's not *my* fault, is it?'

'And you didn't get any idea what Shane might have done to upset Billy?' Daniel asked.

Leila shook her head.

'No, but he's got a bit of a temper on 'im, has Billy. Anyway, Shane and our da wasn't happy about leavin' but nobody don't cross Johnny.'

'Oh, God! What am I going to do?' Zoe wailed.

'I expect he'll come back eventually,' the other girl said helpfully. 'I mean, he can't have meant for ever, can he? Otherwise we'd all have gone.'

'But that's no good, is it? I have to see him *now*! Your mum said he's left his phone behind. Why would he do that?'

Leila shrugged. 'Dunno. Maybe Da made him. Johnny's dead agin us walking out with country folk – outsiders, that is. Says it's always trouble. Sorry, Zo,' she added.

'It's just soooo unfair.'

Leila shrugged and, her protestations apparently at an end, Zoe subsided into brooding silence, chewing one of her fingernails, her cake untouched beside her.

'Have you really no idea where they might have gone?' Daniel asked.

She shrugged again. 'Could be anywhere, we've got family all over. S'possible they've even gone back home.'

'Ireland, you mean?'

Leila nodded and took a sip of her coffee.

Ignoring Zoe's groan, Daniel tried again. 'I assume your mum'll be in touch with your dad. Could she perhaps get a message to Shane that way?'

Zoe looked up hopefully.

'Dunno,' the Traveller girl looked doubtful. 'I'll ask, but if Da doesn't want our Shane to talk to you . . .'

'Shane's not a kid! He's old enough to make his *own* decisions!' Zoe stated with some heat. 'It's so not fair!'

Leila looked uncomfortable.

'It's different for us . . .'

There didn't seem to be anything further to be said, so seeing that Leila had finished her cake and coffee, Daniel suggested it was time they got moving. Zoe hadn't touched her muffin but glancing back at the table as they left, Daniel noticed with amusement that the cake had disappeared, no doubt deftly palmed by Shane's sister.

'I don't understand why he'd go *now*,' Zoe said when they were back in the car and on the way back to Hawkers Yard. 'All he could talk about, the last time I saw him, was the race and buying his horse back. I can't believe he'd just go off and give it all up.'

'You don't understand how it is with us,' Leila said. 'And anyway, he bought the mare before he went.'

'Bought it?' Zoe repeated, swivelling round in her seat to look at the other girl. 'When?'

'The day before he went. Told Da he wasn't gonna leave her behind, so they took her with them.'

Zoe stared at her for a moment or two longer, then faced front again, slumping into her seat and gazing moodily ahead.

They let Leila out a few yards up the road from Hawkers Yard and Daniel turned the car for Abbots Farm.

'That wasn't a lot of help, was it? I'm sorry,' he said, after a moment, when his companion showed no sign of speaking. 'It seems like a bit of a dead end.'

'Well, at least I know why he hasn't answered my calls.'

'Why hasn't *he* called *you*, though? You would have thought he could find a way. I mean – borrow a phone or even use a landline. It sounds as though he's bowing to family pressure.'

'He wouldn't do that!' Zoe said with certainty. 'Anyway, I doubt he knows my number. I wouldn't know his if I didn't have my mobile with me.'

'What about email?'

'We never have. We normally message each other, you know, Snapchat or something.'

'Facebook?'

'It's not really his thing . . .'

'Looks like you're a bit stuck, then. What is it with you Myers women and your men?'

'You're not giving up?' Zoe asked sharply. 'You promised!'

'That I did not,' Daniel stated firmly. 'I said I'd help if I could and I have tried, but you must see this makes it almost impossible to track him down. Besides which,' he added, 'he hasn't got your money any more. According to Leila, he's spent it.'

'But I still need to find him. I can't just leave it at that. I've got to get that money back somehow.'

'I really think you'd do better to come clean to your mum. She might be cross to start with but I'm sure she'd lend you the money to get the jewellery back. After all, she wouldn't want you to lose it, if it's been in the family.'

'No! I can't do that! You mustn't tell her – please, Daniel! She'd blame Shane.'

And rightly, Daniel thought but he didn't reply. With her current worries, he didn't relish the thought of giving Lorna another cause for anxiety but he would tell her about Zoe's predicament, if he felt he had to.

Zoe fell silent, and after a couple of miles had swished by, Daniel glanced her way. She appeared to be deep in thought, which made him feel slightly uneasy but he didn't disturb her.

They were approaching the driveway to her house when she spoke at last.

'I'll go and see Billy Driscoll,' she said decisively. 'I bet he knows where Shane's gone. He must know why, at any rate.'

'I don't think that's a good idea,' Daniel told her. 'If he's not happy that Shane's been seeing you, he's not likely to tell you where to find him, is he? He sounds like a pretty rough character, too.'

'Well, I'll have you to protect me, won't I?' she said sweetly.

'I don't remember offering to take you.'

'If you won't come, I'll go on my own.'

'And how will you get there?'

'I could hitchhike. I've done it before.'

'You,' he said, 'are a devious, manipulating little . . .'

'Cow? Bitch? Minx?' she supplied.

'Well, I wasn't going to say it, but quite frankly, yes. All of the above! I'm beginning to think Shane might have had the right idea in scarpering!'

'That's unkind,' she said making a face. 'When shall we go, then? Tomorrow?'

'Maybe. It depends on work. I'll have to let you know.' If he was being railroaded into confronting Driscoll, Daniel wanted to find out all he could about the greyhound trainer before he went, being a firm believer that to be forewarned was to be forearmed.

'I expect I could get a bus, or hitch,' she mused.

'If I find you've gone on your own, I'll go to your mum and tell her everything,' Daniel told her. 'And that *is* a promise.'

'You wouldn't?'

'Watch me. Be glad to wash my hands of it all.'

Zoe's look turned mutinous.

'Didn't take you for a quitter,' she muttered.

'Well, now you know,' he said serenely.

FOUR

'Daniel?'

It was nine o'clock the next morning and Daniel had just made his second drop of the day. His phone had started ringing just as he was about to pull out onto the road again, and he stopped at the end of the farm track with the engine idling.

'Hello?'

'Daniel? Hi, it's me, Lorna Myers.'

'Hi, Lorna. Are you OK?'

'Yes. I mean, no. I don't know. I've just rung GS – Harvey's work – and they say they don't know where he is. He's not in Hong Kong. He was only there a few days. They're saying he flew back nearly ten days ago and he's now on leave. Apparently he booked it before he went. They seemed surprised that he wasn't with me.' She paused. 'Daniel . . .?'

'Yes, I'm here. Sorry, go on.'

'I don't know what's going on. He's been missing nearly two weeks! What do I do now? If this was all planned then I was never meant to know. Where is he? And . . .' She took a steadying breath. 'And who's he with?'

'I know how it looks but he may not be with anyone,' Daniel began, but Lorna cut in.

'Then where is he? And how did those men know he was back when I didn't? How often has he lied to me like this? I feel like everyone knows what's going on except me!'

'Lorna, slow down,' Daniel advised, when she stopped for a breath. 'I think it's much more likely that Harvey has got wind of the fact that those two charmers are looking for him and is lying low.'

'But why didn't he tell me what's going on? Why didn't he warn me, for God's sake?'

'I can't say for sure but he may have thought it would be better if you knew nothing about it. After all, what you don't know, you can't tell, and if he has got himself into a whole load of trouble, I imagine he hoped he could sort it all out without you knowing.'

'But what sort of trouble? I don't understand how he came to owe those men money, if that's what it is. What's he been doing? Should I ring the police and report him missing?'

'Well, strictly speaking, we don't know that he's missing, do we?' Daniel said. 'He came back from Hong Kong early without telling you but it seems to have been planned. I hate to have to say it, Lorna, but whatever he's been up to, it's unlikely to be legitimate. Those two guys weren't sent by any solicitor's office. If I had to hazard a guess, I'd say maybe he's got himself in a bit deep with the bookies and got himself in hock trying to clear it.'

'No!' Her vehemence surprised him. 'He wouldn't do that. He knows how I feel about gambling. He promised. He actually *promised*, when we got married, that he never would.'

Belatedly, Daniel remembered what Fred had told him about Lorna's brother. Privately he thought that the breaking of such a promise might go a long way to explaining Harvey Myers' secretive behaviour but he had no wish to distress Lorna further while there was no proof. 'Well, for whatever reason, I reckon he's found himself short of cash and gone to a moneylender – maybe to fund an investment that went bad – and now he can't pay it back. You said his accountant was keen to get hold of him the other day . . .'

'He was,' Lorna admitted. 'But he wouldn't tell me why. Oh God, what a mess! What am I supposed to do now? How dare he just bugger off and leave me to deal with all this?'

As Daniel's thoughts had been running along the same lines for the last two days, he could provide no constructive answer.

'What's important now is to make sure you and Zoe are safe. I really don't like you being there on your own.'

'I won't be for much longer,' she said. 'I rang Stephen and he's coming down tomorrow for the weekend.'

'Well, that's something, at least,' Daniel said, endeavouring to keep the doubt out of his voice. As far as he knew, Harvey's son, Stephen, worked as the manager of an art gallery. He just hoped his spare-time activities were more physically challenging, if he was to provide any form of protection to his stepmother should Leather Jacket and his tattooed mate come calling again.

'So where does your mum think you are *this* time?' Daniel asked, as he and Zoe headed for Barnsworthy the following evening.

'Doing coursework at a girlfriend's house,' she replied unashamedly. 'At least, that's what I told her. She probably thinks I'm secretly meeting Shane.'

'You haven't told her he's disappeared, then?'

'No. She doesn't need any more reasons to dislike him.'

'She's just looking out for you, you know,' Daniel said.

'I know, and I love her to bits, but she's wrong about this.'

'Has there been any news on your father?'

Zoe shook her head. 'And the worst thing's happened. Apparently Stephen's coming down for the weekend.' She groaned dramatically. 'I can't stand him! He's just so . . . so pompous! Thinks he knows everything and it's, like, his job to tell everyone how they could do things better. It's seriously annoying.'

'Seriously,' Daniel agreed, but Zoe appeared not to notice his gentle mickey-taking.

'Why did you stop being a policeman?' she asked after a moment or two. 'Didn't you like it?'

'I was asked to leave.' It wasn't strictly true, but easier than explaining the circumstances that had led to him handing in his notice.

'Seriously? Why? What did you do?'

'I, um – fell out with a senior officer.'

'Why?'

'Long story,' Daniel said with a sigh. 'I'd rather forget it.'

'My real father was a policeman,' Zoe said then. 'He ran out on us – Mum and me – before I was even born.'

'Yeah. My father did the same. He was a policeman, too.'

'When you were a baby?'

'No. He hung around longer than yours. I was eight when he left. No warning, no explanation. Mum had four of us to bring up by herself. It was a struggle.'

'But you still joined the police. Didn't your mother mind?'

'She wasn't over the moon but my sister was worse. She's really bitter about it. We don't talk much, but that's life, I guess.' With some relief, Daniel changed the subject. 'Now, the satnav is saying we've reached our destination but I don't see it, do you?'

'It's further along on the left, I think.'

'You've been here before? Why didn't you tell me?'

'Shane brought me on his bike once but it was dark and I didn't really see anything.'

'Did you see Driscoll?'

'No. Shane just nipped in for something. I stayed outside.'

'Well, you're going to do the same again, so get used to the idea,' Daniel told her.

When they eventually reached Barnsworthy and the kennels, which were unimaginatively but helpfully signposted as Driscoll Greyhound Racing, there appeared to be no one about. The kennels consisted of six rows of long, low buildings that might once have been pigsties or hen houses. They were reached by a gravel drive flanked by fields in which a variety of ponies and horses grazed on what looked to be very poor pasture riddled with ragwort and docks and littered with rusting corrugated iron and obsolete agricultural machinery.

Daniel parked in the wider space between the two central buildings, told Zoe to stay where she was and got out to investigate. The yard itself was clean enough. The concrete apron in front of each range of kennels appeared to have been recently swept and the sign on the door to the reception area and office was polished to a high gloss. A broom leaned against the wall at the far end, next to an industrial-sized plastic container of Jeyes Fluid, and a blue-light insect killer lay in wait under the eaves, flashing intermittently as it did its job.

Their arrival had been heralded by a cacophony of barking and before he'd gone very far, Daniel was hailed by a heavily built man in navy blue overalls who had just appeared round the end of one of the kennel blocks.

'Evening. Can I 'elp?' the man asked, pleasantly enough. Black hair was combed and greased back from a widow's peak on the forehead of a deeply tanned face out of which shadowed dark eyes peered shrewdly.

'Billy Driscoll?'

'S'right. Was I expecting you?'

'No. Sorry to turn up unannounced,' he said. 'Daniel Whelan.'

The man wiped a hand on his none-too-clean boiler suit and offered it to Daniel. His clasp was powerful, the palm broad and fingers short.

'So what can I do for you? Are you interested in buying a dog? Looking for a trainer?'

'Not just at the moment,' Daniel said. 'To tell you the truth I'm looking for someone and I thought you might be able to help.'

'Oh? Who?' Driscoll's genial persona shifted to one of wariness. His gaze slid past Daniel to where the Merc was parked.

'Shane Brennan,' Daniel told him. 'He was interested in a horse of mine, but I've lost touch with him and he mentioned working here, so I've . . .'

'Well, 'e don't work 'ere no more,' Driscoll cut in. ''Ad to let 'im go last week. Fact is I'm closin' down. Been in the business twenty-odd years but there's no money in the dogs no more. Tracks are closing all the time. Gonna give up and grow Christmas trees.'

'Yet you were going to sell me a dog a minute ago . . .' Daniel couldn't resist pointing out.

'Can't blame me for trying, now, can yer? Always got a few dogs for sale,' Driscoll told him. 'An' more specially now. Would've put you in touch with a mate of mine, if you had wanted a trainer.'

'It sounds as though you've still got plenty here. How are you going to manage on your own?'

'Not on my own, am I? Got my brother to 'elp. Look, I can't tell you where the boy is. I haven't seen him since he left here. Bit of a waste of space, truth be told.'

'I understood he was your nephew,' Daniel said.

'So what? I got more nevvies than you've had hot dinners, shouldn't wonder. Couldn't tell you where the half of 'em are at any one time.'

Daniel felt that was probably true. He plainly wasn't going to get any useful information from the man but something about Driscoll kept him probing. For one thing, making the boy redundant might possibly explain the row with Shane's father but it didn't explain why Johnny Driscoll should have felt it necessary to remove him from the area altogether. According to Leila, Billy had threatened violence if Shane ever crossed his path again.

'Couldn't you have kept Shane on to help with the trees?' he said then.

Driscoll shrugged.

'You know what kids are today – don't want to get their hands dirty.'

'Shouldn't have thought cleaning up after a bunch of dogs is a very clean job . . .'

'Like I said; he was a waste of space. Now, if there's nothing else . . .?'

'So what happens to all the dogs when you close down?' Daniel persisted, neatly sidestepping the trainer and strolling towards one of the buildings. 'You must have got quite a few here.'

He peered through a doorway into a corridor that ran along the front of a dozen or so individual wire-fronted pens. The leggy inmates bayed at him with renewed vigour and somewhere he could also hear the stentorian tones of at least two much larger dogs. The smell was slightly rank and the inner concrete didn't quite reflect the cleanliness of that on public display outside.

'Some'll go to other trainers; some owners will take their own dogs, and some will end up in rescue, I expect. It's unavoidable. It happens all the time.' Driscoll had moved to stand behind Daniel.

'They only have a working life of about three or four years, don't they?' Daniel said, turning round. 'You must have sent quite a few into rescue in twenty years of training.'

'So what if I 'ave? Look, what's with all the questions? What do you really want?'

At close quarters, Billy Driscoll was an impressive figure. Not far off six foot four, he was broad with it. Daniel was six foot himself, and not used to being towered over, but he didn't step back. On the wall, the insect killer buzzed as another fly met its maker.

'I told you, I'm looking for Shane. I'm just interested, that's all.'

'Well, 'e's not 'ere, and isn't gonna be, so I'd appreciate it if you'd leave now and let me get on with my work.'

'Well, I'll leave you my number and if you hear from him, perhaps you'd let me know,' Daniel said, taking a card from his pocket and offering it to Driscoll.

The bigger man grunted, but took it, nevertheless.

'Not expecting to. Heard 'e's gone north.'

'Well, just in case,' Daniel said, turning away. Beyond a straggling hedge at the side of the yard he could see the brown expanse of a recently ploughed field and further away still, more pastureland and a stand of woodland.

As he approached the car, Zoe spoke through the open window.

'Did he tell you?'

'He says he doesn't know.'

'He's lying!' In a flash Zoe had wrenched the door open, dodged round Daniel's outflung arm and marched over to Driscoll. 'Where's Shane?' she demanded.

Daniel emitted a silent groan and turned to follow.

Zoe was already squaring up to the trainer like a terrier to a mastiff, undaunted by his bulk.

'Where has he gone?'

'I've already said, I don't know,' Driscoll said, visibly annoyed. 'Don't tell me he was buying a horse off you, too.'

'Of course not! He's my boyfriend,' she said crossly, thereby effectively blowing Daniel's cover story, although Daniel doubted the man had believed it, anyway.

'So, you're the little slut who's had her claws into the boy.'

'*What* did you call me?'

'Well, he may have been your boyfriend. Not any more.'

'No. You're wrong. We're going to get married,' she stated.

'Zoe, come away.' Daniel took hold of her arm.

She shook him off.

'Sorry to shatter your dreams, sweetheart,' Driscoll said, ignoring Daniel and leaning towards her with an unpleasant leer, 'but Shane's never gonna marry no country girl, so I should go home to mummy, if I was you.'

'You can't stop us!' she flared up.

'Won't 'ave to. He told me all about yooz. Just stringing you along for what he could get, he was. Never had no intention of takin' it any further.'

'You're a liar!' Zoe said furiously.

'Well, if he's your boyfriend – how comes you don't know where he is?' Driscoll taunted.

'Zoe! Come with me, *now*!' Daniel told her, grasping her arm in an iron grip and forcibly turning her back towards the car, where, sensing the increasingly confrontational nature of the exchange, Taz was barking and showing his teeth at the window.

'I will find him,' Zoe called back over her shoulder.

'Yeah, well, good luck with that,' Driscoll replied.

'Will you just shut up?' Daniel told her roughly, propelling her towards the open passenger door.

'Ow! Get off! You're hurting me!' she said, transferring her anger to Daniel.

Given the thinness of the forearm he was gripping through the inevitable loose jumper, Daniel thought that was quite possibly true, but just at that moment he didn't care overmuch. Pushing her into the seat, he shut the door and went round to the drivers' side.

'I'll leave you behind next time!' he told her through his teeth. 'When I tell you to stay in the car, I expect you to do just that!'

'He was lying!' she protested. 'Anyone could see that.'

'Well, of course he was,' Daniel said, putting the car in gear and swinging it round. 'But there was nothing to be gained by telling him so. I hope you feel better for getting that out of your system because you've ruined any possibility of going back there.'

'I wouldn't want to, anyway!' she declared. 'I hate him. I can't believe he's any relation to Shane. I'm not surprised he hated working for him.'

Daniel raised a hand in farewell to Driscoll as they left but the gesture wasn't reciprocated and they left the premises with the trainer scowling blackly at their departing forms.

'What I don't understand,' he said as they drove back between the fields of dejected-looking ponies, 'is why Driscoll and Brennan had such a falling out. Your friend Leila made it sound as though Driscoll was threatening actual violence if he ever got his hands on Shane, and Shane's dad must have believed he meant it, if he was prepared to carry him off to the other end of the country, or wherever they've gone. It sounds like a lot more than just a row over Driscoll firing him – if that's what happened.'

'I don't know.' Zoe shrugged, twisting a few strands of silvery-gold hair round her index finger. 'The last time I spoke to Shane, he was still working for Billy. I knew he wasn't happy with the way the dogs are treated but he didn't mention anything in particular. I definitely don't think he was expecting to lose his job or anything.'

'Well, whatever the case, I can't help feeling you'd be better off out of that family,' he said, glancing at her as he pulled up at the junction with the road.

'I know you won't believe me but Shane's not like the others,' she said, her eyes all at once shining with unshed tears. 'He's kind and honest. But anyway, I still have to find him to get my money back.'

'Ah, yes,' Daniel said. 'The money. If it was only a short-term loan, how were you intending to pay it back? When is this famous race?'

'In the spring. But there are other races before then,' she added quickly. 'Shane said he'd win the money back in no time once he'd bought her.'

'But he's not here, is he?' Daniel observed, and earned a resentful glare.

'So what do we do now?' Zoe asked as they headed for home.

'I really don't know. We'll just have to hope that one of the family can appeal to his dad's better nature and get Shane to ring you.'

'And if they can't?'

Daniel didn't know.

'Maybe we can extend the loan on the rings to give us some breathing space,' he suggested. 'But I think you'll have to prepare yourself for the idea that you might never get that money back.'

'I was talking to Tom, last night,' Fred Bowden told Daniel over a cup of coffee before the day's work started. Daniel's lorry was being loaded from the warehouse and he had just got back from giving Taz an early morning constitutional round the woods that bordered the TFS depot. They now were sitting in Fred's office. 'He said you'd been in touch.'

'Yeah, I was asking him about the Travellers.'

'You're still helping Lorna's kid, then? You want to be careful, there. Getting mixed up with the Travelling community is never a good idea. But then, you'll know all about that, I suppose, with your background.'

'Mm. I've had my fair share of encounters with them in the past.'

Daniel had given his boss a summary of his first meeting with Zoe, leaving out any mention of the pawning of the jewellery. Now he told him briefly about the visit to the Traveller site and Driscoll's kennels.

'Hmm, Billy Driscoll. It's been a while since I last had any dealings with him and I have to say if I never do so again it'll be too soon.'

'Dodgy character?'

'I'll say. Twisty bastard is nearer the mark. We used to deliver to his kennels years ago. A bit off my patch but I was starting out and it looked like being a lucrative contract with the amount he was ordering. Course, I didn't know him then.'

'What happened?'

'Well, it was OK for the first couple of drops but then he started to drag his heels over payments, cheques would go missing in the post or would bounce, and then finally he tried to make me believe that he hadn't received his full order – not once, but twice! Well, you know how meticulous we are about checking and double-checking the load against the invoice . . .'

'Triple-checking, in fact,' Daniel nodded. It slowed up the process but pretty much eliminated any possibility of error.

'Yes, well let's say Mr Driscoll and Tavistock Farm Supplies had a parting of the ways, and I wouldn't describe it as amicable. I was within days of taking him to court when he settled his final bill. I've got nothing against the Travellers per se, but it's the few like him that perpetuate the bad feeling against them as a group.'

'A rotten apple.'

'Rotten to the core,' Fred agreed. 'And now you say he's thinking of growing Christmas trees. I'll believe that when I see it.'

'Yeah, me too,' Daniel agreed. 'And it seems that he's at the back of whatever made Zoe's boyfriend do a runner. Threatened ABH, I gather, but we don't know why and he's not telling.'

'Tell her to give it up as a bad job, I should.'

'Believe me, I have, but it's a bit more complicated than that.'

Fred grunted. 'Not pregnant, is she?'

'She says not, but he has something of hers – something she's anxious to get back before Lorna finds out.'

'Well, have another word with Tom,' Fred advised. 'He'll help you if he can. He's got a lot of time for you – can't think why . . . Now, as I said earlier, you've got a couple of extra drops today because of Frank being off, but they're not too far off your regular route. Oh, and I should warn you, you may notice that the invoice for Redlands Farm is slightly lower than you might expect; Peggy Branscombe has been a customer of ours for ever and she runs a rescue, so she gets special rates.'

'You're an old softie,' Daniel said, putting his mug down on the table and getting to his feet. 'You'll never be a millionaire.'

'Shut up and get out of here!' Fred growled, waving a hand in dismissal. 'Go on, clear off! You're late. I'll dock your pay if you don't get your arse in gear!'

Peggy Branscombe's delivery was scheduled towards the end of the day and, with lunch a distant memory, Daniel greatly appreciated the tea and scones that she produced as he finished unloading her order.

With only one more drop to make, Daniel was able to stop and chat for a few minutes, during which time he learned that Redlands Farm Rescue was pretty much a one-woman show. Peggy had started by rescuing and rehoming battery hens, and progressed to unwanted sheep and goats. Now she also had a couple of dozen dogs and cats, two elderly cows and three retired horses.

Peggy herself was a lean and wiry woman, somewhere in her late middle years, with a shock of greying frizzy hair and candid grey eyes.

'It's so hard to turn them away,' she said sadly. 'But sometimes I have to. There's only so much money to go round and although I have lots of wonderful volunteers, this is about the limit of what I can cope with.'

Daniel looked round at all the converted farm buildings and beyond, to where animals grazed contentedly in the adjacent fields.

'It must take all your time,' he said. 'Do you manage to rehome most of them, or do some stay for life?'

'I do try to rehome,' she said, 'because then I have room for more, and however much I love having them, I can't give them the individual attention they really need to thrive. It's a wrench saying goodbye, but hearing how they've settled into their new homes is just the best thing ever! We do get some sticky ones, though.'

Remembering Driscoll, Daniel asked, 'Do you often get greyhounds in?'

'Oh, do I ever?' she sighed. 'It's those I have to turn away most often. There is just a constant stream of them needing homes. The trouble is I don't find them easy to place. I've got three indoors that ended up staying.'

'I was at a kennel yesterday,' Daniel told her. 'Billy Driscoll's. I expect you've heard of him.'

'Oh yes!' she said. 'I've heard of him, all right! Anyone in rescue has had dealings with Billy Driscoll at one time or another, and usually lived to regret it. Used to always be badgering me to take dogs. Haven't heard from him for a couple of years, though, thank God! Finally got the message, I suppose.'

'He told me that a lot of his retiring dogs go into rescue, so I guess someone must take them,' Daniel said, polishing off a jammy scone and putting the plate down.

'There's Anya Darby at Longdogs Rescue, out Bideford way. Perhaps she's been taking them, let's hope so . . .'

Daniel thought that an odd remark and queried it.

'Oh well, nothing really. Don't quote me, but he wouldn't be the first trainer who had a retired dog or two – disappear, shall we say? And for some it's a lot more than that. There are people who make a profitable little business helping trainers clear their kennels of unwanted dogs.'

'I've heard that. It's not a sport with the best reputation.'

'And that's the ones that actually make it to the track,' Peggy said sadly. 'They reckon that upwards of thirty thousand are bred for the track every year but only around fifteen thousand are registered to race, so where do the others go? In the ground, probably, or burned. It's one of the many things the industry keeps very quiet about. The trouble is it's self-regulating. The Greyhound Racing Board is supposed to look out for the dogs' welfare but the board is pretty much made up of bookies, and we all know who they look out for!'

Daniel shook his head in disgust.

'I knew it was bad, but I didn't realize it was that bad,' he said. 'But Driscoll tells me he's jacking it all in, so hopefully there'll be a few less unwanted dogs on the market in due course.'

'If it's true, that's the best news I've heard for a long time,' Peggy declared. 'Here, take this last scone for your shepherd. He's been so patient, sitting in the cab.'

'He's used to it,' Daniel said, accepting the treat, nevertheless. 'He'll get a good walk when I've finished. Just one more drop to go, so it won't be long.'

While he was out walking that evening, Daniel found his thoughts constantly returning to Lorna and the disappearance of her husband, and when he got back to his car, he rang her.

She answered the phone with a wary, 'Yes?'

'Lorna? Hi, it's Daniel.'

'Oh, Daniel,' she said, sounding relieved.

'Are you OK?'

'Yes, it's just – I hate answering the phone these days. Every time it rings, I jump and then kind of freeze inside, terrified it'll be those men again.'

'They haven't contacted you?'

'No. I've heard nothing. It's just that it's always on my mind.'

'I'm sorry, I didn't mean to give you a fright. I was just wondering if your stepson had arrived.'

'Yes, Stephen's here. He turned up at lunchtime. It's good to have someone else around but that'll be a mixed blessing when Zoe gets back, I can tell you. They wind each other up no end. He thinks he can give her brotherly advice and she resents it. I'll be tearing my hair out by the end of the weekend, if last time's anything to go by!'

'Have you said anything to her about Harvey?'

'Not really. I don't know what to say. She knows I've been trying to get hold of him but I suppose I'll have to tell her the rest soon. I suppose I've hung on, hoping it'll all be sorted out and she won't need to know but I'd better tell her before Stephen lets it slip – he's not the most discreet of people.'

After Lorna rang off, Daniel continued his walk feeling increasingly unimpressed with what he knew of Harvey's son and pondering the strange mix of street savvy and naivety that was Zoe Myers. He supposed she was quite typical of a modern teenager; in some ways far more grown up than he'd been at that age, but in other ways far less so. They talked the talk and it was easy to forget just how inexperienced they really were.

It was almost fully dark by the time he and Taz returned to the car and he'd just slipped into the driver's seat when Zoe rang him. It was immediately obvious that she was in a state of high excitement.

'Daniel, I've seen him! I know where he is!' she declared, before he'd even had time to speak. 'We have to go – now, tonight!'

'Hold on. Slow down. I presume you're talking about Shane,' Daniel said.

‘Well, of course I am, who else?’ she replied impatiently.

‘Who indeed?’ he murmured.

She ignored him. ‘I’ve seen Shane. He’s in Wales. It was on the MSN news page. Leila hadn’t heard anything and I suddenly thought, what if I do a search for news stories about Travellers, and there he was!’

‘You actually saw him? Was he mentioned by name?’

‘Well, no, not specifically. But it *was* him, I’m sure it was.’

Leaving aside for the moment the all too real possibility, in his eyes, of mistaken identity, Daniel asked, ‘Why was he in the news? What has he done?’

‘He hasn’t done anything!’ she said, rising instantly to her boyfriend’s defence. ‘It was about the police trying to evict a group of Travellers from a site near Brecon. They weren’t doing any harm – I mean, they’ve got to live somewhere. Anyway, they showed a clip of a trotting race and I saw Shane’s dad really clearly and Shane in the background, driving.’

‘Are you sure it wasn’t archive footage?’ Daniel asked.

‘No, because they said the locals had been complaining about the Travellers using the roads for racing.’

‘Yes, I know, but they’ll still use old footage if they haven’t any of the actual event,’ he pointed out. ‘You’d want to be sure before you think about heading off halfway across the country.’

‘But they *were* in Wales. I saw a road sign for Merthyr Tydfil and looked it up. That’s on the edge of the Brecon Beacons. But we need to go soon because if the police do move them on, it might not be so easy to find them again. Google Maps says it takes two and a bit hours to get there, so if we set off right away, we could be there before ten.’

‘Whoa! Steady on! What’s this *we*? You’re expecting me to drop everything and take you to Wales? Now? Quite apart from the fact that I’m working in the morning, it’s a crazy idea! If they’ve been moved on they could be anywhere by now: I’m pretty sure your two and a bit hours would be much nearer three: and what the hell are you proposing to tell your mother when you set off halfway across the country in the dark?’

‘It’s not crazy!’ she said indignantly. ‘I’ve got to find him, to get my money back, so what else can I do? If he’s in Wales, that’s where I have to go. Somebody will have seen them. I’ll tell Mum I'm staying with Sarah for a sleepover. I often do stuff like that, she won't worry. Come on, Daniel. We have to go tonight. Surely you can get tomorrow off. Throw a sickie, or something.'

'You're an unprincipled brat!' Daniel said. 'I feel sorry for your mother. Listen, where are you now?'

'At home. Stephen's here,' she added disgustedly. 'I think Mum phoned him because of Harvey and he's come for the weekend. It's absolutely dire!'

'Has your mum told you about your dad – Harvey, I mean?'

'Well, only that he's not abroad, like she thought, and that she doesn't know where he is, but nothing else. Why, what do you know?'

'Not much more than that.'

'You have to wonder, don't you . . .?' she said.

'What?'

'Well, whether he's – you know – got another woman. Why else would he not be answering her calls? I'm sure that's what Mum's thinking.'

'If he wanted to keep it a secret, he'd surely do better to answer her calls.'

'Well, *I* don't know,' she said, dismissively. 'But what about tonight? What time can you pick me up?'

'I can't,' he said decisively.

'You mean, you won't.' She sounded sulky.

'Well, whichever it is, the result is the same for you. It would be pointless setting off now. It'll be dark soon and we wouldn't get there before eleven, and then we'd have to find them, which wouldn't be easy, even in the daylight. No. Tomorrow, maybe. I'll have to think about it but it won't be until lunchtime at the earliest. My boss is short-staffed so I can't just "throw a sickie" as you helpfully suggested.'

'But, *Daniel*! He could be anywhere by then!'

'Tough. Ask your mum to take you.'

There was a frustrated groan and then, 'What time tomorrow?'

'I'll ring you in the morning.'

FIVE

Daniel half expected to be on the receiving end of a phone call from Zoe at the crack of dawn the next day, but in the event it was Lorna who rang when he was on his way to work after a quick leg-stretch with Taz on the moors.

'Daniel? It's Lorna. Zoe's gone!'

'Gone where?' Daniel asked with a sinking sensation as he pulled his car in to the side of the road. He had a horrible feeling he already knew the answer.

'I don't know. We had a huge row last night and she stomped off to her room but this morning she's not there and her bed hasn't been slept in. I'm worried she's gone off to be with that Traveller boy but I don't know where he lives or anything . . .' She paused. '*You* don't know where she is, do you? She mentioned you last night. Said you'd been helping her. Daniel, what's been going on?'

Daniel sidestepped the question. 'Can I ask what the row was about?' he enquired cautiously. He needed to know how the land lay before he offered any information.

'I suppose so. It was one of those stupid things that escalated out of all proportion. I'd discovered that some jewellery of mine was missing and I asked her if she'd borrowed it. She seemed to think I was accusing her of stealing it and then Stephen stuck his oar in. It was pretty awful but I never thought for a moment that she'd do something like this!'

'Look, I don't know where she's gone, for sure, but I have an idea,' Daniel said. 'Sit tight and I'll be over as soon as I can. Just got to square it with Fred.'

Daniel reached the gates to Abbots Farm in just under half an hour, entered the security code and drove on down to the house, where he saw a gleaming black BMW parked alongside Lorna's 4x4. Looking at the number plate, he raised an eyebrow. Stephen

Myers was doing OK for himself, then, or at least wanted the world to think he was.

Parking his battered Mercedes alongside it, he headed for the front door. It opened before he could lift the brass knocker; Lorna had evidently been watching for him.

'Daniel. Come in. Go through to the kitchen. Stephen's in there,' she added in a lower tone as Daniel passed her in the hallway.

In the kitchen, Daniel found Stephen Myers sat at the head of the table, sideways on, with his legs stuck out and crossed at the ankle. Of a similar age to himself, he was of average height, as far as Daniel could judge, and wore dark brown corduroys and a classic beige fine check shirt over a body that carried a fair few pounds of unnecessary weight. His hair was mid-brown, thick and straight, with a fringe that flopped over his forehead and he looked across at Daniel with confrontation already in his eyes.

'Hi. Daniel Whelan,' Daniel said. 'You must be Harvey's son.'

'Stephen,' the other man confirmed. 'So you're the one who's been encouraging Zoe in all that silly nonsense with the Traveller boy.'

'Stephen, that's not fair!' Lorna exclaimed, following Daniel into the room.

'Isn't it? From what the little madam said, that's exactly what he's been doing.'

'The only thing I've encouraged her to do is come clean to you,' Daniel told Lorna. 'Unfortunately, she wasn't ready to do that.'

'Why didn't you tell me yourself?' Lorna said reproachfully. 'I wish you had, Daniel. She's only a kid.'

'I know, and I wanted to, but the only reason she opened up to me at all was because she trusted me not to tell. She made it very clear at the outset that if I didn't help her, she had every intention of going it alone.'

'You let a schoolgirl blackmail you?' Stephen put in scornfully. 'You're supposed to be the responsible adult in this. And how come she told you in the first place? It makes me wonder what your angle is.'

'No angle,' Daniel said, keeping a tight rein on his temper.

'She knew from Lorna that I used to be in the police force, that's all.'

'Oh yes, I heard about that. You got thrown out, didn't you?'

'Stephen, stop it!' Lorna said sharply.

Daniel chose to ignore him, addressing Lorna instead.

'I knew you had a lot on your mind and I thought if there was a chance we could sort out Zoe's problem without adding to your worries, then it seemed worth trying. For what it's worth, I was intending to speak to you today, Lorna, with or without Zoe's cooperation.'

'Easy to say that now,' Stephen observed with a sneer, and Daniel began to fully sympathize with Zoe's dislike of her step-brother.

'What exactly did Zoe tell you, last night?' he asked, turning away from Stephen to address Lorna, once more.

'How about you tell us what *you* know?' Stephen interjected.

'Well, it was all a bit garbled, really,' Lorna told Daniel, also choosing to ignore her stepson. 'She was in a bit of a mood to start with and then, when I asked her about my mother's rings, she blew up at me and started crying and shouting. There were a lot of things said that would have been better left unsaid on both sides, but basically she said she'd only borrowed the rings. The thing is she wouldn't tell me what she'd done with them – just kept saying I'd get them back in due course and that it was all right because you were helping her. I couldn't make sense of it all and I have to say, Stephen didn't help a lot.' This last was added with a speaking glance at her stepson.

'It wasn't me! She was being bloody rude!' he protested.

'I know she was. But you were winding her up even more,' Lorna told him.

'I think I should explain, at this point, that I had no idea the rings were yours,' Daniel said. 'If I had, I'd never have agreed to help her. Zoe told me they'd been left to her by her grand-mother.'

'Well, technically speaking, they will be hers, one day,' Lorna said. 'I told her that when they came to me, but she really had no right to take them now. But what's she done with them? Please don't tell me she's sold them . . .'

'Not quite. Apparently she took them to a pawnbroker.'

'She's too young,' Stephen put in, glaring at Daniel accusingly. 'You must have helped her.'

'She'd already done it by the time she told me,' he replied evenly.

Lorna groaned. 'Oh God! I suppose that boy helped her. He'd be old enough. Daniel, what's going on? Do you know? Where is she now?'

Daniel made a face. 'I hope I'm wrong but I'm very much afraid she might be on her way to Wales,' he said.

'Wales?' Lorna exclaimed, horrified. 'You're not serious! What for?'

'Chasing after her boyfriend, obviously,' Stephen said. 'Probably got herself knocked up and he's run scared!'

'Oh God, no!' Stricken, Lorna looked to Daniel for reassurance.

'No, it's not that,' Daniel said. 'But I think she probably has gone after him.'

'How? She can't drive.'

'Well, from what she told me, she's no stranger to hitchhiking,' Daniel said.

'Hitchhiking? Zo? Oh God! You think you know your own kid,' Lorna said, rubbing her face and eyes distractedly. 'How could she be so stupid? It's those Travellers, isn't it? That's where she's been getting these ideas from. I should have kept a closer eye on her. Oh God, Daniel! What are we going to do? Where in Wales, do you know?'

'Somewhere in Brecon, she said. She wanted me to take her last night but I said no.'

'Pity you didn't think to let us know then,' Stephen said, sniping.

'As it happens, you're right,' Daniel admitted. 'But it never occurred to me that she would jump the gun and set off on her own. I don't think that was her plan.'

'Until we had that row. Oh, I wish you'd told me,' Lorna said, running her fingers through her hair. 'But the thing is, what are we going to do now? I've tried ringing her but she won't answer her phone.'

'Get the police onto her, I would,' Stephen stated.

Lorna looked at Daniel. 'Should I? It seems a bit extreme. What would they do if they found her?'

'Take her to the nearest station and call you,' Daniel said. 'But you'd have to provide them with a recent picture so they'd know who they were looking for.'

'She'd be so embarrassed and as mad as fire,' Lorna said.

'Serve her right,' came the predictable response from her stepson.

'I think a better idea, if you agree to it, would be for me to go after her,' Daniel suggested. 'If she *has* been hitchhiking, she may not have got far. There's not so many people will stop these days.'

'Except the wrong type,' Zoe's mother said darkly.

'Actually,' Daniel said then, 'let me try ringing her. She was expecting me to call this morning and if she's struggling or regretting her actions, she might just see me as salvation.'

Stephen muttered something disparaging and, glancing in his direction, Daniel said he'd make the call outside.

Standing on the gravel by Lorna's front door, he found Zoe's number and rang it. Quite prepared for her to take her time in answering it, he was surprised when she did so straight away.

'Daniel. Thank God! I thought it was going to be Mum again. You'll never guess where I am.'

'On your way to Wales, I imagine,' Daniel said dampeningly.

'Oh. Mum called you.'

'She did. And I have to say, if you were looking for a way to turn her against Shane once and for all, you've found it. Congratulations!'

'But you should have heard them last night,' she protested. 'Stephen, especially, going on and on. They wouldn't let me explain. What was I supposed to do?'

Act like a grown up and not a spoilt child, Daniel thought, but didn't say it. After all, he'd had a bellyful of Stephen Myers in the last half-hour himself.

'Was Mum terribly worried?' Zoe wanted to know.

'What do you think? Look, where are you, exactly? I'll come and find you. How far have you got?'

'I'm not coming back until I've seen Shane,' Zoe stated.

'We'll talk about that when I get there. Where are you?'

'I'm in Wales,' she said with an unmistakable touch of pride.

'A place called Pontypool. But now I can't find anyone to take me to Merthyr Tydfil. They're all going to Cardiff or Abergavenny.'

'Well, stay where you are,' Daniel told her. 'Your mum's talking about calling the police and Stephen is encouraging her.'

'The police?' Zoe sounded shocked.

'Yes, you know – navy uniforms, flashing lights . . .'

'Oh God, no! It's not funny! Don't let them, Daniel, please!'

'Well, if you promise to stay where you are until I get there, I'll do my best to stop the cavalry,' he said.

'All right. But you will come straight away . . .'

'Yeah, I'll be on my way in a few minutes. You realize you've probably got me the sack, don't you? I'm supposed to be working. My boss is seriously unhappy.' It wasn't quite true. Fred had been – if not overjoyed – then at least understanding, but he didn't think laying on a little guilt would do the girl any harm.

Lorna was jubilant when he went back inside to report his success. Stephen merely scowled.

'Will you really go and fetch her? Are you sure? Thank you *so* much!' Zoe's mother said.

'I feel a bit responsible,' Daniel said ruefully. 'Inadvertently.'

'*Irresponsible*, if you ask me,' Stephen remarked.

'Well, I might as well get going,' Daniel said with a reassuring smile in Lorna's direction. 'Don't worry, I can be there in a couple of hours and she's promised to stay put till I arrive. The threat of being picked up by the police saw to that.'

He headed for the door, pausing as he passed close to Stephen, who was on his feet now, putting more water in the kettle.

'You, my friend,' Daniel said, in a low but pleasant tone, 'are becoming quite tedious! Just saying . . .'

Stephen turned round, glowering, but Daniel merely continued on his way.

Lorna caught up with him as he reached his car.

'Sorry about Stephen – he's insufferable at times. But thank you so much, Daniel. I really don't understand all that stuff about the horse, though. She could have had a horse any time, if she'd wanted it. I mean, she did have one until she outgrew it a couple of years ago and then, with uni on the horizon . . .'

'Yeah, look, it's a long story, which I'll make sure Zoe tells you in full when she gets back. And by the way – you're not in any way responsible for Stephen, so there's no need to apologize, and pain in the backside or not, I'm glad he's here with you. Presumably you've still heard nothing from Harvey?'

She shook her head.

'Well, hopefully no news is good news,' Daniel said. 'What have you told Stephen?'

'Just the basics, no details – not that I know much more, myself. He knows you and Taz scared the men off, though. You'd think he might be grateful.'

'Hmm. Not his sort. OK. Bye for now and keep your chin up. I'll ring you when I catch up with Zoe.'

It began to rain as Daniel was driving across the Severn Bridge and when he reached Pontypool, just before midday, another phone call to Zoe pinpointed her position as in the museum tearooms.

He found her at a corner table, apparently deep in conversation with an elderly couple at the adjacent one. The couple got up to leave as Daniel arrived, smiling and thanking him as he stood aside to let them pass.

'Glad to see you've not been too lonely,' he observed drily as he slid into a seat opposite Zoe.

'They were sweet,' she told him. 'Eric and Kay. Would you believe they come from Devon, too? You come all this way and sit next to someone who lives just down the road.' The dark circles under her eyes were more pronounced but she looked otherwise unaffected by her overnight travel.

'Well, would you believe I've just driven all the way from Devon, too?' Daniel asked in tones of amazement.

'You didn't have to,' she said sulkiness creeping into her voice. 'I was doing OK.'

'So it wasn't you who said, "I can't find anyone to take me to Merthyr Tydfil. They're all going to Cardiff," when I spoke to you earlier?'

'I would have done eventually.'

'Gee, thanks, Daniel, for dropping everything and driving a hundred and fifty miles to come to my rescue,' he said.

'Mum sent you to take me back. Well, I'm not going,' she stated, looking mulish. 'I've come this far and I'm not stopping now.'

'Nobody sent me, I offered. But your mum *was* very grateful. Have you any idea how worried she was?'

'I was going to ring her, once I'd found Shane.'

'And done what? Forced him to sell the horse and give you the money? Joined him on the road? What exactly was your big plan?'

Zoe's gaze shifted upwards, over his shoulder and Daniel turned to find a pleasant-looking woman poised with a notepad and pen.

'Oh, coffee, please. A large one.' He glanced across at Zoe, who had an empty cup in front of her. 'You?'

'Not at the moment, thanks,' she said, then when the waitress had turned away, 'I've already had four. I've been here most of the morning. Well, since it started raining, anyway.'

'We may as well eat something,' Daniel said. 'We've got a long drive ahead of us.'

Zoe's eyes narrowed with suspicion.

'Merthyr's not that far,' she said, watching him closely.

'Devon, on the other hand is nearly three hours away,' he pointed out.

'No! I'm not going back with you!' she declared. 'Not when I've got this close. You can't make me!'

'Keep your voice down.'

'Please, Daniel. We could be there in half an hour and still be home in daylight. Mum need never know.'

'I think you'll find your mum's going to want to know everything. You're going to have a lot of explaining to do when you get home. And anyway, that news footage was from three days ago, they could be anywhere by now.'

'But close. They won't have gone far,' she asserted.

'You don't know that.'

She leaned forward across the table and said in a low voice, 'If you try to force me to go back I'll scream for help and say you're trying to abduct me.'

The waitress arrived with Daniel's coffee, supremely unaware of the tension at the table.

'Will there be anything else?'

'In a minute, maybe. Thanks.'

'Certainly.' The waitress lingered, her head on one side, apparently surveying the floor between the table and the wall. 'We don't usually allow dogs unless they are guide dogs,' she commented quietly.

'He's an assistance dog,' Daniel responded, equally quietly, with an innocent smile. 'And it's very wet outside . . .'

'Ah. That's all right then,' she said with a twinkle. 'Just as long as he stays under the table where I can't see him . . .'

As she moved on to clear the next table, Daniel turned back to Zoe, who was sitting back in her chair eyeing him with hostility. 'If you're going to be childish, I'll take you to the nearest police station, myself, and get them to call your mum.'

Zoe's shoulders slumped. All of a sudden she looked tired and very young.

'Please, Daniel! You know how important this is. Can't we at least try and find Shane while we're here, otherwise it's all been a waste of everyone's time.'

Daniel took a mouthful of hot coffee and sighed appreciatively; it was his first since six o'clock that morning. He was aware that Zoe was waiting for his response and thought it wouldn't do her any harm to wait.

'Please, Daniel?'

'You know I'm supposed to be working this morning,' he said after a long moment. 'My boss has got someone off sick already. I've left him short-handed.'

'I'm sorry.'

'I'd have brought you myself, this afternoon, if you'd waited.'

'I wasn't sure you meant it, I mean people say stuff like that when they just want to shut you up.'

'Yeah, well, that too,' he admitted. 'But knowing you it wouldn't have worked for long. However, I would have insisted you told your mum before we set off – speaking of which, I should ring her and let her know you're OK.'

'Now? Do we have to? Couldn't we wait until we've had a chance to look for Shane?'

'No! How can you even suggest that when your mum's half out of her mind with worry?'

'I didn't mean to frighten her – well, maybe I did, a bit, to start with,' she amended. 'It was Stephen. It was bad enough having Mum mad at me but then he comes along and starts sticking his bloody nose in! I mean, what right does he think he has? He's not even my brother – he's no relation at all – but he just kept on and on carping at me. He makes me want to . . .'

'Spit?' Daniel suggested. 'I met him this morning. We didn't exactly hit it off.'

'You'll know what I mean, then,' she said triumphantly. 'He treats me like a child. He's so bloody patronizing. It just winds me up so much.'

'I do sympathize. But running off in the middle of the night isn't exactly mature, is it?' He put his hands up. 'No, don't spark off at me – I'm not the enemy. Look, I'll text your mum and then we'll have something to eat, because even if you're not hungry, I am. Afterwards, I'll take you to Merthyr Tydfil and we'll have a look around but if the trail runs cold I'm taking you home. We're not going to spend hours chasing all over Wales looking for them. OK?'

Zoe's face lit with a flashing smile.

'Thank you! Thank you soooo much!' she said. 'Shall I get the waitress back? I'm starving!'

With lunch out of the way, the journey to Merthyr Tydfil took a little over half an hour. As they drew closer, Zoe became progressively quieter and Daniel guessed that a measure of anxiety as to her reception was beginning to kick in.

Her apprehension, if that was what it was, was somewhat premature, however. There was no sign of the Travellers anywhere in or around the former steel-working town. Enquiries at a couple of businesses and pubs revealed that they had indeed moved on three days previously, after being turned off an overnight camp in a car park and a second one on some common land at the edge of the town. It was the opinion of all that they little cared where the Travellers had gone, so long as they didn't come back any time soon.

One worker at the supermarket, more open-minded than most, gave it as her opinion that the group would head into the Brecon Beacons.

'They've stocked up well, so I should imagine they'll go somewhere to get some peace and quiet,' she said. 'They're not so bad, really.'

'You'd be in the minority round here with those views,' Daniel told her, paying for his own small basket of provisions.

'I know, but my grandmother was a Traveller,' she explained. 'She settled down, eventually, but she always said that a little respect would go a long way to improving the situation. If you treat people like dirt, how can you expect them to behave?'

Back in the car, Zoe was encouraged by his report, but he was forced to dampen her spirits.

'Have you any idea how big an area the National Park covers?' he asked. 'And if they've hidden themselves away from the park authorities, we haven't a hope of finding them.'

'But we can't turn back now!'

Daniel looked at his watch.

'It's three o'clock, near enough. I'll give it till the light starts to fade, then we go back, OK?'

Zoe nodded but Daniel wasn't fooled by her apparent compliance. He had a strong suspicion that she wouldn't give in gracefully if Shane had still not been found by the time darkness fell.

In the event, their luck was in. The Travellers' convoy hadn't gone unnoticed and by turning back onto the Heads of the Valleys Road and asking at every petrol station, hostelry and business they came to, Daniel was eventually able to gauge roughly where they had left the main road and headed north into open country. He chose at random one of the smaller roads heading that way and, shortly after, an even smaller road that dwindled into a stony track that ran on for a mile or more with a hedge and fields on one side and the open moor on the other.

Having bottomed out the Mercedes a couple of times on the uneven surface, he was searching for a place to turn when they saw a wisp of smoke curling up from behind the shoulder of a hill a little way ahead.

'There!' Zoe exclaimed, pointing. 'Smoke! That must be them.'

'It's possible,' Daniel said, not sure whether to be glad or sorry. He'd embarked on the quest to satisfy the girl, with little anticipation of it proving successful. The possibility that it might be about to threatened to open a whole new can of worms.

'Well, who else would it be?' she demanded.

'Campers?' Daniel suggested, but in reality, the volume of smoke indicated something a little larger than the average campfire. He slowed the car to a halt and in the back, Taz, who had greeted the sight of open moorland with restless excitement, began to whine and pant loudly.

'Why are you stopping?'

'So that we don't suddenly find ourselves in the middle of them with no plan of action,' he said, pulling the handbrake on and turning to look at her. 'Do you have one?'

'Well . . . Not exactly. Do we need one?' she said, shrugging, and Daniel was forced to revise his earlier suspicions that she might doubt her reception.

'OK. Well, what are you going to say, then? Are you expecting Shane to welcome you with open arms? He might do – I have no idea about that – but I've got a strong suspicion that his father won't, and you can't just rock up and say you happened to be passing.'

Zoe looked at him, chewing the inside of her lip, thoughtfully.

'I'll just have to tell him the truth,' she said after a moment. 'I'll say Mum has found out about the rings and I need to get them back from the pawnbroker. He's probably forgotten the deadline's next week.'

If Daniel had any doubts on this front, he tactfully kept them to himself, saying only, 'Did Shane know the rings didn't really belong to you?'

She flashed him an uncertain look.

'Mum told you about that, did she?'

'She did. Just when were you going to tell me? You put me in a very difficult position.'

'I didn't think you'd agree to help me if you knew,' she confessed.

'You got that right.'

'But they *were* going to be mine, one day.'

'Not any time soon. And don't skip the question: did you tell Shane they weren't yours?'

'No. He wouldn't have taken the money if I had.'

Daniel sighed. 'Well, I'm glad to hear that, at least. It seems he has better moral fibre than you have, not that that is any great recommendation.'

'I just wanted to help him.'

'Yeah, I get that, but you have to draw the line somewhere.

If helping someone else means you get into trouble yourself, you need to stop and think very hard. After all, if he really does love you, he wouldn't want you to do that and he's not going to love you any less just because you can't lend him money.'

Zoe flushed darkly. 'You think I'm trying to buy his love! That's so not true!'

'No. I'm saying it's natural to want to help someone you love but sometimes you just have to accept that the best you can do is be there for them. Oh, God! Listen to me,' he said, shaking his head disgustedly, 'Now you've got me dishing out relationship advice!'

'You're not married?'

'Used to be.'

'Children?'

'A boy. Nine-year-old. Drew.'

'What happened?'

'We drifted apart.' *The hell we did!* he thought wryly. The truth was that Amanda had legged it as fast as she could in the other direction when his career had gone pear-shaped. He shook off the unpleasant memories. 'Anyway, this isn't about me, this is about you and Shane and the money. So how do you want to play it?'

Zoe pursed her lips. 'By ear?'

Daniel looked at her for a long moment, then shrugged. He hadn't any better ideas.

'OK. Let's do it, then.'

As they set off again, they passed, parked by a field gate on their left, three two-horse trailers. Daniel slowed the car to look. They appeared to be in fairly good condition and all had tow-bar locks fitted. Through the gate he could see two coloured ponies grazing on the lush grass of the field and wondered if the landowner had any idea they were there. He sighed to himself as he changed gear and continued. It looked as though they had indeed found their quarry.

The track continued over the rise and then curved round the inside of a bowl-shaped hollow. At the bottom the heather cleared to leave a broad swathe of green turf alongside a stream on which were parked maybe a dozen caravans and an assortment of other vehicles. Driving slowly down the track towards them, Daniel couldn't see many people about, and their eventual arrival was heralded only by the barking of a number of dogs, some of which came forward to mill around the car as it drew to a halt.

'Where is everyone?' Zoe asked.

'I don't know,' Daniel said, somewhat unnecessarily. He opened the car door and most of the dogs shied away before renewing their barking from a distance. One or two came closer, ears flattened and tails wagging. He scratched one behind the ears as he took a moment to scan the area and in the car behind him, Taz went crazy at the proximity of the other dogs.

The camp wasn't quite as deserted as it had at first seemed. On the stream side of one of the caravans was the fire that was responsible for the smoke they had seen, and around it sat a number of people, mainly women and children. Several of the youngsters approached the car, keeping behind the line of barking dogs, and after a moment or two one of the women by the fire stood up and looked his way.

Daniel started to make his way over, hoping the dogs would allow his movement, and although they didn't stop barking they gave way, circling around so that they all moved together. A hand tucked under his arm and he found Zoe at his side.

The standing woman spoke when he was ten or fifteen feet away. Middle-aged, as far as Daniel could tell, she had dark hair, lined olive skin and magnificent eyes that were as close to black as he'd ever seen. She wore a long skirt with a lacy cardigan over a vest top, and a conspicuous amount of heavy gold jewellery.

'You lookin' for someone?' she enquired, eyeing the newcomers with some reserve.

'Shane Brennan. He's my boyfriend,' Zoe stated, stepping forward, and Daniel sighed inwardly. *That was subtlety out the window, then.* But at least he supposed it had cleared the air.

The woman's gaze sharpened.

'Is he now?' she replied, tilting her head to one side. 'You'd be Zoe, then. He's spoken about you.'

There was a murmur of agreement from the other women and Zoe shot Daniel a look of triumph.

'Has he? Is he here?' she asked eagerly, but the woman wasn't about to be hurried.

'Oh yes, we've all heard about his little "Country Girl",' she said with a wry smile and several of the onlookers chuckled. Of ages ranging from teenage to very elderly, their mode of dress varied accordingly from traditional to that really only suitable for a nightclub.

'But where is he? Is he here?' Zoe repeated, looking round at the vans, from one or two of which other people were beginning to emerge, including a couple of older men. It seemed, however, that they were content to let the woman do the talking. Daniel wondered if the woman who had spoken was perhaps a kind of matriarch, possibly married to the leader of the group.

'You've come a long way, I'm thinking,' the woman said then, but before Zoe could give vent to her growing frustration, one of the other women stood up and faced them. Dressed in a clinging minidress with fringed boots, she was nearer Zoe's age and undeniably attractive.

'Shame you've wasted your time then,' she said staring boldly at Zoe, who returned her look with no less hauteur.

'Why would you say that?' she demanded.

'Cos he's among his own kind now, ain't he? And he ain't going nowhere, any time soon!'

'Be quiet, Jade!' the first woman snapped and the girl pouted, tossing her thick mane of curly, reddish dyed hair like an actress studying for Carmen.

'I'm sorry, my dear,' the older woman said. 'He's not here at the moment. I'll tell him you called, maybe.'

'But where is he? And when will he be back?' Zoe wanted to know.

'They'm trying the ponies out,' another of the women said, and earned herself a glare from the first speaker.

'Couldn't say when they'll be back. Mayn't be for a long while,' she said, turning back to Daniel and Zoe. 'Best go home. There's those that won't make you welcome.'

'We'll wait,' Zoe declared, with a defiant look at the girl called Jade.

'No, we won't,' Daniel said decisively. He smiled and thanked the older woman and, taking Zoe's arm in a firm grip, turned her away from the group by the fire.

A rough semicircle of curious children and dogs wavered and

gave way before them as Daniel steered his companion back towards the car.

'What are you doing?' she hissed furiously. 'We know he'll be back later. Why can't we wait?'

'Because, A – they don't want us to, and, B – we haven't got time.'

'I'm not giving up now,' she stated. 'Not now we've come this far.'

'I didn't suppose you would,' he said drily, propelling her to the passenger door. In the car he had to speak sharply to Taz, who was still giving voice to his indignation, before saying to Zoe as he started the engine, 'If they've taken the horses out somewhere, presumably in harness, they hopefully won't be far away. Somewhere on the roads around here, I imagine. Let's go and see if we can find them. If we don't, we can always come back here as a last resort if we have time.'

Zoe didn't look happy but made no further protest as Daniel turned the car around and drove back up the rough track and over the rise.

It was a little over half an hour before they came across the Traveller men and their ponies, and with light levels starting to drop under grey skies that promised further rain, the meeting was very nearly catastrophic.

SIX

Daniel and Zoe were negotiating a bend in the narrow road when, with shocking abruptness, they suddenly came face to face with two ponies approaching head on, side by side across the road and travelling at speed. Only the blinkers on their bridles and the breastplates across their chests showed that they were being driven, their drivers sitting low down and out of sight behind their flying heels.

With no time to brake, Daniel swore and swerved as far onto the grass as he was able to without losing his nearside wheels in the ditch and the driver of the animal closest to him swerved into the one on the other side, which in turn mounted the grass verge. The three vehicles drew abreast for a fraction of a second in a flurry of hooves, flying tails and screeching tyres. There was a light clonk as something impacted the side of the Merc and then they were past, miraculously without any apparent injury.

There were two more ponies approaching, some fifty yards behind the first pair and travelling more moderately and in tandem, so Daniel waited where he was, with two wheels on the grass and two on the tarmac. The man driving the foremost of these glared at Daniel in passing, as though the fault for the near collision was his, but the second driver acknowledged him with a touch of his baseball cap, sitting close behind his pony in a lightweight, tubular framed contraption that hardly looked strong enough to bear his weight. The barely-there seat was low down so that the driver's knees and feet were higher and spread wide to allow the animal's hind legs room to move. This was the kind of racing sulky used for trotting races the world over.

Behind the driven ponies came several vehicles, predominantly 4x4s and pick-up trucks, with men and boys observing the race, if race it was.

As the last of the cavalcade passed, Daniel glanced at Zoe.

'You OK?'

She nodded, a little white-faced.

'Well, it looks like we've found your friends,' he observed mildly. 'Was any of them Shane, or could you not see?'

'No, I didn't see him, but I think one of the ones in the cars might have been his dad.'

'Well,' Daniel said, driving on slowly to find a place to turn round, 'I guess we'd better follow them.'

'Shane would never race his new pony on the roads. He's saving her for the proper races and he's always said road racing is too risky for good horses, besides being bad for their legs,' Zoe said, but a note of uncertainty belied the confidence in her words.

'Hmm . . .'

'What do you mean, hmm?' she demanded as he found a pull-in and began to manoeuvre the car.

'Nothing really. It's just that I imagine a group like that could put a fair bit of pressure on a lad.'

'He's not a kid!'

'I didn't say he was,' Daniel returned in soothing tones. 'I just wouldn't be completely surprised if they'd been egging him on to try out his new horse, that's all.'

Zoe muttered something inaudible but Daniel didn't ask her to repeat it.

It took them another couple of minutes to come up with the Travellers again and when they did so, around another bend in the winding road, it was immediately apparent that the two foremost sulkies had met a second motorist on the narrow causeway and this time their luck had run out.

They were travelling across open moorland now and, going over a rise and dropping in a swooping curve into the dip on the other side, the road crossed a shallow stream in the bottom by way of an old stone bridge. One of the sulkies was halted on the grass at the side of the little hump-backed bridge, but one had attempted to cross it and was now on its side at the bottom of the bank, a piebald pony struggling to find its feet between shafts that had been twisted by the fall. The motorized observation fleet were scattered around on the road and turf, and a family saloon was on the bridge itself, one front wing ominously crumpled against the centuries old stone parapet.

People swarmed over the area like ants around a stirred-up anthill, mostly concentrated around the car on the bridge and the damaged sulky beside it, and even at a distance it was easy to see that tempers were well and truly frayed.

'Oh shit!' Daniel breathed, slowing the Merc as he approached the scene. Parking on the verge close to a pick-up truck with enormous wheels, he told Zoe to stay put and got out of the car.

It took a conscious effort not to go straight into traffic officer mode and start ordering the situation but he decided that for the moment the justifiably angry owner of the damaged saloon was holding his own and not in any actual physical danger from the massed ranks of Travellers he faced, so Daniel turned his attention to the stricken pony still struggling in its harness on the other side of the bank.

Splashing across the shallow stream, he took in the situation rapidly. The sulky driver had been thrown from his seat and was now lying on the turf some ten feet away, being administered to by half a dozen of his friends or family. He appeared to be conscious, if dazed, and was cradling his left arm, but Daniel decided he wasn't in any immediate danger and transferred his attention to the pony, which had somehow got a leg the wrong side of the bent shaft and was held there by the twisted leather straps of its harness. Unable to get up it was thrashing about in a way that presented a very real danger not only to those trying to untangle the mess of leatherwork but also to the long, thin cannon bones of its lower legs.

Instinctively Daniel assumed command. A young boy was trying without much success to hold the pony's head and Daniel pushed him unceremoniously out of the way and took his place. Forcing the animal's neck and head flat to the turf, he used his weight to hold it there, effectively subduing its struggles. The warm smell of sweaty horse filled his nostrils.

'Don't faff about! Cut the bloody traces before he breaks his leg!' he snapped at the other two men, who glanced blankly in his direction and then at each other.

'Oh, for God's sake! Haven't you got a knife?' Daniel asked starting to reach into his pocket for his own super-sharp penknife, but apparently their reaction had been merely to the shock of having a stranger issuing orders, for one of them said, 'I got one,' produced it and got swiftly to work.

Within moments the pony's legs were free of the leather traces and the shaft, and as one of the two men pulled the ruined sulky out of the way, Daniel lifted the pressure from the animal's sweaty neck and it surged to its feet, staggering wildly until it found the flat ground beside the stream.

Unnerved by its ordeal, the pony's eyes were showing white and its ears flicked to and fro as it alternatively tugged against Daniel's restraining hand and barged into him with its head. Daniel spoke to it in a low voice, stroking the animal's damp black-and-white neck and scratching it behind one ear, and gradually it stopped trying to break free and began to calm down.

The boy Daniel had displaced at the pony's head was standing a few feet away staring at him. He looked to be around twelve years old and wore jeans and a Man United shirt.

'I think he's OK, now,' Daniel told the lad. 'Sorry for pushing you.'

The boy's only response was a shrug but then he said, 'Her's a mare.'

'So she is.'

The sulky was standing back on its bicycle tyre wheels now but the shaft was badly bent and one of the wheels stood at an angle. It clearly wasn't going anywhere behind a horse until it had been mended and the two men were regarding it gloomily. After a moment, the man who had cut the traces abandoned his companion and came over to inspect the pony, running his hands over her back and down her legs in a knowledgeable fashion.

'She's taken the skin off that leg,' Daniel observed, looking round the piebald ribcage to where a long graze showed from hock to fetlock on the inside of the mare's off hind.

'Bit of a scrape,' the man agreed. 'Bloody stupid driver! Should have given way. He could see we were coming. Horses have the right of way. It's the law.'

Daniel could have said a few choice words of his own about idiocy and the rules of the road but he didn't think they would be well received and there was nothing to be gained by putting the Travellers' backs up, so he held his tongue.

'I'll take her now,' the man said, coming forward and putting his hand on the rein. He was a stocky, middle-aged individual with a heavy signet ring on one finger and a gold chain lying on the mahogany skin of his neck.

'OK.' Daniel stepped back, adding silently, *My pleasure. Please don't mention it.*

Turning round he found the rest of the scene had changed little while the drama with the piebald mare had played out. The man who had been thrown from the sulky was still seated on the ground surrounded by three or four men and boys. His arm was twisted at an awkward angle and from his white face it was easy to see that he was in a great deal of pain.

Daniel stepped towards the group.

'I'd say that might be dislocated. Has anyone called an ambulance?'

Heads turned his way and one of the men said, 'Dunno.'

'Well, you need to get him to A and E,' Daniel said. He left the sulky driver and his mates and climbed back up the bank to the road where the car had been backed off the bridge and its furious owner was inspecting the damage while a plump woman in cropped trousers and what should have been a loose T-shirt stood nervously by the open passenger door, as if ready to dive back inside.

Having looked closely at the crumpled front wing of his car and given voice to his opinion that it would very likely be a write-off, the car's driver took out his mobile phone and proceeded to take photos of it from every angle before straightening up and doing the same for the damaged stonework of the bridge.

He was keeping up a diatribe about the reckless behaviour of the Travellers, which began to morph into a general condemnation of their way of life, and although Daniel could sympathize to some extent he felt the man must either be brave or very stupid, given the numbers of Travellers there were on and around the bridge. Based solely on his policeman's instincts, he decided it was probably the latter.

Two or three of the Traveller men were responding to the man's unwise comments with increasingly angry remarks of their own and when he turned the lens onto them, they stepped forward and the tone of their voices turned distinctly menacing.

Daniel was reluctantly preparing to step into the breach when, faintly, drifting on the breeze across the moorland came the sound of a siren.

A hush fell as everyone on the scene strained to hear with more certainty and after a moment or two, the sound came again. The middle-aged, perspiring car owner gave the Traveller men a look of triumphant self-righteousness, which was almost entirely lost on them as the sound had galvanized them into action.

There followed maybe half a minute of frantic, scurrying activity during which all the Traveller men and boys disappeared into or onto vehicles like water running through a colander; the piebald pony was hitched onto the back of one of the three remaining sulkies and with a clatter of hooves, a roar of engines and a screech of tyres the entire lot funnelled onto the road, streamed up the other side of the hollow and disappeared over the rise.

Daniel found himself alone on the bridge save for the aggrieved car owner and his passenger, and Zoe, who unsurprisingly had disregarded his instruction to stay in the car and was now standing on the far side of the stream staring at the ridge over which the cavalcade had disappeared. As if sensing Daniel's eyes on her, she turned her head and looked at him but, before he could speak, his attention was claimed by an exclamation of outrage from the man by the car, who was also gazing after the Travellers.

'It's outrageous! They can't just take off like that!' he protested, turning to Daniel.

'I think you'll find they just have,' Daniel observed.

'But . . . but look what they've done to my car!'

'Strictly speaking the bridge damaged your car. I suspect, even if they had stuck around, you may have had a fight on your hands trying to prove that the accident was their fault. After all, whatever the police may suspect, there would have been a lot of witnesses prepared to swear that you were in the wrong. And on top of that, I'd be very surprised if they had any form of insurance for you to claim on.'

'But I have a witness, too. Evie was in the car – she saw. And you – you must have seen what happened.'

'No, I didn't,' Daniel said, shaking his head. 'When I came over the hill, it was all over bar the shouting.'

The siren was a good bit closer now and the man looked speculatively at Daniel.

'But you don't have to say that, do you?' he said.

'I'm not lying to the police, if that's what you're suggesting,' Daniel said mildly. 'But I will tell them that I passed the Travellers earlier and they were driving recklessly. That and the sulky they left behind should be enough to back-up your story.'

'Daniel?' Zoe had come onto the bridge. 'We need to get going if we're going to catch them up.'

'They're friends of yours?' the car owner expostulated. 'Oh, that'd be right! You didn't think to tell me that, did you?'

Daniel ignored him.

'We can't just drive off,' he told Zoe. 'The police'll be here in a minute.'

Zoe made a face.

'Do we *have* to? Shane wanted to talk and we didn't get much time.'

'Oh, so he was there. Well, I'm sorry but the answer is yes, we do have to wait for the police but hopefully it won't take too long.'

Zoe looked petulant but the approaching siren was very close now and within seconds blue flashing lights were visible in the encroaching gloom. The police car came over the rise and swooped down to the bridge where it stopped and disgorged two young officers.

Daniel heaved a sigh and waited for the inquisition to begin.

Daniel suspected the two police officers might have been nearing the end of their shift, because they dealt with the disgruntled car owner and the scene of the collision with admirable brevity.

They appeared to accept the tale of woe but the man's complaint against the Travellers suffered a check when the breathalyser was produced and showed that he had been drinking. Not very much over the limit, he was nevertheless invited to accompany the two policemen back to the local station, and having given their details, Daniel and Zoe were free to go on their way.

The light was fading fast now and the first thing Zoe said as they settled back into the Merc was, 'We can't go home until I've had a chance to talk properly to Shane. He said he'd wait for us back at the camp. He's got an idea but he didn't have time to tell me before.'

'All right.'

Zoe looked at him suspiciously.

'*All right*?' she echoed.

'Yes. We've come this far. It'd be a bit stupid to turn round and go home now. Against my better judgement we'll listen to Shane's idea, but we can't be too long. It's not fair on your mum.'

'We won't. Shane said he'd be waiting for me.'

'Well, our first problem will be seeing if we can even find the place again.'

After a couple of wrong turnings, they finally found themselves bumping down the stony track that they had taken earlier. It was overcast and had started to rain again, and consequently was almost dark. Daniel began to wonder what time they would eventually get back to Tavistock and made a mental note to call Lorna again before they set out.

'Shane said he'd wait for us at the top of the rise so we don't have to go all the way into the camp,' Zoe said, bringing his thoughts back to the matter in hand.

'Good. I wasn't especially looking forward to having a conversation with his whole bloody family listening in.'

'Shane says he's not happy,' Zoe said then. 'His father's pressuring him to run the mare on the roads and he doesn't want to.'

'Well, as you said earlier, he's not a kid,' Daniel pointed out.

'I know, but it's not easy when you're living in a group like that.'

'Yeah. *I* wouldn't want to do it.'

Zoe shot him a look that showed his remark had hit home.

'Well, that's why he wants to get his own van,' she said, as if that would resolve all their potential problems.

'So was he one of the drivers today?'

'Yes. It was just supposed to be a tryout but then one of the other guys challenged him . . .' Zoe tailed off, perhaps realizing that she was inviting further remarks about immaturity from Daniel, but he felt he'd already made his point and said nothing.

About fifty yards before the Travellers' camp would come into view over the rise, Daniel's dipped lights picked out the three trailers parked at the side of the track. He switched to sidelights and edged forward, and as they approached, a figure stepped out from the shelter of one of them.

'That's him! That's Shane!' Zoe said, somewhat unnecessarily.

As they got out of the car, the young man stepped forward, holding out his hand to Daniel with a surprising diffidence.

'Hi. Shane Brennan. I guess you must be Daniel. Thank you for looking after Zoe.'

'Pleased to meet you, at last.' Daniel shook the proffered hand, finding the lad's grasp firm. 'But to be honest, I was somewhat blackmailed into this trip and I could cheerfully have wrung her neck a few times over the past few hours!'

'She can be a bit headstrong,' Shane agreed with a fond sideways look at the girl, who was now holding onto his other arm and leaning her cheek against his shoulder.

'Well, thank you very much!' she exclaimed through gritted teeth and punched his arm. He smiled and the closed, slightly wary expression habitual to many of his kind, dissolved into genuine warmth.

For the first time, Daniel felt that Lorna might really have cause for concern over the relationship. By the available light, he could see that the young man was a similar height to himself, with broad shoulders, dark hair and eyes and high cheekbones. With naturally olive skin and that particularly engaging shy smile, it was unsurprising that Zoe had fallen hook, line and sinker for him. He was film-star material; the only wonder was that in a culture where the youngsters often made their vows at sixteen or seventeen, he had made it to nineteen in the single state.

'Well, this is all very pleasant, but we have a problem to sort out and besides,' Daniel added, turning the collar of his leather jacket up against the intensifying rain, 'I'm beginning to get very wet!'

Shane squinted up at the sky as if only just noticing the rain, and pointed at the nearest of the trailers.

'We could talk in there,' he suggested.

Five minutes later, Daniel was heartily regretting agreeing to listen to Shane's idea. Zoe, oblivious to his reservations, was looking from one to the other of them with shining eyes.

'I think it's a brilliant idea! We can do that, can't we Daniel?'

'No! We can't!' he said decisively.

Her face fell.

'Oh, but why? It solves everything. What's the problem?'

'The problem?' Daniel repeated incredulously. 'You two are barking mad, that's the problem! Steal the mare and take her back to Tavistock? I can't imagine how you could possibly think I would agree to it. It's crazy!'

'But it's not stealing! I lent Shane the money, so technically she's mine,' Zoe protested.

'I don't somehow think Shane's father will see it that way,' Daniel observed. 'Does he even know where you got the money for the horse?'

'Not exactly,' Shane hedged.

'So what, exactly?'

'I guess he thinks I bought her with my wages. He doesn't know how much I paid.'

'He didn't ask you?' Daniel queried. 'Or you lied?'

'Daniel!' Zoe exclaimed, indignant on her boyfriend's behalf, but both the men ignored her.

'You don't know my da,' Shane said, looking uncomfortable. 'He's just so . . .' He spread his hands, unable to find the words. 'When he wants something, he just keeps on till he gets it. If he knew how special the mare was, he'd want her and he'd find a way to get her off me. If we was still at Hawkers, I could've kept her in secret but as it is . . . Well, I didn't have time to arrange anything, so I had to bring her along. Thing is, he's beginning to guess, 'specially after today.'

'I bet he got Jimmy to challenge you, just so he could see her go,' Zoe put in, and he nodded.

'Yeah, I 'spect you're right. Look, I should be getting back. I just said I was checking on the ponies. Someone'll come if I'm much longer. Will you do it? It'd be the best thing for the mare to be away from here.'

'No,' Daniel said again. 'The mare may be yours – or Zoe's – but the trailer isn't. And besides, if they come after us, they'd catch us in no time. There's only so fast you can go towing a trailer.'

'But they won't know she's gone till the morning,' Shane pointed out. 'Anyway, I've thought about that. If I can sneak the pick-up out early tomorrow morning and head off, they might think I've taken her. I'll make them think I'm heading north and by the time they find out I haven't got her, you'll be long gone.'

'So why don't you?' Daniel asked. 'Take her north, I mean.'

'Where would I go? If I stayed with family, word would get back and they'd catch me in no time – you don't know how the Traveller network works. Wherever I ended up, Da would put the word out and that'd be that.'

'And what's to stop the Traveller network finding *us*?' Daniel asked.

'Well, they won't know your car, will they? And a trailer's a trailer.'

'As long as they don't remember it from earlier.'

'But you'll be back home in a few hours,' Shane told him. 'Probably before anyone knows she's gone.'

'What'll your dad do if he catches you?' Zoe asked with concern.

'He'll likely go crazy for a bit, but it'll pass,' he told her. 'At least the mare will be safe. If she stays here, Da will make me run her on the roads. He can see she's special and he's already talking about setting up a match race for her but that's not what I want . . .' He stopped talking and stood looking at Daniel.

'Please, Daniel,' Zoe said, wheedling. 'She's my horse.'

'So what are you going to do with her? Sell her to get the money back for your mum?' he asked with some asperity, feeling himself being backed into a corner.

Shane turned his gaze sharply to Zoe.

'It was your *ma*'s money?'

'Oh, look, let's not worry about that now,' she said, glaring at Daniel. 'Are we going to save her or not?'

'But, *Zoe*! If it wasn't yours . . .'

'Oh, never mind that now. She knows about it, now, anyway,' she said dismissively.

Shane gave her a long look, and Daniel felt sympathy for the lad, who was perhaps only just realizing the potential implications of a life with Lorna's headstrong daughter.

'I should go before they start wondering where I've got to,' Shane said then, glancing at his watch and edging towards the trailer door. He held out a ring with two keys on it. 'After midnight would be best, cos Da or Jimmy'll be up for a late check around eleven.'

'We'll do it,' Zoe said, reaching for the keys, but Shane swiftly enclosed them in his hand.

'It's Daniel's decision,' he said, waiting.

Daniel sighed. In spite of himself, he liked the boy. He put out his hand for the keys and ignoring Zoe's hissed, 'Yes!' said, 'The field padlock and the tow-bar lock?'

'That's right,' Shane said. 'Thank you.' He turned, ducked through the low door in the front of the trailer and was gone before Daniel had a chance to change his mind.

Left alone in the vehicle, Zoe gave Daniel an impulsive hug. 'Thank you soooo much.'

Daniel unpeeled her arms from around his neck.

'I can't believe I just agreed to this,' he stated heavily. 'And God knows how I'm going to explain it to your mother. But right now we need to go. If anyone sees the Merc here we're stuffed, good and proper!'

SEVEN

It was raining heavily by the time Daniel and Zoe returned to the field on the moors at half-past midnight and in the meantime they had given Taz a run, returned to the nearest village, found a pub in which to get a meal and phoned Zoe's mother.

It wasn't the easiest of conversations. They had decided not to add to Lorna's worries the knowledge that they were, to all intents and purposes, horsenapping the mare and she was understandably somewhat confused by the turn of events and most especially the plan to bring the mare back from Wales in a borrowed trailer.

Daniel gained the impression that she would gladly have forgone the chance to recover the money her daughter had lost, if only she could permanently disentangle her from the unwelcome association with the Travellers. It said a lot for her trust in Daniel that she accepted his dubious assertion that it was probably the best course of action and he ended the call hoping against hope that her trust in him wouldn't turn out to be badly misplaced.

Now as they slowly drove up with no lights, parked the car close to the trailers and listened to the rain drumming on the roof, Daniel shook his head slightly in renewed disbelief at what he'd allowed himself to be dragged into.

'Come on, then,' Zoe said.

'I don't know how the bloody hell we're going to find any horses in this, let alone the right one!' he replied, looking at the complete blackness beyond the windscreen.

'Shane said he'd left a head collar on the mare so we should be able to pick her out quite easily.'

Daniel wished he had her confidence. In his experience, horses and ponies were flighty creatures on the whole, and the more so at night. Throw in wind and torrential rain and he could imagine all six ponies careering around the field with no intention of letting them anywhere near.

When he had quizzed Shane about the ownership of the field, the Traveller lad had replied with untroubled conscience.

'The bloke's got so much land, he hasn't even noticed the ponies are there. And anyway, it's only grass – it'll grow back.'

'Daniel?' Zoe was fidgeting.

'OK, let's do it,' he said. 'There's an old waterproof in the back. Chuck that on or you'll get drenched.'

'What about you?'

'I'll be OK. The leather'll keep it out for a bit.'

The leather did indeed keep the rain off his upper body but it didn't stop it running in rivulets down his neck or soaking his denim jeans to leg-hugging heaviness. He had a bush hat in the car but was pretty sure the wind would have snatched it from his head in very short order. Glancing sideways, he could just make out Zoe trudging at his side, her slight figure lost in the voluminous folds of the borrowed stock coat. They'd be lucky if they managed to get anywhere near the horses with that thing flapping wildly, he reflected.

His first inclination had been to hook the car up to the trailer ready for loading the horse once they had caught it but the downside of that was that if by any chance they were interrupted by one of the Travellers, a quick getaway hauling the trailer would be impossible. He elected to unlock the tow bar and position the car in advance but then catch the mare and hope that Zoe could hold her while he linked the tow bar and coupling.

At the field gate, Daniel took a small torch from his pocket and switched it on. The padlock was a good quality one but with the key in his hand, that presented no problems. It seemed ironic that they would take such care to lock the gate to a field to which they had no claim whatsoever. He swiftly dealt with the padlock and left the chain hanging.

'OK. Stay close to me,' he said, stepping out across the field. The grass had clearly not been grazed for a while and effectively soaked the lower legs of his jeans within a few strides. He wondered if the farmer had intended to get a late crop of hay off it, in which case he would have little empathy with Shane's comment that it was only grass and would grow back. With six animals grazing it, there wouldn't be a lot left standing to cut after a few days.

As the ground sloped away from the rise and the Travellers' vans in the hollow, Daniel risked shining his torch across the field, his first pass illuminating not only the silver rods of rain lancing down at a forty-five-degree angle but also, by a stroke of luck, the ruby and emerald gleams of four pairs of eyes, low down among the grasses.

Zoe clutched his arm, excitedly.

'Daniel!'

'I see them. Have you got the rope and the carrots ready?'

'Yes, here.'

'Right, steady does it, then. I think it's probably better to talk normally, rather than try to creep up quietly, what do you think?'

'Probably . . .'

'I'm surprised they could trot at all with their bellies full of this stuff,' Daniel observed as they waded on through the soaking grass.

'It does seem a bit risky,' Zoe agreed. 'They could easily get colic, I would have thought.'

As they drew closer to the grazing animals, Daniel risked shining the torch ahead again. This time, three of the four swung their heads up and one of those, he saw with relief, was wearing a head collar.

'That'll be her,' he said to the girl.

'But the one with its head down has a head collar, too,' she responded.

'Shit! Well, that's torn it.'

Two of the ponies began to back away as they approached and as luck would have it, one of those was wearing a collar.

Daniel instinctively began to coo softly under his breath. 'Give me one of those carrots,' he said holding out his hand to Zoe.

She handed him a large carrot and he broke it, hoping the snap would be a sound that the horses would recognize. Now three of the animals held their ground, pricking their ears inquisitively at Daniel's voice, and he moved slowly forward, still cooing.

'It's the one on the left,' Zoe told him, raising her voice just enough to be heard over the wind and rain. 'The other one's coloured, and I know his mare isn't.'

Daniel knew that by coloured, she meant of a broken colour, black or brown and white, piebald or skewbald, and could see, now his eyes had adjusted to the very low light, that all but two of the animals met that description. That made life easier. He transferred his attention to the pony on the left of the group, holding out the carrot as he stepped ever closer.

He was unhappily aware that for ponies in a field of long grass the meagre offering of a carrot was probably not high on their list of temptations, but surprisingly, all the ponies except one stayed where they were, two even reaching out questing muzzles as Daniel came within touching distance. He broke the carrot again, handing out pieces to the two boldest ones and suddenly they were all pushing forward demanding their share.

In the melee, Daniel managed to get a hand on the head collar of his target animal and then clipped on one of Taz's spare leads that he'd taken with him for the purpose. With only a token pull back as she found herself caught, she followed him obediently away from the other ponies, who had now begun to pull rank and squabble upon discovering that there were no more carrots to be had.

'Well done!' Zoe exclaimed falling into step beside him as he headed for the gate.

'Let's just hope she loads OK,' he replied.

'At least no one's likely to come checking on them in this weather. No one with any sense would be out in it!'

'You're not wrong there,' he agreed with some feeling.

The ponies they had left behind made no effort to follow, so Daniel and Zoe had no problem negotiating the gate and, leaving Zoe to hold the mare, Daniel set to work freeing the trailer from its security lock and hitching it to the tow bar of the Mercedes. Inside, the trailer had rubber matting on the floor and a three-quarters full haynet hanging from a ring in the front.

Daniel let down the ramp and adjusting his torch so it hung like a small lantern to illuminate the interior, went back to where Zoe was waiting.

'All ready,' he reported. 'Let's try her, shall we?'

Zoe nodded, leading the pony towards the enticing shelter of the trailer, but as soon as her hooves touched the slatted slope of the ramp, the mare threw up her head and swung away, towing the girl with her.

'You'd think she'd be glad of a chance to get out of the rain,' Zoe remarked, bringing her round for a second try.

This time the pony jibbed before she got to the ramp, wheeling round and barging into Zoe, so that she slipped on the wet ground and almost fell. Having caught her off balance, she then towed her for several yards before Zoe recovered enough to dig her feet in and attempt to slow the animal down.

Swiftly, Daniel followed, reaching for the pony's head collar and bringing her to a halt.

'Let me try,' he said.

'Gladly,' Zoe said, crossly. 'She's already stood on my toe!'

'It might help if we knew her name. I should have asked.'

'Oh, I did ask, it's Juno.'

Daniel took hold of the improvised lead rein and turned the mare back towards the trailer. Instantly, she dug her feet in and would have swung away if it hadn't been for his firm hand on the rein.

''S OK, Juno. Come on, girl,' he said, soothing her, but her head was up and her ears flicking back and forth. With his free hand, Daniel scratched the still dry fur under her mane. 'Atta girl. Come on. Come with me, little one,' he went on and once again began the cooing sounds that had apparently calmed the ponies earlier.

After a moment, it seemed as though it was doing the trick again; Juno's head lowered and she snuffled Daniel's sodden leather jacket.

'Good girl. Come with me, there's a good lass.'

Gentle but steady pressure on the lead rein met only slight resistance before she gave in and followed him to the foot of the ramp. Here she stopped again but with a little encouragement she placed her front feet on the slope and, apparently finding it no cause for alarm, stepped forward at Daniel's side and into the dry calm of the trailer.

'Shall I put the back up?' Zoe had followed them and was now standing at the bottom of the ramp.

'Yes, please, but gently,' he told her, tying the mare to the string from which the haynet hung. Moments later, the teenager quietly opened the small door at the front of the trailer.

'I don't know how you did that,' she said softly as he bent to come out through the door, himself. 'It was seriously impressive!'

'I'm not really sure, myself,' Daniel admitted. 'It's kind of instinctive but it seems to work.'

'You could make a mint as a behaviourist.'

'I'd be a fraud,' he said, shaking his head. 'And anyway, dogs are more my thing.' He checked on the mare again and found her pulling at the haynet with apparent contentment, closed the door and headed forward to the car.

'That's not what it looked like to me,' Zoe said as she took off the overlarge waterproof, turned it inside out and slid into the passenger seat, stowing the wet garment at her feet. 'My feet are absolutely squelching.'

'My feet are dry but I'm not sure these boots will ever be the same again,' Daniel said ruefully as he eased the car forward, feeling the unaccustomed heavy pull of the trailer behind. He was only using sidelights and could barely make out the edges of the uneven stony track that would take them, eventually, back to the road. 'I hope the old girl can cope with the extra weight,' he said then. 'She's not in the first flush of youth.'

'She won't break down?' Zoe sounded alarmed.

'I sincerely hope not.'

As the track dipped, Daniel risked switching to headlights and five bumpy minutes later the Merc's tyres found the blessed smoothness of the road and both Daniel and Zoe breathed a sigh of relief.

Ten minutes later, cruising along the main road, Daniel glanced across to his passenger and found her fast asleep with her head against the side window. He shook her arm to wake her and gave her one of Taz's fleece blankets he'd pulled from behind the seat.

'It's a bit hairy but it'll be more comfortable than glass.'

'Thanks.' Zoe folded it up, positioned it under her head and moments later was asleep once more.

Daniel heaved another sigh, this time of resignation, and concentrated on the road ahead. At the safe speed for towing, it was going to be a long old night.

It was, in fact, half-past five in the morning when Daniel stopped the Mercedes at the gates of Abbots Farm and got out to enter the security code for the gates. It was still raining, as it had been for the whole journey; a steady, unremitting drizzle that starred and spread every light that hit the windscreen, and Daniel's eyes felt stretched wide with concentration. At just over halfway, they had stopped at the motorway services for a break and to give the mare some water.

Unlikely as it was that anyone would steal a horse, on a service-station forecourt at a quarter to four in the morning, Daniel had nevertheless taken no chances and he and Zoe had taken it in turns to go into the brightly lit building for coffee and loos.

Thankfully, Juno had been quiet, probably tired, Daniel thought, from having to adjust her weight and balance over so long a period. She drank gratefully from Taz's bowl with only a momentary hesitation at the strangeness of the vessel.

Taz had been liberated for a few minutes to stretch his legs and attend his own call of nature, and caused a startled flick of the mare's ears when he peered in the door to see where his bowl was being taken.

With sleepy eyes, Zoe stayed awake just long enough to drink coffee and eat a doughnut before dropping off again. Daniel discounted the idea of taking a nap himself, unable to relax sufficiently, even though the probability of pursuit was low.

With a strong coffee inside him, he was just about to set off once more when he caught sight of a police car cruising up and down between the rows of parked cars. As it approached his position, Daniel held his breath and prayed that it wouldn't stop. It wasn't that he expected them to be on the lookout for a stolen trailer – he was pretty sure the Travellers were more in the habit of sorting out their own problems – but it was more than possible, if they weren't on other, more important business that they might notice that the trailer registration number didn't match that of the car, and that could make things very awkward.

His prayers weren't to be answered and his spirits sank as the police car slowed and stopped behind him. He watched in his wing mirror as one of the officers got out of the vehicle and approached the back of the trailer. A moment or two later he came down the right-hand side of the Mercedes and bent to look at Daniel through the side window.

Daniel turned towards him, eyebrows raised in query and lowered the window.

'This your trailer, is it, sir?'

Daniel put a finger to his lips and pointed meaningfully at Zoe before opening the door and getting out of the car.

'No, mine's got a problem with the axle,' he said, then, 'Borrowed this one from a friend.'

'Pretty late of a night to be trailing horses round the country . . .'

'Yeah, well, it wasn't supposed to be this late but it took a while to get hold of another trailer. Such a pain,' Daniel said matching his expression to the words. 'You offer to do a favour for a friend and everything goes wrong.' He fervently hoped that Zoe wouldn't wake up and inadvertently give the lie to his concocted story.

'Your horse, is it?'

'No. Belongs to Zoe's mother. Polo pony. Probably the best you've ever seen! Turns on a sixpence and so light in the hand. Got a great career ahead of her. With a bit more training she'll be worth a fortune! Amazing. You wouldn't believe what people pay for them. Anyway, I was coming up this way so, naturally, I offered to pick her up. That was before I realized my trailer had a problem, of course—'

'You need to change the registration plate,' the officer pointed out, cutting him off. 'The trailer and the towing vehicle should match. Where are you heading?'

'Devon. Tavistock,' Daniel said. 'Sorry. With everything else that was going on, I flat forgot about the numberplate. To be honest, I was just so pleased that we'd found a trailer we could use.'

'Yeah, well, get it sorted when you get back, before you go anywhere else with it,' the policeman said. 'Drive carefully.'

'I will, and thank you,' Daniel said, and with a final look into the trailer at the champion polo pony, the officer got into his car and it moved on.

Daniel went round to the back of the trailer, ostensibly to check on Juno, but actually watching the squad car's progress. It seemed, however, that its occupants now had only one thing on their minds and that wasn't Daniel or his trailer. They reached the front of the car park, found themselves a space and headed into the service-station buildings with every appearance of two men in search of much-needed refreshment.

Back in the car, Daniel found Zoe stirring. She looked sleepily at him.

'I heard voices. Who was it?'

'The police.'

'What?' Her eyes snapped open.

'It's OK. He wasn't looking for us but, sod's law, he noticed that the plate on the trailer didn't match the car. I bent his ear with a story about the mare being a polo pony. Gave him so much detail that in the end he couldn't wait to get away. All he really wanted was a coffee,' he finished with a smile. 'I was just hoping you wouldn't wake up and say something awkward. Anyway, they've gone now and we should get back on the road.'

Zoe nodded and Daniel started up, easing the Merc into motion and heading back down the slip road onto the motorway once more. By the time he had rejoined the sparse flow of traffic, Zoe was asleep and he drove on through the darkness, hoping he wouldn't encounter any more eagle-eyed traffic policemen in the last couple of hours of the journey.

Now, as he slid back into the driver's seat and pulled the door shut, Zoe opened her eyes and blinked first at him and then at the gates, illuminated in the headlights.

'We're home,' she said. 'That didn't take long.'

'Went by like a flash,' Daniel agreed drily.

'I think I may have slept a bit.'

'I think you may have slept a lot.'

'We had coffee,' she said as the gates began to swing open and Daniel eased forward. 'And there was a policeman. I remember that.'

'Mm. Well, that was nearly two hours ago.'

'Seriously? God, I'm sorry. I haven't been much help, have I?'

'Not much you could do anyway.'

'I could have talked to you to help pass the time.'

'I'm used to driving and night shifts, so it wasn't a problem. And anyway, I thought you probably needed the sleep,' he said.

They trundled slowly down the drive towards the house and as it came into view could see lights on in some of the windows.

'Oh, God! Mum,' Zoe said as the reality of the homecoming settled on her. 'This isn't going to be easy, is it?'

'I imagine not,' Daniel said. 'But I guess we need to get this little girl settled in first, so you'll have a few minutes to prepare yourself.'

'I could do with a few days,' Zoe said with feeling, as the car and trailer continued past the house and down to the stable yard.

They had, in fact, only been in the yard a couple of minutes when Lorna appeared, wrapped in a waterproof coat against the persistent drizzle, but instead of commenting on either the pony Daniel had just unloaded or even Zoe's behaviour, she clearly had other matters on her mind because her first words were of heartfelt relief.

'Oh, Daniel. Thank God you're back, it's been awful!' she exclaimed, and as she came into the lighted interior of the stable he was settling the mare into, Daniel could see that she looked even more stressed than the last time he'd seen her. She glanced around the stable and outside. 'Where's Zoe?'

'I'm here.' Zoe came out from behind Juno, her expression a strange mixture of defiance and apology.

'Oh, Zo!' Lorna exclaimed with a sob in her voice. She stepped forward and pulled her into a tight hug, kissing the top of her head. 'Don't ever do anything like that to me again!'

'Lorna, what's been going on? Have those men been back?' Daniel asked sharply.

'No, but they rang. It was horrible – so frightening! And the police . . .'

'What men?' Zoe asked.

'The police? What did *they* want?' Daniel cut in, tying the mare to a ring in the wall.

'To tell me they've found Harvey's phone,' she said, over her daughter's head.

'That's a bit odd. They're not normally in the business of returning lost property. I wonder why *they* took an interest.'

'Well, Stephen rang them about Harvey, yesterday. I told him we'd decided not to for now but he wouldn't listen. He kept saying he might have been in an accident or something, although someone would have called us if he had, wouldn't they? But he said the police should know, anyway, and that it would look suspicious if we didn't report him missing. I'm sorry. You know what he's like.'

'It's all right,' Daniel said. 'He's probably right. It's been a while now. You should have heard something. What did the police have to say – anything else? Where did they find the phone, did they say?'

'Apparently some boy they picked up for something else had it but he claimed he just found it by the side of the road. I don't think the police believed him.'

'And about Harvey?'

'They are going to come round and see us later this morning.' She freed a hand from hugging Zoe and ran her fingers through her hair, pushing it off her face. 'It's all a nightmare.'

Zoe pulled away from her.

'Is someone going to tell me what's going on? What did you mean about "men" calling? What men?'

Lorna looked at her and then glanced at Daniel, as if just remembering that she had meant to keep it from her daughter.

'Some men came looking for your dad – for Harvey,' Daniel told her. 'We don't know who they are but they weren't particularly pleasant.'

'The other day?' Zoe asked. 'When Mum was upset and I found you hugging her?'

'That's right.'

'Well, for God's sake! Why didn't you tell me what was going on?'

'Because we don't really know,' her mother said. 'And I didn't want to worry you. I thought it must all be some horrible mistake and that Harvey would turn up and sort it out.'

'But he hasn't,' Zoe stated, flatly. 'So what now?'

'I don't know,' Lorna admitted helplessly, looking at Daniel again.

'I guess now the police are involved it's out of our hands, really.'

'Do we tell them about the men who're looking for him?'

Daniel nodded.

'If they're watching this place they'll know you've spoken to the police, so there's nothing to be gained by keeping quiet. Anyway, Harvey's been back for three weeks now and hasn't been in touch so you have to think that he either isn't intending to or he can't, for some reason.'

'You mean, he could be dead?' Zoe asked flatly.

'Oh, Zoe!' her mother sounded shocked but Daniel felt it was more at her daughter's bluntness than at the idea itself, which would have almost certainly occurred to her at some point.

'I'm sorry, Mum, but it's possible, isn't it? It's what we're all thinking.'

'It's possible,' Daniel agreed. 'But it's not the only possibility. Let's wait and see what the police have to say, shall we? Now, can you get me some hay for our champion polo pony, here?'

'A polo pony?' Lorna asked, interested in spite of her anxieties.

'Not really. Just a story I spun for an over-interested copper we met when we stopped at the service station on the way home. I gave him way more information about her imaginary prospects than he wanted. You should have seen his eyes glaze over!'

Lorna subjected the pony to a critical survey, seeing, in the glow of the stable light, a well put together chestnut mare of about fifteen hands with a deep chest, sloping shoulder and a pretty head.

'Well, she's a nice-looking animal,' she said. 'I suppose that's something.'

'Yes, and she seems to have a pretty good temperament. She's been very well behaved considering she was dug out of her field in the middle of the night in a rainstorm, boxed up and carted halfway across the country!'

'Oh, goodness! I'd almost forgotten you'd been up all night. You must be exhausted! I still don't really understand why you didn't wait till morning but never mind for now. I'll get you some breakfast and then you must have a sleep. There's a bed made up in the spare room.'

'Well, I could do with getting my head down for an hour or two, but the sofa will be fine,' Daniel assured her. 'Did the police say what time they'd be coming?'

'No, just "in the morning",' she said, as Zoe came back bearing a full haynet and a fresh bucket of water.

'Should give us a couple of hours, then,' Daniel said, glancing at his watch.

'I'll go and put the kettle on. Bacon and eggs OK? There's plenty of toast.'

'Sounds wonderful.'

Lorna paused in the stable doorway. 'I'm afraid Stephen's about . . .'

Daniel smiled.

'Nothing's ever perfect.'

EIGHT

The police arrived mid-morning in the persons of one Sergeant Naylor and his younger colleague, PC Innes. Daniel's heart sank and he groaned as he saw them emerge from the car.

'Um, second thoughts, I think maybe you'd be better dealing with them yourself,' he told Lorna as she prepared to go and open the door to them.

She paused. 'Do you know them?'

'We have met. I don't think either of us especially enjoyed the occasion,' he said drily.

'But I'd really rather you were there, if you could bear it.'

'I will if you want, but I'm not sure it would be helpful. Besides, you've got Stephen.' Her stepson had received Daniel with a marked absence of joy earlier that morning.

She pulled a face.

'Please, Daniel.'

He gave in and when the two police officers were shown into the kitchen, took up a position leaning against the worktop near the back door.

Sergeant Naylor, who in the interim had added weight to a figure that Daniel didn't remember being exactly athletic in the first place, was in his early fifties and balding. He had about him an air of everything being too much trouble and when Lorna introduced Daniel as a friend of the family, spared him only the briefest of glances.

His colleague, gingery-blond and slightly built, gave Daniel a longer look from pale-lashed blue eyes and frowned slightly. Daniel merely nodded and if he had been recognized, PC Innes kept the fact to himself.

'Mrs Myers, I understand from what your stepson told us over the phone that you haven't seen your husband for nearly three weeks, is that right?' At her invitation, Sergeant Naylor had seated himself at the kitchen table and now took out a tablet and flipped the cover open. He fished a pair of glasses out of his pocket and put them on before prodding at the device with a stubby forefinger. Innes hovered for a moment and then pulled out a seat for himself, sliding into it as though he half expected it would be frowned upon.

'Yes. But that isn't unusual,' Lorna said. 'He often works abroad and I don't always know when he's going to be back. It depends how things go.'

'But presumably he normally stays in touch?' Naylor was concentrating on the small screen before him, and Daniel got the impression that perhaps technology wasn't really his thing.

'Yes, of course, from time to time.' Lorna's complexion turned a little pink as she replied. 'But he's very busy. It's pretty full-on when he's working abroad.'

'And when did you last hear from him, this time?'

'He sent me a text message a few days after he got there.'

'There being?'

'Hong Kong.'

'And he sounded normal? Not worried about anything, as far as you could tell?'

'No.'

'Do you still have that text on your phone, by any chance?' Naylor asked.

'Yes, I have.' Lorna picked her phone up from the kitchen worktop and opened her messages. She passed it across to the sergeant, who read it and made a laborious note on his tablet.

'How many mobile phones does your husband have?'

Lorna looked taken aback.

'Just the one, I think. I mean, I don't know. He's never contacted me on another one . . .'

'And during this trip, he didn't ring you at any time from a landline.'

'No.'

'We'll be contacting the phone company to get a complete log of his call activity,' Naylor told her. 'So what made you start to worry, this time?'

'Well, I hadn't heard from him for a few days and then someone contacted me wanting to get in touch with him. They were under the impression that he was already back from Hong Kong and so after a day or two, when he didn't come home, I rang GS, who told me he'd been back for ten days.'

'GS?'

'Giradelle Santini.'

'And who was this person who wanted to find him? A friend? Or a business contact?'

'I don't know.' Lorna glanced helplessly at Daniel. 'I'd never seen them before. There were two of them. I didn't get the impression they were friends. They were working for someone else. They didn't say why they wanted him but they did seem pretty keen to find him.' She and Daniel had agreed that this was all that needed to be said about the visit of the two men the previous Monday as Daniel was keen to keep his own part in the confrontation quiet. It was the version they had told Zoe and Stephen.

Naylor followed her glance and his gaze hesitated on Daniel for a moment before finding Lorna again.

'So how did they contact you?'

'They came here,' she said. 'Just turned up.'

'Can you describe them?'

'Um . . . Stocky, I suppose. Average height. One thirty-something, one a bit older. Quite roughly spoken – cockney maybe. Not educated.'

'They didn't give their names?'

'No.'

'You have security gates. How did they get in?'

'I let them in,' she confessed. 'I was expecting a delivery so when they buzzed I opened the gates. Maybe I should have been more careful but then I wasn't expecting any trouble.'

'Of course not. And how did the men behave? Were they at all threatening? What did they say?'

'I told you,' Lorna said. 'They wanted to know where Harvey was and when I said he was abroad, they didn't believe me. They were a bit overpowering but they didn't actually do anything; they just said to let him know they were looking for him.'

'You didn't report it, though?'

'As I said, they didn't do anything, and I thought when Harvey got back he would sort it out.'

'And what did you think when you discovered that Mr Myers had been back for all that time but hadn't been in touch? Weren't you worried?'

'Of course I was.'

'But you still didn't contact us . . .'

'Well, no. He's a grown man. I didn't think you'd consider him a missing person just because he hadn't called his wife for a few days and I didn't think he'd be too pleased to be hunted down if . . . well . . .'

'If what? Where did you think he might be?'

'Nowhere! I mean, I didn't know!' she protested. 'GS said he'd put in for leave . . .'

'But he hadn't told you that. Did you think he might be with someone else? Another woman, perhaps?'

'No!' Her denial was instinctive but moments later her shoulders fell and she said, 'I don't know. I don't know anything any more. But he's never given me any cause to . . .'

'Can you give me some idea of your relationship with your husband?' Naylor cut across her failing voice. 'How would you describe your marriage?'

Lorna frowned momentarily.

'Well . . .'

'I'm sorry, but we have to ask. If you'd rather answer these questions in private . . .' He glanced at Stephen and Daniel, once again letting his gaze linger on Daniel for a fraction before turning back to Lorna.

Yes, you remember me but can't recall from where, Daniel thought. *Long may it continue.*

'No, I don't mind,' Lorna said, in answer to Naylor. 'Our marriage is like many, I imagine. He works long hours and we both have our own interests but when we're together we are OK.'

'And what *are* Mr Myers' interests?' Naylor was trying to input information on his tablet but after a muttered oath, he pushed the device across the table to his colleague. 'Why don't *you* do something to earn your keep for a change?'

PC Innes fielded the tablet and began, deftly, to work it, apparently inured to the sarcasm of his older colleague.

'Harvey doesn't have a lot of down time,' Lorna said then. 'He's a bit of a workaholic, really. He used to be into adventure sports as a young man, but after he hurt his back in a skiing accident, most of that had to stop. He was also quite a keen sailor and had a yacht down at Plymouth, but he sold it last year.'

'Why was that, do you know? Has he been having money worries?'

'Not as far as I know. I think he just wasn't getting the use out of it. It always seemed to need something doing to it. I remember him saying it would be cheaper and less bother to just charter a boat when he wanted to go out.'

'And has he?'

'No. Not often. Well, once or twice, to start with, but not lately.'

'So as far as you know, he isn't in any financial trouble?'

It was Stephen who answered. 'Is it likely? He has a very senior and well-paid position with Giradelle Santini – you *have* heard of them, haven't you?'

'Of course,' Naylor said. However, watching him, Daniel wasn't at all sure he had. 'But just because he's on a high salary doesn't mean anything. Even millionaires run into money problems sometimes. Anyone can overspend. It's just a matter of scale.'

'We have separate bank accounts,' Lorna put in, 'so I don't really know, but he's never said anything and I haven't noticed him spending more than usual. If anything, less.'

'It's not always cars and holidays,' the sergeant said. 'Unwise investments can suck a man dry in no time at all.'

'Finance and costings are my father's business,' Stephen put in. 'He's hardly likely to make that kind of mistake, is he?'

'Anyone can get into trouble with stocks and shares,' Naylor commented. 'You're at the mercy of the market. Well, we'll be requesting access to his bank details in due course, so not to worry for now.'

'Why would you do that?' Stephen demanded, pulling out a chair at the head of the table and sitting down opposite the policeman. 'My father is missing, he's not a criminal! What gives you the right to go nosing into his affairs?'

'The law gives us the right,' Naylor told him with unruffled calm. 'Your father has not been seen or heard from for three weeks and his mobile phone has been either lost or stolen but not reported missing. I'd say that is cause for a certain amount of alarm, wouldn't you? From his banking history we'll be able to tell, not only the state of his finances but where and when his credit and debit cards were last used. We'll be in contact with his work, too – this Gerald el . . .?' He looked at Innes impatiently.

'Giradelle Santini,' his colleague supplied without a flicker.

'Exactly what position does your father hold?' Naylor asked Stephen, as though it was something which Lorna, as a woman, might not know.

'He's a senior negotiator,' she told him before her stepson could reply, and there was an unmistakable edge to her tone. 'He's worked for them for twenty-five years.'

'We'll interview his colleagues and see if he may have spoken of his plans to any of them. It's surprising how often people's workmates know more about a person than their family do,' he added, with the superior air of one imparting information to the uninitiated.

Pompous knobhead, Daniel thought with disgust, easing his weight from one foot to the other.

'So, as far as you know, your husband wasn't worrying about money. Did he seem himself, the last time you saw him? Not depressed or anxious? Was he in good health? Any doctor's appointments lately?'

'Not that he told me about,' Lorna said, shaking her head in bewilderment. 'Apart from his bad back, he's always been pretty fit and healthy. Why are you asking? What do you know?'

'Well . . .' The sergeant paused as if unsure whether to share his knowledge. Apparently deciding in favour of it he said, 'We had Mr Myers' phone unlocked – that's how we came to contact you. It appears it was last used on Sunday the nineteenth, three days after he last contacted you. He made a couple of calls that went unanswered, which we're in the process of following up, and then, late that evening, composed a text that was never finished or sent. That text was to you. It said . . .' He beckoned impatiently to his constable. 'The text message, Innes, let me have it.'

The constable swiped and tapped at the screen of his tablet for a moment or two, then passed it over.

'It said,' Naylor continued in a colourless voice, as if he were reading from a textbook, '"My darling, please forgive me and don't hate me for this. I swear I never meant any of it to happen. If I can . . ." That's where it ended,' he said, looking across at Lorna. 'Do you have any idea what that might have been about?'

Looking at Lorna, Daniel saw the blood drain from her face as she stared fixedly at the police officer. The silence lengthened.

'Mrs Myers . . .?'

She shook her head, the movement barely perceptible.

'No. I don't. I mean, that doesn't sound like him at all, he's always so . . . well, confident, sure of himself. Are you sure . . .?'

'I never heard anything so ridiculous!' Stephen cut across her before Naylor could speak. 'That's not Dad – it can't be. Didn't you say you found the phone on some kid?'

'Yes, we did, but—'

'Well, there you are then.'

'Kids commonly use stolen phones for gaming or to sell on, but aside from the fact that there was no evidence that the lad had been successful in unlocking the phone at all, it's hardly the kind of message a sixteen-year-old would compose, is it, sir? And although it was never finished, the text was intended to be sent to Mrs Myers.'

'So what? My father would never commit suicide!' Stephen declared. 'That is what you're trying to say isn't it? Well, you're wrong. The idea is ridiculous. He'd never do that!'

'I'm afraid we none of us know what we would be capable of if we were backed into a corner,' the sergeant said sadly. 'There may be some other explanation for the text and the fact that the loss of his phone has gone unreported, but it's my business to consider all the possibilities.'

Stephen made a disbelieving noise but could apparently think of no further protest and subsided into silence, contenting himself with glaring at Lorna, clearly blaming her for his father's uncharacteristic behaviour.

'Do you know where the phone was found?' Daniel asked.

Naylor turned to look at him, his gaze narrowing a little.

'We can't be sure. The lad says it was just on the side of the road but he's not someone overburdened with conscience, if you get my drift. Hopefully when we get a full report from the phone company we'll be able to track its exact movements from the time your husband re-entered the country. The lad may be telling the truth, but it's equally possible that he stole it from Mr Myers' car or even, as he was apparently interrupted before he finished the text, from Mr Myers himself.'

'You think he was mugged for his phone?' Lorna exclaimed, shocked.

'No, not necessarily. Merely that we have to consider all possibilities. It is, however, a very expensive phone,' Naylor said, turning back to her.

'But then, why wouldn't he report it?' She apparently saw the answer in his face, because she rushed on, 'No. If he was hurt, somebody would have found him by now, wouldn't they?'

The sergeant nodded.

'You'd have thought so. As I said, Mrs Myers, we don't have the answers for you, at this stage we're just considering the possibilities.'

'There is another possibility,' Daniel put in quietly. 'Looking at all this, house, land, lifestyle, one could imagine that he's a very wealthy man . . .'

Naylor looked at him again, his attention sharpening.

'We've met before, haven't we? Daniel – what did you say your surname was?' He frowned, plainly trying to remember the details.

'Whelan. Yes, we've met.'

Innes was more on the ball.

'The Moorside case,' he said, looking at his colleague. 'Mr Whelan found the little girl.'

'Ah, yes. Of course.' Naylor's expression showed no overwhelming gratitude for Daniel's input on either that or the current occasion. 'Well, yes, of course, we always consider the possibility of kidnap in these sorts of cases,' he said, transferring his attention back to Lorna. 'But there have been no demands,' he raised an eyebrow at her and she shook her head, 'and I would have expected something by now if that were the case.'

To his side, PC Innes cleared his throat.

'The car . . .?'

'Yes, I was just coming to that,' Naylor snapped. He turned back to Lorna. 'Did your husband drive himself to and from the airport?'

'Yes. Nearly always.'

'This time?'

'Yes. Oh! His car? Have you found it?'

'Not yet. If you can give Innes the details, we'll get it on the database and hopefully when we find it we shall be a bit nearer to discovering where Mr Myers is – or at least where he has been since returning from Hong Kong.'

It was nearly half an hour more before Sergeant Naylor and his largely silent sidekick finally departed. Naylor had asked still more questions about Harvey Myers' home life, wanting to know about other members of the family, and even Zoe was summoned and quizzed about her relationship with her stepfather; leading questions which she answered briefly and coolly.

'We'll be in touch, but it goes without saying,' Naylor said as he turned to get into the car, 'that if you hear anything from your husband, or remember anything else that might have any bearing at all upon his disappearance, however small, you should let us know.'

'It might go without saying,' Stephen observed as the car disappeared up the long drive, 'but he still had to say it, didn't he? Officious prick!'

'Did you hear him?' Zoe said incredulously. 'He was gagging for me to say that Harvey had tried to touch me up. That would have made his day.'

'Tiresome, he might be, but he wouldn't be doing his job if he didn't ask those questions,' Daniel said, reluctantly defending the sergeant.

'Of course, you would know, wouldn't you?' Stephen sneered. '*Ex*-copper.'

'I would, wouldn't I?' Daniel agreed equably.

'Oh, God, Stephen! Don't start!' Lorna snapped. 'Things are bad enough without you being obnoxious, too!'

'So what now?' Zoe wanted to know as they walked back into the kitchen.

'We wait, I suppose.' Lorna sighed, putting her arm round her daughter's shoulders and giving them a quick squeeze. 'Shall I put the kettle on?'

Before anyone had a chance to answer, the telephone on the wall beside the door began to ring and Lorna froze, looking at Daniel with a stricken expression. 'Withheld,' she said.

'It's OK,' he said, stepping forward to lift the receiver. 'Yes?'

'We told the Myers woman no police,' the voice said. 'The boss won't be happy.'

'The police were only here because Harvey Myers is missing,' Daniel stated.

'Missing. Hiding. Call it what you like,' was the reply. 'But tell the pretty lady the boss is getting impatient. She's got forty-eight hours. If her hubby hasn't shown himself by then, things will start to get nasty.'

'She doesn't know where he is,' Daniel protested. 'Whatever he's done you can't blame her!'

He was answered by the dialling tone. The man had already gone.

He replaced the phone in its cradle and turned round.

'Oh, my God!' Lorna breathed, her eyes wide. 'How did they know the police were here? Are they watching the house?' She glanced at the window as if expecting to catch someone in the act of doing so.

'The drive or the road, maybe,' Daniel said. 'If the number's traceable, the police will be on to it, because they'll check your phone records as well as Harvey's, but I'm pretty sure these guys'll be using an unregistered mobile, so I don't suppose it'll tell them anything.'

'So what do we do now? What did they say?'

'They just wanted us to know they saw the police car, that's all.'

'Were they angry? What will they do?'

'It's Harvey they want. I think they'll just wait,' Daniel said, hoping he was right. 'But keep your eyes open and your wits about you, just in case. Best not go out alone, if you can help it.'

'What about school?' Zoe asked with a hopeful look in her eye. 'Should I stay away?'

'As long as someone can see you safely onto the bus, I should think you'd be fine,' Daniel said. 'But no bunking off or going into town on your own.'

'Of course not,' she responded, the picture of innocence, but Lorna gave her a look that told Daniel she wasn't taken in by her daughter's act.

'What about your rings?' Stephen asked Lorna. 'And all this running away to Wales business? It seems to me she's got some explaining to do.'

Zoe rounded on him, eyes flashing but Lorna was before her.

'So she might have but it's absolutely no business of yours!' she told him, coldly. 'Zoe and I will sort that out between ourselves.'

Bravo! Daniel said under his breath. Stephen glowered at each of them in turn before heading for the door, saying over his shoulder, 'Forget the coffee, I'm going out.'

Moments later the front door closed behind him with something perilously close to a slam.

'That'll teach us!' Zoe observed.

'He may poke his nose in where it's not wanted,' her mother said, 'but on this occasion he is right, you know. You do have questions to answer.'

Zoe bit the inside of her lip.

'I know.'

'I'll just go and check on the mare,' Daniel announced, putting his jacket on. Instantly, Taz was on his feet, pleased to be on the move again. It had been a long and boring night and morning for him.

'No coffee?' Lorna enquired.

'When I come back. Won't be long.'

He let himself out of the front door and stood for a moment in the porch, sheltering from the rain and watching Stephen's car disappear along the drive towards the road. He saw the brake lights come on as he approached the gateway, but Stephen had a remote key and before long the gates had opened and he was gone. With the surrounding shrubs it wasn't easy to see the gates themselves and Daniel glanced back at the indicator light on the keypad inside the front door which turned from green to red when the gates were secure once more.

Heading down to the stables, he reflected on Naylor and Innes' visit. He was pretty sure that they, like him, regarded the Harvey Myers affair as more than just a simple 'Misper', or missing-person case. With the discovery of his mobile phone, its loss apparently unreported, the unexplained absence of the businessman had assumed far more sinister connotations. If the man were alive and well, Daniel could think of no reason why he wouldn't have at least contacted his phone company to get his account locked down, but this had not happened. So where was he?

The unsent text message had added another dimension to the mystery. What was it that he had been going to tell Lorna? Was he about to confess to infidelity? It seemed hardly likely that he would have addressed her as My Darling, if he had been about to admit to having a mistress, unless perhaps the affair was over and he was full of remorse. But then why admit to it at all as Lorna, if she was telling the truth, had no idea that he'd strayed in the first place?

The rain suddenly intensified and Daniel ducked his head and ran for the overhang in front of the stables, Taz leaping and bounding happily at his side, threatening to trip him up.

'Get out of the way, you great oaf!' Daniel exclaimed, laughing as he reached the shelter.

Making his way along the row he peered in at the newest occupant. Juno was standing at the far side of her box, head low and one hind foot tip-tilted, her rich chestnut coat liberally dusted with sawdust and wood shavings from her bed. Her haynet had hardly been touched and she was obviously weary but Daniel thought she looked happy enough. At the sight of him in the doorway, she straightened up and lifted her head enquiringly.

'It's all right, little one,' he soothed, opening the lower half-door and going in. 'Nobody's going to hurt you. You're quite safe here.'

He approached her slowly and stood at her shoulder, scratching her neck under the soft brown mane, and after a moment she turned her head towards him and snuffled the pocket of his leather jacket. He found her a couple of Polo mints, which she crunched with appreciation, and they stood together in companionship for several minutes until a low growl from Taz made them both look round.

'Who is it?' Daniel called out.

'It's me. Shane.' The voice came from a few feet away.

'All right, Taz. Quiet now,' Daniel told the dog, and the growling stopped.

Moments later the youngster appeared in the doorway.

'Nobody ain't gonna creep up on you, are they?' he observed, admiringly.

'That's the general idea,' Daniel agreed, giving the mare a final scratch behind her ears.

'She seems to like you,' Shane said. 'She can be a bit nervy with strangers but you've got a way with you.'

'Well, we spent the night together,' Daniel joked. 'So how did you get in? Over the fence?'

'No. Through the gate when the bloke in the Beemer went out,' Shane said without apology. 'It stays open just long enough if the driver gets a move on and he seemed to be in a hurry, right enough.'

As Daniel left the mare and joined the lad outside the stable, he saw he was wet through, his dark hair plastered to his head and his denim jeans sodden with rain. His upper body was clothed in a fleece, which showed a fine sheen of moisture over it under the lights and was almost certainly soaked through as well.

'You made good time,' he observed. 'Did you drive?'

'Only to start with,' Shane said, 'and then I had to ditch the car cos I knew my old man would be looking for it.'

'But you must have had a good head start, didn't you?'

'A couple of hours, maybe. I didn't like to go too early, in case I woke them and they saw the mare was gone. But he'd have put the word out, see? Declan Brennan doesn't like to be crossed and we have family everywhere. He'll have been on that phone before you could scratch your arse and have half the community on the lookout for me. You've no idea the way it works,' he told Daniel. 'I'm hoping he thinks I've gone north with the mare to my granma Brennan's. I threatened to, a couple of days ago, and it'll take him a while to check that I haven't. They don't see eye to eye.'

'So did you hitch?'

'Yeah. Got a ride almost all the way down. That's how it goes sometimes. Another day and you'll be lucky to be picked up at all.'

They had turned round and were leaning on the half-door looking at the mare.

'She's a nice-looking animal,' Daniel said.

'Yeah. I really think I could have got somewhere with her,' Shane said wistfully. 'She's the best I've ever driven, by a mile.'

'But not now. I guess now she belongs to Zoe's mum, by virtue of the fact that it was her jewellery you pawned to buy her.'

'I didn't know that! Zoe told me her gran had left it to her. You have to believe me.'

'I don't have to, but as a matter of fact, I do.'

He subsided a little, looking over the half-door at the mare again.

'What do you think Mrs Myers will do with her?'

'I have no idea. She said she looks as though she could be a useful polo pony, but you can ask her yourself when you come up to the house.'

Immediately, Shane appeared shut down and wary.

'I don't think that's a good idea.'

'Nevertheless, I think you should. You're trespassing on her property, after all.'

'But she's always been against me, Zoe said, even before she knew about the jewellery.'

'Have you given up the idea of a future with Zoe?'

'No! That is, I don't know,' Shane amended. 'What chance have we got now?'

'None at all if you don't try and build bridges,' Daniel said bluntly. 'I'm not saying it'll be easy, or even that it'll be possible, but she's a reasonable woman and I think, whatever her initial reaction, when she calms down she'll respect you for trying.'

Shane shrugged his shoulders slightly.

'I guess so . . .'

'Tell me something,' Daniel said then. 'Why did you lose your job at the kennels?'

Beside him, he sensed the youngster going very still.

'How do you know about that?'

'Zoe talked me into taking her to Hawkers Yard to try and find you.'

'I'm surprised they told you anything. What did they say?'

'Well, we spoke to your mother but you're right, it wasn't her that told us.'

'My sister, Leila,' Shane said disgustedly. 'She never could keep her mouth shut.'

'Well, apparently she overheard your dad and Billy Driscoll arguing.'

'I imagine everyone on the site heard them,' Shane said. 'They almost came to blows before Johnny stepped in.'

'Johnny Driscoll, Billy's brother?'

'Yeah. He's all right, Johnny is, not like Billy, but when he says jump, we all fuckin' jump!'

'So what started it all? Why did you get the push?'

Shane shrugged again.

'It was always going to happen. I hadn't been there all that long but we were always butting heads. I didn't like the way he was with the dogs. I love animals, me. To Billy they were just a way to make money, dead or alive.'

Daniel's eyes narrowed.

'What do you mean, dead or alive?'

Instantly the shutters came down.

'Nothing. It was just a way of speaking.'

'Leila said the argument was partly about you seeing Zoe.'

Again the slight shrug.

'I dunno why. They knew I was seeing her pretty much from the start. You can't keep anything to yourself around the yard – especially with a little blabbermouth like my sister on the case.'

'So why was Billy threatening you?' Daniel persisted. 'Why did Johnny send you and your dad away?'

'It was family business.'

Daniel watched him for a thoughtful moment.

'You know, you can have me on your side or not. It's up to you, but it might make quite a difference. I'd say you're probably in a fair bit of strife with your own community, right now, and Zoe's mum isn't likely to be your biggest fan, so I wouldn't turn down the chance of an ally, if I were you. Just a thought . . .'

Shane pushed a loose stone around with the toe of his boot

on the concrete at his feet, then he spoke without raising his gaze.

'You'd take my side?'

'I might. If I thought you were being straight with me.'

There was another long pause and the stone got rolled around some more.

Finally, 'I found out about a scam Billy was running with the dogs,' he said.

'Doping?' Daniel was under no illusions about the state of the greyhound racing industry.

'Nah. Well, yeah, I mean he was doing that, too, but I always knew about that – everyone does, except the Saturday night punters.'

'So . . .?'

'Well, the dogs are only fit to race for three or four years,' Shane said. 'And that's a good dog; most of them retire at two and a half and some of them never do any good at the track and are on the slag heap at eighteen months. People don't think about that side of it. They can live till twelve or fourteen. That's why there's so many greyhounds in rescue centres.'

'So what scam is Billy running?' Daniel had a feeling he knew, but he wanted to hear it from the lad.

'When the dogs retire he takes money from the owners – the decent ones – and promises to find their dogs a good home.'

'But he doesn't.'

'No.' Shane didn't elaborate; he didn't have to.

'And the other owners?'

'They pay him to make the dogs disappear,' Shane said bitterly. 'Young dogs, most of them. Nothing wrong with them except that they've served their purpose. And then, like as not, they'll go out and buy another dog to run.' He was silent, staring at the ground. 'It's their eyes. They're so trusting, you know? He wanted me to help him, once; to hold them while he did it. I refused.'

'What does he do with the bodies?' Daniel wanted to know.

'Buries 'em. He's got plenty of room. I never saw it but I think he may take dogs from other people, too. Davy let something slip once.'

'Davy?'

'His other brother.'

'So, why doesn't Billy get him to help?'

'I think he does sometimes but it upsets him. He's a bit simple is Davy but he wouldn't hurt a fly. To be honest, he's not much help to Billy apart from the donkeywork but he does what he's told and that suits Billy. They're an odd pair but they're like this.' Shane held up two fingers, twisted together.

'So when you found out what was going on, what then? Did you face him with it? Threaten him?'

'I told him I wasn't happy, right enough, but he said he wasn't doing anything illegal. He said, by law, he was allowed to put dogs down.'

Daniel frowned.

'That's not strictly true. I believe you're allowed to put your own dog down but I'm not sure about other people's. It's a bit of a grey area and it's certainly not encouraged. If you didn't like what he was doing, why didn't you leave?'

'Yeah, easy for you to say, isn't it? I needed the money, see? Jobs aren't easy to come by for my kind, you know. And, anyway, it's not like I ever thought he was an angel.'

'So, why the big row if it wasn't about that? Why did he sack you?'

'I dunno. He just lost it one night. I'd left something at work and called back in to pick it up. I had Zoe on the back of my bike and she'd gone to look at the dogs while I nipped into the office. Billy saw her through the window and went mad.'

'At her?' Daniel wondered why Zoe hadn't mentioned it when they had been to see Billy.

'No. He just said, "Get that fuckin' country girl out of here!" I said she wasn't doing any harm but he wouldn't listen. He wanted to know what I'd told her, but I hadn't told her anything.'

'About the dogs?'

'I suppose so. I mean, we'd got better things to talk about. She knew I wasn't happy there but I didn't give her all the details. She'd have thought I should do something, wouldn't she? She doesn't understand what it's like with us. I mean – Billy's family, you know? It's not easy.' Shane looked a little shamefaced.

'I can imagine.' Daniel wasn't unfamiliar with the internal politics of the travelling communities. Their lives were governed by various codes of honour that would seem almost incomprehensible to the average person.

'He wanted me to say I'd finish it with Zoe but I said I wouldn't – that's when he totally lost it. He's living in the past, is Driscoll – both of 'em are. Even my da wasn't like that about it when he found out. He didn't like it but he knows times are changing. It's not such a big deal any more.'

'Well . . .' Daniel squinted out from under the overhang at the rain that was still battering the gravel of the yard as if directed earthwards by some great celestial hose. 'I'm going to make a run for it back up to the house. There's a coffee waiting for me. You coming?'

Shane hesitated.

'What are your other options?' Daniel said reasonably. 'I'm assuming you won't be going back to Hawkers Yard any time soon, and if you're serious about Zoe . . .'

The youngster stared out at the rain, took a deep breath as if mustering his courage, and then nodded. 'OK.'

NINE

The atmosphere in the kitchen of Abbots Farm could not have been described as genial, but Daniel felt it could have been a lot worse. Credit had to go to Lorna, who, having already had the morning from hell, recovered with commendable self-control from the initial shock of having the boy who had corrupted her daughter ushered into the very heart of her house.

Daniel was under no illusions that had Shane not arrived in his company, the introduction wouldn't have gone anywhere near as well as it had.

'Sorry I was a long time,' he had said, preceding the Traveller into the kitchen. 'The mare's fine. A little tired, maybe, but OK. Is coffee still on offer?'

'I can put some more on,' Lorna said, reaching for the kettle.

'By the way, I found Shane down by the stables, checking on the mare. I suggested he come up and meet you.'

Lorna turned with the kettle in her hand. She frowned, then good manners won the day and she nodded almost imperceptibly.

'Shane.'

'Mrs Myers,' he replied, looking acutely uncomfortable.

'Well, you'd better come out of the rain,' she said, continuing on her way to the sink.

Zoe, showing a sensitivity to the situation, refrained from adding extra strain by any great show of affection, but she couldn't keep the delight out of her voice as she greeted him.

'Hi. I don't understand. How did you get here? No, never mind. Come and sit down. You'll have coffee, won't you?'

Shane pinched the fabric of his jeans.

'I'm a bit wet for sitting.'

Lorna turned and looked more closely at him.

'You'll need to get those clothes off and in the dryer,' she said, her maternal instincts winning out over her natural antipathy.

'I don't have any others,' Shane said, reddening a little.

'I expect there's something of Harvey's you can borrow while yours are drying,' Lorna told him. 'Wait here.'

While she was gone, Daniel made the coffee and Zoe and Shane took the opportunity for a rapid, whispered consultation. Moments later Lorna was back with a pair of corduroy trousers and a shirt and jumper over her arm.

'They're only old ones – for gardening and bonfires. They may be too big but there's a belt. You can change in the utility room,' she added, waving him in the direction of the back door. 'And put your things in the dryer while you're there.'

'Thanks,' Shane said, taking the bundle of clothes and heading that way.

When the door closed behind him, Zoe went to her mother and gave her a hug.

'Thank you. I love you, Mum.'

'It doesn't mean anything,' Lorna warned her, returning the hug briefly before disengaging. 'I couldn't let him sit there in soaking wet clothes, could I? I'd have done the same for anyone.'

'Well, thanks anyway.'

The Traveller lad was powerfully built and the borrowed clothes fitted remarkably well. He came back into the room looking very self-conscious, accepted the mug of coffee Daniel offered him and went to sit beside Zoe. In the utility room behind him, they could hear the tumble dryer turning.

'Have you eaten?' Lorna asked, the words coming almost grudgingly, as though hospitality was a habit she couldn't shake, even when the guest was plainly unwelcome.

'Yeah, I had breakfast at a truck stop,' he said, adding 'Thanks,' as an afterthought.

Having done her duty, Lorna leaned against the worktop and regarded the youngster with an intensity that clearly unsettled him.

'I suppose I should thank you for returning what has become my property,' she said after a long moment. 'But to be honest, I don't really have any use for another horse, however nice she may be. What I *do* want, however, is my jewellery back.'

Shane cleared his throat. 'I don't have the money until I sell the pony,' he told her.

'But what about the race?' Zoe cried. 'Can't it wait till after the race? Then we'll have the money.'

'No, it can't.' Lorna's tone brooked no argument.

'It doesn't matter,' Shane said soothingly.

'It matters to me!'

'We'll just have to wait,' he told her. 'There's plenty of time. But we must get your mother's rings back. I'm sorry,' he said looking Lorna in the eye. 'I'd never have done it if I'd known. I misunderstood what Zoe meant.'

'I think it very much more likely that you were misled on purpose,' Lorna said, fixing her daughter with a steely gaze. 'Zoe and I have already had words about that, so I'll say no more. But those rings belonged to my mother and grandmother and I want them back as soon as possible, so I'll lend you the money to redeem them and I'll go with you to get them back. You can pay me back when you're able to.'

'I can go,' Zoe suggested, but Lorna shook her head.

'I think not.'

Zoe looked slightly sulky but Shane nodded. 'Thanks.'

'I'll go with you, if you like,' Daniel offered, more worried about Lorna's safety away from the house than the possibility of Shane absconding with the money or the rings.

'Really? Would you?' Lorna looked relieved. 'But what about work?'

'There's always lunchtime, if I'm close enough. I can let you know once I get my sheet for the day, if that's OK?'

'Fine, thank you.'

'Now,' Daniel said, swallowing a mouthful or two of his coffee and regarding Shane thoughtfully over the rim of his mug, 'what are we going to do with you?'

The youngster looked taken aback.

'Me? I'm all right.'

'Where will you stay, though? You can't go back to your people at the moment, I imagine, and you say you're short of cash . . .'

'I've got some,' Shane said. 'But I can doss anywhere.'

'Is Stephen planning on staying, do you think?' Daniel asked Lorna.

Now it was her turn to look startled.

'I don't know. I imagine so, with what we've found out today . . . Why?'

'Oh, just thinking aloud. No, it was a silly idea, anyway. Tell you what, you can stay with me for a day or two,' he told Shane. 'If you don't mind sleeping on the couch, that is.'

Shane eyes narrowed. He quite plainly wasn't accustomed to outsiders considering his well-being.

'Why?'

Daniel shrugged.

'Why not? But if you'd rather not, I won't lose any sleep over it.' He stood up. 'Think about it. I'll be back later but for now I'd keep out of Stephen's way, if I were you.'

Leaving Abbots Farm behind, Daniel turned the Mercedes' nose north-west. It was a relief to leave the charged atmosphere of the Myers' home behind and give himself some space to think. He hoped it wouldn't be too uncomfortable for the young Traveller, but as he left Shane and Zoe had been talking about heading down to the stables to see Juno, so he supposed they would be OK.

Mindful of Shane's comment, Daniel had stopped the car outside the electric gates until they had closed once more and made a mental note to advise Stephen and Lorna to do the same.

He was on his way to call in on the greyhound rescue kennels Peggy Branscombe had mentioned. A visit to Google had provided him with the address and the name of the woman who ran it, and although he could have emailed her, he always preferred to speak in person, when possible.

He had no real reason to search her out, at all, it was just that after talking to Shane that morning, and remembering his conversation with Peggy, he was becoming aware of a strong desire to bring Driscoll to book over his treatment of the dogs at his kennels. Even though he had apparently shrugged off Shane's doubts, Daniel suspected that Billy Driscoll might have a lot more to hide than the youngster even dreamed of. There was just a chance that someone such as Anya Darby, who was involved in the industry, might have heard something or at least be able to suggest someone else he could talk to.

He found Longdogs Rescue on the outskirts of a small village near the town of Bideford. An earlier phone call had ensured that Anya would be in, and she came out of the house as Daniel drove into the small, untidy yard.

She was much younger than he had envisaged, a slim and attractive woman of about his own age wearing a skin-tight pair of jeans and a fleece, with a waterproof parka slung round her shoulders against the rain. Tendrils of dark hair had escaped from their binding and whipped about her face in the wind. Her skin tone indicated some Asian blood.

'Oh!' she exclaimed as Daniel got out of the car. 'I thought I'd have time to feed the puppies before you got here. They're on four feeds a day at the moment.'

'No worries, I'll come with you, if you like.'

'Um . . . OK.' With no further ado, Anya set off for the nearest of a row of low-roofed buildings that looked suspiciously like pigsties. Opening a door in the end of it, she ducked inside, holding it open for Daniel to follow.

'It shouldn't take long. They're just being weaned and they're eating like gannets,' she told him over her shoulder as she moved towards a food-preparation counter. Her voice was accentless and educated.

'I'm assuming it was an unplanned litter,' Daniel said, closing the door behind him.

'Well I'd have to have rocks in my head to breed more greys when I've already got seventy-five in rescue, wouldn't I?' she replied with some asperity. 'Ex-breeding bitch. They thought she hadn't taken but hey ho, five weeks later and here we are; six more little unwanted people. Poor buggers!'

'Is six a normal litter?'

'Pretty much average,' Anya said, heating milk in a microwave and adding it to some kind of pelleted food. 'I did once know of a bitch who threw fifteen. Hasn't ever happened to me, thank God! Six more mouths is bad enough.' She tested the temperature of the milk with a finger and then carried the two rectangular bowls towards a door at the far side of the area.

Daniel hurried to open it for her but she turned sideways and pushed it open with her hip. Following her down a short corridor with pens on both sides, Daniel looked right and left at the tall, long-nosed occupants pushing forward excitedly at the sight of their benefactor. There were a few squeaks and whines but otherwise, surprisingly little noise considering the numbers. The area was well-ventilated but also quite warm. The inevitable dog smells reminded Daniel of the police kennel blocks at Dog Central, as it had been fondly known.

'They're in here,' Anya said, stopping beside an enclosed pen that had piles of cardboard and fleecy bedding on the floor. 'You can get the door for me, if you want to be useful, but mind you don't let any of the pups out.'

Daniel did as he was told. From the back of the pen a doe-eyed chestnut-and-white greyhound uncurled herself and, stepping carefully over the six drowsy puppies at her feet, came forward on stilt-like legs to greet her visitors, with flattened ears and a gently waving tail.

'Hello, Penny,' Anya said fondly and while the puppies, fully alert now, attacked their milky meal with noisy gusto, she rewarded the bitch with handfuls of dry food from her pockets, the love she had for the dogs evident in her dark expressive eyes.

Ten minutes later they shut the door once more and Anya invited Daniel back to the house.

'Have you really got seventy-five dogs here?' he asked as they divested themselves of wet coats and shoes in a warm kitchen where half a dozen more greys and lurchers occupied beds and blanket-strewn corners.

'Sixty-eight at the moment,' she said, releasing a cascade of dark hair from its binding before winding it into a knot and securing it once more. 'But there are a few more coming in on Tuesday.'

Daniel watched her appreciatively as she gathered mugs and coffee and lifted a flat-bottomed kettle from the Aga. Her face was fine-boned, her eyes large with luxuriant lashes, and if her mouth was a little too wide for classical beauty, it in no way subtracted from the whole. With her boyish figure, she could have been a model, although she was probably lacking a few inches in height. She turned round and Daniel realized he'd been staring.

'Well, you'll certainly know me again, if you see me,' she said with a slight smile.

'I was just thinking you could probably make a packet modelling and support the dogs that way,' he said candidly.

'Well, actually, I do do a little,' she admitted. 'But I don't make a packet. It's photographic modelling, mainly; catalogues and such. I don't enjoy it, but it's the only way to keep this lot going.' She put a mugful of coffee and a packet of dark chocolate digestives on the table in front of Daniel and motioned him to sit down.

'Do you do this all on your own?' he asked.

'Good God, no! I'd be run ragged! I have several really great volunteers, one of whom is due back from her lunch any time now,' she said, glancing at her watch. She sat opposite him and helped herself to a biscuit. 'So, what can I do for you? You said you're a friend of Peggy's and something about an article you're writing. I can't interest you in adopting a dog, by any chance?'

'Sorry, no. Although I love all dogs, I'm a GSD man. My lad's in the car.'

'You *can* have more than one dog, you know.'

'I know, but my lifestyle wouldn't suit. Taz fits in because he's really well trained. I don't think a greyhound would work for me.'

'Oh well,' she said resignedly. 'Can't blame me for trying.' She dunked her biscuit and swiftly ate the soft bit, waiting for him to explain himself.

'Well, the truth is, I work for a feed company and I delivered to Peggy the other day: that's the extent of our friendship, I'm afraid, but we did have a long chat about greyhounds and your name came up.'

'It would,' she agreed.

'I told her I'd been to see Billy Driscoll,' Daniel continued, and the face Anya pulled when she heard the trainer's name told him all he needed to know about her feelings in that direction.

'Driscoll told me that most of his dogs go on to good homes or into rescue when they retire, but someone who used to work for him made me think it's far more likely that they never leave his premises.'

'Well, they certainly don't come here,' Anya said. 'And I'm in regular contact with the local rescue community, as you can imagine, through Facebook, if not in person, and as far as I know it's very rare for any of Driscoll's dogs to turn up for rehoming. At one time they did, but not for a long while.'

'So what do *you* think happens to them?'

'What you said: I think they're killed,' she said bluntly. 'And not by a vet, either.'

'By Driscoll.'

Anya's brows drew down.

'Sorry – who exactly are you?'

'Daniel Whelan: ex-cop, delivery driver, friend of Peggy Branscombe, animal-lover.'

'So there's no article on greyhound rescue?'

'No. Sorry. I might just have been a bit economical with the truth, there,' he admitted.

'So why am I feeding you coffee and biscuits and not just kicking you out – which I'm well able to do, believe me,' she added. 'I was a tae kwon do international as a teenager.'

'You'd be well within your rights to kick me out. In fact I'll save you the trouble and go peacefully,' he said. 'But I think you and I have an interest in common – or rather a disinterest. Billy Driscoll.'

'OK,' she said slowly. 'I'll believe you – because of Peggy. But given that we both apparently dislike Driscoll intensely, what can we do about it? I've told both the police and the RSPCA that I think he's killing dogs and burying them on his land, but without proof . . . And one of the coppers told me that it's not actually illegal as long as it's done humanely. Can you believe that? He said they'd be more likely to do him on environmental issues – polluting his land, for instance – than for killing the dogs.'

'Unfortunately, I think he's probably correct,' Daniel said. 'But I'm pretty sure the scale of the operation might make a difference, and if I'm right, Driscoll's quite possibly taking dogs from other trainers, too.'

'Bastard!' she said. 'That would explain the slight slow down in greys coming into rescue around here over the last eighteen months or so. Not a huge fall in numbers, but noticeable. I just put it down to the decline in the industry in general.'

'Is it on the decline?'

'Well, it's still a multimillion-pound business for the bookmakers but, yes, thank God! It is slowly going down. Only thirty or so tracks left now and roll on the day when they close the last one.'

'And your job will be done.'

Anya gave him a pitying look.

'I don't think that will ever happen,' she said. 'And anyway, there are plenty of other dogs needing help.'

'There are indeed,' Daniel said sadly. He drained his coffee mug. There didn't seem to be anything else to say but he felt oddly loath to leave and, analysing his reasons, realized that he found the blunt toughness of Anya Darby more than a little attractive, partnered, as it was, with undeniably striking looks.

'So what do you plan to do about Driscoll?' she asked then, interrupting his wandering train of thought.

'I'm not sure yet, but it annoys me intensely that he should get away with this. I think I'll do a little more digging – literally, perhaps, if it comes to it.'

'Well, I'd be careful, if I were you. I had a few silent phone calls when I started asking questions and one thing the police did say was that he wasn't a man to get on the wrong side of.'

'Yeah, I'd already worked that one out. I'll be careful,' Daniel said. He pushed his chair back and stood up. 'Well, I'd better let you get on . . .'

Outside there was a scrunch of gravel and the sound of a bicycle bell.

'That'll be Sue, my volunteer for today,' Anya said. 'Have you eaten?'

'Er, no.' Daniel was a little taken aback.

'Neither have I. Fancy some company? There's a decent pub in the village.'

'OK, why not?'

'Well, that's not the most flattering acceptance I've ever received, but never mind,' Anya said, taking a dry jacket from a hook on the back of the door.

'Do you make a habit of asking strangers to lunch, then?' Daniel asked quizzically.

'Only hot ex-cops,' she said easily and then laughed at Daniel's embarrassed roll of the eyes.

Outside, Daniel headed for his car but she hung back.

'It's not far. We can easily walk it.'

'Actually, I've got a better idea,' Daniel said. 'Let's go to Barnsworthy.'

'*Barnsworthy*?' For a moment she was bewildered but she caught up with impressive speed. 'Ah. I'm sensing this has something to do with our friend, Billy . . .'

'I thought we could have lunch at his local,' Daniel suggested. 'A kind of working lunch. I had thought of going there anyway but a couple having lunch would be far less noticeable than a guy on his own.'

Anya pulled a wry face.

'Flattered, I'm sure, but glad to be useful. Let's hope Billy isn't there, then.'

'If you'd rather not, I understand,' Daniel told her. 'Would he recognize you?'

'Well, we've met,' she said, sliding into the passenger seat and turning to look at Taz, who was turning in excited circles in the back, pleased to have Daniel where he could keep an eye on him. 'But it was a while ago: he might not remember.'

'Oh, he would!' Daniel said, sending a smile her way.

'OK. You've redeemed yourself a little,' she said. 'I might even forgive you, if lunch is particularly good.'

There turned out to be two pubs pretty much equidistant from Driscoll's kennels, and in the absence of any more informed reason, they chose the one that was more visually attractive. The Reckless Toad was on the other side of the road from the village pond and its sign bore a stylized picture of the amphibian poised at the side of a road with a 1920s car swishing by, complete with a young couple in period costume.

Inside, they found it to be full of old-world charm and also a fair number of customers. However, with the lunchtime service drawing to a close, Daniel managed to secure a table for Anya and himself without any trouble and went to request a menu.

Casual enquiries at the bar revealed that they had chosen the wrong hostelry if they wanted to run into the Driscolls, and the coolness that accompanied the information told Daniel that there was no love lost between his host and the Traveller family.

'It was more a case of not wanting to run into them,' he told the man, and the ambient temperature instantly rose a degree or two.

'Well, you're safe here, then,' the barman told him. 'They're not welcome here and they know it! Not that they'd want to, really. After all, the Blue Boar is Johnny Driscoll's pub.'

'He owns it?'

'As good as.' The barman looked from Daniel to Anya and back again. 'If you're wanting to eat I should warn you that the kitchen closes in twenty minutes.'

'Yes, please.' Daniel tucked the menus under his arm and carried the drinks back to their table.

A couple of minutes later, their choices made, he was back at the bar.

'So what was this I heard about Driscoll finding a Saxon ring on his property?' he said, when the barman had relayed the food order to the kitchen.

The barman snorted.

'Was it on his property?' he asked. 'Or was it up on old Ruben Callow's? That's the question.'

'So who's Ruben Callow?'

'Owns the farm that backs onto Driscoll's place; up on the hill behind. There's known to be earthworks up there and every summer the university lot come out and dig there. Far be it from me to comment but there's some as might suggest that Billy Driscoll's ring most likely came from there one dark winter's night. Still,' he went on, warming to his topic, 'if that's the case, he didn't do himself no favours claiming it for his own – aside from the money the museum paid, of course . . .'

'Why d'you say that?' Daniel asked, obligingly following his cue.

'Well, he gets plagued by metal detectorists, doesn't he? And Billy Driscoll is not (and that's with a capital N) a sociable kind of bloke! Lost count of the people who've come in here complaining that they've been thrown off his land. Within his rights to do it, I suppose, but there's ways and there's ways, isn't there?'

Daniel agreed that there were, but before he could say anything else, a hand touched his shoulder and Anya appeared by his side.

'I was getting lonely,' she said in reproachful tones.

'Oh, sorry. I was just talking to . . .?'

'Kenny,' the barman supplied, his eyes resting on Anya with warm appreciation.

'. . . To Kenny, about our friend Driscoll,' Daniel told her. 'Apparently he's a bit territorial.'

'A bit?' Kenny snorted again. 'That's the understatement of the year, that is!'

'So, what does he do?' she asked, settling herself onto a barstool.

'Well,' the barman said, with the air of one settling down to a cosy chat, 'for a start, he's got a couple of sodding great Dobermans. And if they don't scare you, the rumour is he's got a shotgun stashed away somewhere, too. Waved it in someone's face, he did, once.'

'Didn't they call the police?' Anya asked.

'Yeah, but when the police asked him about it, he denied all knowledge. Well, there's a surprise!'

'So they didn't follow it up?'

'Can't do nothing without they get a search warrant, I suppose,' Kenny said wisely. 'It's a bloody joke, isn't it? Pardon my language, miss,' he added as an afterthought.

'Don't mind me,' she said.

'So who did he threaten with the gun?' Daniel wanted to know.

'Some local kids who went looking for treasure on his land one evening. They weren't doing no harm, but it was just after the business with the backpacker and old Driscoll was still mad about that, I reckon.'

'A backpacker?' Daniel prodded. 'What was that about, then?'

'Well . . .' Kenny began but was interrupted by another customer wanting to be served. He leaned towards a doorway at the rear of the bar and shouted, 'Darren! There's thirsty customers waiting out here!'

Moments later a plump youngster with acne and a scant millimetre of dark hair appeared, wiping his hands on a cloth, his eyes searching for the expected queue of people but finding only the one.

'As I was saying,' Kenny continued, 'this backpacker arrives in the village; he comes here first, asking about Driscoll and the Saxon ring. It was only a couple of months after he found it and it was in all the papers, you see, so we had loads of people turning up around then. But this chap, he wanted to know everything and he had this green bag which I thought at the time was fishing gear but looking back I reckon it was a metal detector. Anyway, he wanted a room but we didn't have any – not that I was particularly sorry, cos he was a bit of a rough-looking character; a bit down at heel, if you get my drift. So I sends him over to the Boar and I presume they had a room for him cos he was seen around the village for a day or two.' He paused to wet his whistle from a pint of beer that stood, half drunk, on the shelf behind him.

'Anyway,' he went on. 'Long story short, this backpacker chap apparently chanced his arm wandering onto Driscoll's land one evening and ran into Billy, himself, with one of his dogs – the Dobermans, I mean. Well, nobody knows exactly what happened, but the way the chap told it, he played the right to roam card but Driscoll was having none of it. Threw him off, he did. Bodily, if the man is to be believed. Claimed he was bitten by one of the dogs, too, but none of us ever saw any proof of it.'

'So what happened then?' Anya asked. 'Did he report Driscoll?'

'Nah. I'm not sure the chap was the kind who'd want too much to do with the police, himself, if you get me? He spent all day in here, drinking and threatening all kinds of repercussions. He certainly talked up a good fight while he was fuelled by alcohol, but come last orders he disappeared and the next day he'd moved on. As far as I know, he's never been back. I think one taste of Billy Driscoll and his dogs was enough for him, as it is for most people. There were others, of course. Still are, occasionally, but Driscoll's got the place fenced in like a prison camp and there's signs up everywhere telling folks to keep out. Most people take the hint, 'specially as nothing else has ever been found there, as far as we know. Ruben Callow's, they've found all sorts up there. Not that Ruben's there any more, it's his son, now . . .'

Having found an audience, Kenny was loath to lose it, and Daniel and Anya learned a lot more about the village, its residents and recent history than they particularly wanted to. Daniel tried to steer the conversation back to Driscoll and his proposal to close the kennels and plant Christmas trees, but it was plain that Kenny regarded this idea with scorn.

'Well, he's ploughed that four-acre field on and off for a couple of years so we assumed he was getting it ready for something, but Christmas trees? That'd take hard work, that would,' he said. 'Can't see Billy getting his hands dirty with anything like that – unless he's thinking of employing foreigners to do it for him for next to nothing. That'd be more his style.' He dismissed the idea with another of his derisive snorts and had started to tell them about a friend of his who had planted an orchard, when a young girl dressed in black appeared from the kitchen bearing two plates of food and calling Daniel's name.

Daniel and Anya seized on this diversion with some relief and followed the waitress back to their table where Anya's jacket draped over a chair had kept other potential diners at bay, leaving the barman to transfer his attentions to the next unwary customer.

'Phew! Talk about verbal diarrhoea!' Anya said, when the waitress had left them. 'Donkeys should hang on to their legs.'

'Mm, but a detective's dream. All that info with hardly any prompting, and he was so caught up in himself he won't remember anything about us in an hour or two. Not that he's likely to repeat the conversation to Driscoll, anyway, by the sound of it.'

'So, this obsession with keeping trespassers out, and most especially those coming armed with metal detectors and spades – that would tie in with the idea that he's been burying greys on his land,' Anya said. 'If he did steal that Saxon ring and then pretend to the media that he'd found it on his patch, it was the stupidest thing he could have done!'

'Yeah, he definitely didn't think that one through, did he? But then again, it was a few years ago now, so he maybe he didn't have so much to hide. I guess he keeps ploughing the field so no one will notice when he digs another part of it up.' Daniel applied himself with pleasure to a beautifully cooked steak for a minute or two, before saying, 'You know, I wouldn't mind having a chat with that backpacker, if I could find him . . .'

Anya frowned.

'How on earth would you go about that? It was ages ago, we don't have a name and besides, from what our friend Kenny was saying, he didn't sound like the kind of guy who would probably even have a home address.'

'Yeah, it's probably a forlorn hope but worth a look through Mispers if we can get a name. Missing persons,' he translated, seeing Anya's raised eyebrow. 'I was a cop, remember? I still have contacts.'

'Oh, OK.' Anya carried on eating for a few moments before asking the question that Daniel had come to regard as almost inevitable. 'So what happened? You seem pretty young to be an *ex*-cop. Didn't you like the job? I mean, I always thought it was a vocation – like being a nurse or a vet . . .'

'Yeah, well, it just didn't work out.' Daniel kept his eyes on his plate.

'In what way?'

'Maybe I just wasn't cut out for it,' he said, weary of repeating the story.

'Do you know what?' Anya said. 'I think you were, but I sense I'm trampling all over a sore spot in my hobnailed boots, so I'll shut up and we can talk about the weather or the price of bread.'

'Or the price of greyhounds,' Daniel suggested with a slight smile. 'I'm sorry. There's no great secret, it's just that some of the memories are a bit difficult to cope with, that's all. I guess I went into it for all the right reasons as a youngster – you know, thinking I could make a difference and all that – and I stupidly thought we were all in it for the same reasons. I soon got the heads up on that one, but sadly I never learned to keep my big mouth shut.'

'Ah, I'm sensing you got on the wrong side of someone with clout, am I right?'

'Exactly.' Daniel blessed her quick understanding.

'Did you get the push?'

'Not quite, but as good as. They were making it impossible to do my job. In the end,' he paused, his expression bleak, as the memory came stabbing back, 'well, someone got hurt – badly hurt – because of it, so I had no choice; I handed in my notice.'

'That's tough,' she said. 'Sorry. I probably shouldn't have asked.'

Daniel shook his head, dismissively.

'You weren't to know. It's just still a bit recent, a bit raw.'

'So is Taz a police dog?'

'Yes.' Daniel put his hand down to where the German shepherd lay quietly under the table; ruffled the soft fur and then felt a quick, warm lick. 'I was lucky. Taz was injured just before the trouble kicked off and was temporarily off duty, so he wasn't immediately reassigned. Then, when it was clear that I wasn't going to be going back into the dog unit, the vet signed him off for good as unfit to work.'

'But he's OK now.' Anya peered under the table at the dog.

'Yeah. Like I said, I was lucky and that vet was a very good friend of mine.'

'Oh, that's nice!'

'Yeah, well Taz and I have a pretty special bond, but having said that, he'd probably have settled down with his next handler without so much as a backward glance. He's young and he just loves to work. I sometimes wonder if I did him any favours taking him away from all that.'

'I reckon that vet knew you'd need a mate,' Anya said softly.

Daniel pursed his lips and nodded.

'Yep. And he wasn't wrong. Anyway, tell me about you. How did you come to start the rescue?'

'I didn't. It was my mum. Although I think it was in my genes,' she admitted. 'At uni I was always joining protest groups and organizing marches to save whales or provide vet treatment for working animals abroad. Mum and I had decided I should do law so I could tackle all these issues from a legal standpoint but then she died quite suddenly and I was left with a kennel full of dogs to look after. I came home to take over and I've been here ever since. To be honest, I came back with the idea of rehoming what dogs we had and then closing the rescue down, but the trouble was I found I just couldn't turn new dogs away, so it's never happened.'

'Do you ever wish you'd carried on and got your degree and a career?'

Anya shrugged.

'Now and then, perhaps, but to be honest I don't have much time for regrets: it's pretty full on with all the enquiries, home-checking and fundraising. And besides, someone's got to look out for the dogs – they can't do it for themselves. It feels like a never-ending struggle most of the time but it has its rewards. It sounds unbearably cheesy but the feeling when you find a fantastic home for one of the dogs makes it all worthwhile. Especially if it's one of the sticky – that is to say, long-stay – ones. Dogs are such intelligent, sensitive creatures. It's so wrong that they should have to spend their lives cooped up in cages.' She stopped. 'Sorry, I'll get off my soapbox now.'

'No, please, don't apologize! I couldn't agree more. But, you could always go back to uni later on,' Daniel said.

'I could,' she agreed. 'But I don't suppose I ever will. For one thing, I'm a bit of a free spirit and for another, I can't see how I would ever be able to afford it. No, it's OK. I'll just see where life takes me.'

When Daniel settled the bill on the way out, he asked the barman if he happened to recall the name of the backpacker they had talked about.

'He sounds a bit like the brother of a friend of mine, who chucked in his job one Friday evening and went off with only a rucksack and a couple of walking poles. He's never heard from him again.'

'As I recall, he only gave us one name,' Kenny said, frowning as he tried to remember. 'Something odd, it was – something biblical like Saul or Solomon. What was your friend's brother called?'

'Oh, nothing like that,' Daniel said, feigning disappointment. 'Just plain old Archie Wade.'

'No, wasn't Archie. The more I think about it, the more I think it might have been Saul.'

'I suppose he could have changed his name. How old was he, roughly? Just out of interest.'

'Difficult to say. He had a beard, see? Difficult to tell under a beard, but I'd say late thirties, early forties at a guess. He was a bit of a character, as I said. Appeared out of the blue and disappeared the same way.'

'Oh, well, never mind. Thanks, anyway.' With a wave of his hand Daniel followed Anya from the pub.

'So I'm guessing there isn't really an Archie Wade,' she said, giving him a sideways look as they emerged into rain that had diminished to a steady drizzle.

'I expect there is *somewhere*,' Daniel said, operating the remote key and then lifting the tailgate for Taz to jump in.

'Well, I'm pleased to see you've got your priorities right,' Anya said ironically, letting herself in.

'Well, you can open your door; Taz, though he can do many things, hasn't yet mastered opening the back of the car.'

'So, I'm guessing that the mysterious Saul, aged forty-something, of probably no fixed abode, won't be all that easy to find,' Anya said as the Mercedes swished along wet country roads on the way back to Bideford.

'No. A bit of a lost cause, that one, though it might just be worth checking with a name like that – always supposing it was his real name. Oh, well, it was a good meal and I enjoyed the company . . .'

'Yeah, I can see how Kenny might become your new bestie,' Anya said thoughtfully and Daniel flashed her a smile.

'So, is there a Mrs Whelan or a partner?' she asked after a moment. 'You don't wear a ring.'

'There was. Not any more. Just waiting for the paperwork. I have a son, though. Drew. He's nine and a really good kid.'

'Lives with his mum?'

'Yes.'

'Do you mind?'

'I don't have much choice. He visits.'

'Must be hard . . .'

'Mm. And you?'

'Nope. Nobody. Mum dead and Dad long gone. A sister in Germany, that's all. She's married with kids.'

'I can't believe you don't have a boyfriend,' Daniel said, as plain speaking seemed to be the order of the day.

She pulled a face.

'From time to time, I do, but they mostly can't hack it with the dogs. My life is pretty much working, walking and dog poo, and not necessarily in that order! A lot of guys are surprisingly squeamish about that sort of thing. They mostly last a couple of months at the most.' She spoke lightly but Daniel thought he detected a note of bitterness and wondered if beneath the tough, competent exterior, she was quite lonely.

'They're idiots, then,' Daniel said, without thinking.

'Thank you,' she said simply. 'Do you have family?'

'Yes. Two brothers and a sister.'

'Close?'

'Once, but not so much now,' he said. The truth was, he only saw them at family gatherings; maybe a couple of times a year, at most. His sister had become antagonistic after he had followed his father into the police force as a career and discouraged him from visiting his mother, saying that it upset her.

'Are your parents still around?'

'Mum is. My father, too, is long gone.'

'Bastards!' she commented. 'Have you ever tried to find him?'

'No. Thought I might have come across him when I was a copper, cos he was, too, but I never did. I mean, he left and never bothered to make contact, so why should I?'

By the time he dropped her off at her gate, the rain had intensified once more and water was running in rivulets down the sides of the road. In addition, a squally wind had risen and trees and hedges were being tossed and buffeted, scattering yellow and brown leaves.

Anya surveyed the weather gloomily, telling Daniel that there was a stream at the back of her property that had a tendency to flood.

'Sandbags at the ready, if this goes on,' she prophesied. 'Will you come in for a coffee?'

'I'd love to,' Daniel said truthfully, 'but I'd better get back.'

'OK. I've got plenty to do, anyway,' she said lightly. Then as she opened the car door, 'Do you have a card or something with your number on? Just in case I hear anything . . .'

Daniel fished in the glove compartment and produced one.

'Or maybe we could do Sunday lunch again, one day,' he suggested.

She flashed a smile.

'You never know . . .'

TEN

Stephen had still not returned when Daniel dropped in to Lorna's on his way home and far from the explosive atmosphere Daniel had dreaded finding at the house, it seemed that Shane, now wearing his own clothes once more, had succeeded in winning Lorna over, at least partially.

'It's a pity about his background, he seems a nice enough lad,' she told Daniel as they drank coffee at the kitchen table.

'He can't help who his family are, any more than the rest of us. Where is he now? Or should I say, where are they?' he said, as Zoe was missing, too.

'Down in the yard, filling haynets for tonight. Shane wanted to do something to help and Zoe went too, predictably. It'll be the first haynet she's filled in years!'

'Amazing what infatuation can do,' Daniel observed. 'Have you heard from Stephen?'

'No. I imagine he's trying to make a point by staying away all day, but actually we're all much happier when he's not here. Oh, dear! Is it awful of me to say that? He *is* Harvey's son, after all.'

'I can't see that that makes any difference, he's not a blood relative, and anyway, you forget – I've met him and he is obnoxious!'

Faintly, they heard the swish and crunch of tyres on the gravel outside and a car door thump shut.

'Speak of the devil,' Lorna said with a resigned expression.

Moments later, Stephen had let himself in through the front door and was shaking his wet coat onto the flagstones of the kitchen floor.

'Thanks for that,' Lorna said drily. 'Can't you put it in the boot room?'

'If you want.' Stephen took the coat through to the room where Daniel knew there was a low sink for washing muddy dogs and a heated bench for drying them. As he came back, he said, 'Heard any more from the police?'

'Not yet. Only that they're assigning us a family liaison officer. She'll apparently call in tomorrow. One thing you should know, though . . .'

She was interrupted by the sound of the back door opening and suddenly the two wet spaniels burst into the kitchen, tongues lolling from open mouths and stumpy tails wagging at eighty miles an hour. They circumnavigated the room, greeting the humans and stopping for a quick how-do-you-do with Taz, then Bailey stopped beside Stephen and shook vigorously, covering his lower legs with a shower of muddy water.

'Oh, for God's sake! Bloody dogs!' he exclaimed, stepping backwards and looking down at his trousers in disgust.

'Zoe! Call the dogs, please. They're soaking!' Lorna called out.

'Well, how was I to know the door would be open?' came the indignant reply.

The dogs disappeared into the boot room and the door clicked shut, only to open again as Zoe and Shane, divested of their wet coats, came into the kitchen.

Stephen transferred his attention from the state of his trousers to the newcomers and his frown deepened.

'What the fff . . .?'

'Hello, Stephen,' Zoe said airily.

Shane Brennan lifted his chin in the face of Stephen's obvious hostility and stared him straight in the eye.

Good on you! Daniel thought, liking the boy more with each meeting.

'Please don't tell me this is the bloody Gypsy who's caused all the trouble,' Stephen implored Lorna.

'This is Zoe's friend, Shane,' Lorna said as if making the introduction at a party. 'My stepson, Stephen.'

Shane nodded in Stephen's direction but Stephen wasn't prepared to play along.

'You're not serious?' he asked Lorna, totally ignoring the younger man. 'The bastard who led Zoe on and then stole your jewellery. Two days ago you told her to stay away from him and now you're inviting him into your house! Have you gone mad?'

'He didn't steal the rings!' Zoe flared up instantly. 'I told him they were mine. He had nothing to do with it!'

'He ran off with the money, though, didn't he?'

'It wasn't like that!'

'Be quiet, both of you!' Lorna said sharply.

'But he's twisting everything . . .' Zoe complained.

'Quiet!' she repeated. 'This is my house and I won't have a slanging match in my kitchen. Nor . . .' she went on over the top of renewed grumbling from both sides, 'will I be told who I can or cannot invite into it. So if you can't be civil to each other then don't say anything at all. And that goes for both of you.'

Shane fidgeted.

'Perhaps I should just go,' he said quietly to Zoe.

'No!' she cried. 'He doesn't have to, does he, Mum? He can't go home.'

'No. To be honest, he's the best behaved of all of you,' she said.

'Well, if you think I'm going to stick around with that – that heathen, here, you can think again!' Stephen stated.

'Well, of course, it's your decision,' Lorna replied coldly.

Stephen stared at her in disbelief.

'You were glad enough to see me when I arrived; when *you* called me, I might add.'

'That's true. I thought you should know that your father was missing and, I'll admit, I did feel rather nervous after those two men came looking for him, but I'd forgotten just how insufferable you can be when you choose to.'

'Way to go, Mum!' Zoe murmured, echoing Daniel's own sentiments, but was quelled by a fierce look from her mother.

'Well, if that's how you feel,' Stephen said through gritted teeth, his face flushed with fury.

'I'm afraid it is. I've tried to get on with you for Harvey's sake but I have to say you don't make it easy. Now, this is your father's house and you're welcome to stay but please, for the love of God, try and keep your nose out of what doesn't concern you and your comments to yourself.'

For a long moment, Stephen said nothing, his face reflecting the struggle that was raging inside but then he apparently came to a decision.

'I'll stay because I want to find out what's happened to Dad, but I'm not sharing a house with a flaming Gypsy! If he's staying here, I'll find a room in the village.'

'Suit yourself,' Lorna told him.

Daniel cleared his throat.

'Um . . . My offer still stands, if that would help.'

'That's kind,' she said. 'It's up to Shane, really.'

'Actually, we had a better idea,' Zoe put in. 'If I'm allowed to speak, that is . . .' Attention turned to her and she went on. 'We were looking at the hayloft – Shane and I were, just a minute ago – and we thought he could easily stay there. It only needs a bit of a sweep out and we can find him a sleeping bag. It'd be perfect.'

'But it's got all those old boxes in there,' Lorna protested.

'There's still plenty of room and he doesn't have to stay in there all day. It's only for sleeping, really.'

'A hayloft?' Daniel enquired doubtfully, imagining hay and straw in bales and loose, rats and mice and rafters strung with cobwebs.

'It's not as bad as it sounds,' Lorna told him. 'It was converted into living accommodation by the people before us and has running water and electricity – even a chair and the bare bones of a bed, though no mattress. He could have the one from the box room, I suppose,' she added, thoughtfully. 'If he really wants to, of course. It's a bit spartan.'

'I don't mind,' Shane said. 'I've slept in a lot worse places.'

'I bet you have!' Stephen muttered.

'We were thinking he could have the cushions off the chair instead of a mattress,' Zoe said.

'I see you've got it all worked out,' her mother said. 'Well, I'll leave you two to sort out the details then, if you're sure you're happy with that.'

Shane nodded, his face giving little away, but Zoe's delight more than made up for his lack of expression.

'That's brilliant!' she cried, taking his arm and shaking it. 'Thank you so much. Let's go and sort it out now.'

'I imagine Shane might like something hot to drink, seeing as you've only just come in,' Lorna suggested. 'And I should warn you, there's a condition attached. The room is for Shane only. It is completely out of bounds for you.'

'What? Not during the daytime, though . . .'

'Any time. Take it or leave it,' Lorna stated in a tone that brooked no argument.

'Oh, Mum!'

Her mother shook her head.

'It's no good *Oh Mumming* me.'

'But that's embarrassing! I'm not a baby.'

'No. You're fifteen and a minor.'

Zoe's face assumed a petulant expression but Shane soothed her.

'It's OK, Mrs Myers. We don't – I mean, in my culture . . . What I mean is, marriage is important to us,' he finished with a rush, his face reddening. 'It's why mostly we get married quite young.'

'How quaint. A virgin,' Stephen commented, and then put his hands up as Lorna shot him a warning glance.

'But you didn't?' she asked the Traveller boy.

'I was engaged before. But the girl, she got poorly, so we had to wait and then, well, she died last year,' he finished.

'Oh, I'm sorry,' Lorna said. 'That's sad. She can't have been very old.'

'Seventeen. It was her breathing. Asthma.'

Stephen made a noise that could have signified disbelief, gathered up his phone and keys from the table and headed for the door.

'Do I take it you're staying?' his stepmother asked.

'Just till we find out about Dad,' he said.

'Well, don't you want a cuppa? I was just going to make one.'

'Later, maybe,' Stephen said without turning his head, and moments later, the door shut firmly behind him.

Accepting an invitation to the evening meal, which Stephen took in splendid isolation on a tray in the sitting room, Daniel didn't leave Abbots Farm until late that evening, at which point nothing further had been heard from the police regarding Harvey's disappearance. This didn't surprise him overmuch. He knew from experience that the family wouldn't necessarily be instantly apprised of every development. Time would be taken to evaluate any new information before the decision was taken as to when, or indeed whether, it should be shared with the waiting relatives.

Some of the conversation over the meal was inevitably about Harvey, and Zoe commented that Shane's extra muscle might come in useful if the two men who had come searching for him were to show up again.

Lorna, who seemed to have done a complete about-face where the Traveller boy was concerned, said that she sincerely hoped his muscle wouldn't be called upon. Daniel, for his part, thought it unlikely that Leather Jacket and his friend would risk another visit to the property now they knew the police were involved, but if they did, he put more faith in Shane's protective abilities than Stephen's.

He left with the promise that he would do his best to finish work early the next afternoon and meet Shane outside the pawnbroker's that was holding Lorna's rings.

For once, luck was on Daniel's side. Aware of his mission over the weekend and interested to hear an update on that and the rest of Lorna's troubles, Fred Bowden greeted him with the news that the workforce was up to full strength once more, with the return of the driver who had been on sick leave, and then offered to take on a couple of Daniel's more local drops in the van to shorten his day.

Taking advantage of this offer, Daniel finished his last drop at just after four o'clock and, having hosed down the lorry, was in Tavistock heading for the retail premises of the pawnbroker, which styled itself as an All But New retailer, at just before five.

Ahead of him, outside the shop, he could see Shane Brennan lounging against the wall waiting for him, as he had promised he would be, and Daniel hoped that within a very short time this part, at least, of the Myers' problems would be resolved. Lorna had transferred the necessary funds into Daniel's current account – a cash injection that, he thought wryly, would give his bank manager a severe shock were he to become aware of it.

When Daniel was within fifty yards of the pawnshop, he saw Shane straighten up as something on the other side of the road caught his attention. Following his gaze he saw, in the mouth of an alleyway between two shops, two men forcibly restraining a much smaller figure and realized, with a muttered oath, that it was Zoe.

Shouting 'Oi!' Daniel broke into a run and, weaving between parked cars, ran across the road towards the three, eliciting a blast on the horn from an approaching motorist.

Swift as Daniel was, Shane was there before him, grasping the shoulder of the nearest man and pulling him away from Zoe, who cowered back against the wall. The man, who Daniel recognized as one of the two who had visited Lorna, swung a right hook at the Traveller but Shane was ready for him. Ducking easily, he bobbed up inside the man's guard and caught him a stinging blow on the jaw that rocked him back on his heels.

Following him into the fray, Daniel pulled the second man round, twisted his arm in a lock that forced him to his knees and growled into his ear, 'Who sent you? You've got ten seconds before I break your elbow!'

To add credibility to his words, he applied pressure to the joint, drawing a squeal from his captive, who he could see was once again the man with the scorpion tattoo.

'We've been here before, haven't we?' he added with a grim smile. 'Other arm this time, though. I like to be fair.'

To his left, Daniel could see Shane's man getting slowly to his feet, wiping a thin dribble of blood from his lip. The Traveller stood over him, daring him to make another wrong move.

'Myers owes money,' the tattooed man said between gritted teeth.

'We'd guessed that much,' Daniel told him, applying a little more pressure. 'Tell us something we don't know.'

'Aaah. He'll fucking kill me if I blab!' the man cried.

'And I'll break your arm if you don't,' Daniel promised. 'Your choice. Pain now or trouble later.'

'You can't do that. It's broad daylight!'

'Nobody's looking,' Daniel told him and indeed, a glance round showed him that the few souls who were in the vicinity were hurrying out of it with heads down and eyes averted. 'Besides, you started it!'

In spite of the words, he was well aware that even as he spoke, the chances were that someone, somewhere, was on the phone to the police and just at the moment he was almost as eager to avoid that particular confrontation as he felt sure his captive was.

With the attention no longer on her, Zoe slipped between Shane and Daniel and out on to the pavement.

'I'm waiting,' Daniel told his man, leaning once more.

'All right! Fuck it! All right, I said!' the man squawked. 'Gregg – Felix Gregg! Now fuckin' let go!'

'Are you fuckin' mad?' Shane's man hissed furiously at his partner. His anger was music to Daniel's ears; it meant that in all probability the name his man had given him was the right one.

'There, it wasn't so hard, was it?' Daniel asked, letting his man straighten up. 'Now if I were you, I'd leg it before the police get here, unless of course you want to press charges? No,' he observed, as flinging back further obscenities, the two men took to their heels, as of one accord, down the alleyway, 'I didn't think you would.'

When they had disappeared from his sight, Daniel turned to find that Zoe had found security in Shane's strong arms and buried her face in the front of his jacket.

'Are you OK, Zo?' he asked.

She turned her head and nodded, her long lashes spiky with tears.

'What the hell did you think you were doing? I thought we'd made it clear that you shouldn't be out and about on your own . . .'

'School's only just back there,' she said pointing up the road. 'I knew you'd be here. I didn't think it would matter . . .'

'Well, now you know.'

'She's learned her lesson,' Shane put in quietly. 'She doesn't need a bollocking.'

Daniel sighed.

'No. You're right. But that was too close for comfort. What did they say to you, anything?'

She sniffed and felt in her pocket for a tissue. Her mascara had started to run and her pale face looked even more wan than usual.

'They wanted to know where Harvey is – well, they called

him my daddy, as if I was a kid. I said I didn't know and that the police were looking for him, too.'

'What did they say to that?'

'Nothing really. They just looked at each other, and one of them started to say something and then you two came running over.' She blew her nose and mopped delicately under her eyes with a corner of the tissue.

'All right. Well, as long as you're OK. Now I think we'd better get off the street before someone arrives with awkward questions. We'll have to report this but not here and now, I think.'

Crossing the road they pushed through the door of the brightly lit pawnbroker's, where they encountered a hurriedly dispersing crowd of staff and customers, who had clearly been drawn to the window by the drama across the way.

At the service counter, the young man who served them was polite and efficient, and if his gaze seemed irresistibly drawn to Shane's grazed knuckles, it wasn't to be wondered at. It probably wasn't every day that they had a scene from some TV action show played out on their doorstep.

As Daniel entered his PIN number to complete the payment, a flash of fluorescent green caught his eye and he turned to see a police car cruising slowly down the street. It slowed to a halt opposite the shop before pulling away once more, its occupants apparently satisfied that the reported disturbance had resolved itself without their intervention. Within seconds the car had disappeared from view and Daniel turned back to the matter in hand.

'They think if they take long enough, it'll all be over before they get here.' This cynical observation was made by an older man who had been hovering a little behind the one who was serving, perhaps wary of trouble from the newcomers, in view of what they had just witnessed.

'Disturbance? I didn't see anything, officer,' Daniel said.

'Me neither,' the man agreed with a laugh. 'So what did Mr Gregg's boys want with the little lady? It's not their usual style.'

'It's a long story,' Daniel told him. 'Suffice it to say, they've got the wrong end of the stick. So, do you know Felix Gregg?'

'Not *know*, exactly, but we know *of* him. Let's say he sends a lot of custom our way.'

'So what is it? Bookmaking? Gambling? Lending?'

'All of the above. Usually steers clear of minors, though,' he added with a glance at Zoe, who stood within the protective circle of Shane's arm. 'Your young lady, is she, Shane?'

Shane nodded, giving Zoe's shoulders a squeeze. Zoe smiled faintly, her eyes on the display case under the glass counter.

'Well, that's all sorted, then,' the young assistant said, handing Daniel the receipt. 'And here are your items. Thank you for doing business with us.'

Daniel took the three small ring boxes, the contents of which had been carefully checked by Zoe at the beginning of the transaction. He held them out to her.

'There you are. Hold on to them this time, OK?'

Zoe nodded, slipping the rings into a tapestry bag she wore over her shoulder, but her eyes were still on the cabinet. She pointed at a row of watches near the front.

'Harvey had one like that,' she said.

The assistant looked blankly at her.

'Do you want to buy a watch?' he asked.

'No. It just looks like one my stepfather used to own, that's all,' she said.

At her words the youngster's older colleague moved forward to take his place. 'It's a popular watch; mass produced,' he said.

'Expensive-looking for a mass-produced one.' Daniel raised an eyebrow. 'And a good make.'

'Yeah, well. Obviously, what I mean is, you can buy them in good quality jewellers. It's not a limited edition, or anything. But it's a very nice watch.'

'My stepfather's one had an inscription on it. My mum gave it to him for their anniversary.'

'That's nice,' the man said, without moving. Then, finding himself fixed by an unblinking stare from Zoe's wide grey eyes, 'Are you interested in buying the watch?'

She shook her head.

'No, I just wondered . . .'

'It doesn't have any inscription, if that's what you're thinking,' he told her.

'Oh, OK. It just reminded me of Harvey's, that's all.'

'Has he lost one?'

'No. That is, we don't know.'

'Do you mind if we look at it?' Daniel asked. 'Just out of interest . . .'

'Of course. No problem. I'll deal with this. I expect you've got plenty to be getting on with,' the man told his younger assistant, who coloured slightly and disappeared through a door at the back of the serving area. The man took a key from his pocket and unlocked the cabinet.

Moments later, he produced the watch and laid it almost reverently on a soft mat on the counter top, as if it were indeed a precious designer piece.

'May I?' Without waiting for the answer, Daniel picked the watch up and examined it closely, noting the logo of a very exclusive maker painted in gold on the dial. 'Do you have a magnifying glass?' he asked.

'Somewhere around,' the man said, casting about him vaguely. 'Why, is there a problem?'

'Not as far as I know,' Daniel said.

After opening and closing a couple of drawers, the man opened his hands, palms upward, and announced that the magnifying glass seemed to have gone walkabout.

'Never mind.' Daniel unzipped an inner pocket in his jacket and took out a chunky penknife. 'I've just remembered there's one on here. Useful for lighting campfires, I suppose, if you've left your matches at home.'

The assistant smiled humourlessly and watched as Daniel inspected the watch even more closely.

Eventually he closed the penknife and put the watch back on the mat.

The assistant was waiting with raised eyebrows and Zoe was also watching him intently.

'Everything OK?' the man asked.

'Yes. Why wouldn't it be? It's genuine, as far as I can see.'

'So, are you interested in making a purchase?'

Daniel shook his head ruefully.

'No, it's beyond my budget, I'm afraid.'

'It's half the price you'd pay for it anywhere else.'

'So it may be, but even if I had that kind of money to spend on a watch, it wouldn't last five minutes with me; I'm a bit hard on my watches. I do know someone who might well be interested, though. He's been looking for one of those for ages.'

'Yes, well, it's a very good watch,' the man said smoothly, scooping it up and back into the cabinet. 'Beautifully made. Very exclusive. Pieces like this tend to do better at auction, so your friend had better be quick.'

'Yes, I can see how it's worth so much. It's not often you get that combination of exclusivity and mass production, is it?' Daniel agreed with wonderful innocence. 'I'll send my friend along to have a look.'

The man favoured Daniel with a narrow-eyed look but quickly recovered his smile and silky smooth manner.

'Good. I'll look forward to seeing him.'

Safely outside the shop, Zoe said, 'For a minute I thought it might actually be Harvey's, when you asked for a magnifying glass.'

'And it might still be,' Daniel said. 'There wasn't an inscription – you could see that, anyway, but where was it on his? Round the outside?'

'Yes. Round the rim.'

'That's what I thought. I might be mistaken but that surface looked suspiciously rough under the lens. It could be wear and tear but it looked too even for that, as if the surface had been filed.'

'And your friend?' Shane asked.

'Sergeant Naylor,' Daniel said. 'I think he should take a look sooner, rather than later. I might just ring him now.'

In the event, Sergeant Naylor was impossible to contact at that moment, being off duty, but Daniel was promised that his message would be passed on to the officer in charge of the case, right away.

'I hope it is,' Daniel said, after relaying this exchange to the others. 'In spite of my rather poor attempt at a cover story, I have a feeling our friend in there wasn't fooled.'

'If that *was* Harvey's watch . . .' Zoe's voice tailed off. 'That's not good, is it?'

'No, it's not.' There was no point in denying it; Zoe was an intelligent girl. 'But it needn't be the blackest scenario. It's just possible that if he's in real financial trouble, he might have pawned it himself, or even that he gave it to this Felix Gregg guy as settlement of a debt and he's sold it on. There are several possible explanations, and hopefully the police will get to the bottom of it. The older man seemed to know you, Shane,' he added then and left the statement hanging.

Shane shrugged.

'Yeah, the family do a bit of business with them from time to time,' he said. 'That's why I came to this one with the rings.'

Discovering that Shane had recovered his motorbike from a mate who had been repairing it for him, Zoe announced her intention of riding pillion to the house until Daniel pointed out that she had no protective clothing.

'Shane's got a spare helmet,' she told him. 'I've used it before.'

'I very much doubt he's got a spare set of leathers to fit you, though,' Daniel said, and then, as she started to protest, 'No buts. If you'd seen the aftermath of as many motorcycle accidents as I have, where the riders weren't wearing the correct kit, you wouldn't even contemplate it. It's not just a graze we're talking about; even at low speeds the tarmac will take the flesh off right down to the bone.'

Zoe made a face that showed that, in common with many of her age group, she didn't really think something of that sort would ever happen to her, but she gave in and accompanied Daniel back to the car park where he had left Taz guarding the Merc. The dog stood up and stretched hugely, making the kind of chatty German shepherd noises that indicated his happiness to see Daniel back.

'You left the back up,' Zoe said.

'Well, I don't think anyone was likely to try and steal it, do you?'

She watched Daniel fondling the dog.

'He always looks so friendly. Would he really bite someone?'

'Absolutely, if I told him to, or if someone tried to steal his car. But he'd warn them first and once they've seen his teeth, most people don't take it any further,' Daniel said ruffling the fur on Taz's head. 'You're a big scary monster, ain'tcha, boy?'

ELEVEN

Told of the confrontation with Felix Gregg's thugs, Lorna was deeply shocked.

'Are you sure they didn't hurt you?' she asked her daughter for the third time.

'No, I told you, they just grabbed my arm and swung me round into the alleyway but then Shane came and hit one of them and Daniel got hold of the other one. They were amazing!' she added, but her eyes were on Shane as she said it. 'Shane's going to teach me some self-defence. Did you know that elbows are one of a girl's best weapons?'

'I just don't know what you were thinking of!' Lorna said, again for the third or fourth time. 'After all we said the other day. How can you have been so stupid?'

Zoe looked heavenwards.

'OK, so we've established that it wasn't the smartest thing to do, but I'm not likely to make the same mistake again, so can we *please* drop it now?'

'I'm going to try Naylor again,' Daniel said, picking his phone up and heading for the hall, but a buzz from the gate intercom made him hesitate.

Lorna looked stricken.

'I'm not expecting anyone.'

'Well, it's not likely to be Gregg's men,' Daniel told her.

She pressed the button and asked, 'Who is it?'

'PC Radcliffe, your family liaison officer, and PC Innes,' a female voice replied, and Lorna pressed the button to operate the gates.

Five minutes later, Daniel opened the front door to the two officers and they blew in on a gust of wind and a scatter of driven raindrops. It was dark outside now, and the beam of the security lighting illuminated silver rods of rain hammering at forty-five degrees into the gravel of the drive.

'Phew! It's a rough night!' Radcliffe said, removing her waterproof jacket and looking for somewhere to put it.

Daniel introduced himself, took both coats and hung them on one of the already overburdened hooks in the boot room. Water began, immediately, to collect in a puddle on the stone floor beneath.

In the kitchen, Radcliffe introduced herself to the family; a tall, strongly built woman with blonde hair tied back and an air of easy competence. Once more, PC Innes was cast into the shade.

In the time it had taken Daniel to answer the door, Shane had made himself scarce, to be replaced by Stephen, who had presumably overheard the introductions.

'My name is Yvonne and I have been assigned as your family liaison officer,' Radcliffe told them. 'A kind of go-between, if you like, who will keep you updated on the investigation and answer any questions you may have – or try to,' she added with a smile.

'I have a question,' Daniel said. 'Has anyone acted on the information I phoned in about the watch?'

'I'm sorry?' Radcliffe frowned. 'What watch? I think I must have missed this . . .' She turned to look questioningly at Innes, who merely shrugged and looked bewildered.

'About two hours ago . . .' Daniel consulted his own watch. 'Nearly three, now, I phoned in to speak to Sergeant Naylor but he wasn't there, so I left a message.'

'His shift is over,' Radcliffe confirmed. 'Who did you speak to?'

'The duty sergeant; Agnew, I think his name was. I told him that we had seen a watch that might possibly have belonged to Harvey Myers for sale in the pawnbrokers on King Alfred's Street in Tavistock. He assured me that he'd pass the message on, but if he did, it obviously wasn't to you.'

'No, obviously not,' she said with heavy emphasis. 'I'll chase that up.'

'The sooner the better,' Daniel suggested. 'I wouldn't bet on it being around for long. I'm afraid the assistant probably picked up on our interest. I got the feeling he'd rather not have shown it to us after Zoe mentioned Harvey.'

'Right, I'll make a call now,' Radcliffe said. 'Can you describe the watch to me?'

When Daniel had done so, she unclipped her radio and headed for the door into the hall.

'Oh, and while you're about it, we now have a name for the man who sent those two men to find out where Harvey is. We had another little run-in with them in Tavistock. They were trying to pump Zoe for information. They work for a man called Felix Gregg.'

Radcliffe paused.

'They told you that?'

'After I pointed out that it would be the good and Christian thing to do.'

She favoured him with a cynical look.

'Right. I don't think I need to know any more about that.'

With a slight shake of her head she left the room.

'I'm sorry,' Zoe said as the door closed behind her. 'I didn't think when I said the watch looked like Harvey's. I mean – it just didn't occur to me that it would matter. Do you think he knows something? The man in the pawnbroker's, I mean.'

'Probably not. But he may have already had his doubts about where it came from,' Daniel told her. 'Don't worry. You couldn't have known.'

When Radcliffe returned, a couple of minutes later, it was to report that there was no news on the matter of the watch but it was being attended to, which Daniel took to mean that the information he had provided had probably not reached the intended quarter and someone was, at that very moment, getting a rollicking for it.

Lorna had been making coffee and both Radcliffe and Innes accepted a mug, sitting themselves at the big kitchen table with everyone else.

'Is there any news on Harvey?' Lorna asked, joining them.

'As regards your husband's whereabouts, sadly not,' Radcliffe said shaking her head. 'You can rest assured as soon as we have any leads on that front, you will be the first to know. However, that doesn't mean we've been idle, we've been in touch with Mr Myers' employers and also his bank, life-insurance company and financial adviser. I'm afraid what we've discovered may come as something of a shock to you . . .'

Lorna stared at her, saying nothing, but the mug in her hands began to shake and she carefully placed it on the table.

'Well?' This was Stephen, an edge to his voice. 'Don't keep us waiting.'

'I'm sorry to have to tell you that Mr Myers' financial affairs are in something of a mess. It appears that over the last eighteen months he's been spending well beyond his income and as a result has severely depleted his capital. In short—'

'Spending? On what?' A deep frown creased Stephen's brow.

'Well, we don't have all the details as yet.' This was Innes speaking up for the first time. 'But he's made a number of very large cash withdrawals and also he appears to have accounts with several bookmakers.'

'No!' Lorna's sharp rejection cut through the constable's soft West Country burr. She shook her head, her face pale. 'No, not that. He promised he wouldn't – he promised! It was the one thing I asked of him when we got married.'

'You must have got that wrong,' Stephen said, ignoring his stepmother's outburst. 'My father has an exceedingly good income. He's worked for Giradelle Santini for twenty-five years; he's their top negotiator. His salary is practically obscene!'

'Yes, well that might well have been true six months ago,' Radcliffe agreed. 'But it seems your father has recently taken a substantial cut in his salary, due, as I understand it, to a large number of unplanned absences. He is still well paid, no doubt about that, but is now regarded for all intents and purposes as a part-time employee.'

'But he's always working!' Lorna protested. 'I mean, he's away from home more than he's here. Always has been. Nothing's changed.'

'It's ridiculous!' Stephen interjected, scowling at the two officers.

'I'm sorry, I know it's a lot to take in,' Radcliffe said sympathetically, 'but the hard fact is that he may well have been away from home but much of the time, he wasn't at work. I'm afraid, from what we've managed to uncover so far, it looks as though your husband has been spending much of his time and money on various forms of gambling, from playing the stock market online to horse and dog racing. Also, in the light of what you tell me of the connection with Felix Gregg, there's a strong possibility he's been drawn into other forms of gambling as well. Mr Gregg is known to us as someone who runs high-stakes poker games, and I mean, very high stakes!'

'But he promised!' Lorna repeated, as if stating the fact could disprove Radcliffe's statement. 'After Stuart, he wouldn't do that to me.'

'Stuart?' she queried.

'Mum's brother.' It was Zoe who answered. She dragged her chair closer to her mother's and put her arms round her. 'My uncle. He had an addiction to gambling and, well – in the end he . . .'

'He killed himself,' Lorna stated bluntly. 'It was just awful – unbearable, not being able to save him. Harvey knew that. He knew how badly it affected me because I'd had a breakdown just before he met me. So you see, you must be wrong – he would never do that to me!'

'I'm sorry,' Radcliffe said gently. 'His phone records provide the proof. As you of all people know, gambling is hugely addictive. Remember the text message on your husband's phone. ". . . Please forgive me and don't hate me for this. I swear I never meant any of it to happen . . ."'

'But why? Why would he even start?' Tears filled Lorna's eyes and Zoe hugged her tighter. 'I could understand it, in some ways, with Stuart because he wasn't well off but Harvey didn't need money. He had enough to buy everything he needed.'

'The thrill?' Radcliffe suggested. 'The adrenalin rush? Maybe after twenty-five years, his job just wasn't giving him that any more. You said he was keen on adventure sports until he injured his back.'

'I saw him at the dog track,' Zoe put in, suddenly. 'A few weeks ago.'

'*You* did?' Lorna asked, twisting in her daughter's arms to look up at her. 'And what were you doing there?'

'I was there with Shane. We didn't stay long. He wanted to pick up his wages cos we were going to catch a film. My boyfriend used to work for Billy Driscoll,' she told Radcliffe. 'Not any more, though.'

'Your boyfriend? There was nothing in the notes about a boyfriend . . .'

Zoe's face flushed pink.

'Well, I'm not supposed to be seeing him . . . Mum doesn't – didn't – approve.'

'And his name?'

'Shane Brennan.'

If Radcliffe noticed the defiant lilt to Zoe's voice she gave no sign of it.

'From Hawkers Yard?'

'Yes,' she admitted warily. 'Why? Do you know him?'

'We haven't met but I know of the family,' Radcliffe said diplomatically.

'I knew it!' Stephen exclaimed, triumphantly.

'Shane hasn't done anything wrong!' Zoe protested.

'So you say you saw your stepfather at the greyhound track?' Radcliffe said, focusing on the matter in hand. 'When was this, can you remember? And which track? Poole?'

'No. Not that far away. I don't know, exactly. We went on Shane's bike. I couldn't really see where we were going, but it only took half an hour or so. It was a few weeks ago – maybe a couple of months. August? I can't remember.'

'Must have been a flapping track, then,' Radcliffe said, looking at her colleague. 'Yarnbridge, at a guess. It's the only one I'm aware of around here.'

'Flapping?' Lorna asked.

'Unregulated,' Innes supplied. 'There used to be hundreds of them at one time. Thankfully not so many now, although a new one will pop up now and again. Barnstaple and Bideford were used in the heyday of the sport but they closed a long time ago. Basically anyone can turn up and run a dog under any name. Some trainers use them for starting pups on the quiet, but to all intents and purposes they're just another opportunity for the bookies to fleece the public.'

'Dog tracks are not the most wholesome places at the best of times and flapping tracks are even worse,' Radcliffe agreed. 'A rough crowd and, I imagine, little care for the welfare of the dogs. It shouldn't be allowed but unfortunately it's quite legal.'

'And Shane took you to one of these places?' Not surprisingly, Lorna looked unhappy at the thought.

'Only to find Driscoll. We didn't stay.'

'And you saw Harvey there? Why didn't you tell me?'

Zoe squirmed.

'Because I knew you wouldn't like that I'd been there,' she said. 'And you'd have blamed Shane.'

'And I'd have been right, as it happens,' Lorna said, but without much heat. Her eyes were shining with tears and she was clearly still struggling to come to terms with the magnitude of Harvey's betrayal. 'But you knew he was gambling and you didn't tell me . . .'

'He told me it was a work thing. A group of them were there, he said, and he said not to tell you because it would upset you. I didn't want him to tell you I was there with Shane, so we kind of struck a deal . . .'

'Oh, Zoe,' her mother said reproachfully.

'I'm sorry. But I didn't know there was any problem, did I?'

'Was Billy Driscoll one of your stepfather's group?' Radcliffe wanted to know. 'I ask because Driscoll's was one of the numbers on Mr Myers' mobile phone.'

'No. I saw Harvey when I was waiting for Shane. Driscoll was down near the traps.'

'What about Mr Myers' car?' Daniel asked. 'Has that been found?'

'No, not yet.' Radcliffe looked at him. 'Sergeant Naylor tells me he's had dealings with you before. I gather you were involved in the Moorside case, earlier this year. Don't mind me asking but what exactly is your connection with the Myers family?'

'Daniel's a friend,' Lorna spoke up.

'That's a matter of opinion,' Stephen muttered into his coffee mug.

'I work for Tavistock Farm Supplies, as I'm sure you know. I was making a delivery to the stables and walked in on Felix Gregg's two er – employees, shall we call them, when they came to find out where Harvey was.'

'And again, today,' she observed.

'Yes.'

'What took you to the pawnbrokers, Mr Whelan, and what was Zoe doing there?'

'Daniel was redeeming something for me,' Lorna said. 'Zoe is at school in Tavistock but she shouldn't have been in town on her own – we've made that very clear, believe me!'

'Forgive me for asking, Lorna, but are you in financial difficulties, too?'

'No. It was a family matter . . .'

'It was me,' Zoe interrupted, flushing darkly. 'I wanted some money for something and pawned some jewellery.'

'But you are underage,' the constable stated. 'Are you saying the pawnshop loaned money to you?'

Zoe shook her head.

'I took my boyfriend with me.'

'Ah.' Radcliffe looked as though she had a fair idea of the situation.

'Bloody Gypsy!' Stephen interjected, scowling. 'Wouldn't be surprised if he had something to do with Dad being missing.'

'Stephen!' Lorna was shocked.

'Why would you say that, Mr Myers?' Radcliffe asked, her face intent.

'Because he's a bigoted racist!' Zoe said furiously. 'Shane's got nothing to do with Harvey – why would he? It's ridiculous!'

'Stephen?' Radcliffe was still watching him and he shrugged, looking a little awkward.

'Well, Travellers; they're all thieves and scroungers, aren't they? Everyone knows that.'

'To be honest, such generalizations aren't particularly helpful, are they?' Radcliffe told him, relaxing a little. 'Accusations based simply on personal dislike are not evidence. As for thieving, I can tell you that your father's credit and debit cards haven't been used for the best part of three weeks, so whatever might have happened to him, petty theft doesn't appear to have been the motive. The last occasion was to place a sizeable bet on a dog race with an online bookmaker. It appears this wasn't successful.'

'Oh, God!' Lorna breathed. 'Three weeks?'

'Seventeen days to be precise,' Innes said. 'The same day he composed the text message . . .'

'Oh no! I know what you're getting at,' Stephen said hotly,

'but it's just ridiculous! You don't know my father; if you did you'd realize how crazy that is. He'd never do anything like that. Anyway, he didn't send the message, did he? He probably wrote it when he was feeling a bit low and then thought better of it. That'll be what happened.'

'It's possible,' Radcliffe agreed. 'But then, where is he? He doesn't have his phone and he's not using his cards . . .'

'Perhaps he's staying with someone,' Stephen suggested. 'He wouldn't need to spend money if he was staying with someone.'

'True. But who?'

'*I* don't know! That's your job! You find him.'

'But as you rightly said, we don't know your father,' Radcliffe said with commendable patience. 'We have followed up every contact you gave my colleagues last time and also all his work contacts. So far, nothing. If your father *is* staying somewhere, we have to conclude that he doesn't want to be found.'

'Well, if this Gregg person is sending thugs after him, I'm not surprised! Maybe you should be asking *him* where my father is.'

'If he knew,' Daniel pointed out quietly, 'he wouldn't be trying to find out from Lorna, would he?'

'We will be speaking to Mr Gregg,' Radcliffe assured him. 'But in the meantime, is there anyone else any of you can think of, however unlikely, that Mr Myers might have taken refuge with?'

Lorna shook her head.

'No, I really can't. I've given you all the names I could think of.'

'Stephen?'

He shook his head, too.

'Zoe?'

She shook her head.

'No, no one. I didn't really have a lot to do with him. I mean, we've never been particularly close.'

'And your boyfriend?'

She frowned.

'Shane? He's never met him.'

'You said he took you to the flapping track where you saw your stepfather.'

'Well, yes,' Zoe said, her colour heightening a little. 'But that wasn't, like, a meeting. I told you; Harvey was really uncomfortable that I'd seen him there and Shane was looking for Mr Driscoll. When he came back to find me, they didn't even speak.'

'OK, so Zoe; you say your father – sorry, Harvey – was in a party from work. Did you recognize anyone he was with, that night?'

She pursed her lips and shook her head.

'No. I mean, that's what he told me but when I saw him, he was pretty much on his own.'

'OK. That's fine. Thank you. We may need to speak to Shane sometime. Can you give me a contact number?'

'You can do it right now,' Stephen told her. 'He's here. Skulking around down at the stables.'

'He is *not* skulking!' Zoe shot a venomous look at her stepbrother.

'Well, what else do you call it when he takes off at the first sign of the police car?' he asked. 'Must have *something* to hide, if you ask me.'

'In my experience it would be far more unusual for a member of the Traveller community to stick around, given the choice, and who can blame them, really?' Radcliffe observed, with a telling glance at Stephen.

From his expression, it was clear that Radcliffe was in imminent danger of being added to his blacklist.

'Maybe you could ask him if he'd mind talking to me,' she asked Zoe, then. 'It can be in private, if he'd prefer. He's not in any trouble, it's just routine.'

Zoe nodded.

'Shall I go now?'

When she had gone, Radcliffe looked at Lorna and Stephen with a mixture of resignation and sympathy.

'I'm sure I don't have to tell you that the signs aren't encouraging. I'm not saying we should give up all hope of finding Harvey fit and well, but I think you should prepare yourself for the possibility that the news won't be good.'

'No!' Stephen pushed back his chair and stood up, his finger stabbing in the constable's direction. '*You* need to do your job – not spend your time coming round here spreading lies about my father! You don't know him; *I* do. If he's got into financial trouble, he'll get himself out; it's what he does, for fuck's sake! It's his job. He's responsible for millions of pounds' worth of other people's money – he's not going to top himself just because of a few gambling debts, is he?'

Radcliffe remained impassive in the face of this impassioned outburst, but Lorna uttered another, unhappy, 'Stephen, please!'

'No. You accept what she's saying, if you want to, but he's my father; I know him and it's obvious it's all lies! I'm not giving up on him.'

'Nobody's asking you to,' Daniel put in, quietly. 'The officer's just doing her job.'

'Who fucking well asked you?' Stephen demanded. 'And what are you doing here, anyway? This is family business. We don't know anything about you and you're very keen to take sides with that bloody Gypsy – who's to say you haven't got something to do with my father's disappearance?'

'Daniel's here because I asked him for help,' Lorna replied, calmly, but Stephen was on a roll now.

'So what is he – your lover? Have you been screwing him behind my father's back? He's away a lot, isn't he? Leaves the coast clear for you to carry on with whoever you want, doesn't it? And no one any the wiser. No wonder he doesn't want to come home—'

'Stephen!' Lorna cut through his vitriol, really angry now, and he finally stopped, red-faced and breathing as though he'd been running a marathon.

'To be honest, I couldn't care less what you think of me but you're way out of line talking to Lorna like that and I think you should apologize,' Daniel suggested quietly.

Stephen turned to look at him, his lip curling unpleasantly.

'Fuck you!' he said, pushed his chair back and left the room, swinging the door open so violently that it rebounded off the corner of the dresser. Moments later they could hear him making his way upstairs.

Into the void left by his going, Innes remarked matter-of-factly, 'Stress takes some people that way,' and, in spite of the charged atmosphere, Daniel had to suppress a smile. He had a feeling he might have misjudged the young constable.

TWELVE

'Daniel, it's Anya.'

It was the next day and Daniel had stopped the lorry in a car park on the edge of Dartmoor to give Taz a good run in his lunch break. It was a place he'd parked before, its location ideal to let him walk on the rising ground of the moor while keeping the vehicle in sight the whole time; important as he still had a good half of his load on board.

'Anya.' Daniel was surprised but pleased to hear from her. He had found himself thinking about her a few times in the last couple of days. 'What can I do for you?'

'Well, it might be what I can do for you,' she said, intriguingly. 'If you're still interested in our friend Billy Driscoll?'

'I am,' he said, stopping and turning to the side to shelter his phone from the weather. It had been raining non-stop all day and was beginning to run and pool on the roads, catching unwary motorists. With the ground clearance of the lorry he had not been affected too badly, but he'd passed several stranded car drivers, up to their axles in water with engines flooded by the wash from their own or other vehicles. Doom-mongers were already beginning to draw parallels with the onset of weeks of flooding, a couple of winters before.

'So, what have you found out?' he asked Anya.

'Well, nothing concrete, as yet, but I've had a call from a lady called Emily Rathbone. She's a long-time greyhound enthusiast who's had one or two racing dogs of her own. I've known her for quite a while.'

'Not the kind of friend I'd have picked for you,' Daniel commented.

'Well, no, not on the surface, but although I haven't been able to get her to see the error of her ways so far, she is, at least, an owner with a conscience. She has supported my rescue very handsomely over the years and the dogs she's owned have retired into her keeping – until now, that is. Unfortunately, when her last dog retired, she already had so many, she didn't have the room to keep it at her home, so, unknown to me, she made an arrangement with Driscoll, who's been training for her since her previous trainer retired. Anyway, apparently he offered to look after the dog in comfortable retirement, in return for which she pays him a not inconsiderable fee.'

'I see.' In the light of what Shane had told him, Daniel thought he probably did see, quite accurately.

'Mm, well, it so happens that one of Emily's other retired dogs has been suffering from spondylosis – something greys are prone to, especially ex-racers – and last week it sadly had to be put to sleep. So, Emily now has room for Lily at home, which pleases her, as well as promising to save her a good deal of money.'

'Let me guess,' Daniel cut in. 'Driscoll hasn't got the dog any more.'

'Well, he hasn't admitted as much, yet, but he's told her it's not convenient for her to pick the dog up at present – apparently there is a virus in his kennel. This was a month ago, since which time he's avoided her calls. Emily isn't stupid, however, she's still got contacts within the industry and they have told her that there's nothing wrong with Driscoll's dogs – he was, in fact, at a race meeting last week with some of them. So she has begun to get suspicious and plans to call in on Driscoll unannounced and demand to see her dog.'

'Ah,' Daniel said. 'That might not be the best idea. I trust you managed to dissuade her.'

'Well, not exactly,' Anya said. 'She was aware that Driscoll might not be too happy to find her on his doorstep, which is why she asked me if I'd go with her . . .'

'And you said . . .?'

'Well, I couldn't let her go alone, could I? But then I thought of you.'

'OK . . .' Daniel said slowly. 'And when have you planned this pleasure trip for?'

'We thought perhaps Wednesday – tomorrow,' she said. 'Unless you're busy?'

'I can't think of anything else I'd rather do,' he said drily.

'Great! Will you be OK to pick us up on your way, if Emily comes here?'

They agreed a time and Daniel put his phone back in an inside pocket, wondering whether the proposed bearding of Driscoll in his den was really such a good idea. He found that Taz had returned to his side and was regarding him eagerly; conveying his impatience with a series of high-pitched German shepherd nose whistles.

'I know; I know,' he told the dog. 'We came out to walk, not to talk. Well, come on then – what're you waiting for? Sitting there whingeing when you could be chasing bunnies!'

Taz jumped up at him and then bounded off, happy to have got Daniel moving again.

By the evening of the following day, the rain had finally stopped but the wind was rising once again and the weather forecast on Daniel's cab radio was full of dire predictions for the next few days. 'The calm before the storm' was the cliché of choice and while some of the accumulated surface water began to drain away, some people could be seen busily filling sandbags in preparation for worse to come.

Daniel drove to Longdogs Rescue in happy anticipation of spending more time with Anya, but wishing it could be in less potentially unpleasant circumstances, and more particularly without a third party along for the ride.

In her yard, sandbags were very much in evidence and rain-water had collected in a long muddy pool outside the kennels.

'Still dry inside?' he asked as Anya appeared in the doorway of her house, accompanied by a wiry, elderly lady with greying blonde hair cut in an ageless bob and tanned skin that showed pale in the crow's feet at the corners of her eyes. Daniel suspected she might spend a lot of time outside or more probably abroad. Both ladies wore anoraks and wellies, and Anya had on a leather bush hat, the shadow of which seemed to accentuate the clean, sculpted lines of her face.

'Dry at the moment,' she said. 'But the roof of the end kennel is leaking, so I've had to bring two more dogs inside. I can hardly move in there! Daniel, this is Emily Rathbone. Emily: Daniel Whelan, a friend of mine.'

Daniel shook Emily's hand, murmuring a greeting and, emboldened by her introduction, leaned forward and exchanged air kisses with Anya, who favoured him with a quizzical look as they parted.

The journey to Driscoll's kennels took longer than it had on Daniel's previous visit because the roads in the vicinity of Barnsworthy were already suffering from the bad weather. The village pond by the Reckless Toad had overflowed and one side of the road was closed to traffic. As they slowed to negotiate the flood at a sensible speed, Emily cast a nervous look at the trees that lined the lane ahead, which were bowing and tossing in the strengthening wind.

'I hope we don't get stuck. I should feel it was my fault,' she said, leaning forward to speak between the front seats.

'I don't think it's very deep,' Daniel said, reassuringly. 'As long as the trees stay up, we should be OK.'

'Yes, that's what I was worrying about,' Emily said. 'Are we nearly there?'

'Haven't you been before?' Daniel asked.

'No. My old trainer died – a heart attack; it was very sudden, and I was in a bit of a hole because his son wanted to wrap up the business as soon as possible. I was introduced to Mr Driscoll on a race night and he offered to arrange the transfer of my dogs. I can't say I took to him at the start, so I suppose it was poor-spirited of me not to turn him down and look for someone I liked more, but I was under pressure to move them and he more or less took over. But the thing is, he doesn't encourage owners to visit. He says it upsets the dogs. Well I love my dogs and when he told me that, I'd probably have taken my dogs somewhere else if I'd just been starting out, but I only had Lily and her sister left and they were both close to retirement, so I just went along with it. The thing is, at my age, you sometimes take the easier option just to avoid a fuss,' she added, with a touch of wistfulness.

The appearance of the signpost to the kennels forestalled any further comment and in the rear-view mirror, Daniel could see Emily glancing from side to side as they drove down the track, doubtless taking in the untidy state of the paddocks either side, visible even in the gloom of the overcast evening.

As the Mercedes drew up in front of the kennels, Daniel noted the absence of Driscoll's van with a certain measure of foreboding.

The obvious disadvantage of a surprise visit was that they might have chosen a time when the man was out.

'Oh, I hope he's here. I'd hate it to have been a wasted journey for you all,' Emily said, echoing his thoughts, and through the open window of the car they could hear the barking of dogs somewhat bigger and fiercer than the greyhounds.

'Apparently, he's got a couple of Dobermans,' Daniel told the old lady. 'But it sounds like they're shut in. Shall I go and see if anyone's about?'

He had only just stepped out of the car when the door in the corner of the yard opened to reveal a large figure in a bottle-green boiler suit. Seeing Daniel, he took a step backwards.

'That's Davy. Billy's brother,' Anya said, leaning across the seat.

Daniel had guessed as much.

'Hi, Davy!' he called in a friendly fashion, remembering what Shane had told him.

'Billy ain't here,' Davy said, starting to pull the door shut between him and the uninvited visitors.

'Davy, wait!'

Davy shook his head, looking anxious, but the door remained at least partially open as Daniel approached.

'No, I can't talk to you. I'm not supposed to speak to visitors,' he said. 'Billy doesn't like it.'

'But Billy's not here, is he?' Daniel said with what he hoped was a reassuring smile. 'So if you don't tell him and I don't, he won't know, will he?'

'He'll find out,' Davy said looking from side to side and then, bizarrely glancing upwards, as if expecting his brother to be watching him from on high. 'I'm not s'posed to talk to people, see?' he repeated and the door began to close again.

'But that doesn't mean me, does it?' Anya's voice spoke softly from behind Daniel and Davy hesitated once more. 'We're old friends, aren't we, Davy?'

'Billy says I mustn't talk to no one when he's not here,' Davy said, becoming ever more agitated, but his eyes rested on Anya with obvious pleasure.

'Where is Billy, then?' Anya said, and Daniel stood to one side and let her take over the conversation, as Davy seemed drawn to her, unsurprisingly, he felt.

'He's at the track, trying out some yearlings,' Davy told her.

'Which track, Davy?'

'Yarnbridge.'

'Well, that's all right then, isn't it? You can talk to us.'

'I suppose so.' Davy didn't seem to see any flaw in this rather vague reasoning.

'Davy knows all the dogs by name, don't you, Davy?' she continued, smiling at him.

'Yeah. I like the dogs, they're my friends.'

'Which one's your favourite?'

'Binky. She's pretty, she is, and she licks my face when I go in to feed her.'

'Can we see Binky? Can you show her to us?' Anya asked.

Davy looked worried again and shook his head.

'I'm not s'posed to let anyone in to see the dogs. It's security. They're valuable dogs, you see.'

'We won't touch her. We'll just look through the door,' Anya told him. 'You know I wouldn't hurt them, don't you, Davy? I love the dogs, too. I've got lots of dogs.'

Davy glanced doubtfully at Daniel.

'Daniel loves dogs, too,' she assured him. 'That's Daniel's dog in the car.'

Davy took a step forward and peered at the parked Mercedes, from which Taz stared back intently. He returned his attention to Anya.

'Well, I s'pose it wouldn't hurt. Billy couldn't have meant you, could he?' he reasoned, giving himself permission to accede to her request, as he so obviously desperately wanted to.

'No. I've known Billy a long while, haven't I?' Anya said, following up her advantage. She smiled again and Davy's mind was made up. He came through the door and shut it carefully behind him.

He led the way along the front of the enclosed kennel block to the door, and taking a key from the pocket of his boiler suit, opened it and went inside. Hard on his heels, Anya and Daniel followed, and Emily, who had joined them quietly as they crossed the yard, fell in behind.

A decidedly doggy smell assailed their nostrils as they made their way down the corridor, but the kennel area appeared clean and was lit with daylight from several grid-covered windows in the outer wall.

'We'll just look, won't we?' Davy repeated as he led the way almost to the far end. 'Not go in.'

'No, we won't go in,' Anya agreed.

He began to name the dogs as they passed.

'Susie. Jess. Rosco. That's Jimbo, he's bad tempered, he is. Lewis. And here's Binky,' he said then, pointing through the meshed top of one of the kennel doors. 'She's my friend. She's pretty – like you,' he added, looking shyly at Anya and then just as quickly away, blushing furiously.

Daniel looked through the mesh at a black greyhound bitch with a white nose and bib. She was indeed a pretty creature and her coat and eyes shone with good health. She stretched and wagged her tail at the sight of her visitors, coming forward to the door.

'She kisses me when I put her food down,' Davy told them again, returning Binky's fond look.

'She's lovely,' Anya said warmly. 'I'm not surprised she's your favourite. I think it's very clever of you to remember all their names. So where's Lily's kennel, then? Do you know?'

'Lily?' Davy turned with a frown. 'Lily's not here.'

'Are the retired dogs kept somewhere special, then?'

'Lily was old and poorly,' Davy said, looking sad. 'She's not here any more.'

'Poorly?' Emily spoke up sharply and Davy turned to look at her, as if noticing her for the first time. 'I wasn't told she was unwell.'

Davy nodded sagely.

'Billy said she was poorly. He says it's not fair to keep dogs when they are old and poorly.'

'So what happened to her? Did the vet see her?'

'She's not here any more.'

'Did the vet see her?' Emily's tone hardened and Davy began to look uncomfortable. Anya put a hand on the older lady's arm but she shook it off. 'Did she go to the vet?' she repeated.

'Vets charge an arm and a leg. Billy doesn't need a vet to tell him when an animal's poorly,' Davy stated, reciting the phrases as if by rote.

'Balderdash!' Emily retorted, and Davy took a step back,

flinching as if she had struck him. 'Billy has a duty of care to the dogs – it's what he's paid for! Lily's my dog. He should have consulted me. What has he done with her?'

'You should leave,' Davy said, sidling past them in the narrow corridor and beckoning to them to follow. 'You shouldn't be here. Billy wouldn't like it. I shouldn't have let you in. Billy will be angry. Please come now. Please . . .'

Emily was quite clearly not prepared to leave without following the matter up but Anya moved in front of her, putting out a hand towards Davy.

'It's OK, Davy. Nobody's blaming you and we won't tell Billy you let us see the dogs. Don't get upset, please.'

Davy's eyes locked onto hers, pleadingly.

'You won't tell Billy?'

'Of course not.'

'It's just that he gets so mad at me cos I do stupid things.'

'What does he do when he gets mad?' Daniel asked quietly. 'Does he hurt you, Davy?'

Davy shook his head vigorously. 'No! No, he's good to me, Billy is. It's only what I deserve. Not many people would put up with me.'

'It's *not* what you deserve, Davy,' Anya told him. 'You're a good man.'

'I'm a good man,' Davy repeated.

He had stopped in the doorway and was gazing at Anya with something akin to worship in his eyes. If she had told him he could fly, he would have believed it, Daniel thought.

'I love the dogs, me,' Davy said then. 'I want to keep them all but Billy says it's kinder to let them go. Billy doesn't need to pay a vet to tell him what to do . . .'

'Yes, I expect Billy knows what he's doing,' Anya said with an irony that was completely lost on the younger Driscoll. 'We'll go now and come back when he's here, OK?'

Davy nodded with obvious relief and led the way back to the yard, casting frequent looks back over his shoulder to reassure himself that they were all following.

Once outside, Davy seemed disposed to hurry back to the sanctuary beyond the gate once more but Daniel had one more question for him.

'Do you know a man called Harvey Myers, Davy?'

Davy's eyes widened in alarm once again and he shook his head so rapidly that his cheeks wobbled.

'Billy doesn't like me talking about the owners.'

'So Mr Myers owns a greyhound?'

Again the shake of the head.

'No. I don't know where he is. He hasn't been here. Billy doesn't let me meet the owners. They don't come here.'

'Is Mr Myers an owner, Davy?' Unsure as to why Daniel was so keen to know, Anya nevertheless followed his lead.

The look that Davy turned on her was beseeching.

'You mustn't ask me questions. Billy will be mad at me. I say stupid things. Most people wouldn't put up with me. If I didn't have Billy I wouldn't have anywhere to live . . .'

'It's all right, Davy. We won't ask any more,' she said. 'We'll go away now and we won't tell Billy you let us see the dogs, so it's best you don't tell him, either.'

'Before we do, though, Davy,' Daniel said quickly. 'I want you to take this, and if you're ever in trouble or worried about anything, you can give me a call.'

Davy regarded the card he was holding out as if it was a stick of dynamite, even going so far as to take a step back. He shook his head, emphatically.

'Billy wouldn't like it.'

'I suggest you don't tell Billy. Put it in your pocket or somewhere safe and it'll be there if you need it. Billy need never know.'

Davy looked from the business card to Daniel's face and then, in an agony of indecision, to Anya.

'I think it's a good idea, Davy,' she said. 'Daniel's a good man. He'll help you if you ever need it. Take the card and keep it safe.'

Davy scanned her face for a long moment, and then, without making eye contact with Daniel, reached out and took the card, tucking it into his boiler-suit pocket, while looking hurriedly about him as though worried that his brother might suddenly appear. The evidence hidden, he immediately started to back away.

'You need to go now,' he said, making shooing movements with his hands.

'We're going,' Daniel reassured him.

Emily had fallen quiet now and was looking thoughtful; Daniel guessed that the pathos of Davy's situation had tempered her anger.

Within moments, Davy had disappeared through the gate and they heard bolts being drawn. Back in the car, Emily was the first to speak.

'The man's a monster! Billy Driscoll, I mean, not Davy. Not to mention an out and out criminal. He's killed my dog, hasn't he? He's killed Lily.'

'It looks like it,' Anya said sadly. 'I'm sorry. I was afraid that might be the case. It's not the first time.'

'How can he get away with it?' Emily demanded. 'Just killing dogs like that?'

'He gets away with it because a lot of owners are so pleased to have their older dogs taken off their hands, they don't ask questions,' Daniel said.

'If I'd known what he was like, I would never have agreed to let him have my dogs,' Emily said bitterly. 'I blame myself for not doing more research, but to be honest, I had no idea people like Billy Driscoll even existed. I mean, he's a licensed trainer! Why hasn't anyone complained about him, before now?'

'Oh, they have,' Anya said with heavy emphasis. 'But it's a self-regulating industry, practically run by the bookies. I expect all he would get is a slapped wrist and a warning to be more discreet. After all, doping is rife, and you can't tell me that the GBGB aren't aware of it!'

'But the owners of the other dogs . . .'

'As Daniel said, I suspect many of them are just glad to have the dogs taken off their hands and don't enquire too closely as to the details. Or maybe, like you, he spins them a story about happy retirement and goes on taking a reduced fee to look after the non-existent dog. Easy enough to invent a sudden illness or accident to account for its disappearance, if the owner should develop a conscience and come looking.'

Emily sighed.

'I feel unbelievably stupid,' she said. 'Poor Lily.'

'So, who's Harvey Myers?' Anya asked Daniel. 'A friend of yours?'

'Husband of a friend, or perhaps I should say he *was* the husband of a friend. He's gone missing and I have to say it's not looking very rosy.'

'You think he's dead?'

'Well, either that or he doesn't want to be found. The police are involved but so far they haven't—'

'And he had greyhounds?'

'I don't know. It was just a shot in the dark. He apparently knew Billy and as he had a gambling problem it's possible he had a dog. Or maybe he tapped Billy for insider information.'

Whether Harvey had ventured into ownership or not, Daniel was intrigued by Davy's response to his query about Lorna's husband. At first he had trotted out his stock answer that Billy didn't like him talking but when Daniel had pressed him he hadn't said that he didn't know the man but that he didn't know where he was.

'So what now?' Anya's question cut through his train of thought. 'Do we go back another day? It seems a bit pointless now we've lost the element of surprise. I don't hold out much hope that Davy will keep quiet about our visit, do you?'

'No,' Daniel agreed. 'Even if he tries, I think he'll probably give the game away. That's why I think it might be an idea to drop in on Billy Driscoll's little track session. I imagine you know the way to this track at Yarnbridge?'

'I do indeed.' Anya's eyes gleamed with a martial light.

When they reached the rural town of Yarnbridge, Anya directed Daniel to a business park on the outskirts where they eventually drew up outside a large modern building which, apart from its size, was indistinguishable from many of the others they had passed on the way in. It appeared to have been fashioned in sections from huge green-painted panels with the only windows, long horizontal panes, high under the shallow overhang of the roof. To Daniel's relief, light glowed from behind them. He had begun to wonder whether they would reach the track only to find their quarry gone. They drove on alongside the building and, rounding the end, found Driscoll's navy blue Transit parked next to two other vans and a pimped-up truck.

Daniel got out of the car, let Taz out and went on a fact-finding mission.

A large sliding door was labelled 'No Public Access' and underneath that the words 'Reception & Booking' with an arrow pointing towards a glazed entrance further along the wall, but there was also a smaller door let into the sliding one and trying this, Daniel found it to be unlocked. He opened it and peered into a dimly lit interior. There was no one about, but he could see a brighter light further off.

Looking over his shoulder to where the two ladies stood waiting, he said, 'It's open. I'm going to take a look. You can stay here if you'd rather.'

'Absolutely not!' Anya declared. 'That is, I'm coming – I can't speak for Emily.'

Daniel couldn't read the older lady's expression in the semi-darkness but she gamely announced her intention of going with them.

'OK,' Daniel said. 'Quietly until we see what's what.'

With Taz padding at his heels, he opened the door and stepped through, followed closely by the others.

They found themselves in what appeared to be a delivery area lit by a couple of inadequate wall lights, but between the machinery, stacks of plastic-wrapped goods and untidy piles of discarded pallets, a largely uncluttered central walkway led to another sliding door that was partially open, allowing a shaft of light to spill through from the area beyond.

Taz cast about eagerly, scenting, and Daniel had to call him to heel as he cautiously led the way through the open door. They emerged between banks of plastic seating into the bright lights of a huge stadium around the perimeter of which was an oval sand track, some eight yards wide. The sand had been rolled but several trails of paw prints showed where dogs had recently run.

In the centre, near a cluster of what looked like low hurdles, a huddle of men stood talking. A number of wire-muzzled dogs were standing or lying nearby, their thin skins protected from the cold by coats. Most of the men had their backs to the newcomers and none of them had yet noticed their arrival.

Anya caught at Daniel's arm to stop him.

'That's Les Mollahan,' she said softly. 'The one Billy's talking to: the one with the baseball cap. He's a trainer, too. Sells most of his cast-offs to China and the Third World, bastard that he is! Been had up for assault, too. You want to watch him. He's nasty.'

'Good job I've got you to protect me, then,' Daniel replied with a wink.

'Hmm. Now's probably the time to say that I lied about being a tae kwon do international,' she told him. 'I did do it for a while, but only at the village-hall level.'

'Oh! We'll have to rely on Taz then, I suppose,' Daniel said affecting disappointment. 'Are you OK, Emily? You don't have to do this, you know, if you don't want to. You can stay here.'

Resolutely, Emily shook her head.

'No. I'll be fine. Go on.'

The track and the centre of the oval were open to the elements and as Daniel's group stepped out onto the running surface, a light drizzle drifted down.

Although their feet made little noise on the sandy track, the sudden attention of a couple of the greyhounds alerted the men to the arrival of uninvited guests, and Daniel and the others had barely reached the central area before first one, then all of them turned.

Including Billy, there were five men in the group, and Daniel could also see a dark-haired boy of perhaps eleven or twelve who had been hidden from view. Faces that had turned in enquiry quickly became wary in response to a half-heard comment from Billy, and by the time Daniel and the two women reached them, the group were ranged in a line with hostility writ large in both face and posture. As on many occasions before, Daniel was grateful for Taz's watchful presence at his side.

Without looking, he was aware that the dog had taken a step beyond his usual position at his knee and was tense with anticipation. Like most of his breed, Taz was no slouch at reading body language, and like Daniel, he clearly found little to reassure him about the men they were facing. He steadied the dog with a quiet word.

'Ms Darby.' It was Billy Driscoll who spoke first. His eyes flickered over Daniel and he frowned slightly as if trying to remember when and where they had met.

'Mr Driscoll,' she returned, coolly.

Daniel noticed that one of the other men, a tall, well-built individual also came to attention at her greeting. His black hair formed the same widow's peak as Billy's, and Daniel guessed that this was Johnny Driscoll, Billy's elder brother and head of the Driscoll clan.

'So what can I do for you?' Billy asked. 'If you want me to train a dog for you, I'm afraid I shall have to disappoint you. My kennels are full.'

From the outbreak of laughter that greeted this statement, Daniel surmised that Anya was known to most of the group and they therefore knew how preposterous the idea was.

'As a matter of fact, I heard you were giving up the dogs and going into another line of business,' Anya said. 'I was thinking of throwing a party.'

'Kind of you but I can't make it,' Driscoll said, assuming a tragic air and provoking another burst of amusement. Anya flushed dark with anger and Daniel took over.

'We came to see you because Mrs Rathbone here is worried about her dog. She's paying you a considerable sum to look after it and, not unnaturally, would like to see it to check on its welfare,' he said. 'She says you aren't answering her calls.'

'I must have missed them.'

'She left messages.'

Billy's expression hardened.

'I'm a busy man. I was intending to call within the next day or two.'

'And what would you have told her? That her dog is happy and healthy?'

'Of course. All my dogs get the best of care.' He looked at Daniel with intense dislike. 'I remember you. You came to the yard with that little slut Shane was seeing. What's your interest in all this?'

Daniel ignored the question.

'So you'd be happy for Emily to visit and see for herself?'

Billy frowned.

'There's no need. I can assure you, the dog is fine.'

'But she wants to. She's fond of her dog.'

'Yeah well, the thing is, I don't encourage visitors; it's disruptive and the dogs are very sensitive to changes in routine. It can make the difference between winning and losing.'

To Daniel's right Anya uttered a scornful sound but while he agreed with the sentiment he kept his own scepticism hidden as he said calmly, 'Nevertheless, I'm sure you agree she's within her rights to ask to see her dog. What's more, she's got room at home now, so she's decided to have it back.'

Billy's frown deepened. The other men exchanged silent glances and Daniel thought it likely they knew him well and could guess fairly accurately at his predicament.

'Ah, now I remember,' Billy said, as one for whom the light has finally dawned. 'I have so many dogs, as you know, I sometimes lose track; yours is the little tan bitch . . .'

'Black,' Emily supplied.

'That's right, black. I've been meaning to call you but I couldn't find your number. I'm afraid she had an episode of bloat. The breed is prone to it, as I'm sure you know, deep-chested as they are. No warning and nothing we could do. My vet said it was kindest to let her go. I'm so sorry.' He produced a sympathetic half-smile.

'You're sorry but it didn't stop you continuing to take her money,' Daniel observed coldly.

'It's only just happened,' Billy stated. 'I will, of course, be refunding Mrs Rathbone any overpayment. But remind me, again – why is this any of your business?'

'Because I've made it my business.'

'What are you – some sort of professional busybody?'

'No, it's just a hobby,' Daniel said evenly. 'And while we're asking questions – does Harvey Myers have a dog in training with you?'

If he hadn't been watching Billy Driscoll so closely, he would have missed the momentary narrowing of his gaze, for Driscoll recovered instantly, shaking his head and saying, 'You may not be a professional, Mr Whelan, but I am, and I wouldn't dream of sharing the details of any of my clients with you.'

'So he is a client . . .'

'I didn't say that.'

'But you know him.'

'I know *of* him, certainly,' Driscoll admitted. 'I saw him at the track now and then. Someone pointed him out to me, I forget why. He didn't have a dog with me – or anyone else as far as I know.'

'He has your number on his phone.'

'So have any number of people, I imagine. I don't make any secret of it. Now, if you don't mind, I have business to attend to.'

Dismissing the visitors by turning his shoulder, he said something under his breath to one of the other men that made him nod and smile.

'Why do you talk about him in the past tense?' Daniel asked, raising his voice.

Billy stopped and looked back.

'I wasn't aware that I had,' he said smoothly. 'And if I did, it's probably because I haven't seen him around lately. Perhaps he ran out of money. It's well known that he's a serious punter, he's tried to touch me for a tip a time or two, but I'm not in that line of business, am I? I expect that's why he had my number. Now, if you know what's good for you, you and your lady friends should go back to wherever it was you came from and leave me alone!'

'I still want answers about Lily!' Emily protested, trembling. 'And I shall want to see the vet's report.'

'Yes, all right. I'll send it to you,' Billy said, not troubling to hide his impatience.

'I wouldn't hold your breath, Emily,' Anya advised her. 'I have a feeling you'll be waiting a long time.'

The trainer curled his lip.

'I'd forgotten what a troublesome little bitch you are!' he commented.

'I think that's enough!' Daniel said quietly.

'Oh, don't worry about my feelings, Daniel. Being called a bitch is a compliment, as far as I'm concerned!'

Billy shot her a look of intense dislike and made to turn away once more but then paused, leaning towards Daniel.

'You want to watch it – being a busybody can be a dangerous hobby! I've known people have nasty accidents. You might even call it an extreme sport, if you get my drift . . .'

Distrusting his intent, Taz took a pace forward, lifted his lip and rumbled deep in his throat. Putting a hand in the dog's collar, Daniel returned Driscoll's stare.

'Threatening people can be pretty risky, too,' he commented. 'Just saying . . .'

Billy's eyes narrowed still further, glinting with anger, but whatever his intention might have been it was forestalled by his brother, who put a hand on his arm and advised him that enough had been said. Shaking Johnny's hand off, Billy cast a final look of dislike in Daniel's direction and turned away. As the other men followed, the one Anya had named as Les Mollahan sneered and raised two fingers at Daniel and his companions. The young boy also lingered, staring curiously at them, black-eyed and surly, before he was called away.

THIRTEEN

The rain and wind intensified during the night and when Daniel turned up for work the next day, it was to be greeted with the news that there was flooding and potential road closures on several of the routes the TFS drivers regularly used.

'Did you hear about the Greek tanker that's run aground off Torbay?' Fred Bowden said as he passed Daniel a restorative mug of coffee in the office after his early morning run with Taz. 'Got carried off course in the storm last night, they reckon.'

'Heard something about it on the radio on the way in,' Daniel said. 'Something about illegals coming ashore in a boat, wasn't there?'

'Yeah, a whole load of 'em in one of the tanker's lifeboats and apparently they're saying there's more aboard. Tricked into working their passage, I gather. They were in a bit of a state, by all accounts, poor bastards!'

'Must have been desperate to launch a small boat in this weather,' Daniel agreed. 'I wouldn't care to try it.'

'Slavery, basically,' Fred said. 'You'd like to think mankind had progressed beyond that in this day and age, wouldn't you?'

'The savage isn't very far beneath the surface in some people,' Daniel observed sadly, reflecting briefly on the Driscolls and their cronies.

'How's Lorna doing, by the way? No news, I suppose. Have the police turned up anything at all?'

'Not that they're sharing with her,' Daniel replied. 'I assume they're working through all the usual channels but if they've got any leads they're keeping them to themselves. However, when we went to redeem the rings at the pawnbroker's, we saw a watch Zoe thinks might be his. The police are following it up but we haven't heard anything, as yet.'

'Oh, Christ! That's not good however you look at it,' Fred groaned. 'How's she taking it?'

Daniel pursed his lips.

'She's keeping it together but I don't know for how long. It's not only Harvey being missing, it's the financial side of it. If he's run himself deep into debt, where's that going to leave her? She's not stupid; she knows she wouldn't be able to maintain a place like that on her own, and there's the horses – they're her life.'

Throughout the long, difficult day's driving, Daniel found his mind running back and forth over the unpleasant business of Billy Driscoll and his fraudulent activities. He was amazed that the owners he trained for would accept his reluctance to have visitors at the kennels, but then again, given the disinterest shown by many of the owners at the end of the dogs' short careers, maybe that wasn't as surprising as it at first seemed. To Daniel, for whom Taz was not only a partner but a friend, the idea of looking upon a dog as a mere commodity for occasional amusement was totally alien.

Munching on a tuna baguette in a roadside cafe at lunchtime, he found himself thinking about Emily Rathbone and her very real distress upon discovering the fate of her own greyhound. She may have been guilty of seeing only what she wanted to see, but the blinkers were well and truly off now, and she had been horrified to learn that Daniel and Anya suspected that Lily was just one of many dogs that Driscoll had routinely slaughtered.

How many of the other owners had been deceived into paying for the care of dogs that no longer existed it was impossible to tell, but it would be a risky business and Daniel thought the trainer was probably shrewd enough to know which of his owners he could tap in that way, and which it would be safer not to.

He thought again of Shane's abrupt dismissal. Given that the lad had already known that Driscoll was killing dogs and disposing of them on his land, what had prompted the trainer to not only sack the boy but practically hound him out of the area?

Had it been the discovery that Shane was on intimate terms with Harvey Myers' stepdaughter that had so worried Billy Driscoll?

The fact that Shane had been seeing a non-Traveller had been no secret at Hawkers Yard so it seemed Billy Driscoll's extreme reaction must have been due to who she was, rather than what she was. So why was that important? Had he been pulling some kind of scam on the businessman? Did Shane have information that might incriminate him? But if that was so, why hadn't the boy mentioned it during the furore over Myers' disappearance?

Even though Shane seemed honest enough, himself, Daniel knew enough of the Travelling community not underestimate the strength of the youngster's ties of loyalty to his race and heritage.

In the event, despite his dislike for his former employer, had blood ties proven stronger even than his feelings for Zoe or had fear of reprisals tipped the balance? Remembering how Shane hadn't hesitated to wade in when Zoe had been waylaid in Tavistock, Daniel was inclined to doubt that. Perhaps sacking the lad had been a pre-emptive strike on Driscoll's part and Shane either didn't actually know anything or didn't realize the significance of it. He made a mental note to talk to the young Traveller again.

The sudden warm heaviness of Taz's long black muzzle settling on his knee reminded him that he had almost finished his baguette and the dog was expecting his customary crust.

'Got a sausage here, if he'd like it,' the burly man behind the counter offered. 'Been hanging around a bit long, this one; can't really sell it now.'

'He'd love it,' Daniel assured him, draining his coffee cup and casting a disenchanted look at the rain streaming down the windows.

'Here you are, boy,' the man said, coming round the counter and holding the titbit out to Taz. The dog's eyes sharpened but he made no move towards it.

'Sorry. He won't take it from you,' Daniel told him. 'He's been trained not to.'

'Sensible,' the burly one said, undismayed. 'He's a beautiful dog. I love shepherds but the wife wanted a Labradoodle. Bet this chap could make good use of those teeth,' he added as Taz accepted the sausage from Daniel as if he hadn't been fed for a week.

'He could bring you down, no problem, if I told him to,' Daniel agreed.

'I'll make sure I give you the right change, then,' the man joked. 'Take care out there – it looks nasty!'

'It is,' Daniel replied with feeling.

His phone began to ring on his way back to the lorry and he answered it as he swung back up into the cab.

'Daniel, it's Lorna.'

'Hi, Lorna. Is something wrong?'

'Um . . .' she sniffed. 'Yes. Yvonne just called. They've found Harvey's car.'

'Oh, right. Where was it?'

'Near the coast, she says. Hidden in some trees.'

'That's interesting.'

'Yvonne says it's possible it was dumped there by joyriders. It's not necessarily where Harvey left it. There was some damage, apparently. It's been taken off for forensics.' There was a pause and she sniffed again. 'It doesn't look good, does it?'

'Not brilliant, I have to say,' Daniel admitted. 'But let's wait on the forensic report, shall we? Speak to you later.'

By the time Daniel had finished all his allotted drops for the day, the rain had slackened off a little, although the wind was still as strong. By a strange twist of fate or serendipity, he found himself with an empty lorry just up the road from Driscoll's training yard.

Seeing the signpost to Barnsworthy, he made an instant and completely unpremeditated decision to go that way and five minutes later parked in a handy pull-in just a hundred yards from the kennels.

Stepping down from the cab with Taz bounding eagerly after him, he locked the vehicle and headed along the lane. Kenny, the barman at the Reckless Toad, had mentioned a footpath leading across Driscoll's land, and Daniel found he was curious to try it out.

A couple of minutes later and a quarter of a mile down the road, Daniel stopped beside a rickety stile that was almost completely hidden by an overgrowth of brambles and blackthorn. In the long grass of the verge, he could see the stubby remains of a four-by-four timber post and after hunting around discovered the rest of it; a six-foot length of timber, now broken in two, with a small pointed sign at the top bearing the familiar symbol of a walking person that signified a footpath. It didn't require a university education to guess how it had met its fate.

Taz came to attention and Daniel turned to see a woman with two springer spaniels approaching along the puddly tarmac of the lane. He smiled and she smiled back briefly, her face all but invisible with her collar turned up and a waxed hat pulled low over her eyes.

'Good luck if you're planning on going along there,' she said as she drew level. 'You'll need a pair of wire cutters and a machete.'

'Is it that bad?'

The woman stopped; the two spaniels strained towards Taz, who ignored them in his usual lofty fashion.

'We've all given up trying,' she told him. 'We've complained to the council and the Ramblers' Association and anyone else we can think of, but they never seem to do anything. It's a shame because it's the only way to get to Fowlers Wood apart from going round the roads, and that takes for ever.'

'So who owns the land?'

'Chap called Driscoll. Billy Driscoll. Runs the greyhound kennels back along the road, there.'

'And he doesn't like people crossing his land. Is he running stock on it?'

'No, that's the thing. He doesn't do anything with it, as far as anyone can tell, except keep ploughing it up. I don't know why, I mean, he never plants anything. Some people wonder if he ploughs it just to keep us off it.'

'Has anyone tried talking to him about it?' Daniel asked, all innocence.

The woman snorted derisively.

'Yeah, right! Look, I'm not normally judgemental but the Driscolls are Travellers – Gypsies, and Billy and his brother Johnny, who owns the pub, give even *them* a bad name, d'you know what I mean? You don't stir up trouble with either of them unless you want both of them on your case, *and* all of their friends and relations as well, probably.' She pointed at the stile. 'Just try and see how far you can get along there and then you'll see the kind of person you're dealing with.'

'Does he actually come out and confront people?'

'He doesn't have to,' she said bitterly. 'He's made it so difficult to use the path, nobody ever tries any more. No one local, at any rate. The last time I used it, someone was letting off a gun in the copse. Now, he may have been shooting pigeons or something but I wasn't about to take any chances with my dogs running loose. Anyway,' she cast an eye up at the clouds which were beginning to produce the kind of large, heavy drops that usually presaged a downpour, 'I'm going to get home before I get drenched, yet again. Good luck, and don't say I didn't warn you!'

Thoughtfully, Daniel watched her hurry away, tugging her collar up even higher as the rain intensified, then turned back to the overgrown stile and footpath.

'Well, Taz. Shall we give it a go, lad?'

The dog looked up at him, whining his impatience, and moments later Daniel had negotiated the sloping, wobbly plank of the stile, pushing his way through the stiff twiggery of the blackthorn. Brambles tore at his jeans and rainwater sprayed off the vegetation, soaking the denim as he jumped down into the field on the other side. Pig netting had been stretched across the rails but Taz made short work of the obstacle. For a dog who had been taught to climb a ladder, a stile was no problem.

In the field, Taz began to run to and fro, his nose down, but remembering the woman's comments about gunfire, Daniel called him to heel. He wasn't about to take any chances with his safety.

A sign nailed to a tree in the hedge on his right bade walkers to keep to the footpath and on his left a double strand electric fence ran parallel, a scant two feet away from the hedge to ensure that they did so, in spite of there being no stock in the field.

Daniel trudged through the wet grass, wishing he'd got his heavy duty walking boots on instead of his work ones, and in the far corner of the field found another stile buried deep in the overgrown hedge. This one, too, was broken and had, he discovered, two strands of barbed wire stretched above it.

Taking his penknife from his pocket, Daniel unfolded the wire cutters and snipped through the wire and some of the encroaching vegetation. With this removed, he was able to vault the remaining rails, followed with ease by the dog.

Now they were in the famous ploughed field, or at least in a wired-off strip of land running down one side of it. As in the previous field, the corridor set aside for the footpath was barely two feet wide but this field had a ditch running along the hedgeline, which had recently been dredged out. This meant that the choice was either to walk in this channel – at present running with at least eighteen inches of dirty water – or on the mounds of muddy residue that had been heaped to the side of it.

Daniel had no wish to do either and nor was the plough particularly enticing, especially after several days of heavy rain. He stood surveying the scene.

The field was a good four acres in size. Just how many dead greyhounds lay buried under the turned soil was anyone's guess and as long as the ground was kept under plough, no one would ever notice if it had been freshly disturbed. At present, large areas of the ridged soil were beginning to disappear under pools of rainwater, and although Daniel pulled a small pair of binoculars from his jacket pocket, there was nothing untoward to see.

Taz, who had sat at his side without being told to, was now gazing out across the mud through rain that was once more beginning to fall in earnest. Suddenly he started to whine, looking up at Daniel.

'What is it, lad? D'you know what's out there? Can you sense it? No! Get your filthy paws off me!' This was as Taz whined again and jumped up at him. 'I know. It's a poor walk, isn't it? Let's go back before we get drenched.'

As he turned, his attention was caught by a movement on the far side of the field, where it bordered the yard itself. He paused, scanning the hedgerow through the binoculars for several minutes, but saw nothing. Finally he turned away, unsure what was out there and whether he'd been seen. There was no way of knowing, but he felt pretty certain that if he *had* been seen he would also have been recognized. Even from a distance and without binoculars, the presence of the German shepherd would have seen to that.

The already rough wind grew steadily worse as Daniel drove back to the TFS depot and his journey was made slower and more circuitous by a fallen tree on his original route. The rain had returned in torrents and the windscreen wipers were struggling to cope with it. With water rebounding off the already streaming tarmac it was difficult to see where the pools of water were and Daniel had to keep his wits about him on the way back.

'You've been a long time.' Fred came out of the office to meet him as he returned the keys to the lockable cupboard in the hallway. 'Trouble on the road?'

'A little. It's pretty intense out there,' Daniel said, rubbing tired eyes. Taz padded in behind him and shook the rainwater from his fur. 'Made all the drops OK, though. Is everyone else back?'

'Yeah. You're the last apart from Lofty – he just phoned in. He's found himself on the wrong side of a fallen tree and is having to detour. Bugger of a night, it's going to be! I was going to take Meg out, too – it's our anniversary – but I think we might stay in and get a Chinese instead.'

'Congratulations! If I'd known I'd have bought you a bottle of something. Give her a kiss from me, will you?'

'I will not, you cheeky bastard! She's far too fond of you already! You got time for a coffee?'

'Even if I hadn't, I'd make time. I'm gagging for a cuppa. I've been walking.'

'In *this*?' Fred asked, incredulously as he went through into the office.

'I had my reasons,' Daniel said, 'and it wasn't raining quite this hard at the time.'

'So, where was this walk?'

Taking off his jacket and hanging it over the back of the chair, Daniel sat down thankfully and told him about Driscoll's field and what he'd learned about it.

'So what now?' Fred asked. 'Will you tell the police?'

Daniel shrugged.

'Tell them what? I have no actual proof, only suspicions.'

The long journey back to the depot had given Daniel plenty of time to mull over those suspicions and he was just wondering whether to share with Fred the burgeoning extent of those when he was interrupted by the ringtone of his phone. Fishing it out of his jacket pocket, he frowned. 'Don't recognize that. Sorry, do you mind . . .?'

Accepting the call, he heard a male voice say hesitantly, 'Um, is that Mr Whelan?'

'Yes,' Daniel said cautiously, trying to place the caller.

'You said I could ring you, if I wanted to. You gave me a card with your number on.'

Recognition clicked in.

'Davy? Davy Driscoll?'

'You said I could call if I wanted to,' he repeated. He sounded agitated.

'Is something wrong?' Daniel asked, seeing Fred raise his eyebrows.

There was a long pause and he began to think Davy had ended the call.

'Davy?'

'Yes, I'm here.'

Daniel could hear someone talking in the background and wondered if Davy was ringing from a pub.

'Where are you, Davy?'

There was more background noise then Davy said, 'Can I talk to you?'

'Yes, go ahead.'

'Not now cos Billy might hear,' came the reply. 'He wouldn't be happy if he knew I was talking to you.'

That was probably the understatement of the year, Daniel reflected.

'OK. So shall I ring you back later?'

'No!' The single word conveyed panic and Daniel's interest was piqued. What had happened to make Billy Driscoll's brother so anxious to speak to him?

'I need to meet you,' Davy said. 'Can you come now?'

'*Now*? Have you seen the weather, Davy? Can't it wait?'

'No! You must come.'

'Is it Billy, Davy? Has he done something?'

There was a pause and then Davy said, 'It's what I seen. He doesn't want me to talk to you.'

'Can't you at least tell me what it's about, Davy?'

There was a long pause.

'Davy?'

'No,' came the answer, and then, 'It's about the dogs but you mustn't tell Billy.'

'I'm not likely to, am I?'

Daniel gave up on the idea of getting any real sense out of Davy over the phone; he was clearly uncomfortable using it and becoming more incoherent by the moment.

'OK. Where are you?' he asked.

'Can you come to the pub?'

'Which one? In Barnsworthy?'

'No. In Bovey Trent. The Jack of Spades. Just you. Nobody else. You won't bring anyone else, will you?'

'OK, but what about you? How will you get there?' Bovey Trent was a good five miles from Driscoll's yard, a fact that strongly recommended it to Daniel.

'I can borrow the truck, driving's easy,' Davy said, sounding relieved now that Daniel had agreed.

'Won't Billy want to know where you're going?'

'No, I won't tell him, so he won't know,' came the muddled reply. Then after a pause and more background noise, 'He's not here.'

'Well, wouldn't it be easier if I came to you, then?' Daniel asked.

'No! He might come back.'

The idea of setting out towards Barnsworthy again, so soon after his difficult journey back, wasn't one that attracted Daniel overmuch, but Davy's need to confide seemed urgent, so he agreed to meet him in an hour's time.

'Just you,' Davy said anxiously. 'You mustn't bring anyone else.'

'Just me,' Daniel told him and cut the connection.

He found Fred looking at him with a large measure of disbelief.

'I think I caught most of that and if you're about to do what I think you are, you must have rocks in your head!' he stated. 'If ever I heard a set-up – that was it. And not a very good one, at that!'

'It was certainly clumsy,' Daniel said, gratefully accepting a mug of coffee. 'So clumsy, in fact, that it could almost be a genuine call for help. After all, I did leave him my number for just that purpose.'

'You're not serious?'

'Look at it this way – Davy loves the dogs; what if he thinks I can stop Billy from hurting them? He might just take that chance.'

Fred shook his head. 'I don't see it,' he said. 'You forget, I've met the Driscoll brothers a time or two and my impression was that Davy was shit-scared of Billy.'

'Absolutely terrified!' Daniel agreed. 'But what if Billy has done something that's really upset Davy? People like him can be very stubborn when they get an idea in their head and if there's a chance that he can tell me something to incriminate our friend Billy, then I want to hear it.'

Fred frowned.

'Is there something you're not telling me? This *is* just about the dogs, isn't it?'

'To be honest, I'm not sure,' Daniel said. 'That's why I want to go. Yes, I know,' he added, holding up his hand to forestall his employer's protest. 'It's risky; but after all, a pub is a public area by its very name and I'll have Taz with me.'

At the mention of his name the German shepherd raised his head enquiringly and Daniel put a hand down to fondle the dog's soft ears.

'You're not seriously planning to go alone? Let me come with you.'

Daniel shook his head.

'And what are you going to do – sit in the car? How will that help?'

'I could at least watch your back.'

'I've got Taz to do that. Look, if Davy sees I've not come alone he'll just as likely take off without saying anything. I'll be careful, I promise. Besides, it's your special day. You're having a meal with Meg, remember?'

'She'd understand,' Fred stated, but Daniel could tell that his reminder had hit home. 'All right, maybe she wouldn't, but look, I really don't like this. If Davy does tell you something important – you'll call the police, then? Promise? No heroics.'

'Absolutely. Look, why don't I get Shane to meet me there?' he suggested after a moment. 'He's handy in a dust up, if it should come to that, and Davy knows him.'

'Well, I suppose so, though I'd be reluctant to trust one pikey to help me against another. They're tight as a nun's underwear, those Travellers!'

'What do you know about nuns' underwear?' Daniel asked, amused. 'No, Shane's all right. I think I can trust him.' He drained his mug. 'Well, I'd better get going, in case I get held up again. The roads won't get any better.'

He was on his way out the door when Fred spoke again.

'Look, call me, will you? When it's over – let me know you're alive . . .'

Daniel smiled.

'OK, Daddy.'

The roads were, in fact, getting steadily worse as Daniel headed north-west, the Mercedes' tyres swishing on the streaming tarmac and the windscreen wipers battling an almost constant wall of spray. It was a relief to leave the main roads behind and turn into the narrow lane signposted to Bovey Trent.

Badgered by Fred, he had rung Shane before setting out but was foiled by an answering service on which he left a brief message. He had no way of knowing how soon, or even *if*, Shane would pick up the message, but there was no time to do anything more if he was to meet Davy in anything like the hour he'd promised.

The rain eased a little as he drove between the sheltering high banks and hedges of the Devon lane, but the wind seemed, if anything, stronger. The headlights showed the hedgerows and trees swaying violently from side to side, and leaves and small branches littered the tarmac.

It wasn't a road he was familiar with and it seemed to go on for ever. Houses were few and far between but presently he came upon a cluster of stone barns at a crossroads where a sign promised that Bovey Trent was only half a mile distant.

As the car drew level with the barns there was a half-seen blur of movement to his right, a dark shape filled the window beside him and something hit the side of the Merc with a resounding thud.

Too late, Daniel braked and swerved. The tyres lost traction on the wet surface and the vehicle slid sideways to impact with the grass bank on the other side of the road.

The conditions and the width of the lane meant that he was barely doing thirty miles an hour and the rain-softened ground cushioned the shock but Daniel had no thought at all for the potential damage to his car. A glance in his wing mirror confirmed his worst fears and in a flash he was out of the car and running back to where a crumpled bicycle lay in the road and, beside it, face down, the bedraggled figure of a child.

Shock drenched him like icy water.

'Shit!' he muttered, kneeling next to the kid who was lying ominously still. 'Where the hell did you come from?'

It was a boy. Razor-cut dark hair had been covered by a baseball cap that now lay some feet away, and he wore loose jeans and a leather bomber jacket, both wet and streaked with mud. On what little could be seen of his face, there was an ominous smear of red, and a fringe of dark lashes lay unmoving against the soft, dirt-streaked skin of his adolescent cheek.

Daniel bent close.

'Can you hear me?'

There was no response and, aware of the potentially fatal consequences of moving the child, he sat back on his heels and reached for his mobile, putting his other hand gently on the boy's back to feel for movement.

To his relief, he could feel the lad's heart thudding strongly and as he flipped open his phone case he thought he saw a flicker of movement from the dark lashes.

'Can you hear me?' he repeated, raising his voice to be heard over the howling gale, his own heart thudding to match the child's. Behind him, shut in the back of the car, Taz began a frenzy of barking, but at that moment he had no time to spare for the dog.

Suddenly the boy turned his head and opened his eyes. Rain coursed down his muddy face and the pupils were as black as coals.

'Course I can fuckin' hear you!' he said, his vigour shocking after the stillness of a moment before.

With a swipe of his hand he sent the phone spinning out of Daniel's hand and even as he remembered where he'd seen those dark, challenging eyes before, something crashed into the back of his skull and he fell forward, consciousness leaving him before he even hit the ground.

The last thing he heard as darkness closed in was Taz's furious barking.

FOURTEEN

Consciousness seeped back slowly.

Last to leave, sound returned first, but muffled and muddled, like voices in another room. There was a droning sound but also people talking. Daniel couldn't be bothered to try and make out what was being said.

A sense of movement was next to force itself into his awareness: subtle, slightly rolling and interspersed with short, rumbling bumps. His right cheekbone, hip and shoulder seemed to be bearing the brunt of the bumping and his head ached dully. A smell of diesel, dogs and wood resin filled his nostrils and he felt slightly sick.

As he lay still, fighting the nausea, his mind processed the information and arrived at the conclusion that he was lying in the back of a moving vehicle of some kind. He couldn't recall why he should be and instinct bade him be still until he was able to make more sense of it. His arms were in front of him and his wrists felt tight and uncomfortable. Tensing the muscles unobtrusively, he discovered that they were tightly bound.

'Is he awake yet?'

It was the first thing he'd heard that made any sense, and the voice came from somewhere forward and above his head. The reply was startlingly close, the pitch boyish.

'Nah. Out for the count. You got him good!'

Another voice, from the front; full of agitation.

'You shouldn't have hit him. What if he dies? What then?'

Davy, Daniel thought, and memory began to return, bringing with it a measure of disgust at how easily he'd been duped. One of the oldest tricks in the book and he'd fallen for it like a novice. Even as he chided himself, he knew that the master stroke had been using the child to lure him from the car. If it had been a man lying at the roadside, he'd have been far more wary; perhaps released the dog. But the boy had been good, he had to admit. He imagined it was far from the first time he'd used that trick. There had probably been a string of people in the past that had been only too happy to pay handsomely to keep such an 'accident' quiet.

'He won't die,' came the confident answer. 'I didn't hit him that hard. He'll have a headache, that's all.'

'But . . . what if he does? We'll be in trouble, won't we? If he dies?'

'The only trouble will be if you don't keep your fucking mouth shut!' The speaker, who could only be Billy Driscoll, was struggling to control his temper. 'Just give it a rest, will you? All you have to do is keep quiet; that's all you have to do, but even that seems to be beyond you!'

'I will. I will, Billy. I'm sorry.' Davy sounded deeply upset.

'Yeah, well, do as you're told and it'll all be over soon. And you . . .' he added, presumably to the lad in the back. 'I want to know as soon as he begins to wake up, OK?'

'Yeah. Course.'

Even with his eyes shut, Daniel was aware of the boy leaning over him and willed his body to stay relaxed even though he was lying on thin rubber matting on the ribbed floor of the van, and he would dearly have liked to cushion his face against the bumpy ride of the rough country road. His mind was operating a fair way below capacity but instinctively he felt that having his abductors believe he was still unconscious might prove to be an advantage, somewhere along the line.

He could hear the tyres swishing through standing water on the road and at one point the driver swore as the nearside wheels hit a pothole. Daniel's ears rang as his face rebounded off the matting and the ache in his skull stepped up a notch.

He was wondering how far they had come and how long he

could keep up the pretence when the van slowed and then turned sharply to the left, its wheels crunching on gravel. It came to a halt, its engine still running, and then Daniel heard a second vehicle pull in alongside. Over the rattling of the idling van he heard the unmistakable sound of Taz's furious barking and knew it must be the Merc. The dog would be beside himself with rage at having a stranger taking Daniel's place in the driving seat and being unable to reach him.

Moments later the van door opened on the passenger side and a voice said roughly, 'Budge up, Davy. Christ, that bloody dog half-deafened me! Lucky that grille was there or he'd have fuckin' had me – no hesitation! He's a big bastard, too!'

The van rocked slightly as the newcomer climbed in, slamming the door behind him.

'God, it's a rough night!'

'What're you gonna do with him, Johnny?' That was Davy.

'Who?'

'The dog.'

'I dunno. Leave 'im there for now, I s'pose. He's not going anywhere, is he? You got the key for the barrier, Billy?'

'Nah. We'll force it. It's old wood,' came the confident reply. The van moved forward slowly, there was a soft bump and moments later the engine revs began to rise, the bodywork shuddering as it pitted its power against some unseen obstruction.

It was an unequal contest. After only a few seconds there came a loud crack and the vehicle lurched forward to the accompaniment of a cheer from the boy at Daniel's side. The tyres were definitely running over gravel now, bumping in and out of puddles, and Daniel imagined they must be driving along a track. He tried not to think about the intended destination and what was planned for him.

In the front the newcomer was speaking; 'What about Whelan?'

'He's still out of it.'

'OK, though?'

'Yeah. Still breathing, Frankie says.'

'Thank God for that! We don't want another body on our hands! Right, let's get a move on. The sooner we finish clearing up this fuckin' mess you've made, the better!'

'It's not *my* mess,' Billy protested.

'Whatever you say, you were responsible. If you double-cross people it stands to reason they're gonna get mad.'

'Well, how was I to know he'd staked a bloody fortune? He didn't tell me he was planning to do that.'

'I imagine you led him to believe he couldn't lose – I've seen you at work before, don't forget!'

'Yeah . . . well, the suckers deserve what they get, don't they?'

'Suckers or not, you can't blame 'em for getting angry, can you?'

'He *was* angry!' Davy put in, speaking up for the first time. '*Really* angry. He was shouting and pushing Billy. I don't like people shouting . . .'

'It's OK, Davy. Try not to think about it, eh? It's over, now.'

'How was I to know he'd react like that?' Billy demanded. 'He just went mad!'

'The fact remains that if you'd come to me instead of trying to cover it up yourself, we wouldn't be in this fucking mess! And as for letting the boy have the bloody watch – what were you thinking?'

'I didn't give it to him. He must've pinched it. I didn't know he had the brains to pawn it.'

'He's probably watched you often enough,' Johnny retorted.

'Nobody wanted it any more. I just wanted some money,' Davy put in. 'I didn't think it would matter.'

'That's why I do the thinking for you!' Billy said savagely. 'Jesus! If you had half a brain you'd be dangerous!'

'Cut it out!' Johnny snapped. 'It's not his fault. You're supposed to keep an eye on him but it seems you can't even manage that! If Ray hadn't been on the ball and called me when this Whelan character went snooping around the shop, you'd have been in deep shite, I can tell you! The police were onto it before the cat could lick her arse, but luckily he'd ditched it by then.'

Billy responded with a disgruntled muttering that Daniel didn't catch and Johnny apparently decided to ignore.

The concentration required to hear what was being said over the rattle and drone of the van meant that Daniel was almost caught out when Frankie suddenly poked him in the chest with a sharp forefinger, and he only just managed to stop himself reacting.

'He's still knocked out,' he reported in a voice chock full of importance.

'That's good. You keep your eye on him, Frankie,' Johnny told him.

For Daniel, the effort to maintain his pretence was increasing the further they went and after a series of four bruising potholes, he was about to admit defeat when he heard a curse and the van slowed to a rapid halt.

'Fuck!' Billy exclaimed with deep feeling. 'Now what?'

'Well, either we sit here moaning or we get out and move it,' came the reply.

'We'll never shift that!'

'Well, have you got a better idea? It's probably not as heavy as it looks.'

The passenger-side door opened and the van rocked as Johnny got out, instructing Davy to follow him and, still grumbling, Billy went to join them.

The youngster in the back scrambled to look between the front seats, while raised voices from the front of the vehicle suggested that the endeavour to move what Daniel guessed was a fallen tree wasn't going well.

In the next moment, the lad returned to his side, gave his shoulder a shake and then, apparently satisfied by Daniel's stillness, opened the back of the van and jumped out, slamming the door behind him.

Daniel wasted no time. His eyes snapped open and cursing the nylon cord that bound his wrists he got to his hands and knees and scrambled crabwise towards the front of the vehicle. Squeezing between the seats, he slid awkwardly into the driver's seat, bashing his knee on the steering wheel.

In the time since he was behind the wheel of his own car it had become almost completely dark and now the van's lights shone out, illuminating a puddly forest track that stretched away between close ranks of coniferous woodland and, in the foreground, the pole-straight trunks of two fallen fir trees lying across it. The circumference of the trunks wasn't more than eight or ten inches but they were long and one had fallen across the other. As far as Daniel could see, the Driscolls were making little or no progress.

Rain was still falling, though it had slowed to a misty drizzle that was blown against the windscreen like sea spray, defeating the efforts of the wipers to keep it clear.

Glad of the covering noise of the wind, Daniel tried two positions before finding reverse gear and then, releasing the handbrake, he grasped the steering wheel clumsily between his bound hands, stood on the accelerator and drove the van backwards for twenty or thirty yards before sending it into an arc towards the trees at the side of the track, preparatory to turning it round.

Unable to pass the steering wheel through his hands, turning it back in the opposite direction was a frustratingly slow business and Daniel was horribly aware that the Driscoll brothers would be racing back up the track to intercept him.

As the front wheels came round, Daniel let go of the steering wheel to change gear, took his foot off the brake and then floored the accelerator once more.

He'd reversed too far. In the instant before the gear bit, the front wheels rolled back off the edge of the gravel and onto the rain-sodden grass that bordered the trees.

With a sinking heart, Daniel heard the engine note change as the wheels began to spin; water and grit sprayed up into the wheel arches and the van settled deeper into the muddy grooves they were cutting for themselves.

The van quite clearly wasn't going any further.

He was stuck.

The idea of trying to escape three men and a boy on foot and with his hands tied was a non-starter. Likewise, the woods were coniferous and the close-planted ranks of fir trees offered no place to hide; their lower branches were no more than unadorned sticks, and a thick carpet of fallen needles on the forest floor suppressed all vegetation.

Even as Daniel accepted that he was beaten, the van door was hauled open and a fist reached in to grasp the front of his jacket and haul him unceremoniously out of the vehicle. He staggered, trying to keep his feet on the marshy ground beside the track, in which he was assisted by the owner of the hand, whose powerful hold kept him upright.

'Going somewhere?' a voice sneered.

Torchlight flashed, making Daniel screw up his eyes, and

simultaneously an unseen fist smashed into the side of his face. His head snapped back and round, and the next thing he knew, he was lying in a puddle on the soft, spongy moss beside the van.

Icy water instantly soaked his jeans and shirt and seeped into his half-open mouth. He raised his head slightly, spitting it out, and in the poor visibility felt rather than saw a booted foot come to rest some eighteen inches away from his midriff. A darker shadow fell as someone bent over him.

'I said, "Are you going somewhere?"' the voice repeated, and followed the words with a vicious boot to the ribs.

The breath left Daniel's body with a whooshing noise and he instinctively curled round the pain in his torso in self-defence, catching a third blow on his knee.

'For God's sake, Billy!' someone said explosively. 'We don't want to fuckin' kill him! He's tied up, leave him alone!'

For not the first time that evening, Daniel found himself in the unexpected position of agreeing wholeheartedly with Billy Driscoll's older brother. He uncurled a little, experimentally, and lifted his head once more, spitting a mixture of water and blood. He ran his tongue over his lips, one side of which felt sore and swollen, and pain stabbed his midriff when he breathed too deeply.

Depressedly, he thought he probably had at least one broken rib, but the truth was that he'd probably got off lightly. If Billy Driscoll had been allowed to continue, the consequences could have been severe. Daniel had seen the results of many beatings when working the streets of Bristol and knew how surprisingly little it can take to damage internal organs beyond repair. The way TV and film heroes absorbed and apparently shrugged off endless blows was the stuff of fantasy.

'Well, he's fucked everything up!' Billy was complaining. 'What are we going to do now?'

'You're going to stay here and get the van back on the track, that's what you're going to do. There's plenty of branches around you can use. I'll carry on with Whelan on foot. It can't be much further.'

'On your own?'

'*Yes*, on my own. His hands are tied – what d'you think he's going to do, bite me?'

'You're going to stick to the plan?' Billy hissed incredulously. He leaned towards his brother and said in a low voice, 'Are you mad? We don't know how long he's been awake! That's what comes of setting a boy to do a man's work. I should have checked myself.'

Johnny hesitated, looking down at Daniel.

'No, we'll stick to the plan,' he said after a moment. 'What does it matter if he overheard a family squabble? Who's going to be interested in that?'

Billy muttered something unintelligible and then swore at Davy to get moving and find some branches.

Johnny shone the torch at Daniel again.

'Can you get up?'

By way of a reply, Daniel held up his bound wrists and, after a moment's hesitation, Johnny grasped the cord that secured them and hauled Daniel, wincing, to his feet. Once there, he was turned round and prompted to move by a firm hand in the small of his back.

'Where are you taking me?' Daniel asked, resisting.

'You've been poking your nose in where it's not wanted and it's time someone taught you a lesson!'

'Whatever's going on, it's not worth all this,' Daniel protested, hoping to convince the man that he knew less than he did.

'Shut up and walk!'

'Kidnap and false imprisonment will land you in a lot more trouble than a few dead greyhounds.'

'I should warn you, Mr Whelan, I'm not a patient man . . .'

Shaking his head, Daniel did as he was told. Following the beam of Johnny's torch, he began to walk, limping heavily on the knee that had been on the receiving end of Billy's kick. In due course the two fallen trees were reached and in response to another firm push, Daniel stepped over them and continued along the track.

Trudging through the darkness, he wondered if Shane had received the message he had left on Zoe's phone and, if so, what he had done when he had got to the pub in Bovey Trent and found no trace of Daniel.

He debated the pros and cons of telling the elder Driscoll that there were almost certainly people out looking for him, but he didn't think the man was in receptive mood. Nor did he think it would alter his plans, which didn't, if what he'd said earlier was true, include killing Daniel, so why put him on his guard?

'Stop!' Driscoll said suddenly and Daniel was only too pleased to do so.

Looking around him he could make out very little in the gloom but could see just enough to realize that they had come to a crossroads in the gravel track. After a moment's hesitation, Driscoll turned Daniel to the left and prodded him into action once more.

Gritting his teeth against the pain in his knee, Daniel came to a decision.

'Look, wherever you're taking me, it won't take long for someone to find me. You didn't think I'd come without telling someone where I was going, did you?'

'But you didn't *know* where you were going, did you?' Driscoll pointed out. 'You don't even know where you are. By the time anyone thinks to look here, it'll all be done and dusted. I don't imagine you'll be the only missing person reported on a night like this, do you?'

'They'll find the car.'

'Yeah, well maybe they won't. Maybe all they'll find is a burnt-out shell. Take 'em a while to find out whose it is, won't it? And by then it won't matter.'

Daniel's heart began to thud uncomfortably in a chest grown suddenly tight with fear.

'You'd be stupid to do that,' he said, in a voice that was a thousand times calmer than he felt. 'Someone would be bound to report a burning car. A car just parked somewhere – nobody would think twice.'

'Oh, I don't know. Nobody much out and about in this weather . . .' Driscoll let his meaning seep into Daniel's mind.

Oh, God! He didn't give a toss what happened to the car, which was old and shabby, anyway, but the thought of Taz, trapped inside, barking furiously and helplessly until he could bark no more . . .

Abruptly and without conscious decision, Daniel whirled round and attacked Driscoll, swinging his bound fists into the Traveller's stomach with a force fuelled by desperate fear for his partner.

With a grunt, Driscoll bent double, the back of his head and neck inviting a follow-up blow, which Daniel did his best to supply. But he was off-balance; the unnatural position of his arms and the pain in his knee combined to make his second blow something woefully short of the *coup de grâce* he'd intended and Johnny Driscoll was a big man.

Even as Daniel's clenched fists landed, he knew it wouldn't be enough. Driscoll dropped to one knee but before Daniel could recover sufficient equilibrium for a third attempt, the Traveller surged upward, knocking him aside with almost contemptuous ease. As Daniel staggered sideways, Johnny Driscoll took two measured paces and clubbed him on the side of his head.

For the third time in less than an hour, Daniel hit the ground.

A buzzing darkness filled his head, threatening to overwhelm him, and he was only dimly aware of being hefted onto Driscoll's shoulder. Held in a kind of fireman's lift, with his legs and upper body hanging down, the pressure on his damaged ribs with each of Driscoll's steps made breathing almost impossible.

He couldn't have said, afterwards, whether he remained conscious for the whole of the journey, nor yet how long it took, but eventually, the movement stopped and he heard the screech of rusty hinges close to his head, followed by the dragging of a metal door.

A couple of steps more and Driscoll dropped his shoulder, dumping him unceremoniously on the ground. Still too muzzy to save himself, he landed heavily on a surface that was softer than he might have expected before rolling onto his back.

The beam of Driscoll's torch hit Daniel full in the face and he screwed his eyes shut and turned his head away.

'A little bit of advice for you,' the Traveller said conversationally. 'It goes like this: when someone eventually hears your pitiful cries for help – if they do – you'd do well to forget any names and faces you might think you've seen and heard tonight and just write it off as a bad experience. There won't be any evidence left to find, even if you can persuade the police to come looking – and they don't like messing with us, I can tell you – so I suggest you just keep your fucking mouth shut!

'If I hear you've been spreading rumours or even just talking about us in the wrong tone of voice I'll come looking for you, or one of the family will, and you really can have no idea just how big my family is. You've heard of a starfish, haven't you? Well, that's what my family's like. You can cut off one leg and another one will grow in its place. However long it takes, if you cross us, eventually, one of them will get you, and that's a fucking promise!'

When Daniel didn't answer, Johnny Driscoll turned away, redirecting the torch towards the door.

Daniel watched him go, his departing form outlined against the glow cast by the torch. Dimly illuminated, he could see the arching shape of the end wall and a jumble of tools and oddments of forestry working machinery.

'Driscoll!' he called out in a woefully weak and husky voice.

The Traveller paused but didn't turn.

Daniel cleared his throat and tried again.

'I've got some advice for you, too. If I find you've done anything to harm my dog, I will hunt you down and make you sorry, no matter how long it takes or how many members of your so called "family" try to stop me. And that's a fucking promise, too!'

There was a moment's silence, broken only by the keening rise and fall of the wind outside, then Johnny Driscoll emitted a low chuckle.

'You have the Roma soul,' he said and Daniel thought he caught a note of something that was almost approval, but then the man had gone back out into the stormy night and with screeching metal the door was forced shut behind him. There followed a certain amount of bumping and scraping and then silence. Daniel thought it likely the door had been wedged shut.

Instinctively, his hand moved to investigate his jacket's inside pocket but stopped short as he discovered that it was impossible to reach it with his wrists bound in front of him. Instead, he felt for the shape of his phone through the leather and found nothing. Dimly he remembered the kid knocking it from his hand, just before one of the older Driscolls had clubbed him from behind. Where the phone was now, he had no way of knowing; it was out of his reach.

Feeling dizzy and unwell, he closed his eyes and let his head fall back onto whatever it was that had cushioned his fall. There was a mingled smell of mustiness and pine resin; rolling his head slightly, he felt the unmistakable rough weave of hessian against his face. Mercifully – whether by accident or design he didn't know – Driscoll had offloaded him onto a pile of empty sacks.

Musty they might have been but they were dry and relatively soft. The temptation to curl onto his side and go to sleep was almost overwhelming and Daniel wondered, hazily, if he was concussed.

For the time being he was safe. If the Driscolls had meant to do him lasting harm, they would have done it by now. Something – or possibly a combination of things – he had said or done had got them worried and he imagined that the final straw might have been his exploratory walk along the footpath beside the ploughed field, where he'd suspected he was being watched.

It seemed that the plan was to keep him out of the way while they disposed of the evidence. How they were going to do that, he didn't know, and just at that moment, didn't care. In his current state, nothing seemed to matter very much; after all, it wouldn't bring back the dead.

Faces swam at him through the murky tide of apathy, silently accusing, but Daniel pushed away the pinpricks of conscience and turned onto his side, letting the welcome lassitude take over. For a few blissful seconds darkness and inactivity soothed the throbbing in his head, but there was one face that wouldn't be banished or let him rest.

Taz.

Suddenly recalling Johnny Driscoll's comments about the car, Daniel opened his eyes and sat up, his vision fragmenting and then gradually coalescing as the blood found its way around his skull once more. Everyone else was pretty much in charge of their own destiny, even though they might choose to look to Daniel for help, but shut in the back of the car, the dog was at this moment completely and utterly reliant on him. Even though he knew he had little chance of catching up with the Driscolls before they got back to the Mercedes, he had to try. Concern for Taz had banished lethargy like a well-aimed bucket of water.

Wincing at the combined discomfort of ribs and knee, he rolled over and sat up.

The most pressing concern was to find a way to free his hands. Reaching with some difficulty to the back pocket of his jeans, his fingers located and clumsily extracted the penknife that he customarily carried there. Thanking whatever God might have been watching over him, Daniel managed to open one of the razor-sharp blades without cutting off any of his fingers and then manoeuvred it between shaking hands until the edge of the blade rested on the nylon cord that bound his wrists. Anxiously aware of how close the shining steel was to the thin skin of his inner wrists, he started to saw at the bindings, frustrated by his inability to exert more than the most minuscule amount of pressure.

A minute or two later the cord fell away and, after massaging his wrists briefly to encourage a return of circulation, he made it first to all fours and then to his feet, where he stood swaying slightly and trying to make out his surroundings in the gloom. There was just enough light to see that he was in an arch-roofed building of corrugated-iron construction, pretty much like a Nissen hut. It was about fifteen feet wide at the base and as far as he could see there were no windows. An old Massey Fergusson tractor was parked at one end and there were a number of filled sacks leaning against one wall. A table, a tall metal cupboard, a pile of chopped logs and a few tools completed the contents.

Trusting his weight warily to his bad knee, Daniel hobbled to the door and found it, as he had expected, firmly closed. He didn't think it had been locked before Driscoll had opened it to bring him inside, but there might have been a bolt or a hook holding it shut. When, without much hope, he put his shoulder against it and shoved hard, there was no movement at all and he was reluctantly forced to conclude that he'd been right about Driscoll having wedged it shut from the outside.

Taking a step back, he eyed the door speculatively, but his first instinct – to try and kick it down – was foiled by the impossibility of either taking his full weight on his injured leg or using it to kick with. Gritting his teeth, he threw himself, shoulder first, at the metal panel, but although it rattled under the strain, it stayed stubbornly shut.

Twice more Daniel battered the door with his shoulder, trying to ignore the protest his ribs were setting up, and by the fourth time, he felt the wooden-framed panel give just a little.

Leaning into it, he could see the edge gaping slightly, but only slightly – he could only just get his fingers into the gap. Running his hand up and down the edge of the iron, they encountered the smooth round column of a bolt that had evidently broken free of the housing into which it fitted. However, the door refused to open any further, even when he slotted a broom handle into the opening to use as a lever. Whatever Driscoll had used to wedge it had clearly bedded in to the point where it would move no more and as he leaned on the wooden pole, it snapped under his weight, causing Daniel to crash, face first, into the metal wall.

Daniel swore. He'd wasted five minutes and got nowhere. Driscoll would surely have reached the others by now and be on his way back to the car park in the van. The car park and Taz.

With a groan of frustration, Daniel turned and threw the broken end of the broom across the hut, where it clanged against the mudguard of the tractor and dropped to the ground.

The tractor. He'd driven a similar one, occasionally, when he was a kid.

Was there any chance that the key was anywhere around? Cursing the poor light, Daniel limped across to the cupboard by the wall and opened it. Its shelves were fairly full and his searching hands found glass and plastic bottles of liquids, packets of screws, a pot of paint, several rolls of wire and sundry hand tools but no keys. The table top was similarly littered with the detritus of forestry work but there, after sifting through a pile of papers and knotted lengths of binder twine, his fingers fell upon a single key on a large wooden fob.

As he picked it up the initial surging triumph turned to doubt. It didn't feel much like any ignition key he'd ever come across but nevertheless, he made his way past the hefty back wheels of the Massey Fergusson and peered below the steering wheel to locate the ignition. It was exactly where he remembered it being but the key in his hand wasn't the one that fitted it because that one was already there.

For a moment, he could hardly believe it. Who leaves the key in a tractor in an unlocked shed in the woods? But then he was in the seat, switching the fuel on and, hardly daring to hope that the battery wouldn't be flat, turning the key.

The engine turned over, coughed and spluttered, caught for a shuddering second or two and then died. Daniel waited for everything to still and then tried again, with the same nearly-but-not-quite result. By the fifth time there was a strong smell of diesel in the air and hope was beginning to fade but suddenly, miraculously, the shuddering settled into a regular, if rattling, tickover.

Daniel could have cheered. Finally, something was going his way. There was clearly no way of turning the Massey Ferguson in the narrow hut so, finding the reverse gear after a couple of attempts, Daniel opened the throttle, looked over his shoulder and drove the old machine backwards in the direction of the closed door.

When he was a few feet away Daniel opened the engine up to full power and ducked low over the controls. With a deafening crash the tow bar and then the rear wheels hit the corrugated-iron panel, followed by an appalling screech of tortured metal as the door gave up the unequal battle, twisted on its hinges and burst outwards.

All at once, the tractor was clear of the building and running backwards across the clearing. Daniel stood on the brake but by the time he discovered how woefully poor it was, it was too late and the tractor had reversed into a stack of full-length pine logs. The jolt that nearly shook him out of the dished metal seat stalled the machine and any hope he might have had of using it to chase after the Driscolls faded after several attempts to restart it came to nothing.

Resigned to a long painful walk, Daniel glanced around the clearing and found a choice of two possible tracks. After studying them the realization hit him that he had no idea which way they had approached the hut, and if he chose wrongly, he could end up even further away from the car park where he desperately wanted to be.

Thinking of Taz, he had to quell a rising panic. He'd been too long already. If Johnny Driscoll intended to harm the dog, he'd had plenty of time to do so by now.

Whether that was what he'd intended, Daniel didn't know. If it had been up to Billy, the trainer who had quite possibly killed hundreds, if not thousands of greyhounds over the years, he was pretty certain the dog would have been doomed, but Daniel knew too little about Johnny to make a judgement call. Would he kill the dog out of hand? Daniel didn't know and the uncertainty was tearing him apart.

Standing in the wind and rain was achieving nothing. There was no moon to steer by, so trusting to his instincts, Daniel turned his back on the Nissen hut and taking the track directly in front of him began what, even if he had chosen correctly, would be a long painful trudge.

FIFTEEN

With the overcast sky and the close-planted, tall conifers, the light at ground level was poor and though Daniel could see enough to avoid falling over tree stumps and into drainage ditches, the track he was following disappeared into the gloom both in front and behind.

In addition to his anxiety about Taz, his head throbbed with a dull ache and the pain in his knee was causing him to limp heavily. He cursed the Driscoll family with every step he took.

At the end of the first track, he was confronted by a T-junction and came to a halt, dredging his woolly mind for any scraps of memory that might give him a clue as to which way to turn. The track stretched away to either side with no identifying features but, even if there had been any, Daniel had been in no fit state to notice them for much of the outward journey.

To his left, a three-quarter moon showed intermittently between the racing clouds, whereas to the right there was a faint orange glow through and above the trees, which might have been the lights of a distant town or . . .

Daniel cut the thought off short. It couldn't be that, surely. A burning car would certainly produce a glow but not enough to light up the sky. Would it?

Without conscious decision, he turned in the direction of the glow and hobbled on. The rain was fitful now but the wind still gusted strongly, rushing and howling through the forest canopy. Other smaller turnings came and went and then a fork in the track where he chose the left option, following nothing more than instinct and a vague feeling that he should keep the moon behind him.

He didn't know how much time had elapsed since Johnny

Driscoll had left him in the forestry hut but he knew with a heart-wrenching certainty that Taz's fate had by this time been decided one way or another and was completely out of his hands. He was now driven by the need to know, to be put out of the misery of apprehension.

The fog of exhaustion and depression was made all the worse by the knowledge that he might very well be moving further away from the answer with every step. Stumbling, his injured knee gave way and Daniel rolled and found himself sitting on the running wet gravel with, for the moment, no energy to get up. He looked ahead of him between the two walls of straight-trunked fir trees. It was darker now and the glow he had seen earlier had disappeared.

Had he unwittingly changed direction?

Twisting round he looked back. No; there was the pale reflected light of the moon, just showing behind the scudding rain clouds. So the fiery glow he'd been moving towards had died down or been extinguished, and that could only mean one thing. Driscoll had carried out his threat to torch the car.

Oh God, Taz! Daniel groaned out loud.

Big, strong, loyal, clumsy, graceful, goofy, protective and needy all in one; his dog, his partner and his best friend. He would never see him or sink his fingers into that thick soft fur again. As the realization hit him, Daniel closed his eyes and wanted to die.

After what could have been minutes but may only have been seconds, Daniel found himself lying on the cold wet gravel, his face cradled in the curve of one arm, and forced himself to face facts. Dying wasn't an option, however enticing it might momentarily have seemed. As he pulled himself together, the need for revenge came searing through the misery, giving him a reason to get back on his feet and carry on. He had promised Johnny Driscoll he would pay if he harmed the dog and pay he would, no matter how long it took or what the cost to Daniel, himself.

Driven by renewed purpose, Daniel gritted his teeth and pushed himself up to his hands and one knee, pausing there to get his balance.

Above the howl of the gale a whisper of sound reached his ears only a split-second before something hit him from behind with a force like a freight train.

Daniel's face impacted on the gravel yet again and he grunted as the breath was driven from his lungs. His first, barely coherent thought, even though it defied logic, was that Johnny Driscoll had lain in wait to finish him off. But this was banished an instant later by something cold and wet pushing roughly under his cheek, attempting to lift his face from the ground, followed by a warm gusty breath huffing in his left ear. Definitely not any of the Driscolls.

'Taz?' His incredulous query seemed to please the dog, who renewed his efforts to raise Daniel's head with his muzzle, whining and whistling under his breath, all the while. He was down on his belly in the wet, frantically trying to lick every portion of bare skin he could find and Daniel rolled over onto his back, flung his arms around the wet fur of the shepherd's ruff and hugged him as if he would never let go.

'How'd you get free, you old bugger?' he demanded of the dog. 'I thought I'd lost you! Oh God! It takes ten years off my life every time!'

Taz pulled out of Daniel's embrace and tried to lick his face again, padding round him on the wet gravel of the track, his bushy tail waving as his body bent first one way then the other in his ecstasy.

Finally, laughing, Daniel pushed the dog away.

'OK. Give over now, lad – we've got bad guys to catch. Though how we're going to do that without a car and no phone to call anyone, I'm not sure.'

Back on his feet, one of his problems, at least, was solved; told to 'Find the car', Taz set off down the track with no hesitation and Daniel wished, not for the first time in his life, that his own sense of direction was as good as the dog's.

Judging by the short time it took them to reach the two fallen trees, it seemed that Daniel's sense of direction hadn't, after all, been too badly at fault. However, his injured knee made progress slower than both he and the dog would have liked; the dog showing his impatience by continually running a few yards ahead, then stopping and looking back, before returning to circle round behind Daniel's heels in what he no doubt felt was an encouraging manner.

When the car park finally came into view ahead, a faint

flickering glow still remained as testament to the fate of Daniel's car but what brought him to a halt on the edge of the open space was not the sight of the smouldering wreck but the lights of another vehicle and the silhouettes of two figures moving about in front of it.

Before he even had time to guess at their significance, Taz was running forward, giving full voice to his indignation that anyone should approach his car, no matter what state it was in.

Following on the dog's heels, through the broken remains of a wooden barrier, Daniel heard, above the ever-present rushing of the wind in the trees, not the cries of alarm that often greeted the German shepherd's approach, but an exclamation of delight in an unmistakably feminine voice.

'Taz? Look! It's Taz! Thank God! Where've you been? Where's Daniel?'

Surprised and a little dismayed, Daniel identified Zoe Myers and then, incredibly, Lorna, standing with her arm round her daughter.

'I'm here,' he called out as he drew closer. 'The question is, where the hell did you come from?'

'Daniel! Thank God! Are you OK? What happened? Your face – that looks nasty!'

'The Driscolls happened,' he said wearily. 'Where's Shane?'

'I'm here!' Shane came round from the other side of the sad wreck that was the Mercedes. 'Where did you pop up from? When we first saw the car we were afraid you'd been in it.'

Apparently recognizing the newcomers, Taz had fallen quiet and now returned to Daniel's side, pushing his head into his hand.

'It's a long story, which we haven't got time for now.' He glanced at the vehicle which stood, engine idling and headlights illuminating the burnt-out car, falling rain and trees at the edge of the car park.

'We got your message,' Lorna said. 'Or rather, Zoe did, but as I had the car, we all came.'

'So what happened? Was it Billy?' Shane asked.

'Yeah, Billy and the rest of them.'

'Johnny, too?' In the lights of the car, Daniel saw puzzlement on the lad's face. 'So what happened? We came as soon as we could and did go to Bovey Trent but of course by the time we got there we were too late and you had gone. We couldn't get you on your phone, so we've been driving around looking for you. We were just about to give up when we saw the car, but if it hadn't been on fire, we wouldn't have seen it even then.'

'So it wasn't you that let Taz out?'

'No, we've only just got here. I think it took a long time for your message to get through,' Lorna said. 'The signal is dipping in and out all the time and the power lines are down all over the place. There was a power cut at the pub when we got there. But, Daniel – what's this all about? Something about greyhounds, Shane said, but I still don't really understand.'

Daniel glanced at the Traveller, wondering, not for the first time, just how much he knew or had guessed. Whatever the answer, he obviously hadn't confided in Zoe or her mother.

'It's a bit complicated,' Daniel hedged. 'Basically, they wanted me out of the way. I'm sorry, I haven't got time to explain now, but I'm afraid I'm going to need the Land Rover.'

He turned and limped towards it.

'But what about your car?' Lorna exclaimed as she and the others hurried in his wake.

'I don't think that's going anywhere,' Daniel observed wryly.

'No, but I mean . . .' Lorna's voice trailed away to nothing as she apparently realized that she didn't really know what she meant.

'Where are we going? Billy's?' Shane asked, as Daniel put his hand on the open door of the Land Rover.

'Yep, and as quick as we can.'

'So, what's going on? Why are we going to the kennels?' Zoe demanded, as Shane slipped into the passenger seat beside Daniel.

'Where's Taz? Is he in?' Daniel asked, ignoring her questions.

'Yes, here. In the back with us,' Lorna said.

'Right, well strap yourselves in,' Daniel advised. 'I'm going to have to put my foot down!'

Reversing at speed, Daniel swung the Land Rover round and drove out of the forest car park in a spray of wet gravel and pine needles, turning right as its wheels hit the tarmac and accelerating through the gears like a racing driver. The vintage off-roader shuddered and vibrated at the unaccustomed treatment and Daniel caught sight of the nervous faces of his back-seat passengers in the rear-view mirror.

'It's OK,' he told them. 'I know what I'm doing.'

Although it was now raining heavily once more and there was a certain amount of storm debris lying in the lane, the journey to Driscoll's kennels was mercifully unimpeded by any fallen trees or any significant depth of flood water and they made good time.

Unwilling to place Zoe and Lorna in danger, Daniel parked the Land Rover on the side of the road close to the footpath he had explored that afternoon. He turned the ignition off and for a moment there was silence except for the rush and patter of the wind and rain, and the ticking of the hot engine starting to cool.

'Bloody hell!' Lorna exclaimed shakily.

'Sorry,' Daniel said, flashing the ladies a grin. 'It was probably worse in the back. Now, look – it's important that you stay here. If we're seen, it could spoil everything and there's no cover out there.'

'But why? What's going on?' This, predictably, was Zoe. 'You can't just order us about without telling us anything. It's so not fair!'

'For God's sake, shut up, Zoe! Just do as you're bloody told!' Daniel snapped, pain and fatigue making his temper precarious.

'She'll stay,' Lorna assured him. 'Just be careful, will you? There's a torch under the dash.'

Daniel flashed her a grateful look.

'Thanks,' he said, locating it. 'And yeah, I'll try.'

He opened the door and slid out, aware of Shane doing the same on the other side. Without waiting to be invited, Taz scrambled between the front seats and slipped out of the door before Daniel shut it. Without a word, Daniel led the way towards the overgrown stile, keeping the beam of the torch pointing at the road.'

'So, what *are* we doing here, exactly?' Shane asked.

'Hoping to surprise them but I'm afraid we may well be too late. I'll tell you as we go.'

'What happened to your leg?'

'Your ex-boss stomped on it, charmer that he is,' Daniel replied, grasping the top rail and pulling himself up. The rain was hammering down and the wind whipped the trailing bramble runners into a cat o' nine tails. 'Do you *really* have no idea what we're doing here?'

'Well, I'm guessing it's not just about the dogs, is it?'

'No. I wish it were.'

'What has Billy done this time?'

Daniel half stepped and half slithered off the slanting step of the stile, cursing as his bad knee almost gave way beneath him.

'You remember the watch we saw at the pawnbroker's? The one Zoe thought she recognized.'

'Yeah, of course.' Shane said, following Daniel over the broken stile with ten times more grace.

'Well, she was right. It *was* Harvey's.'

'It was? How do you know? Have the cops found it?'

They had started to trudge along the hedge line, between the blackthorn and the electric fence, where the slight indentation of the footpath was ankle deep in water.

'No. Apparently the guy at the pawnbroker's gave Johnny the heads up about our interest and disposed of the watch before the police arrived.'

'So, how did he know it was anything to do with Johnny?'

'Well, from what I heard, it sounds as though Davy took it in, so I guess he made the connection.'

'*Davy?*'

'Yeah.'

'But how did he get hold of Harvey's watch?'

'That's what we need to find out. I have my suspicions but no proof, as yet.'

'Well, if Davy did pawn the watch, it will have been because Billy told him to. Davy does as he's told. Billy can do no wrong in his eyes; he's got him totally under his thumb.'

'When we visited the kennels, I got the impression Davy was scared of his brother.'

'Yeah, he is, but he's even more scared of upsetting him and being turned out on the street.'

'Is that what Billy threatens him with? Bastard!'

'Don't think he ever would, though,' Shane said. 'Sometimes I think he needs Davy just as much as Davy needs him.'

'You reckon?' Daniel was surprised at the youngster's level of insight.

'He's a bully. Bullies need someone to bully.'

They had reached the second stile now, where earlier, Daniel had cut the barbed wire that ran above the rails. Telling Taz to stay back, he switched the torch off, climbed over and moved just far enough forward to enable him to see past the overgrown hedge into the field.

It was empty. No lights showed and even with the limited available light, he could see that if the Driscolls had indeed been there since leaving Daniel in the woods, they were not there now.

Daniel strained his eyes to scan the waterlogged plough, but although he could make out the boundaries, detail was lost in the gloom.

A low whistle brought Taz to his side, and within moments he had sent the dog off on a mission to quarter the field for any sign that the Driscolls had been there.

Half a minute later, the dog began to bark. Daniel followed his ears and soon saw Taz sitting about fifty feet away and close to the hedge on their left. He had found something.

Stepping over the electric fence, Daniel headed his way as quickly as he could over the waterlogged plough, aware of Shane toiling at his side.

'Damn! Too bloody late!' Daniel swore.

'For what?'

He switched the torch on, pointing it to where the dog was waiting.

'Look.'

Shane squinted into the driving rain, his black hair plastered to his skull like a shining cap and water running off his nose and chin.

'What am I supposed to be looking at?' he asked.

'Over there, where Taz is. Someone has been digging.'

'Burying something?'

'Or digging something up. Or somebody . . .'

'*Somebody*?' Shane echoed, turning to look at Daniel.

'Someone who'd lost everything on a bet gone wrong and blamed Billy, perhaps?'

Shane's eyes widened as the meaning of Daniel's words sank in.

'Oh God! You don't mean . . .? Shit! I hope you're wrong.'

'So do I, believe me,' Daniel said grimly. 'But I don't think I am. Come on, we might as well go and check it out, now we've got this far.'

Together, he and Shane set off over the heavy clay furrows once more towards the site of the disturbance. Drawing closer, it became obvious that Daniel's surmise had been right; someone had been digging. Taz was marking a hole, roughly five feet by three and already almost completely full of water, beside which were lumps and slabs of shining wet clayey earth.

Close by, there were one or two other, shallower holes, as if those excavating had been unsure exactly where to dig. A single tyre track less than four inches wide led away from the side of the hole and off towards the far hedge. Possibly a wheelbarrow track, Daniel thought, though it couldn't have been easy either pushing or pulling it over the muddy ground.

With a word of praise, he released the dog and shone the torch over the area.

In each of the pits, from just below the surface of the soil and disappearing down into the waterline, the earth was densely criss-crossed with a myriad of thin white sticks and stones and it was a moment before Daniel fully realized what he was looking at.

Bones.

SIXTEEN

Even though he had known what to expect, the scale of it was still shocking.

There were dozens and dozens of slim white bones just in the few square feet of ground that had been turned over. Shining the torch over the field, Daniel could see further gleams of white along the waterlogged furrows, where presumably the heavy rainfall of the last few days had washed the lighter topsoil away, and his eyes narrowed as he tried to compute the scale of the slaughter that had taken place over the years.

'How much of the field . . .?' He turned to the Traveller boy.

'I don't know,' Shane admitted, shrugging. 'I think, most of it. Billy used to say he was going to plough the other field, too, to make more room, but he knew I bloody hated it so I never knew whether he was just winding me up.'

'How could you just stand by . . .?' Daniel shook his head.

'What was I supposed to do? Rat on Billy?' Shane demanded, stung to defend himself. 'You don't know how it works in my world. What's within the community stays within the community. I may not like him but he's my bloody uncle! You don't rat on your own family; not when family's all you've got. I mean, if I did – what then? Where would I go? My life wouldn't be worth living! I'd probably be fuckin' dead within a month.'

Daniel sighed, remembering older brother Johnny's threat earlier that evening: '. . . *you really can have no idea just how big my family is . . . However long it takes, if you cross us, eventually, one of them will get you . . .*'

'Yeah, I do know. Sorry, I wasn't thinking. Come on; we should get back to the girls.'

'What you said a minute ago . . . Do you really think Zoe's stepdad could have been buried back there?' Shane said as they toiled back over the heavy, wet troughs and peaks of the ploughed field. The clay clung to their booted feet, building up in layers and making each step more difficult than the last. Taz was the only one who wasn't struggling but even his paws and legs were liberally coated in the yellowy-grey mud.

'I'm afraid so,' Daniel said. 'I heard Johnny giving Billy a bollocking about it, earlier, when they thought I couldn't hear. They didn't actually mention his name but it fits what we know. The police said Harvey's finances were in crisis when he disappeared, presumably due to his gambling, and almost the last thing he did was place a huge bet on a dog race with borrowed money. A huge bet on a dog Billy was running, as it turns out.'

The Traveller frowned.

'Would anyone be that stupid? To put everything on a dog race, I mean.'

'They might, if they'd been told the dog couldn't lose. If the trainer had reason to believe it couldn't lose, shall we say? And you know what gamblers are like – they can convince themselves it's a dead cert. But then, what if the dog broke down halfway through the race, maybe? Might Harvey not, after tanking himself up, go looking for Billy to have it out with him?'

'I know Billy used stuff to hold the dogs back, sometimes. But to kill someone over it . . .? Even Billy wouldn't do that . . .'

'I'm not saying he meant to,' Daniel told him. 'I think it's more likely it was an accident. From what I heard, it looks like Harvey was in such a state he went for Billy. Billy's a big bloke; it's easy to imagine that he might have hit out at Harvey in self-defence, or even just pushed him. Maybe he fell and hit his head – who knows? Then, I suppose it must have seemed a natural progression to bury the body in the field, given that it's already a mass graveyard. It's my guess they probably towed the car away and left it somewhere, with the phone inside, perhaps, to make it look like he'd taken his own life.'

Shane shrugged, clearly very unhappy.

'Well, whatever happened,' Daniel went on, 'they've clearly been here recently and dug something up – something large – and in such a hurry that they didn't even stop to fill the hole in behind them. They know I was becoming suspicious and I think they panicked. They were attempting to keep me out of the way for the next few hours, rather than more permanently, which suggests that, in spite of everything, they don't believe I'm on to them and they're confident they can dispose of the evidence – in other words, Harvey's body, somewhere it won't ever be found. Do you have any idea where that might be?'

They had reached the first stile by now and Daniel paused to try and scrape some of the clay off his boots before climbing over. Shane did the same.

'Not really,' he said, shaking his head. 'Unless . . .'

'What?'

'Well, there was a car once . . . I don't know where it came from but Billy was pretty keen to get shot of it and he dumped it in this old flooded quarry.'

'You don't happen to remember where it is, by any chance?' Daniel asked, hardly daring to hope.

'Yeah, it's about ten minutes away. I know because I had to go along to drive him back. Davy doesn't drive, you see.'

'God, I wish I'd known that when he suggested we meet at Bovey Trent!' Daniel commented. 'He said he was going to borrow Billy's truck. It didn't occur to me that he doesn't drive, though it should have.'

'I can't believe you fell for the whole thing,' Shane said bluntly, as they trudged through the wet grass towards the road, wind blowing the rain horizontally into their faces.

'I know. I think I wanted to believe Davy had a conscience but I guess he was just saying what Billy told him to. The stupid thing is, I was prepared for them to be lying in wait at the pub but I have to say I didn't expect them to use a kid on a bicycle to ambush me on the way.'

Shane squinted at him through the rain.

'Oh, did they use Frankie? That doesn't surprise me. He's Johnny's kid and he's been doing the bike trick since he was five. Made quite a bit of dough in the past till the coppers got wise to it. It's amazing what people will pay to avoid getting their insurance companies involved!'

'He was certainly slick,' Daniel agreed, ruefully.

As they reached the stile, he put out a hand to stop Shane.

'Look, best not say anything to the girls just yet, OK?'

'You think there's a chance you could be wrong?' he asked hopefully.

'No, I'm sorry. I don't think so. But for tonight we need them to keep it together. I don't think this is the time or place for Lorna to find out, do you?'

Shane looked at him for a long moment and then nodded.

'OK. But what shall we tell them? They're bound to ask.'

'Oh, God, I don't know. We'll just have to be vague; try and fob them off.'

'They won't swallow it,' Shane prophesied. 'You know what Zoe's like. She's like a terrier when she wants to know something.'

'Well, I'll leave you to deal with her, then,' Daniel said, flashing him a sweet smile as they headed for the Land Rover. 'Be good practice for you.'

Moments later, having wiped the worst of the remaining clay off their boots, Daniel and Shane were back in the Land Rover. Taz leapt through to the back of the vehicle, where he obligingly shook himself, thoroughly, to the accompaniment of squeals from Lorna and Zoe, before settling himself happily on the seat between them.

'Oh, my God! I'm soaked!' Zoe complained.

'Yeah, me too,' Daniel agreed, unfeelingly.

'Yes, but I *wasn't*!' she pointed out. 'Till your bloody dog shook himself all over me . . .'

'Before we go, has anyone got a signal on their phone? I lost mine when the Driscolls jumped me.'

There was a pause and then three negatives.

'Damn! I thought so. This bloody wind!'

He started the Land Rover and looked enquiringly at Shane. 'Which way?'

'Back towards the main road and then turn right in the village,' he said.

'So, when are you going to tell us what's going on?' Lorna asked. 'And where are we going now? I have absolutely no idea what this is all about. Zoe says this Driscoll man is the greyhound trainer that Shane used to work for, but that doesn't make it any clearer at all. Why did he attack you, Daniel?'

'Because he's got something to hide and he thinks I'm close to finding out what it is,' Daniel said. 'He was trying to keep me out of the way while he and his brother covered his tracks.'

'*What* is he trying to hide?' Lorna wanted to know. 'It's not still to do with the pony, is it?'

'Not directly, no,' Daniel said.

'Does this have something to do with Harvey?' Zoe asked suddenly.

Shane glanced sharply across at Daniel, who kept a carefully straight face.

'What makes you say that?' Daniel asked.

'Well, I saw them together that time at the dog track, and Yvonne told us he'd been gambling, didn't she? Do you think Billy Driscoll knows where Harvey is?'

'I think he may. But I have no proof.'

He looked at Lorna in the rear-view mirror and found her looking very thoughtful, before his attention was reclaimed by the road ahead and a lengthy stretch of flood water. He slowed down.

'What do you reckon?' he asked Shane. 'You know the road better than I do.'

'Should be OK,' came the answer. 'Never heard of any bad flooding here.'

Putting the Land Rover in a low gear, Daniel revved the engine and drove on, keeping to the centre of the carriageway. A wheelie bin floated towards them on the dark water and bumped against the front wing as it was carried past. The water proved to be no more than eight or ten inches deep and presented no problem to the four-wheel-drive vehicle, but everywhere there were signs of wind damage. Trees and hedges were whipping from side to side, shedding leaves and small branches: several fence panels were leaning at crazy angles, and odd pieces of plastic sheeting and black bin bags were caught on gates and branches, and draped like trembling shrouds over shrubs and against buildings.

'So, where *are* we going?' Lorna repeated, as they left the village behind and accelerated along a country lane.

'The Driscolls weren't at the kennels but Shane thinks he might know where they've gone,' Daniel replied.

'You must think it's pretty important, to go chasing after them on a night like this.'

'It is.'

'And it's about Harvey?'

'I think it might be.'

'Well then, shouldn't we just call the police?'

'Please do, if you can pick up a signal,' Daniel told her. 'There weren't many lights showing in the village back there, so I suspect there's a massive power cut that's knocked out the masts.'

'You can always get through on 999,' Zoe stated.

'Not if the masts are down.'

'What about 3G? That uses satellites, doesn't it?' she asked.

'Go for it!'

In the rear-view mirror he saw her head go down as she concentrated on her phone and after a moment she asked, 'What am I supposed to tell them, exactly?'

'Have you got coverage?'

'Not at the moment.'

'Let me know when you have,' Daniel suggested, his full attention on the road again. 'I don't suppose you've got Yvonne's number on you?' he added, without much hope.

'I have,' Lorna said before her daughter could answer.

'Brilliant! If you get a signal, Zoe, try and ring her. On a night like this they'll be run ragged with answering emergency calls; I don't think they're going to be too impressed by a lot of maybes and what-ifs. Now, if you can get hold of Yvonne, or even Naylor or Ennis, that might be more helpful.'

For a couple of minutes, while Daniel navigated the standing water and storm debris on the narrow road, there was silence from the rear of the vehicle while both Lorna and Zoe attempted to get their phones to connect to a network, but their very silence indicated their lack of success.

'Slow down!' Shane said suddenly, grabbing Daniel's arm. 'It's somewhere along here, I'm pretty sure. We went over a rise and the turning was on the right – yes, there it is! There!'

Daniel braked sharply and swung the Land Rover hard right into a trackway that was surfaced with slate chippings. Here he was forced to brake again, for just thirty feet or so off the road was a single-bar metal barrier wrapped in yellow and black tape, which bore a sign warning that the area beyond was private and held no public right of way. A padlock secured the barrier, but a second look revealed that it was unlocked and merely hooked in place.

'They're here,' Shane said. 'Or someone is, anyway. I'll open it.'

'Where did he get the key?' Daniel asked but Shane just shrugged.

'Where does Johnny get anything? He can get pretty much whatever he wants, can Johnny.'

There was a note of pride in his voice and Daniel watched him thoughtfully as he slid out of the passenger seat and went to unhook the padlock.

Moments later, the barrier was swung wide and Daniel drove through.

'How long is this track?' he asked as the Traveller got back in. 'I don't particularly want them to hear us coming, if I can help it. I just want to observe.'

Shane pursed his lips.

'A hundred – a hundred and fifty yards, maybe? At least with this wind, they won't hear anything until we're really close.' As Daniel began to drive on, he added, 'I remember there was a kind of hut on the right, just before we got there. You could pull in there.'

In spite of the feeling of urgency, after what he judged to be about a hundred yards, Daniel cut the Land Rover's speed and switched to side lights only. Nobody said anything but he felt Lorna's hands grasp the back of his seat as she leaned forward to peer at the track ahead.

Barely a minute later, the track widened on his right and he could just make out the outline of a low building. Steering towards it, he discovered a narrow gap existed between its wall and the tree line, and he tucked the Land Rover as far out of sight as he could. With any luck, the occupants of any vehicle travelling back along the track would drive past without seeing it at all.

'OK, so now what do we do?' That, predictably, was Zoe.

'Now, I go and take a look at what they're up to and you stay here with your mum until I get back.'

'Why can't we come too? *I'm* not staying here,' Zoe declared.

'Because it's going to be hard enough for me to get close enough to see without being seen, let alone a whole troop of us. And because if I *am* seen, at best I might have to run for it; at worst – well, it could get nasty.'

'You can't run,' she pointed out. 'You can barely walk.'

'It's getting better all the time,' Daniel lied. In fact, his knee had swollen until the leg of his denim jeans felt tight.

'I don't like the sound of this,' Lorna said, her voice tight with anxiety. 'Do you have to go? Is it that important?'

'I think it may be,' Daniel told her. 'But I'll be careful. I've no intention of being seen if I can help it. I could really do with a camera, would either of you trust me with your phone?'

'You can have mine,' Lorna said immediately, holding it out. 'Daniel, please tell me – Harvey . . . You think he's dead, don't you?'

Daniel took the phone. Her eyes searched his face and he couldn't defer his answer any longer. He nodded.

'I think he might be. Hopefully we can give you some answers after tonight, but I need you to stay here, OK?'

Tears filled her eyes but she nodded.

'OK. But, Daniel, take Shane with you, at least.'

'If he will.'

'I'll come.'

'OK, thanks.' On the whole, Daniel was relieved. Shane might be young but he was tough and, by his very upbringing, resourceful. Whether or not his loyalty was absolute was a matter Daniel would have to take on trust. The Traveller had given them no cause to doubt it, so far, apart from a couple of comments he had made. 'But you stay here with your mum, Zoe – *in* the Land Rover. I don't suppose you've got another torch, by any chance? This one's pretty much had it.'

'That's so not fair!' Zoe exclaimed.

'No, sorry, that's the only one,' Lorna said, talking over her daughter. 'What if . . . I mean, how long will you be?'

'I don't know. It might be a few minutes, it might be quite a bit longer, but if we're not back in, say, an hour, or if the Driscolls drive past and we don't appear, then drive back to the nearest village and call the police. Whatever you do, don't come looking for us, OK?'

Daniel and Shane were out of the vehicle now, but Lorna wound her window down.

'But if they've driven past, surely . . .?'

'They might have more than one vehicle,' Daniel told her. 'But don't worry, it won't come to that. See you in a bit.'

Closing the Land Rover's doors as quietly as they could, Daniel and Shane set off up the track. The slate chippings gleamed dully in the gloom and there was just enough light to see the difference between the swaying walls of trees on either side and the sky above, from which rain still slanted down with unabated vigour. Daniel gritted his teeth and set the pace at a shambling jog, which was the best he could manage in the circumstances.

'Your leg doesn't *look* much better,' Shane observed doubtfully, after they had covered fifty yards or so.

'I lied.'

A low chuckle greeted this disclosure and a moment or two later, Shane said, 'She can be a bit headstrong, can't she?'

'That's one word for it.'

'I like a bit of spirit in my mares.'

'Well, good luck with that one!' Daniel said with feeling. 'By the way, keep your eyes peeled, we don't want to get caught out in the middle of the track if we meet them coming back.'

The track ahead curved round to the right and as they followed the bend they could see a faint glow of light which gradually became brighter. As the track straightened out once more, the source of the light became clear.

'Whoa! Hang on a minute!' Daniel panted, putting out a hand to slow Shane. 'Taz! With me.'

Thirty or forty yards ahead, they could see the black silhouette of a van. It was parked facing away from them so that its headlights and the bank of roof-mounted lights illuminated the area beyond: a metal-framed gate, some eight feet high, in front of a clearing encircled by trees and shrubby undergrowth. Then, as he and Shane paused, watching, it was possible to make out two or three figures moving about in front of the vehicle.

'What d'you suppose they're up to? I really thought we'd be too late,' Daniel said, as they began to move forward, more cautiously this time.

'I don't know. The quarry's really deep and it's been fenced off since a couple of children drowned in it, a year or two back. But Billy had a key when we were here before, so I don't know what's holding them up, unless he forgot to bring it with him. Or maybe they've changed the padlock.'

'Well, at least something is going right for us tonight,' Daniel observed with satisfaction. 'Look, when we get a bit closer, we need to cut into the trees and find somewhere where we can see without being seen. I just want to get some decent photos; what I *don't* want is a confrontation!'

'Suits me,' Shane replied.

In accordance with this plan, when they had halved the distance to the van, they stepped off the track and melted into the deeper darkness of the flanking trees. The ground rose quite steeply as they made their way round the perimeter fence and the undergrowth became dense. Their progress from this point was somewhat less than stealthy but the van's engine was running and they had to hope that that and the stormy weather would mask any noise they were making.

Looking back at the vehicle from the shelter of the trees, it became obvious that lack of a key was the problem. The quarry was ringed by a chain-link fence, supported by galvanized metal posts. There were two gates, joined by a stout chain and a heavy-duty padlock.

A crowbar lay discarded on the slate chippings, but the lock had apparently resisted their attempts to lever it open and now Billy was setting about the chain links of the gate itself with a pair of impressive-looking bolt-cutters.

As they watched, he peeled back a section of chain link some five feet high by three feet wide and stood back, resting the blades of the tool on the ground.

Another man stepped forward, gesticulating, and words were exchanged. Presently Billy set to once more and after taking one shot of the scene with Lorna's phone with the flash turned off, Daniel motioned to Shane to follow him as he moved away round the perimeter fence to get a better view of the quarry.

Around twenty yards from the besieged gate, and having gained several feet in altitude, Daniel found what he was looking for; a place where undergrowth grew thickly right up to the fence to provide effective cover, but with a clear view of the part of the enclosed area lit by the van's headlights. Daniel and Shane hunkered down among the wet brambles and dying bracken, and Taz sat a foot or two away, intent, as they were, on the scene below.

It had clearly been a very long time since any work had been carried out on site. The grass grew thickly through the slate chippings in places, and scrubby blackthorn and rowans were encroaching on the central space where once diggers would have operated. To one side, two Portakabins stood in dismal dereliction, windows smashed, roofs flapping in the wind and what was left of their walls decorated with graffiti until there wasn't room for even one more full stop. A good fifty per cent of the fenced-off area was taken up by the blackly shining pool of the flooded workings, on the far side of which layers of slate rose steeply, like an intricately fashioned dry wall. On the near shore, water lapped darkly at the edges, brimming after the recent rain, and here and there spreading over to join with the gleaming pools on the flat ground.

Almost immediately, Daniel's attention was claimed by movement from the gate area. Evidently, the hole in the chain link had been enlarged to Johnny Driscoll's satisfaction and he now stepped through, followed closely by his young son.

Daniel regarded the boy with deep disfavour as he ran to the water's edge and gazed down, kicking a shower of scalpings into its depths, and had to suppress an uncharitable hope that he might overbalance and receive a ducking in what was almost certainly icy cold water.

'Look!' Shane breathed, at Daniel's side. 'My God!'

Back at the gate, Billy and Davy were struggling to negotiate the jagged hole in the chain-link fence bearing a large and cumbersome bundle between them.

Daniel took Lorna's phone from his pocket once more and, wishing that it was a dedicated camera with a more efficient zoom function, began to take pictures of the scene. The object the two brothers were struggling with was certainly of the right size and shape to be a human corpse and Daniel had no doubt that that was what it was, even though it was swathed in black plastic.

Halfway through the fence, the plastic appeared to catch on a jagged point of metal and even as the watchers heard Davy shout a warning, it stretched and tore, allowing something pale to flop through the opening.

Immediately, Davy recoiled, letting his end of the bundle fall to the ground on the inside of the gate.

Triumphantly, Daniel took several photos, hearing a sharp intake of breath from Shane as his side, while down below, Billy Driscoll directed a stream of invective at his hapless brother.

'Well, don't just stand there! Pick him up, you cretin!' he yelled, after his first fury had found its expression in foul abuse, but Davy was clearly in a state of shock and unable to assimilate even the simplest of commands. He stood staring in horror at the half-exposed corpse at his feet as if expecting it to rise up and demand retribution.

As far as Daniel could see, it was a leg that had come free, but it was plainly more than Davy could cope with and he dissolved into tears like a distressed child.

With an inaudible exclamation of impatience, Johnny strode back towards the pair, pushed his helpless brother out of the way and bent to pick up the lower half of the black-wrapped body himself, bundling the plastic back around the exposed leg.

'Is it Harvey?' Shane asked Daniel in a low voice.

'Well, I imagine so. Unless your uncle is in the habit of

knocking people off and burying them in his field with the greyhounds.' Flippant the answer may have sounded, even to Daniel's own ears, but the memory of his conversation with the proprietor of the Reckless Toad caused a flicker of doubt. Perhaps Harvey Myers hadn't been the only unlucky soul to end up under the clay of Billy Driscoll's fields.

Shane was silent. Daniel glanced his way but there was only enough light to make out the outline of his profile, nothing to give a clue of what he was thinking.

'You OK?' he asked.

'Billy's a headcase. We're not all like that, you know.'

'Yeah, I know. I'm sorry.'

Down on the quarry floor, the Driscoll brothers had reached the edge of the water with their grisly burden and appeared to be engaged upon a heated argument, nothing of which was audible above the roaring of the wind in the trees surrounding the old slate workings.

The boy, Frankie, had drawn close and peered at the black-wrapped corpse with a ghoulish fascination until his father became aware and sent him on his way with a cuff round the ear. Unabashed, Frankie ducked away and resumed his observation a short distance away.

Davy had followed his brothers into the fenced-off area and was now hovering halfway to the waterside looking miserable and uncertain.

Trying to get the clearest pictures he could, Daniel took several more photos on the borrowed phone, noting with dismay that the battery warning light had started to flash.

Apparently reaching an agreement over whatever had divided them, Billy left his older brother standing beside the corpse and headed back towards the van with the purposeful stride of someone on a mission.

'What are they waiting for?' Shane asked.

'Worried it won't sink, I expect,' Daniel replied. He was looking through the images he'd managed to capture on the phone. 'Look, I think I've got all I need here. Let's work our way back round and after Billy gets whatever he needs from the van, what say we pinch the keys and scarper?

'Why not just take the van? If we take the keys they'll notice as soon as the lights go out, and I don't reckon you can do much scarpering, the state you're in!'

'Good thinking, Batman! Lead on!'

Shane didn't move.

'What happens then?'

'Well, as soon as we find somewhere with a phone we'll get the police here. Shouldn't take much persuading, considering what we've seen.'

'The police?' Shane echoed.

'Yes. The police. What else did you think we were going to do?'

Shane was silent and Daniel wished he could see his face beyond just a pale blur beside him.

'Look, I know they're family but you must see that this has gone beyond that. This is murder we're talking about. Or at the very least manslaughter. Keeping quiet would make you as guilty as they are. And you know *I'm* not going to keep quiet.'

'If the police come, they'll all be arrested, won't they? Daniel, Davy can't go to prison. It would kill him. You know what it'd be like in there. They'd make his life hell!'

'He'd be assessed. I very much doubt they'll put him in prison once they see what he's like,' Daniel said. 'But whatever happens, the police have to be informed, you know that. Think of Lorna. Come on. We need to go now or we'll miss our chance.'

He stood up, cursing under his breath as he straightened his knee, and became aware that Shane was staring at him. For a moment, it occurred to Daniel to wonder if the Traveller's loyalty to his own kin was going prove overwhelming and he tensed, ready to defend himself and heartily glad that Taz was on hand.

'All right. Let's go,' Shane said.

Daniel let go of his tension in a long, silent breath.

As they moved away from their vantage point, he had to have words with Taz, who, bored with inactivity, was leaping around in joyful anticipation as Daniel tried unsuccessfully to negotiate the brambles without scratching his legs to bits.

Suddenly, Shane hissed Daniel's name and caught at his arm. He turned back and focused once more on the brightly lit stage below.

Walking back across the quarry floor was Billy Driscoll,

dragging with him a slight figure in skinny jeans and a long coat, who splashed and stumbled into the many puddles in unsuitable ankle boots as she was hurried along.

Daniel didn't need to see the long silky mane of untidily gathered blonde hair to know who it was. His heart sank.

'Shit!' he said forcefully.

Somehow, Billy had got his hands on Zoe.

SEVENTEEN

'Christ! I'm going down there,' Shane said, making to push past Daniel.

This time it was Daniel who put the brakes on. He caught the Traveller's arm and turned him roughly back to stand face to face. Even in the gloom he could see the frustration and anger radiating off the youngster.

'Get off me or I'll flatten you!' Shane growled.

Daniel had no doubt the lad could do it. His well-developed upper-arm muscles could be felt even through his jacket and he knew that bare-knuckle fighting was the chosen method of settling disputes in the Travelling community. Daniel had a few tricks up his sleeve when he was forced into combat but just at the moment, a scrap was way down his wish list.

'For God's sake, Shane, just calm down a minute! It makes no sense to go off half-cocked! That won't help her. What exactly are you planning to do when you get down there?'

'*I* don't know – *something*; I can't just stay up here and watch, can I?' He looked over his shoulder to where Billy and Zoe now stood, in front of Johnny Driscoll. From Billy's free hand trailed a length of rope and more black polythene. Even from a distance they could see Zoe's gaze fixed with wide-eyed horror on the black-swathed shape lying on the edge of the flooded pit. 'They can't let her go; she's seen too much, hasn't she?'

'I'm not suggesting we do *nothing*, but blundering in without a plan is plain stupid!'

'What then?' Shane demanded. 'What *do* we do?'

'Well, our advantage is that they don't know—'

From down in the quarry the sound of raised voices interrupted him and they turned to look. Tempers were fraying. Johnny, obviously deeply unhappy at the latest development, was making his brother aware of the fact in no uncertain manner, and Billy wasn't taking it lying down. As they watched, Zoe tried to take advantage of this distraction by pulling back suddenly and sharply in an attempt to drag her arm free.

All she succeeded in doing was pulling Billy Driscoll off-balance for a moment and inflaming his temper still further. Jerking her towards him, he raised his hand and dealt her a vicious blow across the face which brought her to her knees.

Almost in the same instant, with an exclamation of fury, Shane wrenched his arm from Daniel's grasp and lowering his shoulder, cannoned into him like a charging bull. Caught hopelessly off-guard, Daniel staggered back winded, caught his heel in the looping brambles and fell sideways into a clump of blackthorn.

Taz, unsure of the protocol that applied when two people he knew and liked started pushing each other around, leaped first on Daniel in a frenzy of licking and whining, and then set off in pursuit of Shane, who had already been swallowed by the forest gloom.

'No, Taz! With me!' Daniel commanded as loudly as he dared, staring into the darkness. To his relief the German shepherd heard and obediently turned back.

Struggling to his feet to the accompaniment of heartfelt cursing, Daniel took a steadying breath, gritted his teeth and set off in Shane's wake. He couldn't really blame the boy for his reaction but he wished his frustration had found a less physical outlet.

It seemed that the forest was conspiring to slow his progress as he made his way down the slope through the scrub, brambles and whippy saplings towards the van. Twice, his knee almost let him down and he was forced to pause, holding on to whatever was closest to retain his balance. Taz stayed obediently at his side, panting with excitement, and no doubt mystified as to why Daniel was behaving so oddly.

Finally fighting clear of the waist-high bracken, Daniel slipped and slid down the last and steepest part of the bank beside the track and fell heavily against the van. There, leaning against the vibrating metal skin he had a clear view of the old slate workings and the drama playing out at its centre.

Closest to the gate but with his back to it was Davy, apparently caught in a fog of indecision, and a little further away was the bulky form of his brother Billy, still holding Zoe firmly by the arm. She was on her feet now, her pale hair rain-wet and straggling down her back and her free hand cradling her face. Facing them Daniel could see Johnny and slightly to one side stood Shane, his face intense, talking rapidly and urgently to the older man, gesticulating with his hands.

The boy, Frankie, hovered near the two of them, face upturned, patently excited by the charged atmosphere.

Daniel could just hear Shane's voice over the sound of the van's engine but not well enough to make out any words. He was reluctant to risk betraying his own presence by moving forward until he had had a chance to see how things were going to pan out. As things stood, with Zoe a hostage, there was more advantage in staying hidden.

He wondered what explanation Shane had given for his sudden appearance on the scene, but whatever his niggling doubts as to where Shane's loyalties would ultimately fall if push came to shove, he was sure of one thing: the youngster loved Zoe, and would do everything in his power to keep her from harm, and that, at the moment, was of paramount importance.

It seemed, now, that Billy had rejoined the conversation and more heated words passed between the brothers as Daniel watched; Johnny indicating the black-wrapped corpse behind him and Billy shaking Zoe's arm so violently that she staggered and almost fell again.

Shane stepped towards Billy, his face darkly furious, but Johnny was quicker. He stepped between them, his hands raised pacifically, and then grasped Zoe's arm himself, saying something to his brother and pointing towards the bundle on the ground. His meaning was clear: the body was Billy's problem and he could deal with it.

With a gesture of annoyed resignation, Billy picked up the bundle of rope and polythene he had dropped when he struck the girl, pushed past his brother and went over to the body.

Slanting a sideways look at Zoe, Shane followed him and the

two of them began gathering a few of the larger lumps of slate that lay scattered around the quarry bottom.

Plainly, Harvey's body, if it was indeed Harvey, was to be weighted in time-honoured fashion, to ensure its rapid and permanent descent to the bottom of the pool. It was possible, Daniel thought, that Billy's failure to prepare properly for its disposal was the major cause of the friction between the brothers. It was all taking a long time and Johnny was naturally uneasy.

It appeared that Shane had offered to help but Daniel found it difficult to believe that he did so in the belief that it would help secure Zoe's safe release. As Shane had rightly said, she had seen too much, and Daniel suspected that the only course of action the Driscolls would see open to them at this stage was for Zoe to join her stepfather at the bottom of the flooded quarry.

The lad wasn't naive, so what was he planning? Daniel watched intently, waiting for a clue, while at the back of his mind another question jostled for attention.

Where was Lorna Myers?

It required no great feat of deduction to work out that Zoe had come to the quarry in defiance of her mother's wishes, and Lorna's concern for her daughter's safety would understandably override the instructions Daniel had given her, so why had she not followed Zoe, on foot or in the Land Rover?

It was easy to imagine the strong-willed teenager refusing to listen to reason once her mind was made up, but Lorna should surely, at the very least, have followed her and been here, watching at the quarry gate with Daniel. He peered into the darkness surrounding the van but could see nothing. If she was there somewhere, he silently commended her strength of mind in not rushing recklessly out to the defence of her daughter.

Maybe she had gone for help, instead.

Impatient for action, Taz butted Daniel's leg and pushed his muzzle into his hand.

'In a minute, lad. Just wait, OK?'

Out on the quarry floor, Shane and Billy Driscoll had piled several rocks onto the torso of the corpse and were working to wrap more plastic around it. Shane's face was contorted with disgust as they laboured over the awkward task.

Finally, it was done and the two men straightened up, Shane

wiping his hands on his jeans as if trying to decontaminate himself. At their feet, the black plastic wrapped a shape almost unrecognizable as a body.

Johnny moved forward, pushing Zoe ahead of him while still holding her arm.

Daniel couldn't see her face but everything in her body language spoke of a natural reluctance to go anywhere near the grotesquely bundled form. But against the Traveller's brute strength her struggles were futile.

Johnny looked down at Shane and Billy's handiwork and nodded, and with no further ado, they bent down and picked up the body between them. Shuffling sideways to the very edge of the flooded pit, they began to swing it from side to side, gathering momentum, before releasing it to fly out over the water.

It seemed an age that the corpse hung in the air, turning slowly, before it fell into the shining pool. The water erupted, rising in a curtain to hide it, and sending a glittering shower of droplets out to dapple the surrounding surface. Waves surged back in and then outwards to slop over the edge onto the gravel at their feet and all at once the body was gone.

Beside Johnny, Zoe stood staring with horrified fascination at the point where it had slipped from view, as substantial ripples continued to radiate outwards, lapping at the water's edge.

Turning from his own contemplation of the water, Billy said something to his brother, glancing significantly at the girl as he did so. Whatever it was shook the teenager out of her trance and she instantly tried to back away, tugging frantically against Johnny's grip.

At the same time, Shane reacted, pushing in front of Billy and speaking urgently to Johnny. What passed between them, Daniel couldn't tell, but when Shane turned and pointed towards the slope upon which he and Daniel had recently hidden, things became a whole lot clearer.

Immediately, Johnny turned to look in the direction the youngster had indicated, a frown creasing his dark brow, and then said something to his brother which sent Billy striding towards the gate, a look of eager anticipation on his bronzed features.

'Oh, shit!' Daniel said to the dog. 'Here comes trouble!'

Keeping Taz with him, he retreated swiftly from his position beside the van, moved round the back and came up on the other side.

The chain-link fencing jingled as Driscoll came through the gap out of sight from Daniel's position behind the van. At his side, he heard the German shepherd draw a preparatory breath and quickly clamped his hand over the dog's muzzle to stifle the snarl before it properly got going.

'Quiet!' he hissed.

The steady throb of the engine effectively masked such small sounds as might be made by feet on chippings, and Daniel had no way of knowing if Driscoll had headed up the slope as Shane had obviously intended or whether he might even now be circling the van in search of him.

It was impossible to watch both the front and back of the vehicle simultaneously from where he stood and feeling perspiration running to join the rainwater on his face, he started to back away towards the treeline, glancing rapidly one way and then the other.

It was Taz who spotted the man first, and shaking his muzzle free of Daniel's grip, strained against the hand on his collar and emitted one of his best deep, blood-curdling growls.

Daniel turned to face the greyhound trainer, but even as he did so, Taz's head snapped round and he barked an excited warning.

Daniel threw a hasty look over his shoulder and saw a second, smaller dark shadow approaching from the rear. From its size it could only be the boy, Frankie, and Daniel relaxed a little.

'Gotcha!' Billy Driscoll declared with deep satisfaction.

'Oh, I don't think you have,' Daniel countered.

Diminutive as Frankie was, Daniel felt he would be happier keeping him in sight and began to back further away from the side of the Transit to bring both the Driscolls into view at once. Unfortunately, Billy recognized his strategy and moved parallel with him, the boy following suit. Space between the van and the tree-clad slope was limited and Daniel stood still once more. Running wasn't an option, even had he been in a fit state to attempt the bank behind him. It was either submit or fight.

There was no mistaking the option that Taz favoured, but Daniel wasn't quite ready to loose the dog just yet.

'I've called the police,' he told Driscoll. 'They're on their way.'

'You must have a loud voice, then, cos there ain't no signal down here and you ain't got no phone, anyway,' the trainer responded, and Frankie cackled.

'What do you think you're going to do? Throw us *all* in the quarry?' Daniel asked. 'Give up, man, you can't get away with this! Don't make it worse than it already is.'

'Well, that's where you're wrong. That's a very deep hole and I happen to know it's scheduled to be backfilled in a couple of days, for safety reasons,' Driscoll stated. 'And guess what . . . Johnny's got the contract.'

Daniel felt fear wash over him. He had no idea whether Driscoll was telling the truth but it sounded ironically plausible, and although he had faith that in this technological age their whereabouts would eventually be discovered, that would be of little comfort to any of them in the here and now.

'OK. So what now?' Daniel asked.

'Now you come with me, sunshine.'

'Why would I? You haven't exactly sold the idea to me.'

'Because if you don't, the little girlie gets hurt.'

'But you've already said you're going to kill us all. How much worse can it get? Why wouldn't I just cut and run?'

'You tell me? You've had time. Why haven't you already done it?' the trainer countered. 'Besides, you'd have to get past me first.'

Daniel decided the time for talking was over.

'Taz?' he said, quietly, and saw the gleam of the German shepherd's eyes as he glanced up enquiringly. He pointed at Billy Driscoll. 'Take him!'

Taz needed no second bidding. Silent and swift now the talking was over, he rocketed from Daniel's side and launched himself at Driscoll. The dog needed no light to perform and Daniel needed none to follow the sequence of events.

Driscoll cried out in fear and shock; a scraping footfall or two sounded, followed by the hollow booming of something hitting the side of the van and then a heavy thud.

Taz had got his man down.

'Aahh! Call the fucking dog off!'

Driscoll's demand was answered by a muffled growl, the nature of which told Daniel that Taz was giving the trainer's arm a good shake. This was borne out by a second cry of pain.

Daniel took the little torch from his pocket and switched it on.

The trainer was lying near to the rear wheel of the Transit with his head and shoulders propped against the wheel arch. The arm that Taz held clamped in his jaws was forced up close to his jaw and Daniel imagined that he would be feeling the dog's hot breath on his face.

'See, here's my problem,' he said, conversationally. 'If I call the dog off, what am I going to do with you?' His tone was light, but the problem was real enough and the only solution not one that sat easy on him.

'I'll stay down, I swear it!'

'The thing is: I don't believe you. I think you'd swear to just about anything, right now.'

'Get 'im off, for fuck's sake!'

'All right,' Daniel said, moving forward. He leaned down as if to take hold of the dog's collar but instead, grasped the heavy leather lapels of Driscoll's coat, pulled him away from the side of the van and then slammed him back again with as much force as he could muster. The trainer's free hand, which had started to rise as he divined Daniel's intent, now fell away and the grunt that was shaken from him died away into silence. Excited by the movement, Taz growled again and shook the arm he held between his jaws, but the action elicited no response. Billy Driscoll was out cold.

Shining the beam of the torch on the closed eyes and lifeless face, Daniel searched for a pulse then let go his pent-up breath in a relieved sigh. Much as he disliked the man and everything he stood for, it was no part of his plan to remove him from the action on a permanent basis.

'OK. Out!' he told the dog.

Taz, however, was having too much fun and shook the limp arm again, which drew a severe reprimand down on his head.

Reluctantly, he unclamped his jaws, watching his victim eagerly for signs of renewed activity, but there were none.

Daniel straightened, ruffling the dog's fur.

A whisper of sound from behind had him and the dog whirling

round as one and the sharp pain in Daniel's side coincided with a high pitched scream of fright as, without waiting to be commanded, Taz launched a second attack.

'No-oo, get 'im off me, pleeease!' Frankie sobbed. 'Get 'im off!'

'Taz, no! Out!' Daniel said, instantly, his torch picking out the screwed-up face of the boy.

This time, Taz stood back, instantly, and Daniel reached down to haul the kid to his feet. The torchlight gleamed on metal at his feet and moments later he held a knife with a four-inch blade alongside the torch in his free hand.

That explained the sharp pain, which now manifested itself as a deep soreness in the muscles that ran over his hip. It seemed the strike had hit the bone, with the result that it was painful but not disabling. However, he knew if he hadn't moved at the critical moment, upsetting the boy's aim, the point might well have plunged home a couple of inches higher, which would have been a different matter altogether.

Shrinking away from the hold on his arm, his eyes on the dog, Frankie was doing his best to swallow the sobs which were still rising and in spite of the situation, Daniel was aware of a tinge of pity. However tough and streetwise he seemed, he was only a little older than Daniel's own son, Drew, and could hardly be blamed for his upbringing. It made what Daniel was about to do even more distasteful, but he could see no alternative.

Turning Frankie round, but keeping a firm hold on his arm, he started to walk towards the gate, pushing the boy ahead of him. Pain spread from his hip into his lower back and down his leg as he walked, and he felt the warm slipperiness of blood running.

At the front of the van they stepped into the brilliant glare of the headlights and their appearance plainly unsettled those already there, who had clearly been waiting, with widely differing emotions, for Billy's return, with or without Daniel.

Keeping the boy in front of him, with the knife held conspicuously close to his face, and Taz close to his heel, Daniel started to walk towards Johnny.

They had covered half of the forty or so feet between the perimeter fence and the pool before Johnny reached behind him and produced a small but deadly pistol from somewhere on his person.

'Stop there! Now!' he said, jabbing the muzzle of the gun into Zoe's neck.

Shane started towards Driscoll and then stopped, his fists clenching, as the older man added, 'And you!'

Zoe whimpered, her face crumpling with terror and her whole body visibly shaking. Under the relentless rain, her silky blonde hair was silky no more, flattened to her head and straggling over her shoulders, and her customary dark eye make-up had run, staining her cheeks and accentuating the waiflike fragility of her face. Her eyes, reddened with crying, begged silently for help.

Daniel stopped dead, another such scene playing across his mind. A corner shop: a strung-out addict with a knife, and a petrified girl, willing him to do something, *anything*, to help her.

The flashback was so real, so powerful, it threatened to overwhelm him. His breath caught in his throat as his pulse rate doubled and he screwed his eyes shut momentarily, willing the memory away.

He couldn't allow the past to colour the present. Although terrifyingly similar at first glance, the situation wasn't the same. Johnny Driscoll had already proved to be coolly calculating, far removed from the irrational crackhead, desperate for a fix, who haunted Daniel's nightmares.

He took a deep steadying breath.

'Let her go, Johnny. It's over.'

'And how do you reckon that?'

'You're on your own, mate. Billy's out of it. You can't win; surely you can see that?'

'But I've got something you want.'

'And I've got something of yours,' Daniel responded.

'Frankie, you OK?'

'The dog bit Uncle Billy,' Frankie said in a shaky voice. 'And then it bit me.'

'Did it hurt you?'

'A little bit. It's my arm.'

Johnny returned his attention to Daniel.

'You'll pay for that,' he promised.

Daniel didn't attempt to justify what Taz had done. He didn't want Johnny Driscoll to know he'd sustained further injury, and he had no doubt that the Traveller would applaud his son's attack rather than considering it ample provocation for the dog's attack.

'He'll live,' he said. 'But that's nothing to what he'll get if you don't let the girl go.'

'You won't hurt a kid,' Driscoll stated confidently.

'You don't know me. And you don't know what I'm capable of.'

'You won't hurt the boy.'

'I was a police officer. I got thrown out because I almost killed a child,' Daniel told him, aware that Shane had turned to look at him, frowning.

'An accident.'

'No.'

There was a pause, then Driscoll said, 'I don't believe you.'

'You've got no worries then, have you?'

Driscoll eyed him narrowly.

'Let the girl go,' Daniel repeated.

'In your fucking dreams!' the Traveller growled. 'I can shoot you *and* the girl before you can scratch your arse!'

'Taz, behind me!' Daniel said and, hating the necessity, hooked an arm round the boy's chest, lifted him off his feet and held him in front of his own body like a shield. Frankie kicked and squealed briefly and then fell silent, trembling.

'Just how good a shot *are you*, though?' Daniel asked. He walked forward a few steps, stopping on the edge of the flooded pit, which looked bottomless and blackly menacing. Johnny Driscoll swore; the boy wriggled again, and Daniel suddenly realized that what he was scared of was not the gun in his father's hand but the water.

'He can swim . . . *can't* he?' he enquired.

This time the response from the terrified boy was unmistakable and Daniel was hard put to hang on to him.

'Tut, tut,' he said, shaking his head reproachfully. 'All little boys should learn to swim. You can never be sure when they might fall into a river, or . . . a flooded quarry, maybe.'

'Dad!' Frankie squealed and Daniel saw Johnny make an involuntary movement towards him, then stop.

'You're fucking dead, Whelan!' his face was filled with loathing.

'So,' Daniel went on. 'You have to ask yourself this: if Frankie were to accidentally fall into the water, would you waste time trying to shoot me and the girl, or would you jump in to save him?'

Driscoll's eyes darted towards the water and back to Daniel, and he licked his lips.

'You won't do it.'

'My God!' he said wonderingly. '*You* can't swim, either!'

For the first time, Johnny Driscoll began to look unsure, and it occurred to Daniel that with all the available light behind him, his own face would be unreadable to the Traveller, no doubt adding to his uncertainty. He kept the pressure up.

'So what is it to be?'

What Driscoll's answer might have been he was never to know, because in that instant their attention was claimed by the wild revving of the Transit's engine. Daniel turned to look over his shoulder just as the van accelerated and with a ringing clash hit the chain-link panels that formed the gates, partially ripping one of them from its steel support and pushing it inwards. The vehicle travelled forwards a few yards before the front wheels ran onto the panel, which snagged on something beneath it, bringing it to a screeching halt.

Behind Daniel a shot rang out, so shockingly loud that it was a moment before he gathered his wits and realized that he hadn't in fact been hit. Glancing back at Johnny, he was just in time to see Zoe take advantage of the distraction to drive her elbow into his midriff.

She must have been stronger than she looked or maybe desperation lent her strength because the man doubled forward with a grunt of pain and Zoe lost no time in twisting out of his grasp. As she tore herself free and stumbled away, Johnny straightened and started to take aim at her, one hand still on his solar plexus but deadly intent in his eyes.

Too far away to do anything, Daniel watched helplessly but just as Johnny's finger tightened on the trigger there was a blur of movement and Shane hit the big man in a flying tackle from the side. Both the shot and the gun were thrown wide as the two of them fell in a tangle of limbs at the water's edge. Rolling a time or two, they came to their feet and started to slug it out with their fists in the time-honoured way of the Irish Traveller men.

His ears still ringing from the report, Daniel stood Frankie back on his feet and gave him a strong push in the direction of the gate.

'Go on! Get out of it,' he urged and to his relief the lad stumbled away as fast as he could.

The van's engine was still revving repeatedly as Billy – if Billy it was – tried to break it free of the tangle of metal underneath but it showed no signs of doing so.

Looking round for Davy, Daniel found him standing a little way off to one side with his eyes screwed shut and hands clamped over his ears. He was swinging his head slightly from side to side, presumably distressed by the gunshots.

Daniel turned back towards Johnny and Shane, just in time to see the youngster floor his opponent with a terrific racking uppercut to the jaw. Johnny Driscoll spun round, hit the ground and rolled onto his face. Pushing himself to his hands and knees, he shook his head as if to clear it while Shane hovered over him, breathing hard.

'For God's sake, don't let him get up! Finish it!' Daniel urged, but Shane, it seemed, was following some sort of unwritten code of bare-knuckle fighting and merely shook his head as the older man started to get back to his feet.

'Shane – look out!' Zoe cried suddenly. Having broken free, she had moved only a short distance before turning to watch the confrontation and now she stood a few feet from Daniel.

Daniel saw the rock in Johnny Driscoll's hand just a split-second before he brought it into play but it was doubtful whether Shane ever saw it. As the youngster piled in once more with a jab to Driscoll's stomach, the hand holding the chunk of slate swung in a vicious arc to catch Shane on the side of his head and knock him off his feet and into the flooded quarry.

The surface of the water surged upwards as the youngster hit it in much the same place as Harvey Myers' corpse had done just minutes before. Zoe screamed and Daniel saw her run forward even as the black water returned to close over Shane's body.

EIGHTEEN

Hoping against hope that the youngster was the one member of his family who could swim, Daniel was robbed of the opportunity to attempt a rescue by the need to deal with Johnny who, though a little the worse for wear, was still on his feet and heading his way.

In his own slightly battered state, Daniel had no wish at all to be drawn into hand-to-hand combat with the bigger man, rock or no rock. He wasn't at all confident that he could succeed where Shane had failed, even though he would have no scruples about using all the dirty tricks in his repertoire.

As Johnny started to move Daniel spoke two words to Taz.

'Take 'im!'

Taz was only too willing. He'd been watching the fight in a fever of frustration, only his rigorous training keeping him at Daniel's side, and now he shot forward like a bullet and fastened his jaws round the big man's forearm, his thirty-eight kilos of muscle pulling Driscoll off-balance and dragging him to the ground.

The Traveller uttered a roar of pain and fury and, excited by the noise, Taz leaned back, tugging enthusiastically. Daniel saw Driscoll's free hand scrabbling on the ground and moments later his fingers closed round another chunk of slate.

A couple of swift steps and Daniel put his booted foot firmly on the man's wrist, removed the rock and flung it away into the long grass and brambles.

'Get the fucking dog off me!' Johnny demanded through clenched teeth.

'Daniel!' Zoe's voice, high and panicky.

Daniel glanced across and saw her standing, knee deep, in the water.

'Where is he? Daniel! I can't see him!'

'Shit!' Daniel scanned the water's surface but there was nothing aside from a few shining ripples to suggest that anything had disturbed it.

'Call your bloody dog off! He's breaking my fucking arm!'

Daniel came to a decision. The dog would be in far less danger of being clubbed if his jaws weren't already engaged.

'Taz. Out!'

With a final shake of his head, the German shepherd reluctantly unlocked his jaws but stayed poised just inches from his prisoner, licking his lips to rehydrate them.

'Now, watch him.'

Driscoll wriggled back a few inches.

The dog moved forward by the same amount.

'Stay still!' Daniel warned. 'And don't even think about picking up another rock or he'll go for your throat next time.'

It was a lie but the other man didn't know that.

Driscoll froze.

Leaving him in the dog's more than capable paws, Daniel turned back towards the pool. With a jolt he saw that Zoe had waded in waist deep, her coat floating on the surface, and was stroking the water with her hands as if by doing so she could clear it and see into its depths. Nothing else broke the black stillness.

'Zoe! Get back!' Daniel shouted, acutely aware of how steeply shelving the quarry sides were likely to be. He tore off his jacket, kicked off his shoes and went into the water in an arching dive, aiming a little to the side of where he had last seen Shane. If by any chance the lad was returning to the surface under his own steam, a head-on collision would be disastrous.

Even though Daniel was already soaked through, the water closing around him was shockingly cold. It was also completely and utterly dark.

He resurfaced and looked across at Zoe, who had retreated to knee depth. He held his hands up.

'Where?'

'I don't know – there, I think.'

Daniel followed the line of Zoe's pointing finger, upended in a duck-dive and kicked sharply for the depths.

The water rushed past his ears and his lungs immediately felt under pressure as he strained to see something, anything, in the inky black world below the surface. Keeping his arms outstretched, he kicked again, helplessly aware that he could miss Shane by inches and never know it.

As he went deeper, Daniel's lungs began to burn, his heartbeat loud in his ears. He kicked once more, spreading his arms and fingers.

Nothing.

Could he risk another kick? How far under was he? How long would it take to get back up? He longed to empty his bursting lungs but knew, if he did so, the reflex action of his diaphragm would cause him to draw in water.

His ears were buzzing now and he bowed to pressure and let a few small bubbles of air escape his lips. The relief was instant but fleeting, replaced by an even greater longing. As his chest contracted involuntarily, he felt panic setting in and halted his descent. His mind urged him to keep trying but his body and all his survival instincts were screaming at him to kick for the surface and the life-saving air beyond.

How long had Shane been under? Two minutes? Three? Even if he did find him, would he be beyond help?

Finally acknowledging defeat, Daniel turned upwards and kicked for the faint silvery glow above him. Even with the natural buoyancy of his air-filled lungs the ascent seemed to go on for ever and he was still some six or eight feet beneath the surface when something bumped his shoulder.

Daniel turned, still rising, and saw a dark shadow drift between him and the light. Reaching out, he grasped the first thing his questing fingertips touched – the hem of a jacket – and when his head finally broke the surface, he pulled with him the limp, drifting form of the young Traveller.

Gasping in lungfuls of sweet air, Daniel turned Shane until his back was against Daniel's chest and his head on his shoulder, then, sculling with his free arm, kicked for the edge of the pool.

As his feet found the steeply shelving quarry side and he had increasingly to take Shane's weight, Daniel's lean reserves of strength threatened to desert him and it took the combined efforts of Zoe and himself to haul the lad's waterlogged body out onto the slate scalpings of the quarry floor.

Once there, the youngster lay frighteningly still, his face an alabaster mask and water draining steadily from his hair and clothes to join the puddled rainwater beneath him. Fighting to steady his own laboured breath, Daniel took the lad's arms and began to pump them to and fro, hoping to force the quarry water from his chest.

A trickle ran from the corner of his mouth and with an urgent, 'Help me!' to Zoe, he turned Shane onto his side, at which point a good deal more fluid ran out.

Knowing that it might very well be too late, Daniel turned him onto his back again and began to perform CPR, counting the chest compressions between the life-giving breaths. As he did he stole a glance around the slate workings and was relieved to see that Taz was still in control of his man.

'Good lad, Taz!' he panted, but the dog was taking his duties very seriously and only the very tip of his tail waved to show that he'd heard.

On the far edge of the lighted area, Davy was crouched, hugging himself and rocking to and fro. Frankie had returned and now stood nearby, watching the drama with round eyes.

Gradually it dawned on Daniel that something had changed.

It was quiet.

The Transit's engine was no longer revving; Billy or whoever was at the wheel apparently accepting that it had gone as far as it was going to.

For a moment, all they could hear was the wind rushing in the trees but it was only moments before the relative silence was shattered by the sudden, insistent blaring of the vehicle's horn. Someone was leaning on it, clearly trying to attract attention.

Continuing to work on Shane, Daniel glanced across towards the gate and the fact that it was *his* attention that was wanted became depressingly clear.

Coming towards them at a shambling run was Billy Driscoll, moving as fast as his bulk and heavy work boots would allow, and in his hand he carried a knife.

Heartily regretting not having hit the man harder or even searched him for weapons when he had had the chance, Daniel faced an impossible decision: abandon his efforts to resuscitate Shane and face up to the trainer or stay where he was and hope that a hitherto unexhibited family affection would stay the man's hand while Daniel worked on his nephew.

In the event, the decision was taken away from him.

Billy slowed to a walk as he approached the group by the waterside.

'You're wasting your time, country boy,' he said, his lip curling. 'The boy's dead to his people, anyway. May as well let him go.'

Daniel was aware of Zoe moving away from her position at Shane's side, but while still continuing to work on the youngster, his mind was occupied with trying to guess what Billy's next move would be.

The shout from Johnny took him by surprise.

'Billy! Look out! She's got the gun!'

'Stay back!' Zoe shouted and looking up, Daniel saw her on her feet with Johnny's pistol held shoulder high, braced in both hands.

'Going to shoot me are you, girlie? I don't think so,' Billy sneered, but he came to a halt, nonetheless.

'I will.'

'Go on, then,' he taunted. 'Might as well get on with it. What're you waiting for?'

Daniel slowly stood up.

'Zoe, don't,' he said quietly. 'Give the gun to me.'

It was not that he cared overmuch what happened to either of the Driscolls, but he did care about Zoe and he knew that if she were to shoot Billy, the psychological impact would almost certainly be severe and long-lasting.

A sudden strong gust of wind rushed through the clearing with a noise like an express train and with its passing the heavens opened, throwing rain down upon the scene in silver spears that felt like needles on the skin.

Blonde hair flattened to her head and eyes huge in her white face, Zoe's hands began to shake and all at once, Billy lunged towards her, reaching for the gun.

In the same instant, the gun went off, jerking skywards, and Zoe stepped back, dropping it as if it had suddenly become hot.

Daniel stepped over Shane's body and aimed a kick at the gun, sending it skittering in the direction of the pool. He was too slow to intercept Billy, though, and once more Zoe found herself taken hostage, this time with a knife at her throat.

Daniel stopped dead, raising his hands pacifically, but Billy's attention was all on the girl for the moment.

'Gonna shoot me, were you, bitch?' he demanded, half lifting her off her feet.

Zoe whimpered, her eyes on Daniel, pleading.

'Don't!' Billy advised Daniel. 'Try anything and I'll cut her. Now call the fucking dog off my brother!'

Daniel hesitated. Once both the Driscolls were free again, the game really would be over, but what was the alternative? With Shane out of it, perhaps permanently, his only back-up was Taz.

'Do it, country boy! Before I mess up her pretty face!'

Zoe was sobbing openly, now, her face crumpled and streaked with mascara.

'*Daniel?*' she breathed. 'Please . . .'

Please, again the flashback and the stifling panic. It couldn't happen again; he wouldn't let it.

The rain continued to lash down, drumming on the ground and turning the surface of the pool to an agitated dance of droplets.

'Come on, country boy . . .'

Daniel's brain raced, searching for a way out.

'Why? You're going to kill us anyway. We've seen too much,' he pointed out, more to stall for time than with any expectation of a deal. 'Go ahead, kill the girl. My dog will tear your brother's throat out before you can do a damn thing about it!'

'*Daniel* . . .' Zoe pleaded brokenly.

Even from where he was, some eight or ten feet away, Daniel could see the shudders that were shaking Zoe's slight frame, and he hated what he was doing.

'I think you're bluffing, country boy,' the trainer hissed. 'You've got ten seconds. Call the fucking dog off or I'll cut her throat!'

Daniel was between a rock and a hard place. He clenched his fists, his heart racing, poised to try and take Billy Driscoll down before he could carry out his threat. It was a chance so slim as to be anorexic, but he could see no other option.

Then, over Billy's shoulder, he caught sight of movement. Davy was approaching, his eyes intent; fixed firmly on his brother's back.

Hoping that his arrival on the scene might prove the distraction he needed, Daniel waited and Billy began to count down. By the time he had got to four, Davy was only feet away, but Daniel was pretty sure the trainer hadn't heard him above the rain, so intent was he on counting and watching Daniel.

At three, Zoe screamed; 'Daniel! *Please!* Help me!'

As if the sound of her distress was a catalyst, Davy ran the last few steps and grasped his brother's arm with both hands.

Billy was caught entirely off his guard. For a moment he quite clearly had no idea who his assailant was. As Davy forced his knife hand away from Zoe's face, Billy let go of the girl and whirled to face the new attack.

In a flash, Daniel had reached Zoe and pulled her out of danger, pushing her behind him as the two brothers struggled for possession of the weapon.

'For Christ's sake, Davy! Leave go of me!' Billy said through gritted teeth. 'What the fuck do you think you're doing?'

Davy hung on grimly, his face contorted with conflicting emotions.

'You were hurting the girl. The pretty girl. You mustn't hurt her! She was crying.'

Billy tried to tug his arm free but to no avail. Furiously angry he shouted in his brother's face, 'All right, I won't! OK? Just leave go of my arm, you moron!'

For the first time, Daniel saw Davy's brows draw down in anger.

'I'm not a moron! You want to hurt the girl. You want to bury her with the sick dogs. She's not sick, she's pretty!'

'She's a little slut, that's what she is!' Billy said, spitting the words in his brother's face. 'Now, let me go or I'll shut you in the coal hole for a week!'

Davy's face registered terror and Daniel guessed that this was a threat that had been used, and maybe even carried out, before. The childlike face hardened and Davy shifted his hands to get a better grip on Billy's arm, his knuckles whitening as he slowly turned the trainer's hand back on himself.

'Davy, for fuck's sake!' Billy cried, his face reddening with the physical struggle. Realizing the danger for the first time, he tried to backtrack but he had pushed Davy too far. 'OK, OK, I won't hurt her, I promise!'

He tried to open his fingers and shake the weapon from his

grip but Davy's hand was clamped round his, trapping the haft of the knife inside, and his strength was inexorable.

'Davy! Davy, lad – it's Billy, your brother. I take care of you, don't I?'

Poised to intervene, for a moment Daniel thought the years of conditioning would tell and Billy would succeed in talking him round. The trainer obviously thought the same himself because his next words were conciliatory.

'I won't punish you, Davy, just give me the knife, eh?'

'I can't let you hurt the girl, Billy, I can't!' Davy was half-sobbing as he wrestled with the opposing pulls of loyalty and compassion.

In the next instant, Billy's face froze on a look of disbelief as their joined hands suddenly stabbed towards him. His eyes rose to find his brother's face and he frowned as if seeing him properly for the first time. When his lips moved what came out was more of a groan than any decipherable words and in a kind of hideous slow motion, he fell towards Davy, grasping his brother's shoulder with his free hand.

Davy said nothing, standing like a statue as, slowly, the strength left the stricken man's legs and he slid to his knees at Davy's feet, his body curling round the agony in his chest. His hand lost its grip on his brother's coat and he collapsed to the ground, his blood mixing with the rainwater that ran towards the pool.

Raising his eyes, Daniel saw Frankie, a few feet away and drawing close with a look of shock on his thin face. Beyond him but also coming closer was Lorna Myers.

Daniel glanced at Davy, trying to assess if he posed any further threat to any of them, and saw what could only be described as the disintegration of his spirit. He was standing looking down at the still body at his feet, his face a blank. Rainwater dripped from the sodden curls of his hair and off the tip of his nose, and his hands and the front of his coat were red with blood.

Slowly, uncaring or perhaps unaware, of the running groundwater, Davy sank to his knees beside his brother and bent over him.

'Billy?' he said. Then louder, '*Billy?*'

'He's gone, Davy,' Daniel said gently. 'Billy's gone.' And as if punctuating the scene, the pounding rain abruptly ceased, becoming instead no more than a misty drizzle blowing in the wind.

Davy gave no sign that he'd heard Daniel but after a moment, he repeated the words, 'Billy's gone.'

Turning his face up to the clouded sky, he then began to keen softly, rocking to and fro, his face a mask of unimaginable grief.

Daniel saw Lorna's face twist in sympathy before she sidestepped the scene of the tragedy and hurried towards her daughter.

Zoe's eyes, however, were not for her mother.

'Daniel!' she cried sharply.

When he turned he found her down on her knees once more beside her boyfriend, but instead of the grief he expected to encounter, her face was shining with joy.

Shane was alive. Lying on his side, ashen-faced and painfully retching water, but alive, nonetheless.

'You son of a bloody gun!' Daniel exclaimed delightedly. 'How the hell did you do that? I was sure we'd lost you!'

'Never . . . give up . . . on a Traveller,' Shane managed between gasps. 'You can't . . . get rid of us!'

'Well, next time you go swimming, don't forget to put your bloody armbands on,' Daniel told him.

A throaty rumble from Taz reminded him that the dog was still guarding Johnny Driscoll, and he turned to look at him.

'I only wanted to sit up,' Driscoll complained. He was lying in two or three inches of water, propped up on one elbow and glaring at the dog with undisguised hatred.

Taz was standing, head lowered and tail high, daring the Traveller – beseeching him, to make a sudden movement, to give him an excuse to close in again.

'Let me get up,' Driscoll demanded. 'How long are you going to keep me here? I need to go to my brother.'

'I'm in no hurry,' Daniel told him, turning away.

'But *I* bloody am! I'm wet through and it's fucking cold!'

'My heart bleeds . . .'

Shane had stopped retching now and was sat up with Zoe's arm around him.

'Oh, my God,' he groaned, looking across to where Davy still knelt by his brother's body. 'Is he . . .?'

Daniel sighed and nodded. Thanks to Frankie's efforts with

the knife, his back was beginning to stiffen. It felt as though the evening had been going on for ever already and he knew that when the police became involved, which had to happen, the aftermath would last all night and probably for days and weeks to come. In his current state of physical and mental exhaustion, the thought was depressing beyond belief.

'What a bloody mess!' Shane said, echoing his thoughts. 'What do we do now?'

'Well, I guess someone'll have to go and call the police,' Daniel said, running through the options in his mind. *He* couldn't go and leave Taz standing guard on Johnny Driscoll. He was the only one from whom the dog would take orders and Driscoll might well see his absence as an opportunity to chance his arm. Shane was in no fit state to go anywhere for a bit and Zoe couldn't drive, so it could only be Lorna, but it was a big ask, after all that had happened.

'Daniel? What happened here?' Lorna asked, breaking in on his thoughts. 'What's been going on? Does this man know where Harvey is?'

With a shock, Daniel realized that Lorna had probably arrived too late to see the corpse thrown into the quarry pool and therefore still didn't know what had happened to her husband.

'It's a long and unpleasant story,' he began, hoping to put off the moment of revelation until after the police had been called.

'The Driscolls killed Harvey,' Zoe stated. 'They threw his body in the pool, I saw them do it.'

Lorna became very still. She looked from her daughter to Daniel.

'Is that true?'

'I'm sorry, Lorna.' It was totally inadequate but he didn't know what else to say.

'Who? Who did it?'

'Billy Driscoll.' He glanced briefly across to where the dead man lay.

'The greyhound trainer?' Her gaze followed his. 'Is that him?'

'Yes.'

'But . . . why?'

'It seems they fell out over a bet, but I guess we'll never know exactly what happened, now.'

'You said you saw them do it,' Lorna spoke to Zoe, who shook her head, tears in her eyes. One of her cheekbones was beginning to darken and swell, the result of Billy's blow.

'No, not actually kill him, but I saw them throw his body in the water. It was horrible!'

'Well, if you'd done as you were told . . .!' her mother snapped, flaring up with sudden anger. 'You could have been killed – you nearly were! And what would I have done then, eh? You didn't think of that, did you? You never think of anyone but yourself and what you want! You're so bloody selfish, just like your father!'

Zoe stood up from her position beside Shane and looked miserably at her mother.

'Mum . . .'

'Don't bloody "Mum" me!' Lorna yelled at her. 'I died a million deaths back there.'

'I thought you'd come after me,' Zoe said, crying now.

'I tried! Of course I tried, but when I backed it up, the bloody Land Rover got stuck in a ditch. Well, I couldn't just leave it there, could I? What if you had all come back and needed to make a quick getaway? You didn't think of that, did you, when you went running off?'

'I didn't know it was stuck. I thought you'd wait.'

'What? You thought I was just going to sit there and let you get yourself killed? I've lost too many – I couldn't lose you, too.' Lorna's voice broke on the last words and with an inarticulate sound, Zoe went to her and they hugged each other as if they would never let go.

After a decent pause, Daniel cleared his throat. He was wet through and beginning to chill now the adrenalin was subsiding, as he imagined they all were. Shane was probably feeling even worse.

'So, is the Land Rover still stuck?' he asked, trying to decide on a course of action.

'No, it's back there. By the gate,' Lorna said, pulling back from her daughter and wiping her eyes. 'I eventually got it going with branches under the wheels. When I got here and saw what was happening I didn't know what to do so I got in the van and tried to ram the gates. I thought it might cause a distraction and give you all a chance to get away. I didn't realize—'

'Hang on – that was you in the van?'

'Yes,' Lorna paused, looking uncertain. 'I didn't know what else to do . . .'

'It was a stroke of genius,' Daniel told her, warmly. 'What happened was bad enough, but it could have been so much worse. What you did was brilliant.'

Looking round, his gaze fell on Davy once more, quiet now but still hugging himself and rocking to and fro. Daniel said his name gently but had to repeat it before Davy stopped and looked at him. Limping slightly from the deep soreness in his lower back, Daniel walked over and held out his hand.

'Leave him, now, Davy. Come away.'

Davy shook his head emphatically, looking away.

'Come on, Davy, there's nothing you can do.'

'I killed him.'

'Billy was going to hurt the girl, Davy. You saved her.'

Davy shook his head.

'No, the angry man. He was attacking Billy.'

Daniel's attention sharpened.

'Which man, Davy?'

'The angry man,' Davy said, beginning to cry again. 'I pushed him and he fell. I didn't mean to hurt him but he was shouting at Billy. I didn't know what to do. He was trying to hurt Billy.'

'You killed Harvey? The man in the water?'

'I didn't mean to do it . . .' Davy sobbed. 'He hit his head and he wouldn't move. I didn't mean to hurt him.'

Daniel watched him for a moment longer, then shook his head sadly.

'It's all right, Davy. I believe you.'

He turned and went back to Lorna.

'I'm sorry to have to ask you but someone has to go for help, there's no phone signal here . . .'

'Me?' Lorna looked around at Johnny, Shane and Davy, seeing, as Daniel had, that there was no other option. 'Yes, I see, of course.' She stepped back, releasing Zoe, who returned to Shane's side.

'Harvey . . . I mean, when did he . . .?'

'Some time ago, I think.' Now, he felt, wasn't the time to explain about Billy Driscoll's field, if she hadn't yet put two and two together. Time enough for that horror when the first shock was over.

'It's not as though I hadn't expected it,' Lorna said. 'When they found his car and phone, I think I knew, but it's different when you finally hear for certain. It's like a little bit of you keeps hoping, even when you know there really isn't any chance.'

'Hey! Someone's coming!'

It was Frankie shouting. Unnoticed by any of them, he had wondered towards the gate and was now standing by the stricken van. Everyone except Davy looked his way.

'Who is it, can you see?' Daniel called out.

'S'not the gavvers. I can't see no blues.'

'The what?' Zoe asked.

'Police,' Shane translated.

Daniel glanced at Johnny Driscoll, still sitting on the wet ground under Taz's watchful eye, but the Traveller looked as mystified as the rest of them. Apparently he wasn't expecting anyone, which was a relief to Daniel. He'd had more than enough excitement for one night.

Frankie stayed where he was for a few seconds more, then started to back away before turning and half-running towards Daniel and the others with fear on his face.

Moments later two men came into sight, walking into the beam of the van's headlights and warily, Daniel went to meet them.

Initially, haloed by the strong lights, he couldn't make out their faces, though something in his way of walking struck him as familiar about one of them. Then one of them spoke, low-voiced and wondering.

'Whew! It looks like we've missed the party. What have you got yourself into this time, my friend?'

'Tom? Tom Bowden?' Daniel was incredulous. 'How the hell . . .?'

'Well, I was having supper with Mum and Dad – it's their anniversary, you know – and Dad told me where you'd gone tonight, which I have to say was singularly foolish. This *is* the Driscolls we're talking about. I thought after I'd answered all your questions, you'd learned enough to know you don't mess with them.'

'I guess I'm a bit slow on the uptake,' Daniel put in, still trying to assimilate his good fortune. Of all the people who could have walked into the quarry that night, there was no one he would rather have seen.

'Yeah, you can bash some people over the head with the facts and they still don't get it!'

As they met, they embraced, Tom slapping Daniel on the back to rob his words of their censure.

'But I don't understand . . .'

'Well, when you didn't call in to say you were OK, we started to get worried, and by eleven o'clock Mum practically ordered us to come looking!' he said as they moved apart.

'Us?'

'Yeah, he dragged me along,' the other man joked, coming forward.

'Fred! I'm sorry, mate! I totally forgot about calling, even if there'd been a signal. But what I really want to know is – how the hell did you find us?'

'3G,' Tom said, walking past Daniel towards Davy, still kneeling by his brother's body. 'Called in a favour. 3G uses satellites. We tracked your phone to about a mile up the road before we lost coverage, but there's not much else around here so this seemed like a good bet.'

'But I haven't got my phone. I dropped it earlier, when the Driscolls jumped me.'

'Looks like they must have brought it along, then,' Tom remarked. 'Lucky for you. My God, what's been happening here? I've called it in, by the way. The cavalry should be here shortly.'

Daniel sighed and shook his head. He was cold, sore and deeply, grindingly exhausted. He turned and indicated the scene.

'I hardly know where to start . . .'

'At the beginning,' Tom suggested, practically. 'You were a copper, my friend. You know that's where we always start.'

NINETEEN

'Try as I might – and to be honest, I'm not, really – I can't feel sorry that Billy Driscoll met a sticky end,' Anya told Daniel.

They were in the late Billy Driscoll's kennel yard at Barnsworthy, where they had been for over three hours, initially checking on the occupants but also sorting out paperwork and ringing the owners, who needed to make alternative arrangements for their dogs ASAP.

Getting SOCO to let anyone into the yard had been a battle, with one jobsworth asserting that it would be off-limits until his men had finished their work. It was clearly ridiculous to suggest that the hungry greys could be expected to wait on red tape and with Anya's fiery determination unleashed, and Tom Bowden's willingness to vouch for her, they had seen sense and allowed restricted access.

Now, breaking for coffee after a busy morning, they were standing at the end of one of the kennel blocks, looking out across the fields to where, behind reams of fluttering tape, a team of boiler-suited men worked in and around a small tent. The boiler suits had started off white, but weren't destined to remain that way for long. Daniel didn't envy them their job. Clayey soil that had already been heavy before the recent rains must now be a nightmare to work in.

'Yeah, I know what you mean. I can't get too upset about it, myself,' he replied. 'It's just a pity he couldn't have gone quietly.'

The whole situation was an unholy mess, really. Harvey Myers's body had been recovered from the flooded pit, along with, Tom had reported, a number of other interesting finds; a comment he couldn't be prevailed upon to explain, but which Daniel took as confirmation that it wasn't the first time the Driscolls had used it to dispose of things.

According to Tom, Driscoll had used quicklime when he'd buried Harvey, in the mistaken belief that it would destroy the body.

'In fact, it does burn a little – superficially,' Tom told Daniel. 'But then it starts to suck the water out of the flesh. Drying it, in effect. If you use enough of it, you actually end up mummifying the corpse, preserving it nicely for SOCO to find. It's not the first time it's happened. In this case, though, once it was in the water I think it would soon have broken down, so it's a good job you cottoned on to what was happening, when you did.'

'Yeah, well, I was almost there; it was just a case of joining up the dots. They actually filled in the final link themselves by panicking and trying to keep me out of the way while they dealt with Harvey's body, which is ironic because if they hadn't, they'd probably have had plenty of time to dig up and dispose of the body under cover of the storm with nobody any the wiser.'

'You'd be surprised how many criminals give the game away by losing their nerve,' Tom had said. 'Makes our life much easier when it happens, but it's usually only the opportunists that we catch that way. I would actually rank the Driscolls as professional criminals but as far as I know they've not strayed into homicide territory before.'

'Will Lorna be OK?' Anya asked as they stood in the autumn sunshine.

'I hope so. It's all been a huge shock, of course, but she's amazingly resilient.'

Sipping his coffee, Daniel found himself thinking about Lorna. Her husband's gambling addiction had left her with very little to her name. The house had been mortgaged and remortgaged, and everything, including the cars and horses, belonged to the bank; even Zoe's university dreams appeared to be in jeopardy.

It seemed particularly hard that she should be bankrupted for a second time by a partner with a gambling habit. He and Fred Bowden had put their heads together to try and discover a way to help her, but then came welcome news from Harvey's accountant. It may have been that Harvey had mistrusted his own strength of character, for in more affluent times he had invested in an insurance policy that *only* paid out on the holder's death and the return promised to be handsome. With that and a generous widow's pension from Giradelle Santini, Lorna and Zoe could afford to start again, on a far more modest scale but at least without fear of getting into debt themselves.

Now Harvey's death had been confirmed, Felix Gregg and the two strong-arm men whose visit had initially flagged up Harvey's disappearance were unlikely, in Tom Bowden's opinion, to trouble Lorna any further. Their high-stakes poker operation teetering, as he described it, on the edge of legality, he thought they would almost certainly cut their losses where Harvey was concerned and move on.

'So, what do you think will happen to Davy?'

Daniel pictured Davy Driscoll as he had last seen him, blank-faced with bewilderment at the turn his life had taken, being led away, gently enough, by two police officers. Johnny had called out words of reassurance but his brother didn't seem to hear them and to Daniel they smacked of bravado, anyway, calculated more to show defiance to the police than comfort Davy.

'Daniel?' Anya's voice recalled him from his drifting thoughts.

'Sorry? Oh, Davy; I don't really know. Mental assessment, obviously, but then . . .? We were all prepared to say that he stabbed Billy in self-defence, or at least, that we couldn't see exactly what happened – which was technically true – but it was pointless when the first thing he said to anyone who spoke to him was that he'd killed Billy.'

'Poor bastard,' Anya said sadly. 'Billy treated him like a bloody slave and I'm pretty sure Davy was scared stiff of him but it was the devil he knew and as such, his security. God knows what he'll do now! With Johnny going down for a good long time, with any luck, he's lost all his close family in one night.'

'Yeah, it's going to be tough, that's for sure. I owe him, too, big time! According to Frankie, it was Davy who let Taz out of the car in the forest car park and for that I will be grateful to him for ever, so if there's anything I can do to help him . . .' He put his hand down to fondle Taz, who was, by order of SOCO, having to suffer the indignity of being kept on his lead.

'You know, I still find it hard to believe that Davy actually killed Billy,' Anya said. 'He's always seemed such a gentle soul, but I suppose everybody has a breaking point.'

'I think Billy making Zoe cry tipped him over the edge.'

Anya nodded. 'You're probably right. He does have a soft spot for women – I don't mean in a sexual way, but I think because he doesn't feel threatened by them.'

'He likes pretty things,' Daniel said. 'He seemed *very* fond of you.'

There was a pause, and then Anya asked suspiciously, 'Are *you* trying to chat me up?'

'I don't know.' Daniel kept his eyes on the scene in the field, but his whole attention was on the girl at his side and he was aware that she was regarding him closely. 'That depends.'

'On what, exactly?'

'On how you'd feel about it, I suppose,' Daniel said, finally turning to look at her.

She pursed her lips and considered the matter, her dark eyes hidden by their long, thick lashes. Finally, she looked up, her head on one side.

'I don't suppose I'd mind . . . too much.'

Daniel took her face in his hands and stared down at her.

'You little bitch!' he said and kissed her.